TWICE DAMNED

CARRIE S. MASEK

MP

Mundania Press

A Mundania Press Production

Mundania Press LLC
6470A Glenway Avenue, #109
Cincinnati, Ohio 45211-5222

To order additional copies of this book, contact:
books@mundania.com
www.mundania.com

Cover Art © 2005 by Stacey L. King
Book Design and Layout by Daniel J. Reitz, Sr.
Production and Promotion by Bob Sanders
Edited by Kathryn Milner

Trade Paperback ISBN-10: 1-59426-075-3
Trade Paperback ISBN-13: 978-1-59426-075-9

eBook ISBN-10: 0-9723670-5-5
eBook ISBN-13: 978-0-9723670-5-9

First Edition • February 2005

Library of Congress Catalog Card Number 2004113971

Production by Mundania Press LLC
Printed in the United States of America

10   9   8   7   6   5   4   3   2   1

TWICE DAMNED

4 Stars! "Masek crafts a near-future vampire story that reads more like a contemporary than a paranormal. Faith and Ritter are fully fleshed-out characters, while the supporting cast and WWII backstory add depth and dimension to this exciting tale."

—Karen Sweeny-Justice, Romantic Times BOOKclub

Chapter One

Waukegan, Illinois
May 16, 2014

Blood. Hunger. Lust. An explosion of red. Red floor, red walls, red air. A girl: thin, naked, dead. Another girl. And another. Black wounds on milky thighs. Gaping throats. Blood- stained breasts.

Another girl. Pink and gold. Arms lift. Veins open. Blood, hot as flame, sweet as life, pouring, gushing, flooding.

Ritter jackknifed off the bed. The image shattered. A dream. Only a dream. He pulled in a shuddering breath and rolled to his feet. It was early, but he dreamed often enough to know his sleep had ended.

He quickly showered, dressed, and slipped into the settling dusk. As always, hunger followed.

⁊⁊

"Thanks." The girl leaned her head against Ritter's upper arm. Unlike most modern girls, she was too short to reach his shoulder. She lisped slightly, and beer tainted her breath. "Shouldn't have tried walking back to the dorm alone. It's not safe."

"Life is not safe." Ritter brushed his lips across her baby soft curls. Baby. That's what she was, a baby. Eighteen years old and out for a night of trouble. He had found her staggering down the bike path, drunk silly and easy prey.

Careful not to frighten her, he gripped her shoulders and turned her toward him. Light from the dormitory spilled across her face. Under black eyeliner and lipstick, her skin glowed with youth and innocence. Black scoop-neck top, black leather miniskirt, black stockings, black shoes. She wrapped herself in darkness, sought it, craved it. If only she knew.

He lowered his face to the curve of her neck, inhaled her fragrance. Under the beer and cheap perfume, the scent of life rose from her. Her pulse fluttered beneath his lips, and his heart matched its pace. He licked the pulse point. "Invite me in." The words scraped his powder-dry throat.

She shuddered and sagged against his chest. "Sure."

The alcohol was catching up with her. If he didn't hurry, she would pass out on him. "Shall I carry you?"

"Can't." She looked up and giggled. "My room's on the fourth floor, and the elevator's broken."

"No problem." Ritter scooped her into his arms and carried her up the steps to the dormitory entrance. She was light, warm, and so alive.

"Wait, the key." She twisted. Her hand seared a path across his chest to a pocket in the skirt. A moment later, she lay back and raised her hand to his gaze.

The key glinted silver, but it was her wrist that caught his attention, thin, blue-lined, enticing. He bent toward the lock. "Open the door."

After two tries, she slid in the key and turned it. Ritter bumped the door open with his shoulder. Several students pored over books in the common room. A young woman in shorts and a T-shirt glanced up and frowned. "Ashleigh, are you all right?" She shoved away from the table and stood. "Why are you carrying her?"

The girl he carried giggled. "Met him at the party. Isn't he hot?"

Other students looked up. Ritter sighed. "Forget the interruption," he said. "Return to your studies." They all obeyed, including the young woman, but Ritter needed a more secluded spot for his purpose. "Which room is yours?" he asked the girl.

"Four-thirteen."

Right to the stairs, up three flights and down to the end of the corridor. He could run the distance in a handful of heartbeats.

A rising wind chased them across the threshold. Harbinger of a storm, it was scented with rain and spiced with fear. Fear—sharp, intense, and growing.

"*Ow.*" The girl struggled in his arms. Without meaning to, he had tightened his grip. He relaxed his fingers and lowered her to her feet. She pushed away from him, staggered, but remained standing. An angry blotch marred her arm. She rubbed it and glared at him. "That hurt."

"I must go." Ritter craved the girl, but not enough to ignore the waves of desperation beating against him. He had tasted that kind of fear before, too often before someone died, and under it ran the faint sepulchral essence of his kind on the hunt. He caught the girl's gaze and held it. "Go to your room. Sleep. I will come when I can." Knowing she would do as he ordered, Ritter turned and ran toward the rising terror. Dinner could wait. He had a life to save.

～～

Faith stared at the two men blocking her path: tall, broad, their faces hidden by the moonless night. Her cell phone was locked in her briefcase, out of power and useless. The nearest security call box was a block away, as was the nearest busy street. Her stomach clenched around a pulse of fear-induced adrenaline and her fingers tightened around the handle of her case. What the hell had she gotten herself into?

She'd worked late in the lab and had missed her ride. Damning her beloved MG Midget and its unreliable internal-combustion engine, Faith hadn't even considered waiting for a taxi. The last time she'd called a cab, it had taken over an hour to show up. It was faster to walk home—forty-five minutes if she kept to well-lit streets, fifteen if she cut through the construction site. The shortcut had seemed safe enough when she stepped from the hospital into the cool breeze and distant lightning of a promised storm. Her only worry had been getting home before the storm hit. Now it looked as if her impatience might cost her life.

"What do you want?" Faith kept her voice steady. "Money?"

The only answer was an ominous chuckle.

"Here." She slipped her purse off her right shoulder and hurled it one-handed as far as she could. It sailed by the men and landed with a clatter on some discarded tiles. They hadn't even tried to catch it.

A stone skittered. Faith turned. Two shadows closed behind her, tall, broad shadows whose shoulders brushed the walls of the new dormitory complex. She was trapped.

A rough hand grabbed her arm. She screamed, the long, loud cry she'd practiced in self-defense class, and stomped down hard. The point of her heel hit the top of her assailant's shoe. He yelped. His grip loosened. She wrenched free. His partner's fingers brushed her sleeve, but he was too slow. Clutching her briefcase to her chest, Faith sprinted past them. She'd been a track star in college and could still run when she had to. Her pumps pinched her toes and slowed her, but she didn't have time to kick them off. She had to reach that security call box. Hit the button, and campus police officers would swarm to her rescue.

Whispered curses and heavy footsteps chased her. She glanced over her shoulder. Even though one was limping, they were catching up. Faith put on a burst of speed, but something grabbed her foot. She stumbled. Her briefcase shot from her grasp, and she crashed to the ground.

Cruel fingers yanked her up and spun her around. A hand clapped over her mouth and pulled her against a massive body. A smell as rank as spoiled lab samples filled her nostrils.

Lightning cracked overhead, and Faith caught a flash picture of the three other men. Built like linebackers, they all wore black jeans and sweatshirts. Merciless faces stared at her from under identical hoods. She was in deep trouble.

The light died. The skies opened in a crashing torrent that glued her blouse to her shoulders and breasts.

"Inside," one of them growled.

Faith struggled and kicked, but they didn't underestimate her again. Keeping their legs away from her flailing feet, they half carried her past stacks of building materials toward the half-finished dorm.

"Let her go." The words came from behind them, softly spoken with foreign precision.

The arm around Faith tightened. The man holding her turned. "Get lost."

Another flash of lightning. A man stood on the path. He didn't seem to realize he was only one against four or that he wasn't as tall or broad as the men who'd attacked her. He stepped closer as the light died. "This is my town. Let her go."

Heat brushed Faith's arms. Like a blast from a furnace, it warmed her despite the pounding rain.

The grip on her slackened. "Let her go," her captor echoed.

"Leave. Now. Do not return."

Faith didn't pause to wonder what the hell was going on. She twisted free and bolted toward her would-be rescuer. "Run! There are four of them and they're—" She slammed into a wet, resilient wall. Instead of running, he'd stepped toward her.

Strong hands gripped her shoulders, steadied her. Even with the rain, she caught a breath of citrus and mint. "Gone. Are you all right?"

He had a nice voice, rich but not too deep. It cooled her panic. "I'm fine. Thank you."

The rain stopped as quickly as it had started, leaving only scattered drips behind. Faith looked behind her. The dark path was empty. Her attackers had vanished into the shadows.

The hands slipped down her arms and away. "You need warmth and safety. Tell me where you live, and I will see you home."

Warm shivers danced across her skin and left her longing for his touch. She wanted to lean into him, to rest her head against his chest. What the hell was wrong with her? She didn't need a hug; she needed to find her briefcase and get out of there. She stepped back. "Thanks anyway, but I can get myself home."

"Not alone. Despite my warning, your assailants may return."

Faith scanned the ground behind her. She couldn't worry about the thugs. She had to find her briefcase.

"It was foolish to walk a deserted path at night. Next time, take the campus shuttle."

"I can't. I live at the Hamstead Arms."

"The apartment complex near the freeway? Most students live on the other side of campus."

The jolt of disappointment surprised her. Even people who could see her assumed she was younger than her thirty-three years, but for some reason, she'd wanted her mysterious savior to be different. "I'm not a student."

The retreating lightning flared, and Faith spotted her briefcase. Her purse lay a few feet beyond it, near where she'd stumbled. She must have caught her toe on the shoulder strap. Glancing around for her attackers, she ran and scooped up her case.

"Do you work at the university?" The words seemed to brush her ear. Faith spun around. Her rescuer still stood on the path where she'd left him.

She took a deep breath and tried to calm her racing heart. Spooked; she was definitely spooked. It took another breath before she trusted her voice. "In a way. I'm here on a grant from the Viral Studies Foundation, researching the link between viruses and birth defects." She grabbed her purse, slung it over her shoulder, and started walking toward him. "My name's Faith: Dr. Faith Allister."

His body stiffened; his head tilted sharply down. Faith wondered if she imagined the faint click of heels. "Good evening, *Fräulein Doktor*. You may call me Ritter."

"Ritter?" The name jogged a memory from college German. "That means 'knight,' doesn't it? Do you make a habit of rescuing damsels in distress?"

"No." He swung into step beside her. Faith wanted to protest, but he was right, damn it. She couldn't afford to walk alone, not tonight. They emerged from the construction zone into the glare of streetlights. Ritter's voice had led her to believe he was her age or older, but beneath a bronze cap of water-darkened hair, his skin was flawless. Not a single line fanned the corners of his eyes. Sharp cheekbones, square jaw, his face was all angles, except for his surprisingly full lips. Sensuous lips, meant for kissing.

Faith looked away. What was wrong with her, fantasizing about a boy who had to be fifteen years younger than she was?

For the two remaining blocks to her apartment, he matched his stride to hers. She led him across the parking lot, into the building, and up the stairs to her fourth-floor apartment.

"Let me see you in." They were the first words he'd uttered since they'd left the construction zone.

"That's not necessary."

"Not for you, perhaps. But I would like to dry off before walking home."

"Yes, of course." Faith fumbled with her key and finally got the door open. There was no reason to be nervous, she told herself. The boy only wanted to get dry. "Go on in. There are towels in the bathroom, first door on the right." She clicked on the lights and forgot to breathe.

Young as he was and pale with cold, Ritter was absolutely gorgeous. His hair had begun to dry, and the lighter wisps curled on his head. His damp T-shirt clung to his broad shoulders and did nothing to hide the well-defined muscle of his chest and arms. Though he wasn't bulky enough for football or tall enough for basketball, she'd bet a week's salary he was some kind of athlete. A soccer player, maybe. He walked to the bathroom, offering her a glimpse of skin-tight jeans. The bathroom door closed, and Faith shook her head. The attempted assault must have shaken her more than she'd realized. She didn't usually ogle college kids.

She stashed her purse and briefcase in her bedroom and caught a glimpse of herself in the closet mirror. Her hair was drying, too, in a dark tangle around her head. Her face was deathly pale. Shock. That's what it was. Shock. A perfectly normal reaction. Faith took a deep breath and walked back to the hall. When Ritter stepped out of the bathroom a moment later, she forced a platonic smile. "My car's in Florida getting a new engine, but can I call you a taxi? It's awfully late to walk back to campus."

He stepped toward her. "I don't need a taxi."

"I'll pay the fare, of course. It's the least I can do after you were kind enough to walk me home."

"Faith." Her name flowed like velvet over her arms and stopped her babbling. He reached out and touched her cheek. "A beautiful name for a beautiful woman."

His eyes were blue, she realized. A bright, clear blue, like glaciers or icebergs. They didn't look eighteen. They looked ancient.

She backed away from his touch. Kept backing until her shoulders hit the wall behind her. "Who are you?"

Faith didn't see him move, but suddenly he was there, only a breath away. "Relax. I won't hurt you." He ran his finger along the skin just above her collar.

A wave of warmth surged down her neck and across her shoulders. Her arms grew heavy, but she raised them, braced her hands against his chest and shoved. "Don't touch me!"

He stumbled back, the surprise on his face almost comical. The warmth vanished.

"I'm very grateful for your help, but I want you to go."

His brow wrinkled, as if he didn't quite understood her. "Go?"

"I'm tired. I want to go to bed."

A slow smile crept up his lips. "I will join you."

Okay, she'd tried nice. Maybe brutal would work better. "I'm thirty-three years old. I do not sleep with children."

"Thirty-three. So old." He stepped toward her again. "You want me. I can taste it."

God save her from inflated male egos. Though she had to admit that in this case some of the ego was justified. A young man as beautiful as Ritter couldn't be used to girls saying no. "What I want is for you to leave."

His expression shifted from seductive to amused. "Amazing."

Faith scooted past him to the door and threw it open. "I'll call a taxi if you want, but you have to wait outside."

"I don't need a taxi." Ritter sauntered toward the door. He paused in the doorway. "You are an intriguing woman, *Fräulein Doktor. Auf Wiedersehen.*" Without seeming to hurry, he strode past the neighboring apartments and disappeared down the stairs.

Faith closed the door and sagged against it, panting as if she'd run a mile. *Auf Wiedersehen.* Though she hadn't studied German in years, she remembered what the words meant: not "good-bye," but "until I see you again." Faith hugged herself. From Ritter's lips, they sounded like a promise.

⊷ ⊶

Faith was on her second cup of coffee the next morning when the doorbell rang. She glanced at the clock over the stove. Seven thirty; Miles was early. Again.

"Just a second!" Groggy from too little sleep, she pushed out of her chair, slogged through the living room to the front door, and peered through the peephole.

Miles stood on the welcome mat, tall, neat, and impatient. Wind never ruffled his thick white hair, lint avoided his perfectly pressed suits. Miles Odell, M.D., Ph.D., S.O.B., had been her boss for the last six months. Though she supposed he was handsome enough in a hollow-cheeked, thin-lipped sort of way, she'd never seen him without a scowl. Faith opened the door, and he greeted her with, "Hurry up, we're going to be late."

"We have half an hour. Want some coffee?"

Miles strode past her to the kitchen. Faith followed, lip-synching his response. "All right. A quick cup."

She poured his coffee and sat down to finish hers. He took a sip and grimaced. "Do you have any sugar?"

"In the bowl in front of you." Where it had been yesterday. And last week. And last month. Miles had scheduled at least one meeting a week since the project began. When Faith complained about the time they stole from her work, Miles switched the weekly status meetings to Saturday morning. Every Saturday since her car died, he'd shown up on her doorstep thirty minutes early. Every Saturday for the last month, she'd had to put on hose and face her boss before she'd finished her coffee.

Faith sipped the Kona blend and sighed. The Viral Studies Foundation had offered her the chance of a lifetime; she wasn't going to throw it away just because the man in charge was an anal idiot.

His spoon clinked against the side of his mug. "Did you ever find those missing blood samples?"

Faith looked up, startled. Ever since she had discovered her files rifled and her samples scattered, she'd been begging Miles to beef up security. Up until now, he'd refused even to discuss the matter. "All but two of them. Unfortunately, they were the most promising."

"Pity." He sipped some coffee from the spoon and nodded as if satisfied. Faith tried not to wince when he stuck the spoon back in the sugar bowl. "You look nice today. Is that a new dress?"

First asking about her missing samples and now a compliment; Miles wanted something. She drained her mug and set it down. "Okay, what's up?"

He cleared his throat. "Another meeting, eight o'clock tonight. Banat's in town, and he wants to see us."

Eight o'clock at night? It was bad enough to waste the morning in meetings. Due to a screwed-up priority system, weekend evenings were the only time she could network with Bradbury University's supercomputer, BUSC, or Essie for short. Faith had been waiting all week to run data through Essie's anomaly-search program.

Faith stifled her protest before it left her lips. From his pinched nose and pressed lips, she guessed that Miles didn't like the idea of the meeting any better than she did. Neither of them had a choice. C. W. Banat, mystery tycoon and chairman of the Viral Studies Foundation, was coming to check on his investment. If they wanted his money, they had to oblige.

Miles pushed back his chair. "Time's wasting. Let's go."

Ignoring his deepening frown, Faith carried the mugs to the sink and rinsed them. She wasn't about to leave her apartment a mess, just because Miles was in a hurry. She grabbed her briefcase but left her purse in the bedroom. The clutch bag she used as a wallet was already in the case, and she didn't need to trip over that strap again. She turned to Miles with her sweetest smile. "After you." She locked the apartment and followed him down the stairs to his blue Lexus.

The storm had blown over, and late spring sunshine shimmered across the parking lot. Miles opened his door and folded himself behind the steering wheel. "Christ, it's already hot in here." He started the car and turned up the air conditioning, while Faith slipped into the passenger seat.

They drove to the hospital in silence. Bradbury University had one of the best teaching and research hospitals in the Midwest. Until a local news station did an "investigative report" on her research, it had also been one of the least known. Now protesters paced the sidewalk in front of the entrance, carrying pictures of smiling babies and placards that read, "Rights from Day One."

One of them shrieked as Miles pulled into his reserved space, and soon they were all shaking their signs and chanting, "Baby Killers," and "Day One, Day One."

Faith wished she'd brought a newspaper to hide behind. "Can't we do anything about those embryo-rights fanatics?"

Miles shrugged. "The court order keeps them across the street.

What more do you want?" He climbed out of the car and Faith scrambled after him.

She followed him around the crowd and up the hospital steps. To work in peace, she thought but didn't say. Without protesters or meetings. The automatic doors slid open, and she stepped into the cool hush of the lobby.

Faith wanted to pause and let the quiet seep into her bones, but Miles was already striding to the elevator. Their lab and offices were in the basement, but they were headed for the conference room on the third floor. She hurried after him. "About the meeting tonight..."

"Banat just left a message saying he wanted to meet. He didn't say why." Miles walked into the open elevator and hit the *up* button.

Faith stepped beside him as the doors closed. A hard, cold knot formed in her stomach. It looked bad, an emergency meeting late Saturday night. She knew how sensitive research foundations were to public opinion. Had Banat had enough of the protests? Was he going to pull the funding? He couldn't, not when she was so close. She knew in her gut she'd succeeded with the two missing samples. The foundation had already spent close to a million on the project. Despite the bad press, surely Banat would realize the value of spending a little more to see it through to the end.

The elevator shuddered to a stop, the door opened, and Miles strode down the hall to the conference room. Faith hurried after him. If Banat and the foundation pulled their funding, the project would die. Six months' hard work down the drain; but worse than that, the Embryo Rights Coalition would win. Faith couldn't let that happen. She wasn't killing babies; she was working to save them, and she wasn't going to let anything stop her: certainly not a bunch of knee-jerk fanatics.

Babies like her brother couldn't speak for themselves. She was their only hope, and she was damned if she'd let them down.

∽∾

Ritter hated springtime. The sun strengthened with every sunrise. During long, pale winter, he could bundle up and—wrapped in scarves and sheltered by a broad-brimmed hat—venture into the day. The bright sun of spring seared his eyes through the darkest lenses and blazed across every inch of exposed skin. He had yet to find a sunscreen powerful enough to keep the blisters from rising. Except for dark, stormy days, spring trapped him in his basement apartment from the early dawn until after sunset.

He barely beat the sun home this morning. After his intriguing encounter with Faith, he'd returned to the college girl's dorm room. Drawn by the dizzying scent of life, he'd knelt by the bed and brushed back her curls. She sighed as his lips touched her throat, as his teeth pricked her skin. It took only a sip to keep him sane for another week.

The girl didn't mind, wouldn't even remember. When she awoke, she'd feel tired but remarkably well. No headache, no hangover. Ritter might be a monster, but he was no parasite. He guarded his prey, shielded them from harm, and purified their blood, even as he stole it.

Hunger dulled, he'd run home, pursued by the threat of dawn. Now, after a few hours' uneasy sleep, he paced his apartment's worn carpet, trapped by the sun and plagued by questions. His kind did not hunt in packs, yet four had attacked Faith. Four against one mortal woman, and still, she had nearly escaped. He'd seen her mad dash for freedom, had watched her legs flash beneath her short skirt. She hadn't faltered or stumbled until her toe caught on the purse strap.

His strides lengthened. Perhaps she always ran in darkness. Her skin was surprisingly fair. The creamy white and rose contrasted sharply with her dark hair and smoky eyes. It was almost as if she avoided the sun.

Most fascinating of all, she had refused him. Ritter had learned long ago to drug his prey with his voice and his eyes. A word, a look, and even the most frightened became willing. Until last night. Last night, for the first time in decades, someone had said no. Faith had said no. Who was she? What was she? Not a monster like himself and her pursuers. Her pulse was too warm, her smile too open. The tip of his tongue brushed his fangs. No, Faith was no monster.

With a grind of gears, his cuckoo clock opened, and the bird cried the hour. Six o'clock. This late in May, the sun wouldn't set until half-past seven. He couldn't return to Faith's apartment for another hour and a half, but perhaps he could call her.

Ritter scooped up the phone, hit the directory-assistance button, and at the tone, carefully recited Faith's name and address. After a chime, a machine voice relayed her number and offered to dial it for him. He scribbled the number on a scrap of paper and answered, "Yes." Moments later, her phone started to ring.

She wasn't home. After four rings, another machine asked that he leave a message. Ritter hung up, disappointed that Faith's voice hadn't been on the tape. Perhaps she was at work. He closed his eyes and envisioned a map of the university. The science building with all its labs was on the other side of campus, but the hospital was right next to the construction zone where he'd met her. Ritter picked up the phone and dialed the hospital. Five minutes later, he hung up smiling. According to the volunteer who picked up his call, Dr. Allister often worked on Saturday. He could find her in her lab—room 17 in the basement.

๑๑

Faith's stomach twisted into knots as she followed Miles into the conference room for the second time that day. Two men stood by the end of the long table. One was about her age, with short sandy hair, a salon tan, and a well-trimmed beard. Armani suit. Rolex watch. Tumi leather briefcase. His elevator stare ran down her body and up again, stopping at her chest and fastening there long enough to make her uncomfortable before finally turning to Miles. What a jerk.

The other, an older man in a conservative, gray tweed suit, stepped forward. "Miles. Allow me to introduce my partner, Phillip Sloan." He spoke in a raspy tenor, as if he'd smoked too many cigarettes in his youth. He looked at Faith and smiled. "And you must be Dr. Allister. May I call you Faith?"

It took her a moment to recognize Banat. His publicity photos made him seem tall and stern. He wasn't. In her sensible heels, she towered over him. He couldn't be more than five feet four. Thin strands of hair tried and failed to hide a wide bald spot. He had pale, plump cheeks and a sweet smile. Though his hair was white, his features were unlined and youthful. Banat looked more like a balding cherub than the head of a multimillion-dollar foundation.

She held out her hand. "Of course. It's a pleasure to meet you, Mr. Banat."

Cool fingers brushed hers, then fell away. "Believe me, the pleasure is mine."

After they exchanged handshakes—Sloan's lingered a moment too long—Miles cleared his throat. "My secretary should have set up the coffee machine before she left. Faith, you know where her office is. Go get it, would you?"

Faith bit back the urge to tell Miles to get it himself. Now wasn't the time to teach her boss manners. "If you'll excuse me."

"Sit down, my dear. I don't need coffee." Banat's gaze slid to Miles and his smile vanished. "You too. I have something to discuss with both of you."

Banat chose the head of the table. Faith took the seat on his right and set her briefcase on the floor beside her chair. Sloan sat next to her. Miles walked around the table and sat on Banat's left. "If you're concerned about Dr. Allister's carelessness, I can assure you, she won't lose any more samples."

"Lose? I didn't lose them; they were stolen. Besides, I—" Faith caught herself before she said too much. This was not the time to admit she'd accidentally violated foundation protocols the night of the break-in. "If you'd let me go to the police, maybe we could get them back," she finished.

"No police," said Sloan, his voice as arrogant as his stare.

"I agree." Banat braced his hands on the table and leaned forward. Without the smile, he looked more like his picture. "We can't afford to involve the police. The media would be right behind them."

"But—"

"The Viral Studies Foundation cannot pursue its work without continued donations. Our fund-raising levels are down twenty percent from last year, mostly due to the unfortunate publicity your project has engendered. The foundation cannot afford further association with such a volatile issue."

Faith sucked in a breath. "Mr. Banat, I know live-embryo research is controversial, but I'm close to unlocking secrets that could save hundreds of lives and prevent thousands of deformities every year. If you'll just let me explain what I'm trying to do—"

Banat raised his hand. "I've read your grant proposal and your status reports. I agree the work is promising, but as the chairman of VSF, the welfare of the foundation has to be my primary concern."

"We could abandon the embryo research," Miles broke in, "and go back to using lab animals."

"We tried that, Miles," Faith said.

"Too late," Banat said at the same moment. "VSF is discontinuing all grants to embryo-related projects."

Faith's throat tightened. Without funding, her work would die. "How long do we have?"

"That depends on you. VSF can't afford to support your research. My partner and I can."

"I don't understand."

Banat smiled again. "As the chairman of VSF, I am bound by the sensitivities of our donors. As a private citizen, I am not. Phillip and I have a great deal of money, more than enough to set up a laboratory and support your research."

Relief bubbled inside Faith and faded almost as quickly. Her research meant everything to her, but why did Banat and Sloan care? "That's an awful lot of money. Excuse me for sounding suspicious, but what's in it for you?"

Sloan leaned toward her, so close that she felt his breath. "We get the patents."

Repressing the urge to scoot away from him, she swiveled to face Banat. His smile no longer seemed so angelic. Ever since the FDA ruled that genetically engineered viruses could be patented like drugs or machines, dozens of companies had sprung up, hoping to cash in on what *Time Magazine* called "The Viral Revolution." If her theory were right and her experiments successful, Banat and his partner would make millions. People would pay anything to ensure a perfect, healthy baby. "I won't sign a confidentiality agreement. My work's too important to keep secret."

Something flickered in Banat's eyes, something dark and at odds with his innocuous expression. "Once the patents are filed, you will be free to publish your findings. Accept my help, Faith. It is the only way to continue your research."

She wanted to refuse. Banat's offer sounded too good to be true. Despite his beguiling smile, he made her nervous. Besides, there was that partner of his to consider. Even if Banat was on the level, Sloan pushed all her warning buttons. She began to shake her head.

"Don't be a fool, Faith." Miles' scowl dug deep grooves between his eyes. "Mr. Banat's right. If we want to complete the study, we have to accept his offer."

"What about the university? Can't we get more funding there? After all, one of its missions is to facilitate research. And we provide work for two post-docs. That's got to count for something."

"Not much. Bradbury U has already reassigned them both to less controversial projects. The bad PR hurts the university, too. Face it, Faith, it wants to get rid of us, almost as much as the Embryo-Rightists do."

"The Viral Studies Foundation will soon announce that it has withdrawn financial support from your project. A short press release, stating that you have suspended the experiments due to lack of funds, and the Embryo-Rights Coalition will be off your back. Move your research to our laboratory and work in peace." Banat's gaze locked onto hers, and a chill swept her body. His eyes were gray and slightly tilted, as her mother's had been. "Think of it, Faith. State-of-the-art facilities, unlimited funding. You don't have to stop at the end of the year, not even at the end of the study. Follow your work as far as it will take you. All we ask is a chance to profit from our investment."

He sounded so reasonable. Faith took a deep breath. It would be wonderful not to run the gauntlet of protesters every day, to know that her files and samples were safe from vandalism. She knew colleagues who had searched a lifetime for the kind of opportunity Mr. Banat was offering her. Why was she reluctant to take it?

The three men watched her, waiting for her answer. If she refused, her work would die. More babies like her brother would die. She couldn't let that happen. "Fair enough. What do I do?"

❧❦

Faith said good-bye to Miles in the elevator and rode alone to the basement. Despite her fatigue—and a case of nerves from last night—she hadn't accepted his offer of a ride home. She still had two and a half hours to access Essie, and she was going to use them.

The elevator doors opened, and she walked past the closed LifeSource blood bank to her lab. She unlocked the door, turned on the light, and booted up her desktop computer.

The vandals had stolen her samples and rifled her files, but they hadn't found her backup, the memory stick she'd accidentally left in her laptop and hauled home in her briefcase. It wasn't an accident any longer; she'd kept her backup with her every moment since the break-in. Since taking data home violated the VSF's protocols, she hadn't told anyone, not even Miles. The stupid protocols didn't matter. The important thing was, she still had the data from the missing samples.

Faith dropped into her chair and typed the network command

and her password. While the desktop hummed, she lifted her brief-case to the table, opened it, and took out the memory stick. It fit in the window designed to hold a business card and contained more data than her year-old laptop. Faith's mouth went dry as she waited for her computer to connect to Essie. She thought she'd succeeded with at least two of the samples, but she wouldn't know until she ran a com-parative analysis of their genetic code.

Finally her computer chimed, and Essie's smiling icon appeared on Faith's monitor. She slipped the memory stick into her desktop, opened the latest file, and keyed in the command for Essie to start the anomaly search. "Okay, Essie, let's check these babies against the N-Double-D-B."

For the last three years, the National DNA Data Bank, the NDDB, had collected genetic information from every infant born in the US, every member of the military, every law-enforcement officer, every con-victed criminal, every teacher, and every candidate for security clear-ance. An individual's genetic makeup was rapidly becoming the new fingerprint, and civil libertarians were already filing suit against the government for invasion of privacy and the trampling of individual rights.

As far as Faith was concerned, the ACLU was missing the point. While she supposed the NDDB might someday be used to keep track of individuals, right now it was an invaluable research tool. The anomaly-search program was just the first use scientists had found for the data bank. In three short years, it had already led to the ge-netic mapping of heart disease and a cure for cancer. The anomaly-search program compared individual genetic codes with the several million codes in the NDDB and created a 3-D map of where the indi-vidual code differed from the norm. The scientist set the parameter for "anomalous," 10 percent of the database, 0.1 percent, or, in Faith's case, 0.0001 percent. The anomalies she was looking for were still very rare, though, sadly, growing more common every year.

Fingers tapping her mouse pad, Faith watched Essie's icon spin. "Come on, Essie. It's not that hard." Another chime, and twenty-three pairs of chromosomes replaced Essie's icon along with the message, "Anomalous genes found: 14, 23." *Yes!* Another keystroke to magnify and highlight the anomalies. Twin lights blinked from the fourteenth chromosome pair; interesting, but not what Faith was looking for. The twenty-third pair, though—both X for a female fetus—lit up like Christ-mas trees. *Bingo.* The first sample's anomalies, right where she wanted them to be.

Progress: she was finally making progress. Despite the stray anomaly on the fourteenth chromosome pair—probably an unintended consequence of her tinkering, which she'd clean up later—the sample showed clear evidence of cell/virus symbiosis. Fanatics had broken into her lab and stolen her work, but they hadn't stopped it. She'd have to rerun the most recent trial, but she knew what the results would be. The embryos in these samples had continued to grow. She'd weakened the virus enough for an organism to survive its initial assault. Phase One was complete. The more difficult, and vastly more important, Phase Two would have to wait until she moved to Banat's private lab.

The door behind her whispered open, and a velvet voice said, "*Guten Abend, Fräulein Doktor.*"

Faith spun around to see Ritter, the young man from the night before. His neatly combed hair was lighter now that it was dry, a honey gold. He'd traded his jeans and T-shirt for pressed slacks and a blue-striped dress shirt. A jacket and dark blue tie comleted the outfit. Except for the wraparound sunglasses, he looked like a young MBA on his first job interview. He pressed the door open with one hand and lounged against the doorframe. "May I come in?"

Nerves made her voice sharp. "What are you doing here?"

A knowing smile tweaked the corners of his lips. "I told you we would meet again."

"How did you find me?" A horrible thought rose in her mind. She was almost sure the goons last night were Embryo-Rightists. Could Ritter be one of them, his rescue a setup to win her trust and give them a better opportunity to destroy her work? At least he couldn't see her screen from where he was standing. She quickly saved the first sample's results, hit <*continue*>, and turned off the monitor. The second sample's results should be waiting for her by the time she got rid of him.

"Elementary, my dear doctor. Invite me in, and I will explain."

Despite her suspicions, Faith had to smile. She loved old black-and-white movies, especially Basil Rathbone's *Sherlock Holmes* series. Maybe she should invite the boy in. Chances were, he was just what he seemed, a college kid who liked older women. And if he *were* an Embryo Rightist, why not use the visit? Banat wanted the fanatics to think they'd shut her down. A hint in that direction might get them off her back even before the move. The chance was worth losing a minute or two of computer time. She'd talk to the kid, mention she was shutting down the experiment, then send him on his way.

Faith pushed back from her computer and stood. "With an offer like that, how can I refuse? Please, come in."

He stepped toward her, letting the door fall shut behind him. "The construction zone where we met lies between your apartment and this hospital, a logical place for a doctor to work. A quick call to confirm that a Dr. Allister is listed in the hospital directory, and *voila!*" He spread his hands and grinned. Serious, Ritter looked like he might be in his twenties. With that self-satisfied smirk, he looked about seventeen, a baby.

A baby who might be a spy. Faith closed her briefcase. "Put like that, it sounds so easy."

"Which is why Holmes hated to explain his reasoning. Once he did, even Watson thought it obvious."

"Are you accusing me of being a doofus, like Watson?" She turned and found Ritter standing close behind her. She tried to back away, but her thighs bumped the edge of the table.

He reached up, and for a moment Faith thought he was going to touch her face. Then his hand rose to the sunglasses. He slipped them off and slid them into his shirt pocket. "Only in the movies was Watson stupid. In the books, his was the sane normality that anchored Holmes' genius. Holmes needed Dr. Watson as much as he needed his violin or his cocaine. Without him, he was lost."

Ritter was only a couple of inches taller than she was, but he seemed to loom over her. She was suddenly aware of her breathing. The air cooled her lips with each inhalation and warmed them with each release. Ritter's lips parted. Each breath matched hers. A warm shiver ran across her shoulders and down her arms. She found herself leaning toward him and had to force herself straight. "Stop doing that."

He blinked and the shivery feeling vanished. "Doing what?"

"Sneaking up on me. Standing too close. I don't know. Just back off."

"As you wish."

The air grew cold as he stepped away, and Faith had to fight to urge to step after him. "What do you want?"

"To get to know you better."

"Why? I must be nearly fifteen years older than you are. Go pick on someone your own age."

"My own age." He spoke softly, his voice tinged with bitterness.

"Okay, I'll bite. How old *are* you?"

His lips twisted, but it wasn't really a smile. "Would you believe eighty-nine?"

Faith snorted. "No."

"Then perhaps I should say merely, 'Old enough to be legal.'"

Legal maybe, but not safe. "That still makes you years younger than I am. I don't date younger men."

He folded his arms across his chest. "Why not? My mother was nearly nine years younger than my father. I understand they were very happy together."

"That's different."

"Sexist, as well as ageist. For shame, *Fräulein Doktor*." His expression remained serious, but his voice rumbled with barely contained laughter.

"What's so funny?"

His eyes crinkled, as if he wanted to grin but wouldn't let himself. "You are."

The hell with dropping hints. Faith stomped to the lab door and flung it open. "Get out."

He stayed right where she'd left him. "But I haven't yet told you why I came. Admit it, you are curious."

"I'll live with it. Out!" She held the door with one hand and jabbed toward the hallway with the other.

Ritter shrugged. "As you wish." He sauntered toward the door, but stopped just before the threshold. Faith could have reached out and touched him, if she'd wanted to.

She clenched her hand and dropped it to her side. "What?"

His eyes, a bright, clear blue in the harsh fluorescent glare, caught and held her. "In order to enter the hospital, I had to run a noisy and unpleasant gauntlet. Allow me to escort you past it when your work is done."

Damn. She should have known the Embryo-Rightists would still be at it. "Don't worry. The protesters usually pack up and go home before I leave."

Ritter's eyebrow tilted. "Usually?"

"I think the goons last night were Embryo-Rightists who followed me from the hospital." The moment the words left her lips, Faith wanted to call them back. Her fears seemed more real, now that she'd said them aloud.

"And yet you plan to walk home again tonight."

"How did you know?"

His lips tipped into a close-lipped smile. "Your fear shows."

Faith tried for a nonchalant shrug and almost made it. "I'm not afraid, exactly. A little spooked, maybe, but not afraid."

"Even so, I will stay and walk with you."

The offer sounded wonderful. She'd been dreading the trek home. Unfortunately, she still had eleven samples to check, and she couldn't do it with Ritter looking over her shoulder. "No. I mean, it's very kind of you to offer, but—" Faith took a deep breath and tried to pull her scattered thoughts together. "The experiment I've been working on is being shut down, and I've got a lot of cleaning up to do. It could be hours. Besides, I'll be fine. I'm not afraid of a bunch of fanatics."

A shadow seemed to fall across his face. "Perhaps not, but I am. Fanatics will embrace any evil in the name of their cause."

The sincerity in his voice raised goose bumps on her arms. Ritter leaned forward until his breath brushed her cheek. "Believe me, Faith; I know."

Chapter Two

Herr Fleischmann was the richest man in Schwarzdorf, though he didn't live in a big house. Herr Rheiner, the mayor, had a big house, three stories of gray slate and red tile; but the biggest house in Schwarzdorf belonged to Herr Othmann, the banker. The first time Ritter Breitmann walked by it with his mother, he was too small to look over the fence and had admired the four-story marvel through the wrought iron filigree. With its fairy-tale turrets and sculpted down-spouts, *Othmannhaus* had been the pride of Schwarzdorf until the bank closed and the Othmann family moved to Dresden. No one lived there now. Weeds overran the grounds in summer. In winter, gales whipped tiles from the roof and banged shutters against the shattered windows.

Herr Fleischmann didn't need a house. Children grown, wife dead, he lived alone in an apartment over his butcher shop. The shop was in the center of Schwarzdorf, across the square from the closed bank. Fresh meat lay like bloody treasure for anyone to covet as they walked past the shop's sparkling plate-glass window. Herr Fleischmann's butcher shop was the cleanest store in town. It never smelled of sour blood or rotting meat. Fresh sawdust covered the wooden floor, and, even on the hottest summer day, the thick walls kept the inside cool. Herr Fleischmann didn't sell ham, or bacon, or pork sausage. His cousin had a dairy. Every Sunday, Herr Fleischmann hooked up his heavy-hoofed cart horse and drove into the country. He'd come back with a side of beef, or sometimes a whole calf, to cut into pieces and set in white trays behind the glass.

Ritter's mother, widowed as long as Ritter could remember, had an arrangement with Herr Fleischmann. She had six hens, good lay-ers, all, and the finest vegetable garden in Schwarzdorf. She traded eggs, onions, and sweet spring lettuce for soup bones and stew meat. Ever since Ritter was strong enough to carry the basket, she had sent him into town to make the trade.

Ritter liked Herr Fleischmann. He was a short, round man with laughing brown eyes. Blood stained his white apron, but his hands were clean. Every time was the same. "Hello, Herr Breitmann," the butcher would say, after the bell above the door rang and Ritter stepped into the cool, sawdust-scented air. "What have you for me today?"

Ritter set the basket on the table next to the scale where Herr Fleischmann weighed his meat. "A dozen eggs," he might say, or "New potatoes, green onions, and peas." His mother sent whatever they could spare. She thought a growing boy needed meat.

Herr Fleischmann would examine the basket's contents thoughtfully, nodding his head and stroking his clean-shaven chin. "Very nice. Wait here."

He'd duck into the back and return moments later with a large, paper-wrapped bundle. "No one wanted stew meat this week," he would say, or "This roast is too bony to sell. Maybe your mother can use it."

Ritter always said the same thing. "*Danke schön,* Herr Fleischmann."

Herr Fleischmann waved his thanks away. "Don't thank me. It's good business, that's all."

The basket was always heavier after the trade. Ritter had to use both hands to lift it from the table. He'd lug the basket toward the door, but, before he got it open, Herr Fleischmann would call out, "Wait. I have a surprise for you." A smile would begin to stretch Ritter's lips. He'd set the basket on the floor and turn. Herr Fleischmann would reach into the deep pockets of his apron, pull out a small, white sack, and grin. "A boy cannot live on meat alone."

There was always candy in the sack, peppermints or gumballs or lemon drops. Ritter's smile would grow until his cheeks ached, but Herr Fleischmann always stopped Ritter before he could thank him again. "Don't let the other boys know," he'd say. "This will be our secret."

Ritter stopped going to Herr Fleischmann's shop when he was ten. With the other children his age, he joined the *Deutsches Jungvolk* and was too busy marching in formation and listening to lectures about the glory of the Fatherland to carry his mother's eggs to town.

On November 5, 1938, Ritter turned fourteen and graduated to the *Hitler-Jugend.* He attended his first evening demonstration four days later. It was a beautiful night, clear but cold. Hard, bright stars speckled the sky. Ritter marched to the village square with the other boys, chilled but proud in the gold shirt and brown shorts his mother had sewn for his new uniform. Singing the *Deutschland Lied,* they circled the square and halted between the men of the village and the newly constructed bandstand. Herr Rheiner was there, and some men Ritter had never seen before. They wore brown uniforms and seemed very tall and grand.

"From Munich." The whisper swept the crowd. "Sent by the *Führer* himself."

The tallest stepped to the center of the platform. The torch light reflected off his white-blond hair, and his booming voice filled the square.

The words washed over Ritter in a meaningless wave, but their rhythm made his heart beat faster. Torchlight flickered across his comrades' faces. They looked as excited as he felt.

The man's speech rose to a final booming word, and the crowd in the square echoed it. "Now. Now. Now." The speaker jumped from the platform and led the crowd in a parade. They marched past the abandoned bank, chanting "*Deutschland, Deutschland, über alles*," and Ritter's heart leapt higher with each word. He was proud to be German, proud of his people, his history, his future.

They rounded the end of the square and headed toward Herr Fleischmann's butcher shop. A single light burned in the upstairs window. Apparently Herr Fleischmann hadn't joined the demonstration.

The tall man from Munich paused, picked up a rock, and threw it toward the shop. There was a crack, like a tree limb breaking, and a crash as the window collapsed over the white trays. Smiling, the man lifted a heavy black boot and kicked out the remaining glass.

Ritter stumbled to a halt. So did a couple of the other boys. Like a single-minded beast, the rest of the crowd surged around them and poured through the broken window.

The shop door burst open. More men ran inside. Metal clanged; wood shattered. Meat and white trays flew from the shop onto the street. Some of Ritter's friends snatched up pieces of meat and ran for home. Too stunned to move, Ritter stayed.

Screams now rose above the mob's roar. High-pitched, barely human. The tide of men turned, flooded back into the street.

One of the last ones out threw down his torch before leaping over the windowsill. The torch flickered. The sawdust caught fire. Red flames raced across the floor.

The mob parted. In the ruddy backlight, Ritter caught a glimpse of Herr Fleischmann. He was barefoot, his nightshirt torn. He held his hands to his face, and blood streamed through his fingers and down his arms. His brown eyes, no longer laughing, bulged with terror. They latched onto Ritter. "Please," he cried. No one else seemed to hear. The men closed around him. Arms raised, lowered, and raised again.

Ritter turned and fought his way out of the crowd, away from his friends, away from the fire-lit horror. He ran home, tore off his uniform and hid under the covers. His mother found him, still shaking, the next morning, but he wouldn't tell her what had happened, what he'd seen.

Fleischmann's butcher shop burned to the ground that night. Herr Fleischmann disappeared. Ritter never saw him again.

Chapter Three

Waukegan, Illinois
May 17, 2014

Faith finally got rid of Ritter by promising to call a cab after she finished. He raised his eyebrows as if he didn't believe her, but at least he left. She returned to her computer and clicked on the screen. The second sample's anomalies shimmered into view. Not an exact match with the first sample, but close enough. Another example of cell/virus symbiosis, and the embryo was still growing. Faith examined all the samples, the ones that had changed, the ones that hadn't, even the samples from embryos that hadn't survived. When she was done, she saved the results to the memory stick. She knew it was borderline paranoid to worry about the fanatics hacking into Essie, but she couldn't help it. The vandals had trashed her lab, but left the door undamaged. If they could get a key to her office, they could get a password to Essie. Faith removed the memory stick from her computer and slipped it into her briefcase. After a moment's thought, she printed out her notes and put them into the briefcase as well.

The anomaly search had taken longer than she expected. Faith had forgotten to eat lunch, and her stomach rattled on empty by the time she shut down the computer and left the lab. Ritter had been gone nearly two hours, but she still half expected to see him waiting for her. Telling herself she was glad he wasn't, she took her keys from the side pocket of her briefcase and locked the door.

"Faith!" Banat's sleazy partner, Phillip Sloan, hurried down the hallway toward her. "Do you have a minute?"

She tightened her grip on the keys. What was Sloan doing at the hospital at 10:30 at night? "Why?"

He stopped next to her, puffing slightly. "I want to talk to you."

Faith's stomach rumbled. She knew Miles would want her to be nice to their new funding source, but she didn't feel up to playing politics. "I'm on my way home. Can we talk in the morning?"

"I understand Odell left you without a ride this evening. I'll give you a lift. We can talk on the way."

Faith knew she should jump at the offer—she was so tired her legs ached and the thought of walking home alone still spooked her—but something in Sloan's smile made her want to clutch her briefcase and run. Faith had learned long ago to trust her instincts, and her instincts said walking home beat accepting a ride from Phillip Sloan any time. She dropped her keys into the briefcase pocket and snapped it closed. "Thanks, but a friend of mine is already on his way to pick me up. He's meeting me in the lobby. We can talk while I wait, if you want." She was pretty sure a busy man like Sloan wouldn't insist on waiting with her. He'd say his piece, then leave.

He fell in step beside her. "The break-in bothers me. Odell says it was fanatics who'll give up once you leave the hospital, but I'm not so sure. We have a lot of competitors out there looking to get a jump-start on their research. Do you keep the lab locked?"

"Whenever I'm not there. With so many master keys, though, it's not very secure." Faith stopped at the elevator and pushed the button.

"And I understand you take your laptop home every night. Are you sure there's no sensitive information on it, proprietary data, thieves might use to reconstruct your research?"

The elevator dinged and the door slid open. Faith walked inside before answering. "Mr. Sloan, I don't care about your competitors or proprietary data. I care about my research. Taking work home is against VSF protocols, but if I ever *did* bring "sensitive information" or pro-prietary data home, you can be sure I'd keep it safe."

Sloan stepped beside her. The door closed and the elevator lurched upward. "Even if there were a fire or someone robbed your apart-ment?"

Faith sighed. She hated hypothetical discussions, especially when she already felt guilty about breaking VSF rules. "I have a fireproof safe in my bedroom. Truthfully, I'd rather keep my work there than in a room that Embryo-Rightists have already broken into. Why, if I hadn't brought my laptop home with me the night of the break-in, I—" Faith suddenly realized she was about to admit to the very security lapse Sloan seemed so worried about. Not the best way to start a relation-ship with her new source of funding. "—probably would have lost that too."

The elevator stopped, and the doors opened. Hoping the heat in her face didn't show, Faith walked into the hallway. Sloan followed her. "You won't have to worry about things like that, once you move to the new lab complex. It's completely secure."

"Great." The word came out tired.

A thin line appeared between his eyebrows. "You're dead on your feet. Call your friend, and tell him he doesn't need to pick you up. I'm driving you home now."

Faith's mouth opened and closed as she tried to come up with a good reason to refuse. "I can't. He doesn't carry a cell phone."

"Then leave a note for him at the desk." Sloan took her elbow and steered her into the lobby.

The evening pressed down on the skylight, making the normally airy ceiling seem heavy and brooding. The volunteer at the desk was reading a paperback; the clusters of chairs usually full of recovering patients and their visitors were empty. All but one. Faith pulled out of Sloan's grasp. "Ritter."

He stood in a fluid movement and stepped toward her. "I arrived early and decided to wait in the lobby, so I wouldn't disturb your work." He extended his hand to Sloan. "Good evening. I'm Ritter, Todd Ritter."

Faith wanted to ask Ritter what game he was playing, but suddenly realized that—unlikely as it seemed—he must have heard their conversation near the elevator and was pretending to be her ride. "Mr. Sloan, I'd like you to meet my friend Ritter. Ritter, this is Phillip Sloan."

Sloan shook Ritter's hand. "Good of you to come, but I'm driving Dr. Allister home. We have business to discuss."

"Your business can wait." Ritter's voice settled over Faith like fine wool, warm, but a little prickly.

Faith expected Sloan to disagree, but instead he nodded. "Business can wait." He sounded distant, distracted.

"You are a busy man," Ritter continued, in the same smooth tone. He seemed to be speaking directly into Sloan's eyes. "Too busy to drive Dr. Allister home. You must go. Now."

"Too busy. Must go. Now."

Ritter turned his head, breaking eye contact. Sloan blinked, and his voice returned to its previous arrogant tone. "Since your ride's here, I'll be going. I'm a busy man, you know." He hurried off without saying good-bye.

Faith turned on Ritter the moment the automatic doors closed behind Sloan. "How did you do that?"

"Do what?"

"Don't give me that innocent look. Sloan was determined to drive me home until you started talking. What are you, a hypnotist or something?"

"Or something. I assume there is no friend coming."

Faith immediately discarded the idea of lying. Unlike Sloan, Ritter would insist on waiting with her until her friend showed up. "No, I just wanted to get rid of him. I don't want a ride. I don't want to talk. I just want to go home. Alone."

Ritter's lips twitched. He'd heard the hint—he just wasn't taking it. "You look half-starved. Let me get you something to eat."

She started to shake her head, but her stomach chose that moment to grumble. Loudly.

The twitch stretched into a smile. "Your stomach says yes."

"Nothing's open this time of night. I'll have a bowl of cereal or something when I get home."

"A bowl of cereal is not a meal. *Al's* is open until midnight. I will take you there."

Al's was a campus institution, rumored to have the best cheese-fries and milkshakes in the Midwest. Doctors at the hospital joked that just walking by the diner was enough to raise a patient's blood cholesterol to dangerous levels. Faith loved its bacon-cheeseburgers. Her mouth started to water, but she swallowed firmly and said, "No. Thank you anyway, but I'm on a diet."

Ritter's eyebrows bobbed up. His gaze left her face and burned a trail down her body. "A diet? You are already too thin."

"No one is too thin. Besides, I'm too tired to walk all the way to *Al's* and back to my apartment tonight. So, if you'll excuse me—"

"You always say no when I ask you something." He sounded aggrieved, almost hurt.

Faith couldn't help smiling. "You didn't ask."

His frown lingered a moment, and then he laughed. It was rough, as if he weren't used to laughing. "Let me rephrase my request. My car is in the parking lot. Please come with me to *Al's* for a decent meal."

Maybe it was the please that did it, or the way the name *Al's* echoed in her empty stomach, but Faith found herself nodding. "I'd like that."

Ritter offered her his arm. Feeling delightfully old-fashioned, Faith moved her briefcase to her left hand and placed her right on his forearm. They walked past the hospital's sliding doors and toward the visitor parking lot. The closest row of spaces was empty. Faith turned to Ritter. "Where?"

"Over there." Ritter nodded toward the far side of the lot. "I don't like to park Greta too close to other cars."

"Greta?" Faith followed Ritter's gaze to a silver convertible parked under a distant light pole. She let out an admiring whistle.

A huge grin flashed across Ritter's face. Faith only caught a glimpse, but there seemed to be too much white between his lips. Before she had a chance to wonder about it, Ritter slipped his hand around hers. He had large hands, callused like her father's. He gently pulled her toward the car. "Come see my pride and joy."

The details became clearer as they hurried across the lot, particularly the three-pointed star poised between the double set of headlights. Greta was a Mercedes. "Two-eighty series?" Faith guessed.

"Nineteen sixty-four 230 SL." Pride filled Ritter's voice. They stopped beside the car. He let go of Faith's hand and stroked the hood. "She was a mess when I bought her, but she cleaned up well."

"I'd say." Watching his hand caress the gleaming hood, Faith pushed back a surge of envy. She wanted the car, not that warm, comfortably rough hand. "My dad collects classic cars, Mustangs mostly. Buys them and fixes them up. I used to help him when I was a girl. That's where my MG is now—with my dad in Florida, waiting for parts."

She eyed the roadster's smooth lines. The top was down, but there was no sign of canvas folded up behind the seats. "She has a pagoda roof, doesn't she? One piece, solid construction. What did you do, leave the top at home?"

Ritter's eyes glinted. "In the garage."

"Aren't you afraid someone will steal her?"

"I don't fear thieves. My alarm system is quite good. Besides—" He pulled his arm gently from under hers and gestured toward the sky. "It's worth taking a risk to enjoy a night like this."

The moon hadn't risen, but stars spilled across the sky in a glittering arc. Wisps of high clouds drifted past, propelled by the same warm breeze that tousled Faith's hair. She sighed. "It is too nice an evening to spend under a roof."

"Would you like to drive?"

"Are you kidding?"

"I never kid."

For once, Faith didn't mind the amusement dancing in his eyes. She held out her hand for the key. "I'd love to."

Ritter hadn't bothered to lock the doors. Faith set her briefcase behind the driver's seat and settled into the leather's cool embrace. She ran her hand over the dark dashboard and grinned. "Nice."

"Turn her on."

She reached back for her seat belt, but there wasn't one.

Ritter must have seen what she was doing. "Greta was built before 1965. She doesn't need seat belts."

"Maybe not legally, but you could get killed driving without one." Faith knew she should get out of the car and walk home, but the lure of driving the little roadster was too strong. She'd be careful tomorrow; tonight she was going to drive. She inserted the key and turned it. The dashboard lit up, and the engine rumbled to life.

Faith drove slowly out of the lot to the street. Ritter chuckled at her caution. "Go ahead, let her loose."

Illinois Avenue was the main artery that ran through campus. Usually crowded with student traffic, tonight it stretched long and empty, as far as Faith could see. "Are you sure you don't mind?"

"I'm sure."

The car leapt forward. Faith slid through the gears; the transmission was as smooth as butter. The power of the engine throbbed through her feet, her hands, and set her whole body humming. Pressed against the seat, she felt her heart race the car, as the speedometer needle swung to the far right. "I don't know kilometers. How fast am I going?" The wind caught her words and flung them away, but somehow Ritter heard.

"Ninety or so. Not bad for your first time." Laughter, joyous, not mocking, filled his voice.

Faith risked a quick glance. Ritter had tilted his head on the back of the seat. He closed his eyes; his lips spread into a grin. The car zipped past a streetlight, and Faith caught another glimpse of his teeth. There was definitely something wrong with them.

The right front wheel hit a pothole, and the steering wheel jerked in her hands. Faith pulled her gaze back to the road, but her mind lingered on Ritter. The light was too dim now for her to be sure, but Ritter's smile reminded her of her own before orthodontia had tamed her aggressive eyeteeth and pulled them into a normal bite.

Faith grinned. Ritter needed braces. Picture perfect, drop-dead gorgeous young man that he was, he had crooked teeth. Now that she thought about it, he always kept his teeth covered, even when he smiled. Not only did he need braces, he was embarrassed that he did. The grin slid into a giggle. She liked him better, knowing he had a flaw.

"What's so funny?"

"Nothing." Faith was glad the darkness hid her expression. "It's just the car. She's wonderful."

"Thank you. You should turn here."

Startled that she'd come so far, Faith took the turn too quickly. The tires squealed, but the car cornered like a dream. Ritter didn't say a word, but she eased off the gas pedal and dropped near the speed limit for the rest of the short drive.

Illinois Avenue had been deserted, but *Al's* was hopping. Faith pulled to the back of the lot and chose a space under a street light. She turned off the engine and handed Ritter the keys. "Thanks. That was wonderful, but you'd better drive on the way home."

"If you wish." He nodded toward the bustling diner. "Shall we?"

Ritter climbed out of the car and waited for her to grab her briefcase before he turned toward the diner. They walked together to the revolving door, then he paused and motioned Faith to go ahead of him. Tickled by his courtesy, she pushed into the scent of grilling beef and hot oil. The line at the hostess station was long, but it moved quickly. Ten minutes later, they slid into opposite sides of a red vinyl booth.

Faith set her briefcase between her feet and reached behind the sugar dispenser for a menu. "What are you having?"

"I already ate." Ritter set his elbows on the linoleum table and leaned forward. "It is after eleven."

"Then why—"

"You haven't eaten." His gaze locked on hers. "Go ahead and order. I will enjoy the company."

That prickly feeling was back. Faith opened the menu and pretended to study the offerings until the tingle faded. "I hate eating alone," she said, when she was sure her voice wouldn't tremble.

"Then I will order a milkshake. I never could refuse a beautiful woman."

Faith lowered the menu. "Are you making fun of me?"

"No." His voice was calm, his expression smooth. "I am enjoying you."

Faith couldn't help it, she had to laugh. "You are the most conceited young man I have ever met."

His head tilted down in a sharp nod that was almost a bow. "Thank you, *Fräulein Doktor*."

The waitress hurried up with two glasses of water. She set them on the table and pulled out a notepad. Dark smudges marred the skin beneath her eyes, but her smile was genuine. "Ready to order?"

Faith ordered a bacon-cheeseburger and fries. Ritter snorted when she asked for a Diet Coke, so she changed her order to a chocolate malt. Ritter grinned and ordered a malt for himself as well.

The decor at *Al's* wasn't fancy, but the service was fast. Faith had just begun to tell Ritter about her father and his Mustangs when the burger and shakes arrived. Thanking the waitress, she picked up her burger and took a bite. It was perfect. The bacon was crisp and salty; the cheese, melty-soft; the burger, so juicy, it dripped down her chin. Faith closed her eyes and concentrated on chewing. "Mmmm."

Warmth brushed her lips. Not a physical touch, but a lingering heat, as if she'd been kissed by a phantom. Her eyes flew open. Ritter's chin rested on the knuckles of his clasped hands. His eyes were half closed, and he stared at her through his lashes with a mixture of envy and hunger that sent shivers down her arms.

"I could watch you eat forever." Ritter blinked as if surprised he'd spoken. He sat back, and the hungry look vanished so completely, Faith wondered if she'd imagined it.

She held the burger out to him. "Want a bite?"

"No, thank you."

Faith brought the burger to her lips, but it was hard to eat with Ritter watching. She set it back down. "How's your milkshake?"

"Good." Ignoring his glass and the straw next to it, he picked up the metal tumbler and took a sip. He shuddered and quickly set it down. "Cold but good."

"Of course it's cold. It's a milkshake."

Ritter's lips twitched. "Cold hurts my teeth. I need something to warm them."

Faith wasn't sure, but that sounded like a come on. She tore the end off her straw's paper wrapper, brought the straw to her lips and blew the paper at Ritter. The wrapper hit him on the nose. "Then order hot chocolate." Ritter stared at her a moment, then tilted his head and laughed. Faith joined him.

Dinner got easier after that. While Faith ate, Ritter talked about his classes. She was amazed by how many he'd taken. She couldn't find a subject he hadn't studied.

She swallowed the last of the burger and pushed the plate away with a sigh. "How long have you been in school?"

"Practically my whole life." He lifted his tumbler. "More milkshake?"

Faith had finished hers halfway through dinner and had been working on Ritter's. "I've already had most of it."

"There's a sip left. It's yours if you want it." He tipped the tumbler and a half inch of frothy liquid slid into her glass. "I'm full, and we must be going. I have to be at work by one."

"What do you do?"

"I work at a warehouse in Waukegan."

"At one in the morning?"

He shrugged. "It's the best time to load the trucks. Are you finished?"

Faith slurped up the last bit of shake and nodded. She reached for the bill, but Ritter snatched it from under her fingers. "My treat. I asked you, remember?"

"But I'm the only one who ate anything."

Instead of answering, Ritter slid out of the booth and headed for the cashier, a pale, black-haired girl who slouched behind an ancient cash register. Faith would have protested, but her stomach was too content. She settled for leaving their waitress an enormous tip. The poor girl looked like she needed the money.

Faith grabbed her briefcase and hurried to the front of the restaurant. She joined Ritter in time to see him hand the cashier the check and a fifty. The cashier didn't take them. She was too busy staring at Ritter. "Do I know you?"

"No." The word rippled across Faith's shoulders.

The girl blinked and dropped her gaze from Ritter's face to his hand. "Oh, sorry." She took the money and handed Ritter his change. Her fingers lingered on his until he pulled them gently back. "Come again." It sounded like a plea.

Ritter nodded and turned toward Faith as if nothing odd had happened. "Shall we go?"

Faith sighed. Nothing odd had happened. Ritter was gorgeous and undoubtedly used to girls' stares. She was the oddity, not the cashier. As hard as it was to believe, Faith was growing immune to Ritter's looks. During dinner, she'd hardly noticed how beautiful he was.

He gestured toward the revolving door. "After you."

"Do you need directions?" Faith asked, as they walked together toward the Mercedes.

Ritter opened the passenger door and waited for her to sit before answering. "No. I am like the homing pigeon. Once I have been someplace, I can always find my way back."

He closed the door, hurried to the driver's side, and slid into his seat. Faith put down her briefcase and automatically reached for the seat belt, but of course there wasn't one. "You really should put in seat belts."

"We will arrive in one piece. I promise." He turned the ignition, shifted the car into gear, and drove out of the lot. Faith forgot about safety as he picked up speed. The wind stroked her cheeks and ruffled her hair. She shut her eyes and pretended she was flying. Long before she was ready for the drive to end, the engine slowed, and Ritter pulled into the lot outside her apartment building.

Faith had expected him to drop her off, but Ritter slid into a parking place and turned off the engine. "May I walk you to your door?"

It was such a sweet, old-fashioned thing to ask. "Of course," she answered, then immediately wished she hadn't. Letting him walk with her meant she'd either have to say good-bye to him on her doorstep or invite him into her apartment. There was no way she was inviting him in, not after the way he'd come on to her the night before. She'd say goodnight on her doorstep, and, with her luck, he'd want a good-night kiss. A kiss. The thought made her cheeks hot. Ritter had great lips. They made it hard to remember how young he was.

Ritter opened the passenger door and Faith climbed out, briefcase handle clutched in sweaty fingers. She walked ahead of him into the building and up the stairs. Maybe if she said good-bye before she reached her apartment, she'd avoid the whole question of kissing. "Thanks for dinner," she said as she approached her floor. "I had a great—"

The words froze on her tongue. Light spilled across the dimly lit hallway, light from her open apartment door. It looked like the Embryo-Rightists had beaten her home.

✖

Faith's throat was as pale as blue-veined marble. Longing roared through Ritter, but he forced his gaze from her fluttering pulse and tried to concentrate on what she was saying. He had fed less than twenty hours ago. The hunger was an illusion.

Her voice stopped before he caught her meaning. She stiffened. He tasted anger, fear. For an instant, he wondered if she had caught a whiff of his bloodlust, but no, her turmoil wasn't directed at him. She stared at a pool of light at the end of the hall. "I locked that door."

The door was solid, by modern standards, and secured with two locks. The light streaming from the gaping doorway told Ritter that two hadn't been enough.

"Stay here." He sprang up the last step and ran down the hallway. Faith matched him stride for stride. He paused just before the open door and caught her arm before she darted inside. "I told you to stay by the stairs."

Her anger beat against his skin. "It's my apartment."

"And you don't know who is in it." Releasing her arm, Ritter stretched his hearing beyond the rhythm of her distracting pulse. Except for the drip of water and the hum of machines, the apartment was silent.

"I don't care." She pushed past him to the door. "Oh, God."

Ritter was beside her in an instant. Someone had torn through the apartment like a Russian platoon. The pictures in the hall had been ripped from the walls and slit from their frames. In their place, someone had scrawled "Day One" in dripping red letters. This was no ordinary burglary.

The scents from her apartment were as jumbled as the savaged frames. He smelled a riot of conflicting perfumes, food—fresh, not spoiled, and a hint of smoke. "Wait here."

He crept past the open powder room—towels and fancy soap littered the floor—and into the living room. White stuffing spilled from slashed couch cushions. A TV, VCR, and stereo lay in a tumble at the foot of the entertainment center. A glance into the dining area showed shattered crockery, but no sign of fire.

Faith followed him into the apartment. "I can't believe they hate me this much."

"Who?" The door to her bedroom stood open. Ritter stepped toward it and the smoky scent grew stronger.

"The Embryo-Rightists."

Bedding, clothing, and singed papers littered the small room, but what interested Ritter was the safe in the corner. Its door hung open on one hinge, and the smell of cordite clung to it like a shroud. "This wasn't about hate. Your thieves came prepared. They were looking for something."

A gasp pulled him around. Faith stood in the door to the room. With eyes gone black and staring, she clutched her briefcase to her chest. "I don't care what Miles says, I'm calling the police."

The chaos around him reeked of frustration. "Yes. And then you must leave. The thieves didn't find what they sought. They will be back."

≈ ≈

Help had arrived within minutes of her call. Both campus security and a Lake County sheriff's car. The deputies took a report and left. The security officer left with them, but returned a few minutes later with coffee, doughnuts, and "a few more questions."

"Thank you." Faith took the cardboard cup from the campus security officer and sipped gratefully. The coffee was cool and weak. It tasted like heaven.

The black tag over the breast pocket read "John O'Connor." O'Connor didn't fit Faith's notion of a security officer. The campus cops she'd seen in the hospital tended to be overweight and balding. This one was younger, thirty-something, with thick brown hair untouched by gray. He was taller than Ritter, but not quite as broad.

Maybe he was moonlighting from a nearby police department.

He righted one of her scattered chairs. "You look beat. Why don't you sit down?" After she did, he held out a bag of doughnuts. "You'll feel better if you have something to eat."

Ritter stepped behind her and put a possessive hand on her shoulder. "Dr. Allister doesn't need food. She needs sleep. Ask your questions tomorrow."

A familiar, prickly warmth washed over Faith, and O'Connor froze. Ritter was doing that hypnosis thing again. She turned, pulling away from his touch. "Stop it."

Ritter frowned and stepped away from her. The prickles vanished. O'Connor blinked. Faith took the bag before he could ask what had happened. "Thank you. I love doughnuts." She glanced over her shoulder. "Ritter, don't you have to go to work?"

"I called and said I wasn't coming."

O'Connor looked from Faith to Ritter. "Who beside your boyfriend here knew you weren't home tonight?"

Faith tried to ignore the wash of heat across her face. "Ritter's not my boyfriend."

"That's right." Leaning against the edge of the table, O'Connor pulled a memo book from his rear trousers pocket and flipped it open. Funny, Faith hadn't noticed him taking notes earlier. "You met last Friday when he saved you from some muggers, but you didn't report the attempted assault or an earlier burglary at the hospital. Why?"

"I wanted to call the police after the lab break-in." O'Connor raised an eyebrow. "Really, I did. But my boss said the publicity would be bad for our project."

"And you're convinced Embryo-Rightists are behind all three incidents?"

Faith clenched her fist until the doughnut bag crinkled. "Who else would want to destroy my research or write "Day One" in blood on my wall?"

"It's not blood."

Faith turned to Ritter, but O'Connor spoke first. "How do you know?"

"The smell. The hallway reeks of tomato and vinegar." Ritter's lips stretched into a slight smile. "And there was a ketchup bottle on the floor by the towels."

Faith hadn't noticed the smell or the bottle, but then, she hadn't noticed much of anything through the shock of seeing her apartment in shambles.

Apparently, neither had O'Connor. He frowned and turned back to her. "Did your boss tell you not to report the mugging?"

"No, I didn't think there was anything to report. Thanks to Ritter, nothing happened."

"Yeah. Lucky him showing up that way." The officer's voice was thick with sarcasm.

Ritter shrugged. "I was walking home from a party and heard the disturbance."

O'Connor closed the memo book and slipped it into his pocket. "Funny thing about parties these days. They're hopping with new designer drugs. Kids, girls mostly, go to them, get stoned, and wake up in alleys or hotel rooms with no memory of how they got there. Some don't wake up at all." A long stride carried O'Connor to within a fingerbreadth of Ritter. "You wouldn't know anything about that, would you?"

Faith surged to her feet. "You don't think Ritter—"

"I don't think anything. Yet." He glared at Ritter's impassive expression. "But I've got questions. Lots of them."

O'Connor topped Ritter by a good six inches, but Ritter raised his chin and matched his glare. They stood, gazes locked. The officer was the first to look away. "It's late. The questions can wait until tomorrow. Dr. Allister, I'll call your office in the morning." He looked back at Ritter. "Don't leave town. I've got questions for you, too."

"Of course."

Faith set down the doughnut bag and walked O'Connor to her door. "Thank you for your help," she said, opening it.

"Just doing my job." O'Connor's gaze latched onto hers. His eyes were brown, she realized, one shade darker than his hair. "Don't trust that new friend of yours. I can't put my finger on it, but there's something wrong about him."

The officer sounded sincere, but he didn't know Ritter. The night air sent shivers up Faith's arms. She didn't know Ritter either. She didn't want to think he had anything to do with the burglaries or the attempt on her life, but he did have a suspicious tendency to be at the right place at the right time. If he hadn't insisted on taking her to dinner, she would have been home and the Embryo-Rightists wouldn't have broken into her apartment. As if he could read her thoughts, O'Connor reached into his pocket and drew out a card. "My pager number. If you run into more trouble, call me. Anytime."

"*Bis später, Polizist.* Later." Ritter walked up behind her and laid his hand on her shoulder. It was warm and oddly comforting. His voice, though, was icy. "Save your questions for tomorrow."

O'Connor didn't even look at him. "Remember, anytime." He nodded to Faith and strode away.

She watched him disappear down the hall and tried not to feel abandoned.

"It's late. You're tired." The warmth was back in Ritter's voice. Faith closed her eyes and let him pull her against his chest. She was tired, deathly tired. "You need sleep, but you can't sleep here tonight. Not on a torn mattress and bedding."

Weariness dragged on her, making it hard to talk. "I hate hotels."

His arms wrapped around her, and his voice settled over her like a cloud of down. "Then come home with me."

෴

"I can't believe I agreed to this." The drowsy warmth had faded during the three-block walk from Ritter's garage to his apartment building. The neighborhood, with its cracked pavement and rundown buildings, made her almost as nervous as the young men who swaggered past them to the pounding beat of techno-rap. Faith's eyes ached with the effort to keep them open, but her brain was clear. Her fingers tightened around her clutch bag. "If you won't drive me to a hotel, I'm calling a cab."

"As you wish. The nearest phone is in my living room." Ritter unlocked the outer door and held it open. "After you."

The urge to refuse washed over Faith, but she shrugged it off. Ritter had been a perfect gentleman so far. Besides, she wouldn't be in his apartment more than a few minutes, just long enough to use his phone. She'd wait for the cab in the lobby. It was worn, but spotless, and the locked outer door should keep her safe.

She stepped over the threshold. Ritter followed, letting the door shut with a muffled click. Instead of turning to a first floor apartment or heading upstairs, he strode to the door beside the stairwell and unlocked it. The door opened silently, revealing a steep, narrow stairway leading down.

Faith stepped back. "You live in the basement?"

Concern lined Ritter's brow. "What's wrong?"

"Nothing." She took a deep breath. "I just don't like basements."

"What is it you fear, the dark or the enclosed space?"

She forced a rueful grin. "Spiders."

Ritter's expression smoothed. "Herr Carter takes excellent care of the building. There are no spiders, even in the boiler room."

"Carter is your super?"

"Yes." Holding the door open with his foot, he reached back and took her hand. "Come."

He led her down the stairs and around a tight turn to a plain wooden door. Faith didn't see any spider webs. Singling out a second key, Ritter unlocked the door and reached in to turn on the light. "After you." He must have sensed her hesitation, because he added, "I do not allow spiders in my apartment."

"It's not that." Faith's fear was ebbing away, and she was beginning to feel foolish. "I'm not used to walking into a strange man's home."

She entered the apartment, and Ritter closed the door behind them. He set his key ring on a table beside the door. "So, you think me strange?" Though he wasn't smiling, laughter lurked in his voice and crinkled around his eyes.

"You know what I mean." Faith followed a short corridor into a cluttered living room. She got a quick impression of too much furniture and too many pictures. There was even an old-fashioned cuckoo clock. At least everything looked clean. "Where's the phone?"

"On the table by the couch. The phone book is in the drawer." Ritter sauntered past her, clicked on a floor lamp next to the sofa, and sat down. The sofa was a soft brown and, like the matching easy chair, looked like real leather.

"Nice place." Faith set her clutch near a small digital clock and reached for the phone.

"Calling a taxi won't do any good." Ritter's voice cut over the sound of the dial tone. "It won't come, not at this hour."

Faith turned her back on him, dialed, and waited. A few minutes later she slammed down the receiver. "No cabs available. Bull!"

Ritter smiled his odd, close-lipped smile. "Stay tonight, and call in the morning."

Faith's anger vanished as quickly as it had come, leaving her more tired than before. "I can't stay here."

He caught her hand and pulled her beside him on the couch. "Why not? My bed is large and quite comfortable."

Somehow, her head settled on his shoulder. Faith wanted to pull away, but she felt too heavy. "I don't put out on the first date," she mumbled.

"Put out." He chuckled, as if he found the phrase amusing. "My dear *Fräulein*, I'm offering you my bed, not my body. I intend to sleep here on the couch."

"I'll take the couch."

"It's too late to argue." His voice was a solid presence, as tangible as the fingers stroking her arm. "Sleep."

She was too tired to fight. Faith closed her eyes and let Ritter's voice carry her away.

❧ ❧

She slept, the deep, trustful sleep of a child. Her head nestled on his shoulder; her curls pressed against his cheek. Ritter reached over and stroked the length of her throat. "Faith?" She did not rise to his summons, as she would if she had fallen victim to his voice. Exhaustion had captured her, not he. Her pulse beat against his fingertip, slow and steady. She snuffled, and her lips parted in a gentle snore.

For once, the blood hunger was still. Ritter smiled. It had been almost a lifetime since he held a woman, simply held her, and watched her sleep against his side. He nuzzled her hair, soft and sweetly fragrant. What would she say, this childlike doctor, if he carried her to his bed and held her through the night? He stifled a laugh. She would be furious, of course. In these modern, disrespectful times, even if he left her dressed, she would assume he had taken unwelcome liberties.

Or perhaps they would not be so unwelcome. Ritter had tasted her desire. Faith found him attractive, and these *were* modern times. His hand slipped down her throat and hovered over her breast. Her chest rose, and her slightly raised nipple brushed his palm. The warmth of it seared his flesh. Ritter yanked his hand back. No. He was not the unprincipled beast the *Polizist* sought. He did not take advantage of women. The irony twisted his gut: a monster with principles. But monster or not, for tonight, he would pretend to be a man.

He bent forward, slid an arm under Faith's stockinged knees, and stood. She was lighter than he expected, a sweet armful of curved warmth. She sighed and snuggled against his chest. Ritter cradled her in his arms a long moment, then kissed her temple. "Come, *Liebchen*. Time for bed."

Chapter Four

Schwarzdorf, Saxony
September 30, 1941

"Happy birthday!"

Grain flew from Ritter's fist as he spun from feeding the hens to face his visitor. Greta had tiptoed into the yard and stood grinning, hands hidden behind her back. The late-afternoon sunshine glittered off her blond braids. Ritter laughed and scattered another handful of grain. "It is *not* my birthday."

Her lips pulled into an adorable pout. "Then I suppose you don't want the cake." She turned to go.

"Cake?" Ritter wove through the cackling hens and caught up with her before she reached the gate. "What cake?"

"This one." Greta grinned and presented him with a small, white-frosted marvel.

Ritter stared at it, mute with amazement. "But how?" he finally managed. "The sugar, the eggs—where did you find them?"

"Your mother held back an egg for me. As for the sugar, I got it from the grocer. When I told Herr Dengler why I needed it, he was happy to sell me a packet."

"When you flirted with him, you mean." Ritter tried to sound stern, but he couldn't help matching her smile. Everyone loved his Greta. Heads always turned when they strolled through the village square together. His Greta was pink and gold, like a porcelain doll, tiny, plump, and beautiful. And sweet. Sweeter than all the sugar in the world.

She flushed prettily. "Flirted? You have wicked thoughts, Ritter Breitmann. Herr Dengler is old enough to be my grandfather."

A grandfather who couldn't keep his eyes off her. Thank goodness she was too innocent to notice how the grocer's gaze never reached her face. Ritter tugged one of her braids, as he had when they were children. "It's still not my birthday."

"I couldn't wait until your birthday, not with you leaving tomorrow." Her smile faltered. "Do you really have to go?"

"You know I do." Ritter gently took the plate and set it on a nearby fence post. He wrapped his arms around her. She smelled of vanilla and baking. "With Uncle Rudi in the army, Aunt Hilde's lonely and needs help in the shop. Who better than her own sister, my mother? And Herr Rheiner offered Mother good money for the house and the chickens. She'll be happy and safe in Dresden, and I'll be free to join the army."

Greta buried her face in his shirt, muffling her voice. "You're only sixteen. Can't the army wait?"

"I don't want to wait. I want to serve the Fatherland. It's my duty, *Liebchen*, and my honor." They'd had this argument before, but Ritter kept his voice patient. "Besides, Herr Rheiner's cousin is a *Panzergruppen* leader with Field Marshall Rommel and the African Tank Corps. They need men to work on the engines. If I wait too long, the war will end, and I'll miss my chance to serve under him."

"You'll be killed."

"I'll be trained as a mechanic." Ritter lifted her chin and kissed the tears from her cheek. "No more gloom. If you make this my birthday, I say it is also Christmas. Close your eyes, and wait here."

Greta sniffed softly, nodded, and squeezed her eyelids shut. Ritter sprinted for the house. He ran to his room, opened his dresser drawer, and took out a small velvet box. A moment later, he pressed it into Greta's hand. "Here. I worked odd jobs all year to buy it for you. Merry Christmas."

She opened her eyes, still shiny from her tears, and stared at his gift. "What is it?"

"Look and see."

Heart pounding in his throat, Ritter waited while Greta turned the box around and opened it.

"I saw it in a pawnshop last Christmas when Mother and I went to Dresden. It's a locket, real silver. Do you like it?"

She looked up and her smile outshone the sun. "Like it? How could I not like it?" Greta pulled the locket from the box and let the chain pour through her fingers.

"See the two flowers with their stems entwined? They're for us, you and me. And the back—I had it engraved."

She turned the locket over. "'You are like a flower.' Oh, Ritter, it's beautiful."

"There's room inside for two photographs. Put yours in one side, and I'll send one of me in uniform for the other. We will sit, side by side in the locket, until I return."

Her chin began to tremble. Ritter took her in his arms and held her close. "After the war, I'll settle in Dresden and work on motor cars. As soon as I make enough money, we'll marry."

She looked up. Fresh tears stained her cheeks. "I'd rather have you poor and alive."

"I won't die. And I'll come back as soon as the war is over." He lowered his lips to hers, a chaste and gentle kiss. "I promise."

Chapter Five

Waukegan, Illinois
May 18, 2014

Faith opened her eyes to darkness. She was lying in bed, between sheets that smelled faintly of citrus. The bed was hard, narrow, and not hers. She sat up. Damp air raised goose bumps on her arms. Where was she?

Memories of the previous night tumbled in her mind. Her ransacked apartment, the blood-red letters, driving to Ritter's place. That must be where she was now, in Ritter's apartment. In Ritter's bed.

At least she was alone and dressed. The elastic in her hose bit the tops of her thighs, and her skirt had bunched at her waist. She swung her feet to the floor, tugging the hem down as she stood. Feeling with one foot, she found her shoes and slipped them on.

The room was intensely dark; the chill gloom, as stifling as a tomb. She wrapped her arms around her shoulders and told herself to stop being silly. Ritter lived in a basement and worked nights. If his bedroom had windows at all, he'd keep them covered to block out the daylight. Of course the room was dark. All she needed was the light switch. Fumbling around, she knocked into a lamp near the head of the bed. She turned the switch and blinked against the sudden brightness.

Her first impression was of books. Except for a tall, thin dresser, every inch of wall space was covered with bookshelves. They stood shoulder to shoulder and reached from the faded carpet, past pipes and a heating duct, to the low ceiling. No wonder the room was dark. The shelves would cover any windows. Stacks of books littered the floor, the top of the dresser, and a small table beside the bed. There were hardbacks, paperbacks, current bestsellers in paper dust jackets, and well-loved tomes with faded covers and tattered pages.

The table held seven books, all with bookmarks in them. Faith picked one up. It was one of the older books, a hardback with the title worn off the spine. She opened it to the title page. *In dem Westen, Nichts*. She'd read Remarque's novel twice, once in a high-school English class, where her teacher had called *All's Quiet on the Western Front* "a classic of modern antiwar literature," and the second time in college, for a German literature course. In both languages, the story had left her chilled and sad. She set the book down and picked up another, a biography of Cardinal Richelieu, in French. The third book was in Russian—she knew the Cyrillic alphabet when she saw it—but the fourth was in an Asian language she didn't recognize. The other three books were in English, a paperback murder mystery, a collection of satirical essays from the 1800s, and a graduate-level treatise on aerodynamics. Not only was Ritter a linguist, but his range of interests was amazing.

Suddenly feeling like a voyeur, Faith restacked the books. Two doors led out of the room. One was tightly closed, the other stood open and revealed a bathroom with a pedestal sink and clawed tub. Though she felt grubby enough for a week-long soak, Faith settled for using the toilet and washing her face. She smoothed her skirt, crossed the bedroom to the other door, and cracked it open.

The room was nearly as dark as the bedroom had been, but, where the bedroom had been silent, the steady ticking of the cuckoo clock filled the room. A flicker of light, from a computer monitor she'd been too tired to notice the night before, caught her attention. Now that she thought about it, she could hear the computer's hum underlying the clock's ticks. The monitor showed a picture of a sunlit meadow. The image slowly changed to snow-capped mountains and then to cotton-ball clouds in a crayon blue sky.

Faith pushed the door wider. "Ritter?" Nothing. The light behind her cut a wedge across the carpet. It lit the end of the leather couch and a pair of long, bony feet.

She stepped into the room. It didn't seem as dark now. She could see a curtained window, a reddish-brown rectangle high on the wall. A green glow from the digital clock bathed the phone and her clutch purse in an eerie light. It was 6:13 AM.

Ritter's feet were white, almost phosphorescent. Faith walked around the end of the couch. He lay on his back, motionless, with one arm draped across his chest and the other hanging off the edge of the couch. He still wore his jeans, but he'd taken off his shirt. His naked chest shone pale in the gloom. The light from the clock fell on his face. It magnified microfine lines on his forehead and around his eyes and bleached the color from his still lips. Ritter looked older in his sleep, and tired. The chill wrapped around Faith's shoulders. Ritter didn't just look tired, he looked empty. Faith shivered. She wished he'd move, that he'd open his eyes, snore, or roll over. He was too silent, too still.

According to family legend, Faith had slept so soundly as a baby that her mother sometimes crept into the nursery and put a hand on Faith's back to make sure she was still breathing. In the dim light, Ritter seemed as still as marble, but surely if she touched his chest, she'd feel movement, the rise of his breath, the beat of his heart. Summoning her courage, she reached toward him.

Her fingertips brushed his smooth, white skin and jerked back. Ritter was as cold as stone, as cold as death. God, he couldn't really be dead, could he?

Nonsense. Faith sucked in a deep breath. The break-in must have bothered her more than she realized. Of course Ritter felt cool to the touch; it was cold in the basement apartment, and he didn't even have a sheet covering him.

She looked down. A dark shadow lay on the floor between the couch and the coffee table. Ritter must have kicked off his cover—not something corpses did. Faith picked it up. She'd expected a sleeping bag or fleece throw, but her fingers recognized the wool yarn and patterned holes of a hand-knit afghan. Smiling at the memory of her grandmother's overflowing yarn bag and ever-clicking needles, Faith spread the blanket over Ritter. He didn't move, not even when she tucked the end around his feet.

Before he'd looked like a corpse. Now he looked like a mummy. What if there really was something wrong? "Ritter?" The name came out a hoarse whisper. He didn't stir.

Light, that's what she needed. She couldn't very well conduct an examination by the clock's sickly glow. She could turn on the lamp beside the couch, but its light would hit Ritter square in the face. She didn't really want to wake him; she just wanted to make sure he was still breathing.

The window. Faith turned and studied the curtain. The bottom was in easy reach. She'd just lift the corner and let in enough clear morning light to make sure Ritter was all right. If she stopped before the light reached his eyes, he'd never know about her foolish worries.

The curtain was soft and surprisingly heavy. Faith raised the corner and stood on her toes to look outside. The window faced an alley, and early morning sunshine streamed down it, white and blinding. She turned and raised the curtain higher. The light flowed down her arm and across the coffee table to the couch. Ritter's afghan was striped in yellow, red and black—the colors of the German flag.

Ritter jerked up. The afghan went flying. "*Himmel!*"

Startled, Faith dropped the curtain, plunging the room into darkness. "I'm sorry," she stammered. "I didn't mean to wake you. I just..." Her voice trailed off. She couldn't very well say she wanted to see if he was alive. "I was just looking for the phone."

"On the table by the lamp—where it was last night." Ritter's voice was tight, as if he were struggling to keep from yelling.

Heat flowed across Faith's cheeks. "I remembered where it was, I just couldn't find it in the dark. You have a lot of tables in here. I didn't want to knock one over and wake you."

"Of course." The edge had left his voice, and he sounded tired. "A moment, please."

The room seemed darker than it had before. Faith could barely make out Ritter's silhouette, a deeper shadow in the gloom. He grabbed his T-shirt, slipped it on, and reached for the lamp.

Yellow light filled the room. Eyes squinted against the glare, Ritter swung his legs off the couch and stood slowly, as if it hurt to move. Faith felt a pang of remorse. If she'd slept on the couch, she'd be stiff too. "Are you all right?"

His laugh was short and harsh. "No." He turned and pointed to floor lamp and table next to it. "The phone is there. The address is 1666 Fallen Way. Now that the sun is up, the cab should come."

Faith stepped toward him. "Thank you for putting me up last night. I'm sorry I woke you."

Ritter closed his eyes. "No, it is I who should apologize. I am not at my best so early in the morning. I would offer to drive you home, but—" He opened his eyes, and a smile flickered across his lips. "It would not be safe."

Faith nodded. "To drive on so little sleep. I understand. I wouldn't ask you to, anyway. I've been too much trouble as it is."

His laughter was softer this time. It rippled up her arms, and suddenly he was in front of her. Though he was barefoot and she was in heels, he seemed to tower over her. He lifted his hand and tucked a curl behind her ear. "You have no idea how much trouble you are." He caught her gaze and held it. His eyes were a bright, hypnotic blue, and she couldn't look away. She didn't want to look away. Slowly his hand lowered. He turned, breaking the spell. "Make your call and go," he said, his voice rough once more. He strode into the bedroom and closed the door behind him with a solid thunk. Faith stared after him a long moment, then grabbed the phone and dialed.

※ ※

Taking deep, measured breaths, Ritter stood by the door and listened while Faith called the cab company. "Fifteen minutes," he heard. "Fine. I'll be in the lobby." The click of the receiver meeting the hook. The muffled clatter of her high-heeled shoes. His door opening. Closing.

She was gone. Ritter sagged against the bedroom door. The movement pulled his shirt tight. He cursed and yanked it off. Lines of blisters, red and beginning to ooze, striped his chest in the pattern of the blanket. "Good morning, sunshine," he muttered.

He had been burned before, when he was younger and more careless. Unlike his mother, who had always put butter on burns, Herr Doktor Übel had told Ritter and his comrades to use ice to control the swelling and pain. He hadn't known much about the monsters he had created. Over time, Ritter had discovered the true cure. A good, long feed would heal him in less than an hour...and kill the donor. His sigh was long and bitter. Treated with cold and salve, the blisters would linger for days. Throwing open the door, he went into the kitchen to get ice.

᠊᠊᠊

Faith paced the lobby. What was wrong with her? She'd bolted from Ritter's apartment like a scared rabbit. Why? Because he'd looked at her with those glacier-deep eyes. No threat lurked in their depths, no come-on, only pain and sharp, bright longing. She'd wanted to heal that pain, fill that longing. For an instant, she would have agreed to anything he'd asked, would have said yes without even knowing the question.

She glared at the basement door. He was good, no doubt about it. She'd seen him pull his hypnosis trick on other people, but this was the first time he'd pulled it on her. Because that had to be what was going on, a hypnotist's trick. She'd never felt so open before, so vulnerable, so willing.

A sharp rap pulled her around. A balding man with a huge beer belly stood outside the lobby door. "You the lady wants a taxi?" he called through the door.

"Yes." Tucking her clutch under her arm, Faith fumbled with the door knob and opened the door. "Thank you for coming so quickly."

"No problem." He turned and lumbered down the stairs to a red, white, and blue taxi.

Faith followed as quickly as her high heels allowed. She gave the cabby her address and climbed into the back. The cab reeked with an eye-burning combination of cigarette smoke and pine-scented air freshener. Faith cracked open the window beside her and let her eyes drift closed. She was so tired. Maybe that was the problem. Maybe Ritter hadn't pulled a trick on her. Maybe her momentary weakness was caused by too much stress and not enough rest. She'd go home, clean up the mess, and buy herself a new safe. Once her work was secure, she could sleep.

Her stomach twisted into a cold, hard knot. She didn't have her memory stick or her notes. She'd taken out the clutch bag to show the police her ID and had grabbed it before leaving the apartment with Ritter, but she'd been so tired, she'd forgotten her briefcase. Her work was still sitting under the dining-room table in her ransacked apartment. Faith leaned forward and banged against the barrier the separated her from the driver. He met her gaze in the rearview mirror. "Hurry, please. I have to get home. It's an emergency."

The cabby nodded, and the taxi surged forward. There was little traffic so early in the morning, and the taxi whipped around the handful of delivery trucks and early risers as if they were standing still. Faith watched a green light turn yellow and prayed he wouldn't stop.

The cab screeched up to her building less than ten minutes later.

The driver slid open the partition. "Quick enough for you?"

Instead of answering, Faith thrust a twenty into his hand and pushed out of the cab. She sprinted into the building and up the stairs.

Her door was closed. Locked. She nearly dropped the key fitting it into the keyhole, but it finally turned and the door opened. If anything, the mess looked worse than it had the night before. Her scattered possessions and slashed furniture seemed even more pathetic with sunlight streaming over them. The sweet-sour smell of ketchup permeated the air. Gagging on the odor, she ran through the living room. Please, God, let the briefcase be there.

It was, propped against the table leg where she'd left it. Faith threw the briefcase on the table, thumbed the combination lock, clicked the latch, and threw it open. Her breath flew out in a *whoosh*. The memory stick and her notes were still inside. Safe.

"Faith? My Lord, what happened?"

Slamming the briefcase closed, she spun around. She didn't know anyone else who got up this early. No one except…"Miles, is that you?"

"Of course it's me." She heard a crunch and a curse. A moment later, her boss stomped out of the hallway. His right shoe, the most expensive brand of running shoe made, and half his calf were covered in white dust. The sweet scent of lily of the valley rose off him in a cloud. Apparently, Miles had found her bath powder.

He was dressed for running, in spandex shorts and a mesh tank top. He had nice legs, Faith noticed with surprise, but his chest was every bit as bony as she'd imagined. "What are you doing here? We don't work Sundays."

"I was on the last leg of my morning run and saw your door open. What happened here? Are you all right?" For once, Miles' hair was mussed. The terry band around his head was dark with sweat. He looked winded and worried, as if he'd run to her rescue, and Faith felt a surge of gratitude.

"Someone broke into my apartment last night. I'm okay, just a little shook up. Want some coffee?" She looked around for her coffee maker and saw it on the kitchen floor. The carafe had shattered, and its pieces mingled with the blue and white shards of her favorite mug. Faith's throat clenched, and she dropped into a chair. "Damn."

A gentle weight settled on her shoulder. Miles' hand. His face creased with concern. "I ran past the Donut Den on my way here. They're open and the coffee doesn't smell too bad. If you're sure you'll be all right, I'll jog home, change and come back with the car. We can grab a cup there." His gaze drifted over the apartment. "I'll bring the number of a good cleaning service. You're going to need it."

Good old Miles, he had that patrician nose-wrinkle down cold. For once, Faith didn't mind that he was predictable to the point of nausea. Predictable sounded good right now. "Thanks."

He nodded and left. Faith grabbed her briefcase and hauled it with her into the bedroom. She wasn't going anywhere without her work, not until she found a safe place to keep it.

Her room was just as bad as she remembered—papers, clothes, and mattress stuffing everywhere. She gathered the scattered garments and dumped them on her dresser. While she had no trouble finding jeans and a T-shirt, her underwear seemed to have vanished. She searched behind the dresser and under the ruined sheets before spotting a shimmer of blue satin on the corner of her overturned night stand. It was a pair of bikini panties. Even though the thought of wearing underwear the thieves had handled made her skin crawl, she stripped naked and quickly put on clean clothes.

Faith's bathroom was a disaster. It would take her hours to find anything, but she had a comb and lipstick in her clutch. She sat on her ruined bed and checked her reflection in the cracked closet door that had once served as her bedroom mirror. Pale as the clumps of stuffing, except for the gray smudges under her eyes—no wonder Miles had asked if she was all right. Faith dug the comb through her hair a few times, trying to fluff it up. She pinched her cheeks and smeared on lipstick. By the time Miles came back, she looked and felt halfway human. She'd found her sandals and was in the kitchen sweeping up her coffeepot. Faith shoved her keys, ID, and some money into her pocket. She left the clutch but grabbed the briefcase before leaving. From now on, her work went wherever she did.

≈≈

"So your place was a mess when you got home last night?"

Faith nodded and tried her coffee. Even in a cardboard cup, it was a fresh, hot lifesaver.

Miles had changed into a polo shirt and pressed khakis. His GQ persona looked out of place among the truck drivers that seemed to be the donut shop's regular Sunday-morning customers. He hunched like a praying mantis over the small table between them. The white plastic surface was sticky with hours-old coffee rings and flakes of sugar glaze. He looked down at it, clutched his cup, and took a nervous sip. "You're lucky you didn't walk in on the vandals."

Nodding, Faith drained her cup and stood. "Want a refill?"

Miles lowered his head for another microscopic taste. "No thanks. You said you got home around midnight. Why so late?"

"I was running an analysis of—" What was she doing, letting her sleep-deprived mouth run away with her like that? Now was not the time to admit to taking work home. "—the remaining samples. Miles, we're finally making progress. Let me get more coffee, and I'll tell you about it." Taking advantage of a momentary lull in business, Faith hurried to the counter. A fresh batch of glazed doughnuts glittered from the cooling rack behind the clerk. They looked wonderful and smelled better. Faith's stomach growled, reminding her how long it had been since she ate that burger. "More coffee, please, and two of the glazed. For here."

She could feel Miles watching her. His impatience beat against her back, but she was hungry, tired, and not about to rush. Faith paid for the doughnuts and walked back to the table, carefully balancing her cup and the two paper plates. She set one by her seat and the other in front of Miles. Maybe the sugar would sweeten his mood. He waited until she sat, then leaned forward, resting his elbows on the dirty table. "What kind of progress?"

Despite her exhaustion, enthusiasm crept into her voice. "One of the remaining samples shows clear signs of cell/virus symbiosis. Two others are probables. The last mutation worked. We've got some keepers."

Miles sat back and beamed. "That's great. And you recorded all the parameters?"

"Of course." The donut was warm. The glaze cracked when Faith bit into it, and filled her mouth with rich sweetness. "Ummm, you should try yours, Miles. It's really good."

"I can't wait to see the data in the lab tomorrow."

"No need to wait." Still chewing, she nodded toward her brief-case. "It's all right here."

He stared at the case, then raised his gaze to meet hers. "Taking data from the lab was inexcusably reckless. If you'd left earlier last night, the vandals could have snatched your briefcase, and we'd have lost all that work."

Damn. Faith swallowed, but the bite stuck in her throat. How was she going to talk her way out of this one? Maybe a strategic diversion. "I did leave earlier. If Ritter hadn't taken me to dinner, I might have walked in on the bastards."

An odd look creased Miles' face. "Ritter?"

"A student I met after work one night. He stopped by the hospital to give me a ride home."

"Ritter. A student you say?" Disapproval laced Mile's voice. "What's his last name?"

Normally, Faith would've told Miles her friends were none of his business, but she was just glad she'd found a way to distract him. "Ritter is his last name." She thought back to when Ritter had intro-duced himself to Sloan. "His first name is Todd."

"Todd Ritter." Miles' expression cleared. He slowly shook his head. "Don't recognize it. How long have you known him?"

"Not long."

"So you don't know him well."

Faith stared at her plate. "That's what the police asked when they came to investigate the break in—how well did I know Ritter." She looked up. "There is something odd about him, but he doesn't have anything to do with those Embryo-Rightists."

"You can't know that for sure." Miles reached out and took Faith's free hand. She was so surprised, she almost spilled her coffee. "I know I've been skeptical about your requests for added security, but the break-in at your apartment has changed my mind. I think we should move our research to Banat's private lab on Monday."

Faith jerked her hand back. "Monday? But we can't, it will take more than a day just to clean out my office at the hospital."

"I thought you wanted extra security."

"I do. It's just…" Faith gestured vaguely with her coffee cup. How could she explain that she didn't trust either Banat or Sloan, that something about their offer made her skin creep? "I hadn't expected to move so soon. I thought we'd switch labs after we finished the current phase of the project."

"It's not just the project. Your apartment's not safe anymore. You have to leave it." Faith opened her mouth to protest that she had a lease, but Miles rode right over her objections. "The fanatics know where you live. They'll be back. Until the heat dies down, you need security. So do I. I called Banat after I got home this morning, and he agrees. There are apartments adjacent to his laboratory complex. They're behind an electrified fence and locked gates, safe and secure. Banat built them for visiting scientists. He's offered to lend each of us an apartment, rent free, for the duration of the project."

"I don't know. This is awfully sudden."

"How much warning did you get with the break-in? Be sensible, Faith. This is the only way to safeguard your work."

Faith raised her cup to her lips to mask her hesitation. Sloan made her nervous, true, but it wasn't like she'd be living with him. Her work—that was the important thing. She set the coffee down. "You're right. When can we go?"

⌗ ⌗

Ritter spoke seventeen languages and could swear in more, but he didn't know a word harsh enough to capture the agony of ice hitting a burn. He filled a zipper bag with cubes from the freezer and carried it to the living room. The lamplight hurt his eyes, so he turned it off before lying on the couch. He took a deep breath and lowered the bag to his chest. "*Himmel*," he whispered, and concentrated on breathing. In, out. In, out. The throbbing slowly dulled. His skin grew numb. When he could no longer feel the ice, Ritter lifted the bag. Most of the cubes had melted. The remainder floated in their comrades' blood. Smiling grimly at the image, Ritter hurried into the kitchen to refill the bag. He knew from experience that the respite wouldn't last.

He was pouring the water into the sink when a discordant note filled his apartment. Someone was demanding entrance into the building. Ritter received little mail and no daytime visitors. Occasionally someone seeking another resident of the six-flat building would hit his button by mistake, but the disturbance was brief and rarely repeated. The note continued, vibrating through the air and calling back the flames to his chest. The idiot was leaning on the button.

Ritter stormed to the intercom by his front door and slammed the switch. "What?"

The note died. "Let me in."

Despite the intercom's distortion, Ritter recognized the voice. Deep. Bitter. *Cole*. Ritter punched the intercom again. "How did you find me?"

"Phone book. Open the door before I fry."

Ritter hit the button for the door and a buzz sounded upstairs. "Come in." His voice sounded as grudging as he felt.

The outside door opened, closed. Heavy footsteps shook his ceiling. Ritter left the apartment and ran up the steps to the ground level door.

"Hurry." Cole spoke softly, but the words penetrated the hundred-year-old oak. Ritter unlatched the door and backed down the stairs to a point that he knew the sun couldn't reach.

"Come," he called.

The door opened with a blast of light, quickly blocked by a tall shadow. The scent of drying blood drifted down the stairs. It grew stronger when the door slammed and darkness returned.

Cole loomed at the top of the stairs. He wore a floor-length, black leather duster and a broad-brimmed black hat. Pulling off the hat, he stuck it under his arm and stripped off a pair of black leather gloves. His dark African face broke into a wide, fanged grin. "For a moment there, I thought you weren't gonna wake up."

"I was already awake. Come. The apartment is down here." Ritter turned and trotted down the stairs. Each step jarred his chest and fanned the heat.

"What's wrong? You smell half-starved."

Ritter kicked his door open and stomped in. Though the dark soothed his eyes, he was starting to sweat. He had to get more ice. Cole followed him into the kitchen. Ritter turned toward the refrigerator, and Cole let out a long whistle. "Shit, what you do, go sunbathing?"

"Very funny." Ritter cracked another tray of ice and dumped it into the plastic bag. "I had a guest, and she opened the curtain. She didn't know."

"And you let her go. Fucking Boy Scout. I would've drunk her dry."

Ritter turned to face him. "Cole, you are the fifth vampire to disturb my peace in the last three days. Why are you here?"

Cole slipped off his coat and frowned at the barely visible specks of blood on the cuff. "I got caught too far away from home, too late in the day. I'm tougher than you, but even with leather and sunscreen, I was starting to sizzle."

"I know why you had to flee the sun." Ritter clapped the ice to his chest and hissed at the pain. "What are you doing in Illinois? Last time I heard, you were in Virginia, hunting pimps and generals."

Cole threw the coat over one shoulder. "I'm still on the hunt. Remember that little snot-nosed captain, the one you called a *Wunderkind*?"

"Miles Odell? How could I forget?"

"He's not two miles from here. Running a research gig out of the university hospital. The same virus shit."

Ritter let the ice drop. "Are you sure? The same?"

"That's what I hear. Calls it something else, though, embryo-virus symbiosis. There was a stink about it on the news—Embryo-Rightists squawking about the 'sanctity of life' to a representative of the Viral Studies Foundation." His lips spread in another grin. "They'd piss their pants if they knew what the bastards were really up to."

Despite his blazing chest, Ritter suddenly felt cold. What was it Faith had said about her grant? Something about studying viruses and birth defects. "What does this foundation have to do with Odell?"

"It fronts the money. The setup feels dirty, but I haven't been able to find out if the board members know the score or not. Odell will tell me, once I find him." The grin faded. "You look like shit."

"Eloquent as always." Holding the ice to his chest with one hand, Ritter gestured toward the living room. "After you."

Cole sauntered into the room with long, casual strides. He tossed his coat at the hook by the door—it caught—and threw himself into the easy chair. Kicking it back, he propped his feet on Ritter's coffee table. "Nice place. How long you been here?"

"Twelve years." Ritter sank to the couch and leaned back. He couldn't believe that Faith would involve herself in Odell's villainy, but he had to make sure. The question was how to find out without setting Cole on her. "What do you know about the Viral Studies Foundation?"

"Why? You want in?"

"To prevent another disaster like the one in '71? Of course."

Cole shrugged. "Don't know much yet. The chairman's connected. He sprang on the charity scene out of nowhere a few years ago, with a shitload of money and nothing to spend it on. Typical laundering setup. Ten months ago, he started pulling in more money and spending less. My sources think he's investing in designer-drug labs."

"Your sources are well informed."

Cole's face split into an enormous smile. His fangs glistened in the light from Ritter's screen saver. "My contacts are well motivated."

The chill from the ice sank through Ritter's numbing skin. Cole was pitiless and relentless. Once he started a hunt, he allowed nothing to interfere. If Cole discovered Faith was helping Odell, even innocently, he would kill her in a heartbeat.

Ritter set the ice in his lap. He and Cole had once been friends. Perhaps that still counted for something. "I met a woman a few days ago. Her name is Faith, Faith Allister. She's a scientist, working on a grant from the Viral Studies Foundation." Cole's eyes narrowed, and Ritter prayed it wasn't already too late. Short of killing Cole, Ritter knew only one way to protect her. "She's under my protection, Cole. Stay away from her."

"So you've met the pretty doctor." Cole slowly stood, and Ritter did too. The ice tumbled to the floor, forgotten. "Saw her on the news, explaining the importance of Odell's research. Friend of yours or not, I'm going to shred her into sushi. She's one of them, Ritter. Another fucking Frankenstein."

"Or an ignorant pawn. You don't know which."

Cole was a head taller than Ritter. He was uninjured and freshly fed. If it came to fists and fangs, Ritter knew he wouldn't win. But he was older than Cole and, in some ways, stronger. Ritter walked around the table and stopped within easy reach of Cole's long arms. He dared show no fear, no uncertainty. Catching Cole's gaze, he put all his years and all his authority behind his voice. "Stay away from her. She's mine."

They stood for a moment, gazes locked.

"I can't." Cole's voice shook with the effort it took to fight Ritter's control. "Not if it means another '71. If Odell and his team make another batch—"

"They won't." Ritter kept the power in his voice, the certainty. "I will prove Faith's innocence and help you stop Odell."

"And if she's not innocent?"

Ritter took a deep breath and released his friend. "I will kill her myself."

Chapter Six

Ritter walked between two rows of beds. A body lay on each, wrapped in a white sheet, motionless and apparently lifeless. He tried not to think of the missing beds and the men they had once held.

"So these are the lucky ones." Cole paced beside him. "A dozen survivors out of...how many?"

They were in the basement of a warehouse, converted to a medical facility for the most secret germ-warfare experiment in history. The room was cold, but Ritter didn't mind the chill; dark, but Cole still needed the dark. So would their charges.

"Out of fifty." Ritter's answer came out tight. He forced a breath, a smile. It would never do to reveal his doubts to Cole. His young friend needed hope, not despair. "Your scientists were right; they successfully weakened the infection. Among my comrades, only four survived out of a hundred." He scanned the rows of sleeping men. "These men knew the risks before they agreed."

"Fuck. Most of them couldn't even read the waiver they signed. Odell promised them a way out of hard labor in an army prison. That's all they knew. Poor bastards—they don't understand the hell they'll wake to. Not yet."

"Odell also promised to seek a cure for this affliction. A cure for them. A cure for us."

"He better keep that promise. I'm sick to death of blood."

Ritter stopped beside one of the comatose patients. A circle of moisture darkened the tape around his hand. "Look. His body rejected the IV needle. It will not be long now."

Cole leaned close. "That happen to me?"

"Yes; it is the first sign of recovery."

"How long, then?"

"One more night, maybe two, before they wake."

Cole touched the damp tape, then straightened. "I don't know if I can do it, Ritter: hand them a pint of blood, smile, and tell them it's going to be okay, when I know it's a fucking lie."

Ritter sighed. He didn't like Odell's experiment, either, or trust the slick *Wunderkind's* promises; but that was why he had to remain and keep watch on him. "There is no need to lie. We will simply help the volunteers adjust to their new life. Help them as I helped you."

He turned and headed toward the door. "Come, we must tell Odell and the others. They have much to prepare."

≈ ≈

"It's not working."

Ritter just shook his head and broke into a trot. He and Cole had been given the night off, but now the first rays of dawn chased them back to the warehouse.

Cole stormed after him. "It's been a fucking week already, and they still go crazy if any of the medical staff come into the room. You had me under control the first day. They have enough blood. They're not hungry, they're—"

Ritter burst into the safety of the warehouse and spun to face his comrade. "Monsters? And what are we? I tell you the same thing I told General White and that *Wunderkind* Odell. Give them time. They will come around." He waited for Cole to enter the warehouse and slammed the door behind him before turning down the hallway to their quarters.

They were housed in a room off the volunteer's ward. Cole walked beside him. Worry had replaced the anger that usually molded his expression. "I didn't say they were monsters; but they're not soldiers, either. They're out of control. Something's gone wrong, and I think Odell better fucking well concentrate on fixing it. And fixing us."

Ritter stopped in front of their door and slowly nodded. "You are right, of course. I will speak to General White tomorrow." He opened the door and motioned Cole into the room. "In the meantime, get some sleep. I will check on our charges."

"Thanks." Cole walked past him into the room, stripped off his boots and pants, and threw himself on his bed.

Ritter continued to the next room. The walls in the new basement of the old warehouse were thick and specially soundproofed. Ritter heard nothing, suspected nothing, until he opened the door to the scent of blood.

It hit him in a heady, intoxicating wave. Blood, lots of it and fresh. Then he saw the volunteers. The twelve massed in a cluster beside the door, snarling and fighting over a mass of bloody rags. "*Himmel!*"

At the sound of his voice, the twelve turned. Their eyes were unfocused, wide and staring. Blood smeared their lips and soaked their hospital gowns. Moving as a unit, they surged toward him.

Ritter leapt away from the door. He didn't dare close it and lock the vampires in with their victim, not when there was a chance the man might still live. No, he must draw the twelve deep into the room and compel them to sleep. Once they were safely unconscious, he could summon medical aid.

"Come," he called when the first of the twelve hesitated at the open door. They turned and followed, pursuing Ritter down the aisle between the beds.

He turned at the end of the row. "Stop," he ordered.

The twelve slowed, but continued forward.

"Stop." The shuffling steps never faltered.

"Fuck." Cole stood in the doorway, without pants or shoes, his expression frozen between horror and longing.

Ritter remembered the feeling. Years ago, he had resisted the lure of blood and saved a woman's life. He prayed his young comrade was as strong. "Cole! Come, I need you."

He didn't have time to see if Cole obeyed. The twelve were almost upon him. Backing into the wall, he funneled all his power into his voice. "Stop!"

The command rolled in a thick wave through the twelve. They shuddered, but kept coming. "Stop!" he called again, an edge creeping into his voice.

Then Cole added his order to Ritter's. "Stop."

The volunteers shuffled another step, then halted.

"Go to your beds," Ritter ordered. "Sleep."

Cole grabbed the nearest by the shoulders and tossed him on a bed. "Sleep."

The rest turned like a single organism and trudged back to their beds. They lay down, crossed their arms over their chests, and closed their eyes. Ritter caught Cole's gaze and nodded toward the heap near the door. Careful to keep his footsteps unhurried and quiet, he walked toward it.

"What the fuck happened?" Cole's whisper shook as he fell into step beside Ritter.

"I don't know." Ritter knelt beside the bloody rags. The shredded uniform held bits of bone, but nothing more. Suddenly, Ritter felt older than his forty-seven years, old and tired. Something glinted from the gore. Ritter picked up a blood-stained star. "I fear General White did not heed my warning to stay away from the volunteers."

"But where's the body? That's not enough meat to fill a shoe box. If anyone was stupid enough to come down here alone, his body would still be here. I mean, they're vampires, not flesh-eating zombies."

"Are you sure?" Ritter's voice sounded as bleak as he felt. "Odell modified the illness, weakened it. Perhaps he changed its effects as well."

"Fuck." Together, they stared at the star. "Odell's gotta find that cure."

Ritter forced a breath. "Yes, he must restore the volunteers' humanity." He looked up and caught Cole's gaze. "And our own."

≈ ≈

"Ritter!" The words sank through layers of sleep. Strong hands gripped Ritter's shoulders and shook him hard. "Ritter, wake up!"

A harsh, choking smell ripped his nostrils. Recognition jolted him awake. *Vietnam. Napalm and burning flesh.* He coughed and sat up.

Cole tugged on his arm. "The warehouse is on fire. We gotta get the fuck out of here."

Thick black smoke curled under the door. Still groggy from his daytime sleep, Ritter swung his feet from the cot to the floor. "The volunteers?"

Cole shook his head. "Flames are shooting from their ward. The fire must have started in there."

"Then they are beyond help." Ritter pushed himself to his feet. "Sunlight is bad, but fire is worse. We burn like kindling. Come."

They were halfway to the door when it burst open. A soldier in fire-proof gear and a gas mask stood framed in doorway. He had a pack on his back and held a nozzle in his hand, a flamethrower.

As Cole stared, disbelief stark on his face, a tongue of flame spurted across the room. Ritter shoved Cole in one direction and dove in the other. The flames blazed harmlessly between them. Without stopping to think, Ritter rolled to his cot, grabbed it and threw it at the soldier. The bedding burst into flames, but the metal frame hit the man, staggering him back.

Cole ran forward and slammed the door shut. "Thanks."

"We haven't escaped yet." The door shuddered as someone threw his weight against it. "We don't have much time."

Ritter ran to the room's one window, eight feet above the ground, heavily curtained. A thin line of sunlight striped the floor at his feet. He smiled grimly and turned. "They think the sun will trap us. Luckily, I overstated our disabilities. Here." He turned, stripped the blanket off the one remaining cot and threw it to Cole.

He caught it with one hand. "What's this for?"

"Wrap it around yourself." Returning to the window, Ritter bent his legs and jumped. He grabbed the pipe overhead and swung on it as though it were a high bar and he, an Olympic gymnast.

A roar sounded outside the room, and the door began to glow. Cole backed away from it. "They're coming."

Ritter kicked his feet up and through the curtained window. Glass shattered, the curtain fell, and sunlight flooded the basement room.

"*Himmel!*" Pain lashed Ritter's bare feet, blazed across his face, seared his hands. Ignoring it, he swung again on the pipe. On the upswing, he let go and soared through the window. More pain: he hit the ground, and the gravel outside the building scraped his burning flesh.

A roar rose from inside the warehouse. They must have breached the door. Ritter crawled back to the window and thrust his hand into the room. "Come!" Cole jumped up and caught his hand. Though his skin had already started to blister, Ritter jerked his comrade up and out of the deathtrap. They stumbled three steps from the window before he fell to his knees.

Swearing, Cole threw the blanket around them both and half carried Ritter down the alley. Ritter wanted to tell him to hurry, that they had to get out of sight before their enemies realized they had escaped, but even through the blanket, the sun stole his strength. It was all he could do to stumble on and pray Cole knew where to go.

After an eternity, he heard a crash and felt the blessed cool of darkness. A few more steps, the creak of hinges, and the blanket fell away. They were in a windowless room, empty except for a pile of cigarette butts. Ritter swayed and collapsed.

Cole knelt beside him. "You look like shit."

Ritter tried to smile, but it hurt too much. *Himmel*, it hurt even to breathe.

Cole's expression grew grim. "What can I do?"

The darkness wrapped around Ritter, comforting, safe. It promised relief from the pain, relief from his memories. Ritter struggled against its seductive pull and used the last of his strength to answer. "Blood. Get blood." Then he closed his eyes and let the darkness carry him away.

☙❧

"Here." From far away, Cole's hoarse voice drifted to Ritter. "Drink."

Ritter didn't move. He couldn't. He heard a muttered curse, felt his head lift, felt something warm press against his lips. "Drink, damn it!"

The smell of life filled his nostrils, the smell of blood. His mouth opened; his fangs plunged into flesh. Blood pulsed into his mouth and he swallowed in huge, greedy gulps. The darkness receded, and strength crept back to his limbs. His eyes opened.

A soldier lay on the ground beside him, dead and drained, another soul on his conscience. Ritter thrust the body aside and sat up. The skin on his hands was white and unblemished; the only remaining pain, the guilt that never left him.

"Better?" Cole sat near the doorway on an overturned crate.

"Much." Ritter nodded at the corpse. "What shall we do with him?"

Cole grinned and stood. "Got it all planned. Gimme your dog tags." Ritter slipped the metal chain over his head and handed it to him.

Cole let the tags swing from his fingers. "Those flamethrowers mean the army wants us dead, right? So unless we want the US of A chasing us all our lives, we gotta make them think we *are* dead. Odell's the one they'll ask, and he's a lazy bastard." Cole knelt and put Ritter's identification around the dead man's neck. "If Odell finds the right number of burned corpses wearing the right tags, he'll declare us all dead and turn his attention to convincing his superiors the whole fucking disaster never happened. All I have to do is find another guard and—slam, bang—once the smoke clears, Odell will have his dead vampires, and we'll be free."

Ritter sighed. "I hate to see the innocent die."

The grin turned to a scowl. "Cut the crap, Ritter. They aren't innocent. Odell and anyone who helps him are the enemy." His lips lifted again, this time in a snarl. "And they just started a war."

Chapter Seven

Waukegan, Illinois
May 18, 2014

Ritter spent most of the day in nightmare-laden sleep. He woke that evening to a high fever and festering burns. Cole was right, he needed blood; but he refused to kill to get it. There was a better—if riskier—way to feed his hunger.

He gave Cole his car keys and directions to the garage he rented. Too dizzy to stand without swaying, he dropped to the front step, and Cole ran to get Greta. Ritter knew of one place he could get enough blood without adding a death to his conscience: the hospital.

It was after nine, and the lobby was nearly deserted. Cole parked Greta in the fire lane by the entrance, but it still took all Ritter's strength to walk through the lobby to the elevators. Cole hovered behind him, as if afraid he would collapse.

"It was stupid to take this chance," Cole said, once the doors closed behind them and the elevator started to sink. "What if the girl at the desk noticed us?"

"I will take care of her on the way out." Talking hurt. The elevator jerked to a stop, sending flames across his chest. Ritter gasped, and Cole grabbed his arm to keep him from falling.

"I sure the hell hope you know what you're doing." The elevator opened and Cole half carried Ritter into the corridor.

"The blood bank is down there, next to Faith's lab." Ritter nodded to the right. "I noticed it when I visited her last week."

The discreet sign read, "LifeSource Blood Services." Leaning against Cole, Ritter managed to stumble to the door at the end of the hall. He listened, but the room behind the door was silent, empty. He tried the knob. It was locked.

"Let me." Cole backed up, spun and kicked the door. The frame splintered. The door burst open. His lips spread in a fang-revealing smile. "Love that cheap modern construction."

The floor tipped. Ritter swayed. Scowling, Cole scooped Ritter into his arms and hauled him past the empty receptionist's desk and waiting area to a large room full of examining tables and medical equipment: the donation center.

It took only a moment to find a refrigerator full of blood. Cole set Ritter down by the open refrigerator door and went back to rifle through the desk. Ritter grabbed a plastic bag and ripped it open. His stomach clenched around the thick, cold liquid, but a moment later, healing warmth spread throughout his body. It cooled his fever, calmed his dizziness. The second pint soothed the burn itself. He could feel the blisters shrinking, his skin knitting to a smooth whole. The third pint restored his strength and sent energy pulsing through his limbs. Ritter tore open a fourth bag but did not drink. He wanted the blood, craved it, but he no longer needed it. He was master, not the hunger. Being careful not to splash himself, Ritter sprayed the contents of the bag across the room. The single pint went amazingly far. When the bag was empty, he dipped his finger into the largest puddle and scrawled, "Day One" on the back wall.

Cole ran in from the waiting room. He scanned the wall and ran his tongue over his bared teeth. "A waste of good blood."

"It gives the police an explanation for the empty bags and a group of fanatics to blame for the break-in." Ritter licked his finger clean. "Come, we must go before someone investigates."

Cole grabbed two bags and shoved them into the deep pockets of his duster. He grinned at Ritter's questioning glance. "Never know when they might come in handy."

Shaking his head, Ritter headed out the door. Cole followed.

They took the stairs to the lobby. Ritter ran up them, buoyed by the blood. He paused at the landing, took out one of the peppermints he always carried, and popped it into his mouth. The taint of blood on his breath tended to frighten his prey, and he didn't want to frighten the girl at the desk.

She looked up when he opened the door. Her brow furrowed, but Ritter walked forward and started talking before she could ask what he wanted. "It's a quiet night. No one has entered the lobby in the last hour."

The girl's eyes widened. "Quiet night," she repeated. "No one's come in."

"In thirty minutes, you will hear a suspicious noise from downstairs. You will call security."

"Thirty minutes. Call security."

Cole stepped up beside him. "She's not the one who saw us come in."

Ritter shrugged. It was hard to worry with fresh blood singing through his veins. He continued to charm the girl in front of him. "You never saw me. Never saw my friend."

"Never saw you."

Nodding, he turned and ran with Cole from the lobby to his car.

Ritter retrieved his keys, thanked Cole and offered to drop him off somewhere, but Cole insisted on coming with him to Faith's apartment building. Moments later, Ritter pulled into an illegal parking space in front of the entrance. It took some persuasion, but Cole waited in Greta while Ritter went into the building.

Despite the blood-induced energy that danced across his nerves, Ritter hesitated at the foot of the stairs.

"What's wrong?" Cole's impatience whispered in his ear. Ritter smiled. His protégé was growing skilled at controlling the powers of his voice. It sounded as if Cole stood right beside him.

"I fear we took too long." He focused his voice on Cole, knowing that a passerby would hear nothing. "It's late. She may be sleeping. Perhaps I should come back tomorrow."

"Perhaps the blood has pickled your brain." Cole sounded disgusted. "One of us is going in tonight. If not you, then me."

"Stay where you are. This will not take long." Ritter ran up the stairs and down the hall to Faith's door. He extended his hearing and caught the faint rustle of movement. She was still awake.

The rustling stopped at his first knock. A tendril of fear wafted under the door and made his bloodlust howl. "It is I, Ritter," he called, hoping to calm her.

Sharp footsteps answered him. Locks clicked, and the door cracked open. Faith glared at him. "It's late. What are you doing here?"

Her fear had shifted to anger. Good. He didn't want her afraid of him. Swallowing his hunger, Ritter allowed himself a careful smile. "I came to check on you. I was worried."

Faith's frown softened. "I'm fine, thanks, but very busy. I'll call you tomorrow." She started to close the door, but Ritter caught it before it latched.

"What are you busy doing, so late at night?" He pushed the door. She stepped back, and it opened wide. "Perhaps I can help."

Faith had changed into denim slacks and a man's work shirt with sleeves rolled to the elbows. She smelled of newsprint, and her face and fingers were smudged with gray. "Thanks anyway, but I'm almost done. One more box to pack, and I'm going to bed."

"You are moving?"

"Yes, my boss offered me a safer apartment, one vandals can't get into. He's bringing a truck in the morning to haul my stuff over there, so if you don't mind—"

The surge of jealousy rocked Ritter. "Cohabiting with your boss is most unseemly."

Her cheeks flared along with her anger. "I'm not 'cohabiting' with anyone, not that it's any of your business. Miles convinced me my apartment was wasn't safe as long as I'm working on the project. We're moving to a new lab, and there are secure apartments nearby. He and I are both moving there. Into separate apartments."

Miles. The name made Ritter's teeth ache. Cole was right, she did work for Odell. God help her if she knew the truth behind his project. "Is your work so important that you are willing to uproot your whole life for it?"

"My work is my life." She took a breath, as if to add something, then let it out in a sigh. "I'm too tired to stand here arguing with you. Come in if you must. I have to pack." She turned and stormed into the living room.

Ritter stepped over the threshold and closed the door behind him. The wall had been cleaned, and pine overrode the lingering smell of ketchup and perfume. He heard a thump and the crinkle of folding newspaper. "What can I do to help?"

"You can leave."

He joined her in the living room. The mess he remembered had been replaced by a cluster of cardboard boxes. Faith knelt in a small, open space, next to a stack of newspaper, a roll of sealing tape, and a utility knife. An open box sat in front of her. She grabbed a sheet of newspaper, viciously shoved a blue china teacup into its center, and slammed it into the box. Something cracked, and Faith winced.

She looked annoyed, frustrated, adorable. Ritter had to fight the urge to lift her to her feet and wrap his arms around her. He was there for a reason, he reminded himself. If he didn't discover what Faith knew about Odell's work, Cole would. Ritter crouched beside her and picked up the matching saucer. "Allow me." He wrapped it in paper and nestled it among its comrades.

A final teacup and a dozen assorted mugs remained on the floor. Ritter lifted the cup and reached for another piece of paper. "What is this work that's so important to you?"

Faith's curious glance turned into a long, searching look. "You really want to know, don't you?"

"Yes."

She sat back on her heels. "I'm a physician with Ph.D.s in both virology and teratology. Virology is the study of viruses. Teratology—"

"The study of birth defects. I know the term."

Faith blinked, as if surprised. "Good; then you may also be familiar with a recent theory that some birth defects are caused by viral infections, rather than by random mutations."

Ritter frowned. "There's nothing recent about that. I had a cousin born deaf and blind because his mother caught rubella while she was pregnant."

Crossing her legs in front of her, Faith leaned forward with her hands on her knees. Enthusiasm brightened her face and voice. "That's different. Your cousin was injured by the virus, but it didn't touch his genetic code. You know how viruses work, right?"

Ritter nodded. "They invade a cell and convert its DNA into a factory to produce more viruses."

"Exactly." Faith beamed at him, as if she were a teacher and he, her star pupil. "Most of the time, the virus kills the host cell. That's what happened to your cousin; some of his formative cells were destroyed, and he didn't develop properly. Sometimes, though, the virus lurks unseen in the cell's genetic material. It may not emerge for years. The virus that causes chicken pox is like that. After the initial infection, viral particles can remain in the victim's cells. They're reproduced as the cells are replaced, but remain dormant until something triggers the virus, and it becomes active again. We call that disease shingles, but it's the same chicken-pox virus."

Ritter shook his head. Instead of fading, the energy that had cured his burn continued to collect inside him. It roared in his ears, making it hard to follow Faith's words. "What does chicken pox have to do with birth defects?"

"I'm working to prove a theory that some viruses can invade the DNA in a developing embryo without killing the cells. Instead, they form a cell/virus symbiosis. In a sense, the embryo becomes a different genetic entity, a virally induced mutation. If my theory is correct, this symbiosis can cause permanent, inheritable changes. That may be the genesis of certain congenital diseases like sickle-cell anemia and hemophilia."

Ritter could taste her excitement, her sincerity. It made his heart beat faster. "So you study the virus that may have caused the bleeding disease."

"No, that virus—if there ever was a virus—has been lost, mutated beyond recognition. I'm studying a different birth defect, a kind of anemia. My brother died of it when he was a few days old." The words were matter-of-fact, but sorrow tinged the air around her. Ritter took her hand and gently stroked her knuckles with his thumb. She closed her eyes, as if shutting out the memory. "I was seven when my brother was born. I remember how tiny he looked, hooked up to all those wires and machines, so pale and helpless. His death almost killed my mother."

She took a deep breath and opened her eyes. "The condition is called Stoker's syndrome. It causes severe sensitivity to light, digestive difficulties, and dental malformations. Most fetuses with this syndrome die before they're born; few live beyond a day or two. To prove my theory, I had to first find a virus that caused genetic changes to fetal cells, identical to the abnormalities found in Stoker's syndrome, and then show that the infected cells could survive and continue to develop."

Her gaze locked on Ritter. "Miles Odell has been working for years on just such a virus. That's why I was so excited when I received a grant to work with him; why I can't walk away now." Her grip tightened. "We've done it, Ritter, completed phase one of the project. We've weakened the virus, so it produces clear cell/virus symbiosis without killing the embryo."

Ritter had a terrible idea of what her "syndrome" must be. "Phase two, then, will be to grow a batch of these embryos to term to see if they are properly defective." His voice sounded harsh, even to his own ears.

Faith twisted her hand from his. "What's wrong with you? I would never, ever inflict such suffering on a child." Her eyes widened and fear washed away her indignation. "Oh my God, you *are* one of those Embryo-Rightists." She sprang to her feet and darted toward the door.

He caught her before she left the room. He swung her around and held her by both arms. "What are you doing then, if not inflicting pain upon the innocent?"

"Let me go!" She struggled, but he held her. Her pulse pounded through the thin fabric of her shirt. It fed his rage and his hunger for more blood. Her gaze met his, and her fear grew stronger.

"Tell me." He pulled her close, lowered his lips to her throat and tasted the salt on her skin. "Tell me what you and Odell plan to do."

She froze the moment his tongue touched her pulse point. "Let me go."

He had to learn the truth before the bloodlust stole his reason. He looked up and held her gaze. "Tell me."

She trembled like a frightened kitten, but her voice remained strong. "The next step is to find a way to repair the damage. I'm not hurting babies; I'm looking for a cure."

⁓⁓

Ritter's expression was set in harsh lines, as rigid and cold as the sculpture of an avenging angel. Dilated pupils swallowed the blue in his eyes, and it suddenly occurred to Faith that he might be on drugs. His hold on her arms tightened to bruising. "A cure?"

Faith struggled against Ritter's iron grip, but she couldn't break free. PCP or speed, either drug, could cause his unnatural strength and his irrational behavior. In his altered state, there was no telling what he might do. She had to keep him talking until she found a chance to escape. Faith fought to keep her voice calm. "That's right. When my brother was born, Stoker's was extremely rare, but more babies are being born with the syndrome every year. More children are dying from it every year. I want to develop a virus that will reverse the Stoker's anomalies: a counterinfection that will put fetal develop-ment back on track and save the lives of those children."

She wasn't sure how much Ritter understood, but the harsh lines melted. "*Gott sei Dank.*" Thank God. It was a whispered prayer. He released her arms, but wrapped her in an embrace before she could bolt for the door. "Oh, *Liebchen*, I feared such terrible things."

He squeezed so hard she couldn't breathe. "Ritter," she squeaked. "You're hurting me."

His arms loosened, but didn't release her. "I would never hurt you." Keeping his left arm firmly around her, he lifted his right and traced her face from temple to jaw. His black gaze burned across her skin. "You are beautiful, *Fräulein Doktor*. Do you know?" His finger brushed her lower lip. "So beautiful."

He was so stoned. "Ritter, please let me go."

Instead of answering, he cupped the back of her head and lowered his lips to hers.

"No," she murmured, but instead of pulling back, he deepened the kiss. His tongue was cool and tasted of peppermint with a dark undertone. The flavor frightened and excited her. She wanted to turn her head, to jerk away, but her traitorous body refused. She melted into him. Strong hands spread across her back and pressed her even closer.

An unnatural heat thrummed across his lips and pulsed from his hands. It filled her mouth, her back, her whole body. She knew she should be afraid, but the heat burned away her ability to fear. She tore his shirt from his pants and wrapped her arms around his naked waist. Splaying her hands against his smooth back, she let the warmth pour into her.

She wanted him. He was too young, crazy, and a drug addict, and Faith didn't care. She wanted him. Needed him. Now. She slanted her mouth and opened it wider, pressing against his lips and the contour of long, hard teeth. He gasped and a metallic taste filled her mouth. Blood. The flavor was stronger and more bitter than the undertone, but that was what the mint had been disguising, the taste of blood. Gagging, Faith jerked back, and so did he.

A thin, red line trickled from the corner of Ritter's mouth. He dabbed at it with his tongue. "*Liebchen*, I—"

Faith broke for the door. The bitter kiss had doused her runaway hormones. She didn't know why Ritter's mouth had tasted of blood *before* his lip started bleeding, and she didn't want to know. She just wanted to escape before Ritter went psycho on her again.

She burst out of the apartment and pelted down the hall to the stairs. There was a pay phone in the first floor laundry room. All she had to do was beat Ritter there. She'd lock the door, call the police, and wait to be rescued.

Ritter yelled something, and she doubled her speed. Taking the steps two at a time, Faith sprinted toward safety. She was running so fast, she almost didn't see the man at the foot of the stairs. He appeared out of nowhere, a tall, dark figure in a broad-brimmed hat. Faith grabbed the banister and jerked to a halt to keep from running him down.

The light above the stairwell spilled over him. He wore a long coat, too heavy for the season, black boots, black gloves. He tipped his face to meet her gaze. He was young, not much older than Ritter. His skin looked like it should be dark brown, but the fluorescent light bleached it to ash. Colorless lips curled into a sneer. "What's the hurry, *doctor*?"

"Cole!" Ritter's voice boomed behind her. "It's not what you think. I frightened her."

They were together. The realization paralyzed Faith. They must both be embryo-rights fanatics. She watched, unable to move while the man Ritter called Cole climbed the first step. "If she were innocent, she'd have nothing to fear. Would you, Dr. Allister?" The sneer spread into a leering grin.

His smile was terrifying, but it took Faith a moment to realize why. It was his teeth. His eyeteeth were too long and sharp, like fangs.

She gasped. "What are you?"

He reached a long arm toward her. "Death."

"No!" A shape hurtled past her peripheral vision. Ritter had vaulted from the third floor landing. He landed on his feet without staggering and stepped forward. "Cole, stop!"

A hot wind raised the hair on Faith's arms, but there was no wind. It was Ritter's voice, his amazing, hypnotic voice. She could almost see it, wrapping around the man in front of her. He slowly turned. "What the fuck are you doing?"

"Back off." The words had an edge to them Faith had never heard before, hard, implacable. "She's innocent, and she's mine."

If she hadn't been so terrified, Faith might have argued that last point. Instead, she watched while, stiff as a marionette, the stranger lifted one foot and lowered it to the floor. The other foot followed. "You're stoned, man. We've got to take her out. If you were straight, you'd see it's the only way. Let. Me. Go."

The wind on her arms grew cold. Goose bumps rose on her exposed skin. Eddies of air she could almost see shifted and flowed back toward Ritter.

"No. We leave. Now." The air thickened between them. Suddenly she could see it, power as clear and insubstantial as heat waves rising from a freeway shimmered around both men.

The man in black shuddered and took another reluctant step. Still facing him, Ritter stepped back and reached for the door behind him. There was a car on the other side, Faith realized, Ritter's car. He opened the door and stepped aside. "Get in the car."

A shrill wail cut through the night air and shattered the shimmering power. It was a siren.

"Fuck!" The tall man dove into the car. Ritter vaulted into the driver's seat. The engine roared, and the car disappeared in a gust of exhaust. Impossibly, she heard Ritter whisper, "*Auf Wiedersehen.*"

Moments later, flashing blue lights streamed into the lobby. The police car squealed to a stop in front of the entrance. The siren and lights died, and the door opened. John O'Connor jumped out. It was a

Waukegan police car, Faith noticed with detached surprise, not one of the campus security vans. He ran into the building, stopped at the foot of the stairs, and stared up at her. His worried expression folded into a puzzled frown. "One of your neighbors reported a disturbance, two men hassling a woman. You okay?"

"Yeah."

"Didn't get another visit from those embryo-rights guys?"

"No." After her suspicions about Ritter, the answer made her feel guilty. "I was just saying good-bye to a friend."

"That boyfriend of yours?"

Faith was too tired to correct the officer's choice of words. "Yes. He was helping me pack." She made a vague gesture toward her apartment. "I'm moving tomorrow."

O'Connor's eyebrows pulled together into a scowl. "Last night you didn't say anything about moving."

"Last night I didn't know I was." The fear and anger that had propelled Faith out of her apartment suddenly drained away. She sank to the steps. "Look, the only one hassling anybody here is you. What's this all about?"

"There was a break-in at the hospital about an hour ago."

"Oh my God." Faith surged to her feet. "Is my lab okay, was there much damage?"

"Your lab's fine. They broke into the LifeSource offices next door. Tore the place up. There's broken furniture and blood everywhere. The perpetrators wrote *Day One* on the wall. In blood this time, not ketchup."

Faith's jaw sagged, but O'Connor just kept talking. "The security cameras were off-line, so we didn't catch the crime on video, but a candy striper saw two men enter the lobby around eight-thirty this evening. One was a tall black guy with a hat, the other a white man, medium height, with blond hair. Real 'eye candy,' according to our witness." Suspicion darkened his eyes. "How long was your boyfriend helping you pack?"

Faith snapped her mouth shut. Ritter might well be one of the fanatics who were trying to destroy her work. If O'Connor was right about the time when the LifeSource office was vandalized, Ritter would have had plenty of time to drive to her apartment after the break-in. Besides, "a tall black guy with a hat" certainly described the maniac who'd wanted to kill her. A maniac that Ritter appeared to know all too well. She had to tell O'Connor everything, how Ritter had shown up unexpectedly, his odd questions, his bizarre behavior, everything. It was the only logical, sensible thing to do. She licked her suddenly dry lips. "He—"

"Wait." O'Connor reached into his back pocket the memo book and a pen. "Okay."

"He was here all evening." The words poured out; Faith couldn't stop them. "Since before supper. Ritter brought burgers, and we ate as we packed. He couldn't be your vandal. He was here with me the whole time."

O'Connor's gaze seemed to bore into her skull, as if he were trying to dig the truth from her brain. "All evening?"

Her nod felt awkward, like her head was too big for her neck. "That's right."

His lips pressed into a thin line. "You're lying."

A guilty flush heated her face. "I can show you the boxes we packed, if you want."

"Don't bother." He slapped the book closed and shoved it back in his pocket. "Call the number on my card and leave your new address on my voice mail. Don't forget, doctor."

"I won't forget."

"We'll talk again." O'Connor held her gaze another moment, then stalked back to his car and climbed in. The engine rumbled to life and the squad car pulled out of the parking lot.

Faith watched it disappear. What was wrong with her? She, Faith Allister, who was almost pathologically honest, had lied to the police. And why? To protect a fanatic determined to destroy her life's work.

She turned and stumbled back to her apartment. Fatigue: that was the only logical explanation. She'd only slept a handful of hours in the last two days—no wonder her mind was muddled. She'd roll out her sleeping bag and get some sleep. Tomorrow she'd finish packing and move into a new apartment and a new lab. She'd give Officer O'Connor a call once she got settled in. Maybe, by then, she'd know what to tell him.

Chapter Eight

"Don't you ever fuck with my mind like that again."

The taste of Cole's anger, chill and bitter, brushed Ritter's tongue. He ignored it and his passenger. Power pounded through him. It echoed in his ears, pulsed through his fingers. Rules were nothing to him; Cole's anger, less than nothing. Faith was innocent. An approaching traffic light turned yellow. Ritter pressed his foot to the accelerator. The car lunged forward, throwing both driver and passenger back in their seats.

The bitter flavor shifted to tart humor. Cole chuckled. "Never seen you this gone. How much blood you take, anyway? A couple of gallons?"

"Three pints."

Cole whistled. "Three pints? That's barely enough to give me a buzz. What have you been living on, two teaspoons a week?"

"Enough to keep me sane. You know my feelings about the bloodlust." Ritter tried to sound severe, but the power pulsed up his throat and stretched his lips into a grin. "I had forgotten the euphoria."

"Euphoria? Man, you are wasted." Cole leaned forward and gripped Ritter's arm. "Listen. We've got to go back and finish the job."

Ritter shook his head. "There is no job. Faith is innocent, Odell's dupe. She thinks she's researching birth defects."

"I don't care if she's Mother-fucking-Theresa. She's working for Odell and she saw me. She may be innocent, but Odell's not. If she tells him what happened, he'll fly. I may never find him again."

A sliver of ice cut the warmth filling Ritter. He slammed on the brakes; Cole slammed into the dashboard. "Odell is your concern. Faith is mine. Leave her alone."

Cole sat back, rubbing his shoulder. "Remember '71?" His voice was tight, strained. "Odell made men into monsters and burned them like trash when he couldn't control them. The bastard is at it again, Ritter. I know it. I feel it. I'm going to stop him, and I'm not going to let anyone get in my way. Not a pretty lady doctor, not even an old friend."

Ritter gripped the steering wheel hard enough to crack his knuckles. "I will not let you hurt Faith."

"How you gonna stop me? I'm not one of your sheep. Your voice is strong, but you have to be there to use it. What will you do when the sun comes up? How will you stop me then?" Cole opened the car door and climbed out. "Go home and sober up," he said, not unkindly. "And forget about the pretty doctor. You won't be seeing her again."

"Stop!" Ritter leapt from the car and ran to the sidewalk, but Cole had already vanished into the shadows. Blood pounded in Ritter's brain, making it impossible to think, but this he knew—once Cole was on a hunt, he never stopped until his quarry was dead. And Cole was hunting Faith.

Vaulting over the car door into his seat, Ritter threw Greta into gear and swung into the opposite lane with a shriek of rubber. Cole was fast, but he couldn't outrun a Mercedes roadster. Ritter pushed the pedal to the floorboard until the speedometer pegged at 240 kph. The force pressed him into his seat, and the wind blasted his lips into a grimace. Ignoring both stop signs and traffic signals, he raced for Faith's apartment. He had to get to her, had to protect her. He was the only one who could.

He roared into the apartment's parking lot a few minutes later. The police car was gone. Ritter jerked the car to a stop and killed the engine. He climbed out of the car, and silence draped over him like a cool sheet. The scents of the night were normal: the cooling engine, exhaust from the nearby highway, green growth. No anger, no fear.

He ran all the way to Faith's apartment. The door was shut, but barely locked. No one had bothered to fix the shattered doorframe; the deadbolt was useless. The only barrier between Faith and those who would harm her was a fragile knob lock. Ritter paused at the door and listened for a hint of movement inside. He heard nothing, not even the ticking of a clock or the hum of a refrigerator. Not a step nor a breath. Could Cole have out raced him? Fear clogged his throat as he gripped the doorknob and twisted it off with a muffled crack.

The door swung open. More silence, and the unmistakable flavor of fear. An icy hand grabbed Ritter's heart and squeezed. He rushed into the living room. Boxes still stood in a haphazard cluster, the last one, still open and half-packed, next to the mugs. The fear was stronger here; not fresh, but flat. The grip on his heart relaxed. The fear was old, probably left over from when he confronted Faith.

The door to her bedroom was closed. Ritter crept up to it and eased it open. The slashed mattress and box springs stood propped against one wall. In the rectangular depression they had left in the carpet lay a sleeping bag, topped by an unmistakable tumble of dark curls. Faith's face was turned from him, but her breath whispered in a slow, even rhythm. The sweet scent of sleep filled the room.

Ritter closed the door. Yawning, he set his back to the door frame and lowered himself to the floor. The rush of blood-driven energy was starting to fade. Fatigue tugged at his eyes, and he let them drift closed. The windows in Faith's apartment were too high for Cole to reach. When he came after her, he would use the front door, and Ritter would be there to stop him.

Ritter took a deep breath and slowly released it. Faith was safe for the moment. Sweet, beautiful Faith, so clever, so frightened, and so bold. The memory of her welcoming lips and daring tongue flooded his mind. She had wrapped her arms around him and welcomed his kiss with an assurance that had been as shocking as it was arousing. He deepened the kiss and she responded, opening her mouth wider and pressing into him. He wanted her, wanted her in a way he hadn't wanted a woman in over sixty years. And she wanted him, or had, until she accidentally impaled his lip on the point of his left fang.

He ran his tongue along the smooth inner surface of his lip. The wound had healed, but his heart still bled. Faith had lunged away from him, her eyes full of fear and loathing. And he had wanted her the more for it. Her fear had enflamed his surging hunger. It was all he could do to hold himself still, to resist the urge to yank her close and plunge his fangs into the hollow of her throat.

Ritter leaned forward and buried his face in his palms. The savor of her fear still lingered in the apartment, stale but enticing. His loins ached, and his teeth throbbed. Both as a man and as a monster, he wanted her. Her even breaths called to him from the other side of the door. "Come to me," they seemed to say, "and take what is yours." He needed only to open the door.

He bit his lip, and blood filled his mouth. The bitter, inhuman flavor overpowered the taste of fear and calmed him. He was there to protect Faith, not rape and drain her. He stood and stepped away from the bedroom door. The room tipped, and he grabbed the back of the couch to steady himself. Cole was right, Ritter realized: he was drunk. The dizzy ringing in his ears confirmed it. Cold blood had always hit him harder than fresh. He had forgotten that, in the pain of his burns. Still, the worst was probably over. The euphoria had begun to ebb. An hour or so of sleep would steady his mind and wash away his troubling desires.

But he couldn't sleep, not surrounded by Faith's scent. And he couldn't leave while Cole still prowled the night. He had to stay and find another way to control his desires.

Work. He would finish Faith's packing. Ritter walked around the end of the couch and crouched by the open box. He shoved the sealing tape and knife aside and picked up the nearest mug. It was heavy ceramic, beige with shiny black cats dancing along its rim. He smiled. For a single woman who lived alone, Faith had an amazing number of coffee cups. The newspaper rustled as he wrapped it around the mug. Ritter froze, but the sleepy rhythm from the bedroom continued undisturbed. He set the wrapped bundle in the box and picked up the next cup and sheet of paper. If he worked through the night, he would finish before dawn.

Dawn. The paper fluttered from his suddenly shaky fingers. For the first time in decades, he had forgotten the dawn. Setting down the mug, he scanned the apartment. It was on the fourth floor, with exposure to the east and south. The thin gauze curtains covering the windows would do nothing to shield him from the sun.

Cole could withstand sunlight better than Ritter, and he had as much as promised to wait until after dawn to strike.

Ritter cursed his blood-thickened brain. He had to do something, but what? If he left now, Cole would kill Faith. If he stayed, the sun would kill him, and Cole would survive to complete his hunt.

Ritter dug his fingers through his hair. There had to be a way to protect Faith. If only he could think.

He could control Cole, but only when Cole was close enough to hear his voice. Cole was younger than he was, less disciplined, and more driven by the bloodlust. His tolerance to the sun was greater, as was his strength. Even his stomach was stronger. Cole could take more solid food: a little bread or fruit, even meat, as long as there was no garlic.

Ritter's lips spread into a fang-wide smile. Garlic. How could he have forgotten?

Only a week after they met, Ritter had walked with Cole past a bustling pizzeria. Just as they reached the door, it had opened with a blast of warm, garlic-scented air. Ritter sneezed, but Cole's eyes and throat had swollen shut. He nearly passed out before Ritter could drag him to clearer air.

They were barely comrades, neither friends nor enemies; but even then, Ritter had thought it prudent to remember that the fragrant rose that made his nose itch and his eyes burn was deadly to his companion.

Ritter pushed himself to his feet and quickly scanned the stacked boxes. As he had hoped, Faith had labeled each box. He quickly dismissed "towels/bathroom" "books/living room," and "silver/kitchen," but "spices/kitchen" looked promising. He moved the box on top of it to the floor, picked up the knife, and slit the sealing tape. When he opened the flaps, a riot of conflicting scents burst from the box in a nose-tickling wave. There was definitely garlic inside.

A large plastic bottle full of garlic powder lay near the bottom of the box. Perfect. Rubbing his nose, Ritter took the bottle to the front door, twisted off the top, and broke the seal. The overpowering scent of garlic hit him like a blow and seared the inside of his nose. Holding his breath, he stepped out into the hall and carefully poured a generous line of powder along the baseboard. Blinking back scalding tears, he closed the door to the apartment; a thin, odorous tendril puffed across the carpet. Cole would go into anaphylactic shock before he could breach that threshold.

Ritter's throat and eyes burned, and his lungs ached. Still holding his breath, he set the empty garlic container on the floor as a warning for Cole and ran down the stairs to Greta. His eyes were beginning to swell, but he climbed into his seat and started the engine. He didn't take a breath until he was out of the parking lot. The air whipped past him, soothed his throat and cooled his eyes.

He cruised down the street and let the wind blow the fuzziness from his brain. The scent of garlic still clogged his nostrils, and he wondered what Faith's reaction would be when she awoke and found the line of garlic at her door. The thought made him smile, but only for a moment. Faith was safe now, but she wouldn't stay that way. The garlic provided only temporary protection. Once she cleaned it up...

Ritter almost wheeled the car around but rejected the gesture as futile. He still couldn't face the sun. The garlic would keep Cole at bay until the movers arrived, and he wouldn't strike when Faith was with others. Though ruthless, Cole was never reckless. Multiple targets diluted the power of his voice. He would wait until he could get Faith alone.

Her laboratory. After her apartment, Faith was most vulnerable at work. She toiled alone in an isolated basement room, and she worked late—well into the night. Worse yet, Cole knew where her laboratory was; they'd passed it after they left the blood bank.

Ritter would have to go there. Maybe he couldn't stay in Faith's apartment and face the dawn, but he certainly could hide in a windowless basement. He turned onto Illinois Avenue and punched the accelerator. The police must have been notified of the burglary at the blood bank. They should have come and gone by now, but even if they lingered, a quick word would wipe him from their memories. Unlike Cole, he could control up to six men at a time, if the room were quiet.

The hospital parking lot was nearly deserted, the overhead lights garish in the predawn gloom. Ritter wasted a moment wishing he had time to return to the garage to get Greta's top, but the horizon in the east had already started to pale. The cloth cover he carried in the trunk would have to suffice. Praying it wouldn't rain, he parked as near the hospital as he dared. It took only a moment to unfold the cover and fasten it over the windshield and along the doors. With the interior covered as well as could be, Ritter locked the doors and ran to the hospital entrance.

The lobby was empty, the desk deserted. Ritter ducked into the stairwell. Though the elevator probably had a surveillance camera, the stairs were not monitored. Smiling, Ritter trotted down to the basement.

He was certain that Faith would come to work after she moved into her new apartment. All he had to do was wait. He would explain the danger she was in and why only he could protect her. A whisper of doubt tickled his mind—after the night before, would she listen to him? But the remains of the blood-fed euphoria pushed it aside. He would bring her to a safe place and keep her there. She would have to halt her research until the danger was past, but even that held a hidden benefit. If she no longer worked with Odell, Cole would lose interest in her. His attention would return to his original target. It shouldn't take long; Cole hated Odell even more than Ritter did. A month at most, and Odell would be dead and Faith could resume her work.

Ritter reached the bottom of the stairs and paused to listen. The corridor beyond the fire door was silent. The only sign of excitement was yellow crime-scene tape across the front of the blood bank. Ritter's footsteps echoed in the empty hallway, as he walked past the tape to Faith's laboratory. The door was locked, but he needed only a credit card and a moment's finagling to get it open. There were some benefits to knowing Cole.

Ritter slipped inside the room and relocked the door. The darkness soothed his still-burning eyes, and he sat on the floor and leaned against the wall. Faith had no idea what Odell really wanted with her research. Ritter knew the bastard well enough to know he wasn't interested in the welfare of unborn children, but Faith was different; she truly believed she was working on a cure. Maybe once Odell was dead, she would find what she sought.

Ritter had abandoned hope years ago, imprisoned it between carefully constructed walls of resignation. He had died once and been reborn as a monster. Nothing could return his humanity. Now a painful longing shattered those walls and blazed through his chest. If Faith succeeded, would her "counterinfection" be strong enough to cure a man?

✿ ✿

A high-pitched buzz vibrated through Faith's skull. Clutching the pillow to her head, she rolled over, but the racket continued. She pried open gritty eyes. Her travel alarm showed 5:00 AM; Miles and his truck would arrive in thirty minutes.

Faith tossed the pillow aside and sat up. Her head hurt. The pale morning light seeping through the bedroom window stung her eyes, but it brightened the room enough for her to see the tiny alarm switch on the clock. She flicked it, and the buzzing died.

Her headache didn't. It throbbed in time to her pulse. Her nose was runny, her sinuses were congested, and a sandpaper rawness scraped her throat. Faith groaned. Perfect, just perfect. Not only did she have to move into a new apartment and pack up her lab today, but she had to do it with a cold.

Drainage from her sinuses tickled her nostrils. Crawling out of the sleeping bag, she reached for the box of tissues on the dresser.

The movement reflected in her mirrored closet door. God, she looked a mess. Her hair stuck out in spikes all over her head, her face was pallid, and her eyes and the edges of her nose matched the red T-shirt she'dslept in.

Cocking her head, she walked closer to the mirror. Faith was prone to colds and sinus infections, but they usually didn't turn her eyes red. She leaned forward and pulled a thick line of goo from her eyelashes. If she didn't know better, she'd say she was having an allergic reaction. She'd sometimes wake up red-eyed and congested during the cottonwood season, but the big trees wouldn't start shedding their highly allergenic fluff for another two or three weeks.

Whatever it was, she'd better get it under control before Miles showed up. For a doctor, he was a real wimp when it came to illness. He'd be whining and blowing his nose for weeks if he thought he'd caught a cold. Faith had boxed up her eyedrops and other allergy medication with everything else last night. Sighing, she turned from the mirror and headed for the living room.

A blast of garlic hit her when she opened the bedroom door. Faith sneezed. Garlic? Blinking her now-running eyes, she held her breath and peeked into the living room.

The boxes had been moved around. Someone had opened one of them, someone who had entered her apartment last night while she slept. Faith waited for the mix of outrage, embarrassment, and violation that had almost paralyzed her after the break-in, but all she felt was confused. If Embryo-Rightists had invaded her home again, why attack only one box? The flaps had been cut, and bottles of spices stood in careful rows beside the open box. This was no act of vandalism.

Taking a shallow breath, she knelt and started putting the bottles back. Someone had broken into her apartment and rifled through her spices, but why? And why did her apartment reek of garlic?

Faith sat back on her heels. She never used garlic. She wouldn't own any but for her last boyfriend. He used to scoff at her insistence that she was allergic to the stuff and would sneak it into as many dishes as possible, hoping to catch her liking one of them. The idiot. She'd cried when she broke up with him. Not because she was sad. It was the garlic he'd chopped into her omelet. He left her with a bottle of garlic powder she'd never opened. Faith checked through the spices. Sure enough, the bottle was missing.

She went to the kitchen. The room was exactly as she had left it, shelves and counters empty. She hadn't forgotten to pack the garlic, so where could it be? This was making less and less sense. The only person Faith knew who valued garlic enough to steal it was her grandmother.

As Bubbie had descended into senility, she'd babbled about vampires, ageless monsters who shunned the daylight and reveled in blood. Her incoherent ranting had confused the horrors she'd suffered in a

Nazi concentration camp with supernatural fairy tales. On Faith's last visit to the nursing home, Bubbie had grabbed her arm with claw-like fingers and begged for garlic. She needed protection from the vampires, she'd cried. She'd escaped once, but they were hunting her again. They came in the night and tainted the air with their blood-stained breath. Faith knew better than to fight nightmares with logic. Promising to return soon, she'd driven to a local farmer's market and bought a braided chain of garlic to hang over her grandmother's bed. Faith had sneezed the whole drive back to the nursing home, but Bubbie's relieved smile was worth a million sneezes.

Her grandmother may have been desperate enough to steal garlic, but Faith wasn't about to believe that some other eighty-year-old dementia victim just happened to wander by last night and break into her apartment, in order to take a dust bath in her garlic powder.

A chill shivered down her bare arms. Ritter claimed to be over eighty, and his kiss tasted of blood. Faith had dismissed Bubbie's stories as the ramblings of a disintegrating mind, but...

No. There was no such thing as a vampire. The dark stranger last night had threatened her with a fang-toothed grin, but once she'd recovered from her shock—after O'Connor had left and she'd dressed for bed—she'd realized the fangs had to be plastic relics from last Halloween.

And Ritter's kiss. A metallic undertone had lingered in his mouth, but that was probably a side effect of the drugs he was on. Ritter and his scary friend might be addicts, vandals, and fanatics, but they were not vampires.

With the movers coming any minute, she didn't have time to worry about why the garlic had spilled. She had to find the mess and clean it up. She sneezed all the way to the front door, intending to pick up the newspaper; but the doorknob came off in her hand. Her indignant gasp set off an even worse bout of sneezing; it looked as though she'd found the garlic. She opened the door and choked on the pungent swirl of air. A line of garlic powder guarded the threshold.

Leaving the paper outside, Faith slowly closed the door. There were no vampires. She knew it as well as she knew the layout of her lab; but she wasn't facing logic here. As with her grandmother's nightmares, reality was unimportant; it was the delusion that mattered. If Ritter's terrifying friend believed himself to be a vampire, he would shun garlic. Garlic across the threshold might be the only way to keep him at bay.

Had Ritter come back to her apartment to protect her? And if so, what did he believe? Was he using a madman's delusion to control him, or was Ritter as crazy as his homicidal friend?

Faith shrugged and turned from the door. She didn't care what Ritter believed. Most of the men she'd dated had been losers, but Ritter was the worst of the bunch. He was too young, too pretty, and too...distracting. Into drugs and wanton destruction. She didn't care what he thought. She didn't care about him at all. In a few hours, she'd move apartments and pack her lab. She'd change her phone number to a new, unlisted one and disappear. She'd never have to speak to Todd Ritter again.

Her stomach ached. Promising herself coffee soon, she hurried back to the living room. She had to find her allergy medicine, get dressed, and sweep up the mess before Miles and the movers arrived.

≈≈

"You're being unreasonable. Banat's sending over a man to pack up my lab. He can do yours as well."

Faith sighed. Miles had been making the same argument all morning, from the moment he stormed into her apartment, still fuming because the movers had arrived more than an hour late. Faith had been grateful for the delay. It had given her time to shower after cleaning up the garlic. She'd stopped sniffling and had finished packing by the time Miles knocked on the door. Now they sat together in his car, outside the hospital entrance.

Miles clutched the steering wheel. "Come with me to the new facility. I need your help to sort out the new equipment. It's state of the art."

It was a new argument, and a tempting one. After working months with pathology department rejects, it was going to be wonderful to use the latest and best. Faith wanted to start as much as Miles did. She just wasn't willing to jeopardize her research.

She shook her head. "I'll do my own packing."

His lips twisted into a forced smile. "I can't afford to argue any longer. I'm meeting with Banat at 10:30. You have my cell phone number. Give me a call when you're done, and I'll drive you over there."

Faith blinked at the unexpected offer. "You don't have to do that. Give me the address and I'll take a cab. Or I can wait and ride in the moving van."

"That'll take too long. Pack your lab and give me a call. Unless you don't trust anyone to carry your precious boxes to the loading dock."

The sarcasm was typical Miles. Faith almost smiled. After so many crazy things had happened to her, it was nice to know she could count on something, even if it was Miles' bad temper. "I don't want to carry the boxes, just pack them. I'll work as quickly as I can." Slinging her purse over her shoulder, Faith grabbed her briefcase, opened the car door, and stepped onto the curb. "Thanks for the ride."

Miles nodded curtly and hit the accelerator. The car lurched forward, snatching the door from Faith and slamming it shut.

Rubbing her stinging fingers, she turned and strode through sliding doors into the hospital.

The cool lobby air felt good. Faith dodged a nurse pushing a new mother in a wheelchair and wove between a uniformed security guard and a man delivering a bouquet of floating balloons. Faith nodded to one of the bobbing, yellow smiley faces and hurried to the relative quiet of the elevator alcove.

Her foot tapped while she waited for the elevator. She was beginning to feel it: that tingle of excitement that went with the start of a new project. Phase one of her research was complete; phase two, about to begin. In a new lab with cutting edge equipment, her work should fly forward.

The elevator dinged, and the door opened. Mary Chapin Carpenter's "I Feel Lucky" drifted over the elevator's speakers. Faith smiled. That's what she needed—luck. With luck, the second phase would come together in a matter of months. Luck and a lot of hard work.

She hummed the tune all the way to the basement. Her humming faltered when she spotted the crime-scene tape across the door to the blood bank, but it didn't die until she got to her lab. She unlocked the door and, holding the door open with one foot, reached for the light switch.

Her hand stopped before she reached it. A shadow huddled against the wall—shadow with light hair and denim-clad legs. She peered into the gloom. "Ritter?"

Blinking as if the light from the hall hurt his eyes, he squinted up at her. "Faith?"

"Of course it's Faith. This is my lab. But what are you doing here?"

He braced his hands on the floor and pushed himself to his feet. "I must talk to you." His words were thick and muddled, as if he had a cold. Cocaine users often had nasal problems. Had Ritter sniffed whatever he'd been on last night?

Faith started to step back. "I don't think—"

"Please." He caught her hand and pressed it to his lips. The warmth of the kiss spread up her arm and across her shoulders. His eyes were blue again: bloodshot, but focused. Concern lined his forehead. "Just listen."

Faith meant to pull free and run for the stairs, but the urgency in his voice stopped her. She nodded and stepped over the threshold. The door whispered shut behind her, cutting off the light. Ritter seemed closer in the dark. She could hear his breathing and smell his unique scent of citrus, mint and—she sneezed—garlic. She yanked back her hand. "It was you, wasn't it? You're the idiot who doused my apartment in garlic powder."

The light clicked on. Ritter looked a mess. His usually neat hair was tousled, and his shirt was wrinkled. He shrugged. "Just the door."

"If it was a joke, it was a lousy one. I'm allergic to garlic."

A thin smile stretched his lips. "So am I."

"Then why?"

Ritter motioned toward the stools by her lab table. "Sit, and I will explain."

Clutching her briefcase, Faith perched on one of the stools. Instead of joining her, Ritter leaned against the wall next to the door. It occurred to Faith that she'd have to get past him if she wanted to leave the room. She tightened her grip on the case. "Well?"

Ritter's self-assurance seemed to drain away. He ran his fingers through his hair. "It's a long story."

"Give me the *Reader's Digest* version."

He lowered his hand. "You know the man who threatened you last night?"

"The one with the pimp coat and the halloween teeth? The one you called Cole?"

"He wants to kill you."

"Oh really? I thought he wanted to dance."

"This is no time for levity." Ritter pushed off the wall and strode to her. He gripped her shoulders. "Your life is in danger."

Faith's heart battered her ribcage, but she met his gaze and held it. "So you half choked me with garlic?"

"It was the only way to keep Cole out of your apartment." Ritter's grip loosened. "I didn't know garlic would make you ill."

"But you knew it would keep him out?"

"Yes." Ritter clasped his hands behind his back and started to pace. "Cole is...different than most men. He—"

"Thinks he's a vampire."

Ritter stopped at the far wall and spun to face her. "What?"

"He thinks he's a vampire. It only makes sense. That's why he wears the teeth and is afraid of garlic. A cross on the door would have worked just as well and wouldn't have given me sneezing fits."

Ritter shook his head. "That's an old wives' tale. Vampires don't fear the cross."

"Old wives' tale?" The conversation was getting stranger and stranger. "Vampires don't mind crosses, but the bit about garlic is true?"

Ritter shrugged. "For Cole, at least. Like men, vampires are not all the same."

Omigod—he meant it. Ritter thought his friend was a real vampire. He wasn't just a drug user; he was deranged. God only knew how dangerous he'd become if she threatened his delusion. Faith's arms began to tremble. She tightened her hold on her briefcase, eased off the stool, and started edging toward the door. If she could distract him for a moment, she'd make a break for it. "So your friend is a vampire?"

Silence stretched between them. Ritter looked down, and when he answered, his voice was little more than a whisper. "Cole is more a comrade than a friend."

The words lodged in Faith's mind, but she didn't bother to make sense of them. As soon as his gaze dropped, she threw open the door and burst into the corridor. The stairs were closer than the elevator. Legs pumping, she sprinted.

She blasted into the stairwell and pounded up the stairs. A moment later, the door crashed open behind her. "Wait!" Ritter called. You don't understand."

Yes, she did. She stretched her legs to take the stairs two at a time.

His heavier strides thundered behind her. "Stop!" The command seemed to grab at her feet. Faith kicked them loose and darted through the door to the lobby.

The sudden brightness hurt her eyes. Sunlight streamed through the skylight and lit the patients, doctors, and visitors below it. Ignoring their indignant cries, Faith plowed through the crowd, determined to get to the door and out of sight before Ritter could catch her.

She was nearly there when his voice boomed in her ear. "Faith!" Startled, she spun to face him, but Ritter wasn't beside her.

Like the restless sea, the crowd had rushed in to fill her wake. Except for the few still glaring at her, most of the people had resumed their conversations. Ritter's pale face gleamed in the relative dimness of the stairwell. He reached toward her, then yanked his hand back as if afraid of the light. His lips moved and his voice tickled her ear. "Don't go where I can't follow. Please, *Liebchen*, come back."

The crazy thing was, she wanted to. Clenching her fingers around the handle of the briefcase, Faith forced herself to turn and push through the lobby doors. For once, a cab stood idling at the cab stand near the hospital entrance. She climbed in and gave the cabby her address.

The adrenaline that had propelled her up the stairs suddenly drained away, leaving her weak and shaky. She flopped her head against the top of the seat and closed her eyes. She hadn't had a chance to disconnect her phone yet. She'd call Miles from the apartment and tell him she'd changed her mind. His assistant could pack her lab. She'd come directly to the secure facility. Knowing how anxious Miles was to please Banat, he'd U-turn on the freeway to come get her. Once there, both she and her work would be safe.

Faith reached down and patted her briefcase. She needed that security to complete phase two of the project—first identifying the genetic changes triggered by Miles' virus and then creating a new virus to reverse them in a living cell. That was the key: reversing the damage without killing the host. Once she discovered that key, the possibilities were endless. In ten years, doctors might have an army of counterviruses at their command. Babies who today would be born sick and dying would be treated in the womb and emerge healthy and perfect. Babies like her brother would live and thrive.

Her work was too important to interrupt for a lunatic, a drug addict who dabbled in hypnosis and ventriloquism. Faith rolled her head and gazed out the window. Ritter had no idea where she was going and no way to find her. She could forget about his crazy warning and his homicidal friend. She and her work would be safe. With any luck, she'd never see Ritter again.

Her eyes started to burn. Blinking, Faith rifled through her purse for a tissue. Damn that garlic, it was making her cry again.

๛ ๛

"Please, *Liebchen*, come back." The hair on the back of Ritter's neck rose, pulled by the power he threw behind his voice. The compulsion rippled across the inaccessibly bright lobby. Anyone else, human or vampire, would have followed his command blindly. Even Faith, staring at him from near the exit, seemed to hesitate. Hope flared. Perhaps this once, she would hear his voice and obey. She held his gaze for a heart-stopping moment, then turned and disappeared into the late morning sunshine.

"No!" Ritter slammed his fist into the wall of the stairwell, punching a hole in the plasterboard. The people closest to the stairwell, a group of nurses clad in identical blue smocks and slacks, stopped gossiping and turned to stare at him.

"You heard nothing, saw nothing." Ritter wiped their memory without even bothering to look at them. He flexed his fingers and grimaced. The knuckles stung, and the tips throbbed from being thrust too close to the sunlight. They were minor pains, though. Faith had run from him, from his call, from his sight, from his protection. Had run from him as if she recognized him for the monster he was. And he had been powerless to stop her.

He pulled the stairwell door closed, and its shadow fell over him like a balm. At least there was one thing to be grateful for: the sunlight that trapped him in the basement was too strong for even Cole's resistant skin. His vengeful friend also was powerless and must remain in shadow until the daylight dimmed. For the next few hours, Faith was safe.

Turning from the door, Ritter trotted down the stairs, back to the basement and Faith's laboratory. Faith loved her work. She wouldn't abandon it for the whole day. She would give him time to leave and then return. All he had to do was wait.

He clicked off the lights and eased to the floor. His eyes burned from staring into the sunshine. Closing them, Ritter sagged against the wall. He was deathly tired, but he didn't dare sleep. Faith would be back soon, and he had to think of an argument strong enough to persuade her to accept his protection.

Frustration boiled inside him. Of all the people he had met since his transformation, why was Faith the only one immune to the power of his voice? Were she any other woman, he would simply compel her obedience. But he couldn't. With the one woman who mattered, he was as helpless as any mortal.

Ritter bent his legs and rested his forehead on his knees. His insides ached. He had wrapped himself in safe indifference for so long, he had forgotten how it hurt to care. He opened his eyes and sat up. He cared. The aching hole in his gut wasn't the familiar worry of a shepherd for his sheep. It was personal. For the first time in seventy years, someone had touched his heart and crept into what was left of his soul. Heaven help him, now he was twice damned.

Chapter Nine

Krankenhaus rechts der Isar
Munich, Bavaria
September 12, 1944

Sunshine warmed the porch of the hospital and spilled over the lap rugs and reclining chairs of the soldiers resting there. To Ritter, they resembled young Rothschilds enjoying the baths along the Rhine—except for the uniforms and the way some stared at the walls, riveted by horrors no one else could see. At first, Ritter had tried to meet those gazes. Now he knew better. He sat in his own chair, knees up, a sheet of paper propped against them. Dipping his pen into the bottle of ink on the table beside him, he leaned forward and began a long-overdue letter.

Dearest Greta:
Please forgive my long silence. Much has happened since I last put pen to paper. I was wounded in an ambush near a small village outside of Rome. Luckily for me, the enemy was loaded against infantry, not a panzer. Still, their shell pierced our armor and destroyed our engine. Two of my comrades were killed instantly, but Captain Krieger and I escaped before the ammunition blew. We were badly injured by machine-gun fire, but were able to crawl to a ditch, where the enemy left us for dead. Our troops drove off the attack and found us some time later. Both the captain and I were sent to a hospital in Munich. I've been here over a month. This is the first chance I've had to write you.
Please don't worry, Liebchen, the doctors are most impressed by my recovery. After we are married, I will show you the puckers the bullets left in my leg, stomach, and back. They're so tiny, it's hard to believe the injury nearly killed me.
Send my respects to your mother and the rest of the village, but save all my love for yourself. I pray our forces will soon be victorious, so I can return and hold you once more.
Affectionately,
Ritter

He lay the pen on the table and blew on the paper to dry the ink. Brisk footsteps, heavier than the nurses' soft tread, marched across the wooden porch floor. They stopped next to his chair. A shadow fell across his letter. Ritter glanced up, then jumped his feet. The letter fluttered to the floor, momentarily forgotten. Unable to stop a grin, he snapped to attention and saluted. "Captain Krieger."

Though not tall, Krieger stood as straight as a poplar. His gray hair, which had grown shaggy on the front, was once again cut close to his skull. He wore a freshly pressed uniform and polished boots, but his weathered face hadn't changed. The skin was still rough and brown, the dueling scar that slashed from the corner of his left eye to the center of his cheek, still straight and pale. The scar closed his eye when he smiled, giving his expression a sinister cast. Behind his back, Krieger's men called him the Pirate. Ritter had served under him for two and a half years. He had followed Krieger into numerous battles and would gladly have driven his tank into hell if the old Pirate had ordered it. Krieger nodded toward Ritter's chair. "Sit. I'm here as a visitor, not your commanding officer."

Ritter sat, but it felt odd, sitting while his captain stood. As if sensing his discomfort, Krieger grabbed a chair and sat in front of him. "The doctors tell me you are fit to return to duty."

"Yes, sir. Fit and willing."

The old man winked a smile. "Excellent."

Encouraged, Ritter burst out with the question that had been plaguing him. "How goes the war? I've heard nothing but grim rumors since I've been here."

The smile dimmed. "We're losing." The words hung in the air like poison gas. Ritter looked around the room to see if anyone else had heard, but the men only sat and stared.

He turned back to his captain. "I know we were losing ground in Italy, but surely elsewhere..."

"We're losing everywhere. Unless the Reich comes up with a miracle, a masterstroke to devastate our enemies, defeat is inevitable." If possible, Krieger's back grew even straighter. "You can help create that miracle."

"I? What can I do?"

"You're being transferred to an elite group, a group dedicated to crafting a weapon so terrible, it will make our enemies turn and run like rabbits."

A hot, proud bubble filled Ritter almost to bursting. At last, a chance to do more for his country than kill and watch his comrades die. "What kind of weapon? A new tank?"

Krieger shook his head. "I don't know. I only know the assignment is very dangerous. It requires men brave enough to embrace the risk and tough enough to survive it. Your recovery from such serious wounds shows your stamina, and you proved your bravery when you dragged me from the burning tank. The job's yours, if you want it."

Ritter shot to his feet. "Thank you, sir!"

Krieger also stood. "Once you finish the special assignment, you'll return to my unit. Take care of yourself, Breitmann. You're a good man, and I don't want to lose you." He bent down and picked up Ritter's letter. "Mail this soon. I doubt you'll be allowed to write your sweetheart, once you start work on the miracle weapon."

〰〰

Ritter's orders arrived three days later. He'd just started a supper of potato soup and rye bread when the door to the hospital mess opened. An SS sergeant, his expression as stiff as his black uniform, marched into the room. Eyes, the color of dirty snow, narrowed as he scanned the room. *"Achtung!"*

The soldiers scrambled to their feet.

"Corporal Breitmann!"

Supper forgotten, Ritter stepped forward and saluted. "Here, sir."

The gray eyes warmed slightly. "Gather your things and meet me by the loading dock. You have five minutes."

Three minutes later, Ritter pushed through the back door of the hospital, lowered his duffel to the ground in front of the sergeant, and snapped to attention. "Sir!"

The sergeant's lips thinned in a slight smile. He nodded toward a troop transport parked near the loading dock. "Get in." Without waiting to see if Ritter obeyed, he turned and climbed into the cab.

Ritter threw his duffel into the back of the truck and clambered up behind it.

"Look, Erik, another 'volunteer.'" The wheezy tenor belonged to a small terrier of a man sitting on the bench in the shadow of the transport's canvas cover. The truck lurched forward, and Ritter dropped onto a bench across from him. The man flashed a grin full of bright, crooked teeth and thrust out his hand. "I'm Fritz Heine, Corporal Fritz Heine."

Ritter took the hand. "Ritter Breitmann, also a corporal."

Heine's grip tightened a moment, as if searching for weakness, then released. "That makes three of us. Allow me to introduce my friend, Corporal Erik Jurgensohn." He nodded to a massive soldier beside him.

Jurgensohn clung to the bench as it bounced beneath him. *"Guten Abend."* Good evening. His voice was deep and heavily accented. Ritter guessed he was from the north of Germany: Niedersachsen or Schwanzig-Holstein.

"Abend." Ritter held out his hand, but the truck chose that moment to turn and accelerate. Jurgensohn held his seat, but Ritter slammed into the back of the cab. Pushing himself upright, he shrugged an apology. "Let's save the handshake for later."

Still clutching the bench, Jurgensohn grinned. "Good idea."

Light from the setting sun now streamed into the covered transport, giving Ritter a good look at his new comrades. They looked about the same age, a few years older than Ritter. Jurgensohn had a broad, open face that made his pale eyes seem small. His hair was longish, straw fair, and ruffled. He had a friendly smile and large, work-roughened hands.

At first glance, Heine's smile was even friendlier. It spread an innocent, engaging expression across his face. Short, dark hair circled a crown-wide bald spot. He reminded Ritter of a medieval friar, jolly and harmless, until he looked into Heine's eyes. They were sharp, narrow, an odd, gray-rimmed gold. They caught the dying sunlight and shone like a cat's. Heine's wrists were small, his fingers long and tapered, with short, well-trimmed nails.

"Were you a tailor before the war?" Ritter asked, remembering the only other man he'd known with such delicate, yet strong-looking, hands.

Heine chuckled. "Hardly."

"He was a pickpocket in Berlin." Jurgensohn spoke slowly, his voice rich with pride. "One of the best."

"One of the best?" Heine snorted. "Don't mock me with faint praise. Rich men used to scurry like rats across Alexanderplatz, clutching their wallets in fear that I'd lighten them. And I did, often."

"And you," Ritter asked, turning to Jurgensohn. "What did you do before the war?"

"He was a dairyman," Heine answered. "His family owns a dairy outside of Bredstedt. He's been milking cows since he was five. That's why he's so big and clumsy. He drank too much milk as a boy."

"And you drank too much *Schnaps*. That's why you're so puny."

Heine grinned, and Ritter realized this was an old and well-worn joke. "How long have you known each other?"

Again, it was Heine who answered. "Three years. We met on the Russian front, but we didn't get to know each other well until the retreat from Minsk."

Despite the continuing bumps, he sat back and crossed his arms over his chest. Obviously, this was a story he told often and with relish. "My squad was ambushed by a Russian tank. I never even saw the damn thing. One minute I was running across a field with my comrades, the next I was on the ground with my guts in my hands. My squad scattered. I heard the tank rumbling toward me and knew I was dead. I was trying to remember how to pray when this big, blond dairyman darted from a nearby stand of trees. He ran straight for me and picked me up like I was one of his calves. I don't remember much after that, just Erik running and the machine gun spitting. The gunner shot him five times in the back, but this oaf was too stubborn to lie down and die."

Heine's eyes glittered like coins. "He didn't collapse until he found the medics."

Jurgensohn looked down and shrugged. "I was lucky."

"We both were. The medics said it'd be a miracle if either of us survived. It took months, but here we are, on the way to a new assignment."

The truck turned again, setting its side to the dying sun. Gloom filled the back of the transport, and the men rode in silence. Before long, the occasional jolt of the tires hitting a pothole shifted to a consistent, tooth-shaking rattle. Ritter peered out the back and saw a cobblestone street and neat houses with autumn flowers blooming in their window boxes. The truck turned once more and jerked to a stop. The door to the cab creaked open. *"Heraus!"* the sergeant called. Out!

Ritter grabbed his duffel and scrambled out of the truck. Heine and Jurgensohn joined him.

"Come!" The sergeant led them into a squat brick building and down a straight flight of stairs to the oddest basement Ritter had ever seen.

Unlike his mother's cellar, a dank hole that smelled of earth and moldy vegetables, the room was large and airy, with whitewashed, windowless walls. The air smelled of soap, fresh paint, and men. Bright lights hung from the ceiling, and posters with inspirational slogans, like Work Makes Life Sweet and What Doesn't Kill You Makes You Stronger, graced the walls.

Beds, arranged in rows of ten, covered the floor. The three nearest the stairway had folded blankets and linen stacked on their naked mattresses. The rest had already been made, though some of the blankets looked rumpled, as if someone had been lying on them. One sported a chess board and the remnants of a game. Beside each bed stood a soldier, frozen at attention under the sergeant's icy glare. "The last men have arrived. Sleep well. Tomorrow we begin." He turned to Ritter and his companions. "Choose a bed and get settled. The morning will come early. *Heil* Hitler!"

The whole room returned his salute. The sergeant nodded, turned, and marched from the room.

The soldiers remained at attention until the footsteps faded. Most flopped back on their beds or clustered around the chess game, but a tall blond with corporal's bars on his shoulders stepped forward. "I'm Heinrich Schmidt. Welcome to Dachau."

Chapter Ten

Lake County, Illinois
August 22, 2014

The numbers on the monitor blurred into a meaningless stream. Damn it, she'd lost track again. After hitting *Save*, Faith rocked back in her ergonomic chair and rubbed her burning eyes. What was wrong with her? Her research had come further in the last three months than in the previous three years combined. She should be pumped and eager to press on. Instead, just looking at the data was enough to make her stomach churn.

She couldn't blame the computer. It was marvelous, perfect. Banat hadn't lied about his research facility being state of the art. For most of the last three months, Faith had relished the luxury of working in a private lab. She had daily access to the best electron microscope she'd seen outside a major university, excellent technical support, and a 24/7 connection to a supercomputer and the national data bank. Banat's research compound was modern, well-equipped and secure—the perfect place for continuing her research.

Faith sighed and rolled her neck to ease the kinks. She was tired; that was the problem. Three months of working nonstop, pausing only for gulped meals and cat naps—no wonder her attention wandered. When was the last time she took a break, had a little fun?

When she went to the diner with Ritter. The memory of him staring at her through his eyelashes filled her mind. Faith shook her head and willed the image away. Ritter was a drug-addled child. She refused to miss him.

A click behind her warned that someone had opened her office door. Since there was no knock, it was probably Miles. She spun around in time to see him stick his head into her office. "I'm heading back to the apartment complex. Want a ride?"

"Across the parking lot?" His brow furrowed, and Faith felt a pang of remorse. "Sorry, Miles. Don't mind me. I'm a bitch today."

Still frowning, he stepped into the room. "Problem with the last trial?"

"No, the raw data looks great. I'm the problem. I just can't..." Faith struggled for a word to capture her growing discontent. "Focus, I guess. My mind keeps wandering."

His expression cleared. "You need a break. Why don't you go back to your apartment and watch a movie?"

Her apartment had come complete with a new coffeemaker, an internet-connected refrigerator, and a digital TV with built-in movie collection. The spacious one bedroom was as perfect as her lab. Faith suddenly realized she'd had enough perfection. She forced a smile. "Good idea, but I think I'll leave the grounds for once. Remember Shawna, the post-doc who was helping me at Bradbury U? I haven't talked to her since we moved out here. Maybe I'll give her a call. We could go to dinner and catch a movie on the big screen."

She expected Miles to nod and say something pompous, but his frown returned. "How? We're miles from the nearest town, and you don't have a car."

"If Shawna can't give me a ride, I'll call a cab."

The frown melted in dismay. "A cab would never find this place. If you don't feel like cooking, come over to my place and I'll fix pasta primavera."

"What's wrong with you?" Faith stood and walked toward him. "You sound—I don't know—scared."

Their gazes brushed, then his eyes shifted to look over her shoulder. "I'm just worried about those Embryo-Rightists finding you again."

"Now you're being paranoid."

"Not paranoid; smart. Those fanatics may still be watching Nick and Shawna. It's safer for you to stay here than to go gallivanting around Lake County with your former research assistant. I order you to stay put."

"Order?" Not trusting herself to say more, Faith turned, removed the memory stick from her computer, and threw it into her briefcase.

Miles stepped up and dropped a heavy hand on her shoulder. "Faith—"

"Move it or lose it." The words squeezed out. The hand lifted. Faith shut the case before facing him. "You have no right to tell me where to go or what to do."

Miles shoved his hands into his pants pockets. "You're right, of course. It's just, with the project at such a critical point, I can't afford to have anything happen to you."

Faith shrugged, too angry to accept the nonapology gracefully.

"Here." Brightening as if he'd just discovered a new retrovirus, Miles pulled a key on a plain steel ring from his pocket. "Banat loaned me a company car for as long as mine's in the shop. It's parked right outside—the white Lexus. Take it. Go out. Have fun."

Jaw loose with astonishment, Faith took the key and clasped the warm metal in her palm. Forget what she thought before; lending her a car was a damn fine apology. "Thank you, Miles."

He nodded and stepped aside. "See you Monday. Go ahead, I'll lock up," he said when she hesitated.

That was all it took. "See you!" Clutching her briefcase, she ran from the room.

༄ ༄

"Born to Be Wild!" Faith cranked up the oldies station and sang along at the top of her lungs. Instead of the worn-out fleet car she expected, the Lexus turned out to be a late model gas/electric hybrid— slick and loaded. With the sunroof open and the windows down, she felt almost as free as she had in Ritter's convertible.

An approaching traffic light turned red. Faith's left foot slammed the car floor while her right foot hit the brake. Damn automatic transmission. That was the only problem with the hybrids: no clutch. Faith loved to ride the power curve, to bask in the full-throated roar of a gasoline engine and feel the acceleration vibrate up her legs and through her body. That's why she loved driving her father's Mustangs. That's why she missed Ritter's Mercedes.

The antilock brakes engaged, and the car shuddered to a stop. Disc-jockey prattle drowned out the engine's quiet hum. Faith was about to change stations when the light turned green. Taking her foot off the brake, she eased on the accelerator. The Lexus rolled forward, smooth as glass. The hybrids were quieter than the old gas-guzzling engines, cleaner and safer, too. So what if they weren't quite as much fun as Ritter's little roadster? The dj talk ended and after a moment of relative silence, the jaunty opening of "Leroy Brown" filled the air.

Faith tapped her foot and hummed along. She didn't need Ritter or his car to have a good time. Since she hadn't been able to get ahold of Shawna, she could go wherever she wanted. She could turn right and head for Chicago. She recognized the intersection she'd nearly run; the road led south to a tollway entrance. She could take the tollway to the Edens and the Edens into the City. Once there, she could cruise Rush Street or hit the jazz joints on the South Side. In her blue silk shift and least sensible heels, she was dressed up enough to go to the Palmer House if she wanted to. It was a hot Friday night, and Miles wasn't expecting her or the car back until Monday morning. With her overnight bag in the trunk, she could make a weekend of it.

Faith continued east. There was too much crime in the city. Not that she was worried about the car getting stolen—the Lexus came equipped with all the latest security devices—but she had three months' worth of work in her purse. Before leaving, she'd tucked her computer's memory stick securely behind her driver's license. Miles would scream if he knew she'd taken all that data from the compound, but she didn't feel safe unless it was with her. Call her paranoid, but after the break-in at her last apartment, she'd lost all confidence in safes. She wanted to keep her work where she could lay her hands on it. No, there were too many purse-snatchers in Chicago to risk going there. Besides, all she really wanted was a good cheeseburger and an old-fashioned movie. The best of both were right here in Lake County.

Fifteen minutes later, she pulled into *Al's* parking lot. It was nearly nine, late for dinner, but early for the night crowd. Faith found a parking space near the door. She set the car's security system, grabbed her purse, and hurried inside. She picked up a campus newspaper from the stack by the register and flipped through the entertainment section while she waited for her burger. Every weekend, even in summer, the University Film Club screened movies in the auditorium at Jackson Hall. Tickets were five dollars a head; free, with student ID. Faith scanned the calendar, hoping UFC wasn't in the middle of a Bergman retrospective. Tonight, she needed to laugh.

She found the date and smiled. They were playing a Jack Benny double feature. *The Meanest Man in the World* had already started, but the second feature—her favorite Jack Benny film, *To Be or Not to Be*—didn't start until ten. Perfect.

The burger smelled wonderful, but it didn't taste as good as she remembered. The malt was disappointing, too. Though cold and sweet, it didn't seem as rich. Under Ritter's appreciative gaze, each sip had rolled over her tongue like essence of chocolate.

Suddenly everything about the diner reminded her of Ritter: the food, the decor, even the tired-eyed waitress. Faith pushed her half-eaten burger aside, threw a five on the table, and stood. She was out to have a good time, not to moon over Todd Ritter. If she hurried, maybe she could catch the end of the first movie. She scooped up the check and hurried to the register.

☙❧

The sun set at 6:56. Ritter pulled back his curtain and watched the eastern sky turn indigo, then black. A three-quarter moon, jaundiced with summer haze, rose an hour later and filled the alley with sallow light. Ritter's cheeks tingled. Without sunscreen, even secondhand sunlight could burn.

He dropped the curtain. His stomach ached and his head echoed with need. He had to hunt, to feed. The bloodlust would kill him if he didn't; kill him as surely as a stake in the heart or a bath of fire. Not that he minded dying; it was the madness he feared. The hunger would drive him mad before it killed him. It already whispered chaos in his mind.

He slapped on some sunblock and exchanged his T-shirt for a red mesh tank-top: the height of fashion to his young prey. He left on his jeans—they were black and tight enough—and pulled the flared hems over the tops of his snakeskin boots. The black-and-silver-scaled toes glittered when he walked into the brightly lit bathroom. He slicked his hair with styling gel and lifted it into lazy spikes, then grinned mockingly at himself. His reflection, pale and drawn, grinned back. Despite what Stoker wrote, not even monsters were exempt from the laws of physics.

Cash in his wallet, keys in his pocket, and he was ready. He locked the apartment door and trotted up the stairs. The heat and humidity of the evening didn't hit him until he stepped from the lobby; even with the sun down, it was like a sauna outside. Ritter strolled the three blocks to his garage and Greta.

He didn't really need Greta during the school year. Dorm parties and fraternity keggers kept him well provided with prey. But summer posed a challenge. With most of the students gone, the dormitories and frat houses were closed. The parties became smaller, more intimate, and harder to crash. He had left several schools because of such summer droughts. Then he enrolled in Bradbury University.

Nestled in the north-eastern tip of Illinois, Bradbury U attracted two kinds of students: hardworking scholars, drawn by its generous grants, and spoiled dilettantes from Chicago's North Shore. The scholars worked during the summer or buried themselves in the intensive summer curriculum. The dilettantes returned to mansions in Wilmette, Kennilworth, or Lake Forest. What they did during the week, Ritter didn't know or care; but on weekends, they and their equally spoiled siblings piled into Lincoln Navigators and headed for Waukegan's warehouse district. The rave scene was alive and well in Lake County. Thanks to it, so was Ritter.

He needed Greta to drive them home, those foolish girls who thought money and looks would keep them safe. They flirted with doom, reveled in it. Alcohol was bad enough, but the designer drugs the rich and stupid preferred stripped their senses and left them doubly vulnerable. Many predators prowled the raves; not only monsters like himself, but evil men, who hunted for gain or to satisfy twisted desires. At least Ritter brought his victims home, alive and unmolested. A pint or so of blood was a small fee to demand in return.

The address for tonight's rave was in his wallet, but he knew the building well: an abandoned dry dock near the Waukegan harbor. It was south and a little east of his apartment, but Ritter turned north toward campus.

He hadn't seen Faith in the three months since she ran into the sun and out of his life, but he couldn't stop looking for her. She hadn't gone far, he was sure of that. Some nights, Faith seemed so close, he could almost taste her. Like tonight. The humid breeze seemed sweeter, as if flavored by her passing. Ritter grinned into the air rushing past him. It wouldn't hurt to check just once more.

At first he had searched secretly, by internet and telephone. Cole wanted Faith, and he wouldn't hesitate to trail Ritter to find her. They knocked against each other more than once, Cole growing increasingly frustrated as the summer passed. He had finally left to investigate rumors of a new viral lab on the West Coast. That was two weeks ago, and Ritter was free to chase the promise in the air.

He drove by the hospital first. The lobby was open, as always, but her lab was locked. Her apartment was next. Cold and dark, it had lost all but a hint of her presence. She hadn't gone back to work, and she hadn't come home.

Ritter sighed and slid into his seat. The flavored breeze was probably a false lead, like Cole's laboratory in Oregon. More from nostalgia than from any hope of finding Faith, Ritter pulled out of the parking lot and headed for *Al's*.

And there she was, framed in the entrance to the diner. Her face was shadowed, but her posture and long-legged gait were unmistakable. She wore a sleeveless blue dress and clutched a small black purse. No briefcase, for once. Ritter steered Greta into the shadow between two streetlights and watched Faith stride to a late-model coupe, unlock the door, and climb in.

He had forgotten how much he loved the swing of her legs, the sway of her hips. Sharper than the bloodlust, longing sliced through him. He needed to see Faith, to touch her hand, to hear her voice. Dry-mouthed and trembling, Ritter gripped the wheel until his knuckles popped. He would follow Faith, see her and talk to her, but not until he regained his hard-won control. Damning the hunger that sharpened his pain, Ritter shut his eyes and ordered his racing heart to slow, his tremors to still.

An engine purred to life, and his eyes flew open. Faith pulled out of the lot and turned away from him, heading down Illinois Avenue toward the campus. When his hands were steady, Ritter shifted into gear and drove after her.

She didn't go far. Three blocks later, she turned and parked across the street from Jackson Hall. Ritter continued past the auditorium and parked in the next free space he found. He wasn't worried about losing Faith. Nine-thirty on a Saturday night in August, there was only one thing happening at Jackson Hall—the UFC's weekend movie.

The film club was screening old comedies this month. Ritter couldn't remember the name of the night's showing, but it didn't matter. He wasn't there for the movie. Hopping out of Greta, he ran down the street to the box office and stepped behind Faith. "*Guten Abend, Fräulein Doktor.*"

She jumped at his greeting and spun around. "What—" Her gaze dropped to his chest, and her words stopped.

Her speechless stare hit Ritter like a shot of blood. He wanted to tip his head back and laugh. Instead, he reached out and brushed a soft curl off her shoulder. Her hair had grown in the last three months. Her eyes were the same, gold-flecked gray, slightly tilted. Lipstick heightened the blush of her lips. He inhaled her fragrance of flowers and musk. And fatigue. He leaned closer. Her cheeks seemed paler beneath their rouge, and the hollows in the base of her alabaster throat seemed deeper. "You work too hard," he said.

At the mention of her work she blinked and met Ritter's gaze. A faint line appeared between her eyes. "What did you do to your hair?"

"Gel." He tilted his head to give her a better look. "Spikes are hot on the rave scene."

"Rave?" She backed away from the ticket window. "I don't do drugs, and I don't associate with people who do."

"Two tickets," Ritter said to the ticket seller, a young man with severe acne. Then he stepped after Faith and caught her arm. "I don't take drugs. Not even aspirin."

She pulled her arm free. "Right. You go to raves to listen to the music." Her tone suggested he would do better trying to sell her the Matterhorn.

Ritter let his lips tip up. "No, I go to meet girls."

"You can't expect me to believe you have any trouble meeting girls. I've seen them practically fall in your lap."

"That's ten bucks unless you have a student ID," the ticket seller interrupted.

Ritter dug into his pocket for his wallet. "It's summer. Most are gone until autumn quarter."

"And if you never use drugs, how come you were sky high last time you came to my apartment?"

Ritter sucked in a breath. When he tried the truth, she ran away. "That was...an accident. I'm afraid Cole is a bad influence."

"Bad influence? He's crazy."

Fear emanated from her, strong enough to made his teeth ache. Ritter stepped forward and spoke in his gentlest voice. "He's also gone. I haven't seen him in weeks."

Faith licked her lips and her heartbeat slowed. "Really?"

"The last time I saw him, he was headed for Oregon."

She took a breath and straightened her shoulders. "Good. But even with him gone, I really don't think—" The lights dimmed and brightened. The heavy lobby doors swung open.

"The next film starts in five." It was the young man again. "You want tickets or not?"

Ritter pulled out his wallet and flashed his student ID. The attendant nodded and slipped the tickets through the portal in the glass.

"Thank you." Ritter grabbed them and took Faith's arm. "Let's go."

She planted her feet. "No."

Ritter couldn't bear to lose her again, not so soon after finding her. His hand slid down her arm to her hand. "I missed you, *Fräulein Doktor*."

She snorted, a husky and surprisingly arousing sound, but at least she didn't pull away. "How could you? You don't even know me."

"I know enough." He wove his fingers between hers. "Come. It's only a movie."

A laugh chased away her lingering frown. "I take it back; you just might need to rave to meet girls. You certainly have no idea how to ask one out."

Ritter lifted her hand and kissed the knuckle above her ring finger. Her warmth teased his lips, and he longed to open his mouth and trace her veins with his tongue. Instead, he raised his head and let his lips spread into a careful smile. "Will you do me the honor of accompanying me to the cinema this evening? Please."

At first he thought she was going to pull away, but her fingers tightened around his. "I'd love to."

～～

The theater lights dimmed, the screen brightened, and the opening credits began to roll. Faith settled in her seat, determined to ignore the distraction of Ritter's hand, still clasped around hers. She was here to watch the movie, she reminded herself. She loved old films. Unlike modern movies, the credits were just that—a simple list of who did what: director, actors, technical crew. She smiled as Robert Stack's name appeared well down on the list. One of the best things about old movies was spotting stars in roles they played before they were famous.

Ritter's well-callused thumb brushed her knuckle. His clasp felt cool, but the gesture shot warmth through her arm. He leaned across the armrest. "What are you smiling at?"

"The movie."

Her words came out louder than she meant, to the annoyance of someone in the next row, who loudly shushed her.

Frowning over her shoulder, she turned to Ritter. Sitting, he was nearly a head taller than she was. She tipped up her chin and lowered her voice to a whisper. "It's one of my favorites."

His breath kissed her cheek. "I have never seen it."

"Then you're in for a treat."

He tilted his head, bringing his lips within inches of hers. "*Liebchen*, you are the treat."

He lowered his head. Ritter was going to kiss her. Despite her best intentions, Faith couldn't pull away. Instead, her lips parted, and her eyes drifted closed.

The music stopped, and a male voice spoke over the auditorium sound system. "We're in Warsaw, the capital of Poland. It's August 1939, and Europe is still at peace." Ritter froze, and Faith's eyes flew open. Abandoning the near kiss, he turned to the cheerful street scene that began the movie. When the "man with the little mustache" appeared, Ritter seemed as horrified as the Poles on the screen. His grip tightened to crushing strength.

"Ow!"

Ritter released her hand but kept staring. The scene had changed. An SS officer was luring a boy into betraying his father. Faith laid her hand on Ritter's arm. It was as still and cold as marble. "Are you all right?"

"Of course." Even his voice was cold.

Suddenly, she remembered Ritter was German. He must be seeing the movie as an attack—on his country, if not himself. "It's just a movie, an old propaganda piece, but a good one. Don't take it personally. The message is anti-Nazi, not anti-German."

"There was little difference in 1939." Before Faith could think of a response to that, he blinked and turned to her. "I'm just surprised," he said in a normal tone. "With the title, I thought the movie had something to do with Shakespeare." His faint smile transformed him back into a college kid. "I don't care much for history."

Considering the range of books in his bedroom, Faith rather doubted that, but she decided to let the comment slide. She patted his arm and turned back to the screen. "They get around to Shakespeare. Just wait and see."

❧ ❧

"What did I tell you?" Grinning, Faith wiped her eyes. Even though her stomach hurt from too much laughing, she felt lighter than she had in months. "There was plenty of Shakespeare."

"Indeed." Ritter gave her hand a gentle squeeze. He'd taken her hand again sometime during the movie. Faith couldn't remember exactly when, but she was in too good a mood to mind.

She returned the squeeze. "So, what do you think? Did you like it?"

"Yes." He sounded surprised.

The final credits stopped, and the house lights came on. In their harsh glare, Jackson looked like the science lecture hall it was during the school year. Tiers of chairs, with desktops folded between them, rose sharply toward the exits in the back. Murmured voices filled the hall as the audience sidled toward the aisles. Ritter stood and nodded after them. "Shall we?"

They pushed through the lobby doors into the velvety evening. "Are you off to the rave now?" Faith asked.

His expression folded into the beginning of a frown. "I suppose so."

"What's the matter, don't you want to go?"

"Of course I do."

"Then why the long face?"

"I don't want to lose you again."

Faith opened her mouth, but no words came. Ritter lifted her hand to his lips. His tongue slipped between her fingers, sending shivers up her arm. His breath puffed warm on her knuckles and cool on the newly slick skin. "Where have you been hiding?"

"I haven't been hiding." Faith's voice was thin, breathy. "I've been working."

Ritter lowered her hand. "Of course. But where have you been working."

Faith almost told him, but the memory of her ransacked apartment stopped her. Over the summer, she'd come to doubt that Ritter was involved in the break-in—his surprise and concern when they discovered her vandalized home had seemed sincere—but until she knew for sure, she couldn't afford to trust him. She gently pulled her hand from his clasp. "Where's the rave?"

The line between his brows grew deeper. "What?"

"The rave. Where is it? I feel like dancing." She extended her arms, threw back her head, and twirled until the hem of her dress billowed around her thighs.

His eyes widened. "You can't come with me."

The pang of disappointment caught Faith by surprise. "Why not? Afraid you won't be able to pick up a girl if I do?"

The truth flashed across his face, truth that his shaking head didn't dispel.

"Fine." The word cut Faith's throat like broken glass. She turned and stomped toward the Lexus.

"Faith." Ritter was suddenly beside her. "You wouldn't want to come. The raves around here are for stupid, spoiled children. You wouldn't fit in. You are too—"

"Old?" Why did it hurt that he agreed with her? "That's what I've been telling you all along. I'm too old for you."

She stormed past him to the borrowed car. Yanking the key from her purse, she shoved it in the lock. "Never mind about the rave. I'll find my own action."

"Faith, wait!"

She threw herself into the car and slammed the door, cutting off Ritter's voice. Turning the ignition, she threw the car into drive and peeled from the curb. So he thought she was old, did he? Faith had outgrown the rave scene while still in college, but tonight, she'd find one if it killed her. She turned on Illinois Avenue and drove east toward Waukegan. Unless things had changed a lot since she was in college, she knew just where to look.

❧

Faith's car squealed around the corner, and Ritter turned toward Greta with heavy feet. The ache in his gut was hunger, he told himself. Faith was working somewhere nearby. He would see her again. He would talk to her and make her trust him; but not now. Now, he had to feed. He climbed into the convertible and headed for the lakefront.

His route took him past shiny new subdivisions and cookie-cutter strip malls. The malls grew older as he drove east. Storefront restaurants, specializing in tamales or southern fried chicken, replaced the ubiquitous fast-food outlets. Turning off the main boulevard, he wove through a maze of one way streets. The neighborhood shifted from simple frame houses, to run-down tenements, to deserted warehouses. Suddenly, a searchlight sliced the sky above the graffiti-covered buildings. Ritter stiffened, then snorted at his foolishness. The film must have disturbed him more than he realized. The powerful beams weren't hunting bombers; they were advertising the rave. He pulled into an empty parking space and turned off the ignition. With the engine silent, he could hear a faint base beat. The party was in full swing.

Ritter left Greta and walked the remaining two blocks to the transformed dry dock. He didn't like to park too close, not since the night two SUVs boxed Greta into a space too tight to escape. He had barely made it out of the makeshift parking lot before dawn.

The two blocks also gave Ritter the chance to change. His posture went first. He relaxed his shoulders and sank into a slouch. He let the boots swing his legs into a swagger. Eyelids half-closed, lips curled into a bored sneer, he became the picture of spoiled modern youth.

The music grew louder as he approached the dry dock. He timed his strides to the techno-pop rhythm and turned the corner into the full force of the stadium-strength sound system, then stopped until his ears adjusted to the barrage of noise. It would be louder inside the building, but the first assault was always the worst. When the sharp stabs had dulled to distant ringing, he entered the parking lot and walked toward the guarded entrance.

When he first discovered the rave scene, the dance-and-drug parties were informal affairs, thrown together by the participants with little organization and even less security. Now raves were big, if clandestine, business, run by the men who profited from the drug trade. They rented large spaces in deserted parts of town and hired bar bouncers and off-duty police officers to keep order. Most of the kids who came to the raves couldn't care less who ran them. The ones thoughtful enough to have an opinion enjoyed the higher-quality sound systems and the freedom from trespassing charges. Ritter often wondered if he were the only one who noticed the hard-eyed men in adolescents' clothes who courted girls with flattery and drugs. Occasionally monsters like himself, more often the men were monsters of the human kind. The girls were always young and pretty. They often left with the men. They rarely returned.

The cacophony stilled, replaced by the roar of shouted conversations. A shriek of feedback silenced them. The emcee was about to announce the next band. Ritter paused just outside the entryway to listen for its name when a girl, unsteady even on the arm of her escort, staggered into him. She was no more than sixteen, tall and fashionably thin. She had dyed her short hair blue. It matched her sheer dress and her knee-high boots. Her blue eyes wobbled as they tried to meet his gaze. "Sorry."

Ritter recognized the man beside her. At first glance, he appeared to be one of the twenty-somethings who hadn't outgrown their childhood. His bleached, spiked hair and pencil-thin goatee could have belonged to any of the boys dancing on the floor. But he wasn't an overgrown child. He was Phillip Sloan, the man who'd had "business to discuss" with Faith, back in May. In the hospital, Ritter had dismissed Sloan as an arrogant nuisance. Outside the rave, the hard lines bracketing Sloan's mouth and his predatory eyes announced he was something more offensive. Sloan tightened his grip on the blue girl and propelled her forward. Ritter's lips twisted. How convenient to come upon his supper so soon.

He stepped after them, but before he spoke, a high voice sliced through the emcee's intro. "Megan!"

The girl stumbled. Sloan swore, but slowed to help her regain her feet. It only took a moment, but in that moment a small tornado blew past Ritter and grabbed Sloan's arm. "Let her go."

The tornado was another girl, shorter and probably younger than her friend. She wore her hair loose, in a mahogany cascade that reached the middle of her back. Her short black dress fit badly: too tight in the bust, too long in the thigh. Ritter suspected the dress belonged to the blue girl, Megan. The tornado was built for the sleek lines and plunging décolletage of an earlier generation. Large eyes, mostly brown with flecks of green, narrowed. "What have you done to her?"

The blue eyes quivered, then locked on the brown. "Lori?"

Sloan smiled, and Ritter could taste the evil in it. Here was one who would prefer two and didn't care if they were willing. "Megan felt a little dizzy and I thought a walk outside would do her good." Sloan's voice was smooth with false concern. "I'm sure she'd feel better if you came with us." He stepped toward the cars, apparently certain the small tornado would come along.

She planted her feet and tightened her grip. "Megan never gets dizzy. Did you slip something in her pop?"

"Trouble?" The guard abandoned his post by the door and swaggered up to the trio.

"Yes," the tornado said, turning to him.

Sloan's grin widened. "No."

Ritter's hackles rose. Some of the guards were off-duty police officers. While they turned a blind eye to the drug use, most would balk at the obvious abuse of young girls. Unfortunately, the approaching guard was no policeman. The tall black man reeked of prison and had the weight-lifter muscles and finger tattoos to prove it. His thick arms barely folded across his chest. "Need any help, Mr. Sloan?"

Sloan glanced around the parking lot. Except for Ritter, the lot was deserted. He stared at Ritter without recognition, then nodded toward the rave. "Go on in. The cover's on me." Apparently convinced he had dealt with the only witness, he turned to the guard. "Help me get these two in the van."

Lori opened her mouth, but the guard slapped his hand over her face before any sound escaped. He wrapped his other arm around her, crushing her arms against her sides, and heaved her off the ground. Ignoring her flailing legs, he hauled her toward a gray conversion van.

"Wha's he doing?" Megan took a shaky step after them. "Tell him to put Lori down."

"Shut up." All pretense abandoned, Sloan hustled Megan after the guard.

The new band took the stage with a blast of sound, enough noise to dilute Ritter's voice. He took a concentrating breath and poured his power into a single word. "Stop."

The power rippled across the parking lot and froze all four. Another breath, more concentration, tighter focus. "Put her down, gently, and release her."

The guard lowered Lori to her feet. His hands relaxed their grip, his arms lowered. Sloan pulled his hand from Megan's elbow, and she started to topple.

"Stay on your feet," Ritter ordered. She tipped back and straightened.

The music continued to throb; the parking lot remained empty. Ritter stepped up to the guard. "Return to your post." When the guard remained still, Ritter sighed and rephrased the command. "Go back inside. It's a slow night. No one's come in or out for the last half hour."

The guard turned and lumbered back to the rave's entrance. Ritter turned to Sloan. "You have lost your appetite for unwilling playmates. Go home, sleep, and dream of me." He bared his teeth. "If I catch you drugging another child, I will rip out your throat and bathe in your blood."

Fear rose from Sloan in tempting waves, but Ritter let him stumble to his van and climb in. Unlike Cole, Ritter didn't enjoy killing his prey, and he was too angry to trust his control.

He watched the van drive away before turning to the girls. Both faces were tilted toward him. Megan's was level, Lori's tipped upward, as if offering her throat. Ritter stepped forward and stroked the tempting vein. Her blood coursed just beneath his fingertips. All he had to do was lower his lips and taste it. His bloodlust leapt, but he ruthlessly thrust it down. The girl before him had risked rape and worse to save her friend. For her sake, he couldn't sample either of them.

Ritter bracketed her face in his palms and gently kissed her forehead. "You saved your friend tonight. Take her home and be proud."

His gaze dropped to her ill-fitting dress. Clearly, she saw her friend's beauty and wanted to emulate it. "And remember that one tonight found you beautiful, as well as brave."

Still lost in the trance, she smiled. Then her eyes focused and her smile vanished. Throwing an arm around Megan's shoulder, she turned a formidable glare on Ritter. "Who are you?"

"No one." Ritter used just enough power to make her believe it.

Her glare softened and slid away from him. Her gaze fell on her friend's bleary expression, and her brow wrinkled. "I told you to watch your drink. Come on, I better get you home."

Ritter stepped forward to help but pulled himself back before the girls noticed him again. The little tornado neither needed nor wanted his interference. Still, he hadn't saved the girls to abandon them to other predators. He lingered in the parking lot and watched Lori half carry her friend to an elderly compact. She eased Megan into the back seat before sliding behind the wheel. The little car sputtered to life and lurched from the parking lot. Ritter waited until he could no longer hear the engine over the music, then turned toward the rave.

Faith's voice stopped him before he had taken a step. "I thought you preferred older women."

She was standing at the corner of the building. The security light cut across her face and made her eyes flash gold. The sight triggered an old memory, but before Ritter could track it down, she strode up to him, her purse swinging angrily. "Those girls couldn't have been more than fifteen."

She must have driven in the back way and parked on the other side of the lot. Instead of the irritation Ritter expected, a strange lightness filled him. Ignoring Faith's frown, he took her arm. "I do prefer older women."

Her scowl deepened, but she didn't pull away. "So you hit on a couple of high school kids because two fifteens equal a thirty?" She sounded indignant and just a little hurt.

Ritter laughed. He couldn't help it. He didn't know why, but her anger delighted him. "I wasn't hitting on them. I was sending them home."

"Right. And the Easter Bunny lays eggs." She was lovely out-of-temper. Her cheeks flushed and her eyes glittered. Her pulse pounded against her collar bones, and Ritter's hunger surged. He had to hunt, and soon, or the bloodlust would take control.

Instantly sobering, he dropped her arm. He couldn't hunt, not with Faith there. "You should go home, as well."

Her eyes widened, almost as if she could read his mind. "I don't care how many children you seduce. I'm here to dance."

"Faith, I—"

She spun toward the entrance and strode inside. "What's the cover?"

The guard started. Apparently the effects of Ritter's voice had lingered, as they often did in the weak-minded. Rubbing his bald head, the guard glared at Faith. "Twenty bucks."

Faith ripped open her purse and pulled out a twenty-dollar bill. She threw it on the table and stormed inside.

"Wait." Ritter ran after her, only to be stopped by the newly alert guard. Fumbling with his wallet, Ritter tried to keep his eye on Faith, but she disappeared into the crowd. He quickly paid the entrance fee and stepped into chaos. Pulsing lights, bone-pounding noise, writhing bodies. The cavernous room was packed.

The blaring song ended and another began. A plaintive soprano mouthed the microphone, accompanied only by the keyboard and the bass guitar. The song was sweet and sad, something about lost love and second chances.

Empty-eyed partygoers shuffled and bumped against one another in time to the amplified music. A thin redhead brushed tantalizingly against Ritter. "Want to dance?"

Her blood sang sweetly from her veins, but he ignored her. A line of dread trickled down the back of his neck. In addition to sweat and expensive perfume, the faint scent of dried blood rode the air. Another vampire stalked the room. Ritter scanned the crowd, hoping against hope that he was wrong, but he soon spotted a tall silhouette next to the band. Cole was back.

Chapter Eleven

Faith plowed through the crowd. Ritter had told her he was going to the rave to pick up girls, but she hadn't believed him until she saw him lower his obscenely kissable mouth to that child's face. His back had been toward her, but she knew a frenching session when she saw one. And that other girl—what was she doing? Waiting her turn? When Faith was that age, girls had more pride.

The techno beat fueled her anger, but as the crowd grew thicker, Faith's dormant party instincts took over. Her headlong drive turned into a weaving pattern. She sidled past entwined couples and dodged elbows jabbing in time to the music.

The song crashed to an end. The solitary dancers stopped, but the couples kept grinding against each other. Looking into their young faces, Faith suddenly felt tired. That's what was what really bothering her; Ritter belonged to this scene and she didn't. She spotted the bar and turned toward it. Right now, she needed a drink.

Only she couldn't get one. Frowning at her request for a glass of chardonnay, the bartender informed her this was a "sweet" rave: no wine, beer, or booze. He bristled when she suggested there might be a few bottles or a keg hidden behind the bar. Faith fought the urge to slap the sanctimonious expression off his face. What right had he to act so superior? Half the dancers on the floor were stoned out of their minds. The partygoers weren't any more sober than they'd been when Faith was in college, they just got their kicks from pills and powders instead of alcohol. Disgusted, Faith threw a five on the bar and ordered bottled water and a glass of ice.

She twisted the bottle open and poured. The ice crackled and the water fizzed. Faith sighed. She preferred still water; carbonation stung her nose. Her throat and mouth were dry, though, so she took a tentative sip.

A deep voice slipped under the band's new song. "Be careful what you drink. Some of the kids get off on spiking the soda."

Faith choked, and the acidic bubbles raced into her nose. She sneezed and turned. John O'Connor, the security officer who'd brought her doughnuts, stood behind her. He'd traded his uniform for jeans, a light-colored polo shirt, and a bright orange vest. "What are you doing here?" she asked.

He turned. On the back of the vest the word *security* was spelled out in black reflective letters. He grinned over his shoulder. "Earning a little extra money. How about you—out on the town with your boy toy?"

"I'm alone." The words sounded almost forlorn. Faith frowned and set her glass on the bar. "I mean, I came alone. To listen to the music and dance."

O'Connor leaned his elbows against the bar. His head nodded in time to the music. "Tonight's band is better than most. My break's coming up. Want to take a spin around the dance floor with an old cop?"

"Old? You're what, thirty-five?"

"Thirty-six next month."

Faith couldn't help laughing. "One foot in the grave."

"And the other on its way." He straightened and slipped off his vest. Folding it, he laid it next to Faith's drink and held out his hand. "Shall we?"

She took it and smiled. "I'd love to."

Faith expected him to lead her toward the dancers, but he drew her close and put his other arm around her waist. He leaned down until his breath tickled her ear. "Ever waltz?"

"Not since junior high."

"Just follow my lead." He stepped forward, and Faith stumbled back. Her heel came down on something soft.

"Shit! Watch where you're going, bitch."

Faith glanced over her shoulder. A young man with spiked hair and the ghost of a beard was standing on one foot behind her, scowling. She started to apologize, but O'Connor swung her around until he was shoulder to shoulder with the boy she'd stepped on. "That's no way to talk to a lady."

The boy puffed up his chest and shoulders as if getting ready for a fight, then his gaze lifted to O'Connor's face. He deflated like a spent balloon. "Sorry."

O'Connor nodded once and swept Faith toward the dance floor. "You shouldn't have been so hard on the boy," she said, trying to recapture the box-step rhythm. "After all, I did step on him."

"That's no excuse for foul language. Get ready to spin." He lifted his arm, and she twirled, laughing, beneath it.

Just when she thought she'd lose her balance, he pulled her close and swung her back into step.

She leaned her head against his shoulder. "I haven't had this much fun since high school."

O'Connor chuckled. "Wait until you try my tango."

The song ended too soon. The band lay down the instruments,

preparing for a break, and Faith started to pull away. O'Connor tightened his grip. "One more song."

"Officer O'Connor—" Faith began.

"It's Detective, but call me John."

"John. You're a wonderful dancer, but I have to get going. I've got a long drive, and it's already past my bedtime."

With flattering reluctance, he let go of her hand and dropped his arm from her side. "Is this where you tell me you just want to be friends?"

She laughed. "No, this is where I give you my home number and ask you to call me tomorrow."

Grinning, he reclaimed her hand and led her back to the bar. Faith's drink, ice half-melted, still sat beside the orange security vest. John leaned over the railing. "Hey, Steve, got a pen?"

The bartender gave Faith the once-over, smirked, and slid a well-nibbled pencil across the bar toward them. John caught it and grabbed a book of matches from a holder near the cash register. Faith told him the phone number for her borrowed apartment, and he wrote it down with bold strokes on the inside flap.

"Faith!" Ritter's voice echoed through her head, as if he were yelling behind her ear.

She jerked around, but he wasn't there. John looked up. "What's wrong?"

"Nothing, it's just—" Then she spotted Ritter, pushing through the crowd toward her. "Ritter."

He shouldered past the people clustered around the bar and grabbed Faith's arm. "You must leave. Now."

John turned and stepped toward them. "Let her go."

Faith yanked her arm free and rubbed the reddened skin. Ritter's grip had hurt. "I don't have to do anything. John and I are going to dance until dawn."

John's eyebrows rose, but he nodded. "Get lost, kid. The lady's not inter—."

"Silence."

John's face froze, lips curved around the truncated word.

Faith glared at Ritter. "How do you do that?"

"With difficulty. Now come. It's not safe for you to stay."

"What are you talking about? I'm with a police officer, for Christ's sake." Reaching behind her, Faith grabbed her glass and gulped her drink. The bubbles had stilled, but the lingering acidity puckered her tongue. "I'm perfectly safe."

"Not from Cole."

A chill clutched Faith's stomach. "Your crazy friend? I thought he was in Oregon."

"He was. But I spotted him near the band when I came in. I have searched the crowd for you ever since."

Faith shook her head. "He wouldn't try anything here. It's too crowded."

"You don't know him. Your only hope is to leave, now, before he sees you."

"Bullshit!" The word came out louder than she expected, propelled by anger and reluctant fear. The music hadn't started yet, and several partygoers turned and stared. Faith shrugged an apology and lowered her voice. "He's probably not even here. You just get off on telling me what to do."

"That's ridiculous." Ritter's voice was rising too, and more people turned to watch them. "You never do what I tell you to."

"Exactly. Take the hint and go away."

Ritter clenched his fists. "I should leave you to your stubbornness."

"Finally, something we agree on." Faith turned to John. He was still staring, empty-eyed, over the crowd. "And let John go. Bring him back or whatever you call it. Make him normal again."

"With pleasure. O'Connor." The police officer slowly turned his head until his blank gaze met Ritter's. "Take Faith and—*Himmel!*"

Faith spun around. Ritter was staring past John's shoulder with a look of horror on his face. At first, she couldn't figure out why; then she saw the tall dark figure pushing through the throng toward them. He looked like a refugee from a costume party in his disco suit and ransom of gold chains. A white hat with a floppy brim hid his face, but Faith didn't doubt for a moment that he was Ritter's dangerous friend or that he'd seen her and was coming after her.

The whine of feedback filled the room, and the band started up again. "No." Ritter's voice was thick with frustration. "Without the music there was a chance, but now . . . I am too weak and there are too many distractions."

He stepped sideways until he was toe to toe with John. His face grew stony. "O'Connor. Arrest that man." He pointed to the rapidly approaching Cole.

Faith grabbed Ritter's arm. "What are you doing?"

He continued as if she hadn't spoken. "His name is Cole Morgan. He's wanted for murder in Virginia. Handcuff him and take him to your car. No matter what he says, do not release him until you reach the police station."

"I don't understand. If he's wanted for murder, John shouldn't release him at all."

The blank look on John's face changed to one of grim determination. "Sorry, Faith." His voice was barely audible above the blaring song. "I'll call you tomorrow." He turned and strode into the crowd.

Ritter took her hand. "Come. We must leave while Cole is occupied." His gaze dropped to the bar and the open matchbook. He scooped it up.

"Put that back. It's John's."

"That's your phone number, isn't it?"

"Yes, but—"

"Cole could use it to find you."

Ritter slipped it in his pocket and tugged on her hand, but she hung back, looking over her shoulder to see the confrontation Ritter had engineered. "What about John?"

"O'Connor will be all right. Cole respects little, but he has a fondness for police officers. He won't hurt your friend. Now come." He pulled again, hard, and Faith had the choice of falling or stumbling after him.

The crowd had surged to the middle of the dance floor, leaving the fringes of the room relatively clear. Faith turned to follow the less crowded path, but Ritter hauled her straight toward the door. "Move." Without looking up, the dancing couples parted for him. It was as if he were Charlton Heston, and they, the Red Sea.

Faith tried to keep up with him, but her feet suddenly seemed heavy, and the room, hot and airless. She was panting and dizzy by the time they passed the guard.

"You parked in the back lot?" Ritter pulled her around the corner of the building without waiting for an answer. Though Faith had to sprint to keep up with him, he wasn't even breathing hard. He ran past the rows of parked cars and didn't slow until he stopped in front of Faith's borrowed Lexus. Through her anaerobic blur, Faith was amazed he recognized it.

Ritter let go of her hand. "Drive home as quickly as you can. I'll go back and make sure your *Polizist* is all right." He turned back toward the warehouse.

"Wait." Faith swayed and caught herself on the hood of the car. The Lexus dissolved into a swirl of dots. She looked up, but couldn't find Ritter in the whirlpool of color around her. "I don't think I can drive."

❧ ❧

Ritter stopped in mid-turn. "What?"

She answered in a torrent of words. "The car—it's spinning. So's the lot. I thought I was just out of breath, but—" She closed her eyes and sucked in a long pull of air. When she spoke again, it was with the careful enunciation of a drunk. "I think someone spiked my water."

Her eyes opened. The pupils were pinpricks in a wall of gold-laced gray. "It tasted funny—the water. John warned me, but I was so mad at you, I didn't think. Now everything's swirly, and I have to leave, and I can't even drive." Her voice caught on what sounded like a sob.

Ritter put his hand on her shoulder. "Don't worry. I'll drive you home. Tell me where you live."

Her whole body twisted with her shaking head. "I can't."

The sound of two men arguing drifted under the pounding music. Ritter thrust out his hand. "We have to leave. Now. Give me your keys. We'll worry about where to go later."

Faith fumbled to open her purse. Ritter grabbed it from her and found her keys tucked in the change compartment. He opened the passenger door, threw the purse on the floor, and pushed her into the seat. The voices were getting louder. He didn't have time for courtesy.

He slammed the door and ran for the driver's side. Cole and the *Polizist* appeared at the corner of the building. Cole's arms were behind his back, thanks probably to O'Connor's handcuffs. He had lost his hat, and his dark gaze glowered across the parking lot. His voice rumbled in Ritter's ear. "You bastard."

Ritter dove into the car, turned the ignition, and threw the automatic transmission into reverse. The car squealed backwards. It was too much to hope that Cole wouldn't notice the make and color of the car, but perhaps if Ritter got it out of the lot fast enough, he wouldn't get the license number. He swung the car around and took a hard left to the street. His shoulder hit the door, and Faith sprawled into his lap.

Holding the wheel with one hand, he pushed her back into her seat. "Put on your seat belt."

She giggled. "I thought you didn't like seat belts." Her words were beginning to slur. Her head tipped back against the seat. "'S a beautiful night. So many stars."

"In the car?"

Her eyes drifted shut. "That's what's wrong with you. No 'magination." She sighed. "An' you're too young an' too pretty. An' a crazy drug addict. Why do I always fall for losers?"

Headlights raced toward them, and Ritter swerved into the right-hand lane. "What?"

"Brian slep' with everything in skirts, Toby lived with his mother, an' Edward had a garlic fetish. Why can' I fall for a decent guy, just once? Mom did. Bubbie did."

Faith thinking him a drug addict bothered Ritter more than he wanted to admit, but he found the thought that she might care for him terrifying. "You don't know what you are saying."

She kept talking as if she hadn't heard. "Such a romantic story. They met in Germany. My grandfather Meyer, my *zeyde*, was an American soldier. He liberated her, and they fell in love."

"Your grandmother was German?"

"No, silly, not German; French. A French Jew. She was a prisoner at Dachau, but she escaped. A German couple took her in. She kept their pictures on the mantle. Their frowns scared me when I was little, but Bubbie always said they were good people." Faith turned and looked at Ritter. "I think you're good people, too, even if you *are* a drug addict. You're nothing like Bubbie's monsters."

A cold weight settled in Ritter's chest. "Monsters?"

"The guards at the camp, I think. Bubbie never mentioned them when I was little, only after she got old and senile. Some days, she'd think she was still in the camp. She'd call me a monster and cry and beg me not to hurt her."

The oncoming headlights lit the side of her face and caught in her eyes. Her irises glittered a hard, bright gold. Ritter's hands jerked, raking the car's wheels against the curb. Faith gazed at him through Fritz Heine's eyes.

Chapter Twelve

Dachau, Bavaria
October 31, 1944

"Corporal Breitmann, can you hear me?"

The syllables swirled past Ritter's ears, nonsense except for the name. Corporal Breitmann. His name was Breitmann, Ritter Breitmann. He was a soldier.

"His eyelids fluttered. I thought he was waking up." A different voice, quiet, fearful. The fear lapped around Ritter. It made his stomach rattle and his throat burn. "See?" the timid voice continued. "He stirs."

"Breitmann." A rough hand shook his shoulder. Sparks of pain danced across Ritter's skin. The voice grew louder, until his head throbbed with it. "Can you hear? Can you speak? Answer."

"Water." The word rasped from Ritter's raw throat. He tried to open his eyes, but couldn't. It felt like all the sand in North Africa pressed against his eyelids. Was he still in Africa? He'd seen men rescued from the desert, parched and delirious. Is that what had happened to him? He couldn't remember. Ritter tried to sit up, but something tightened on his chest, holding him down.

"Drink." A gentler hand lifted Ritter's head. A tube brushed his lips, and he sucked greedily. A thick, warm liquid filled his mouth. It had a metallic taste he almost recognized. His stomach clenched around the first swallow, then relaxed into a warm glow. The warmth spread through his arms and legs, soothed his throat, and stilled the pounding in his head. Too soon, the liquid was gone. The tube pulled away. The hand lowered his head.

Ritter struggled vainly to sit up. "More."

"Later." The quiet voice. Calmer, but still fearful. "Your stomach will rebel if you take too much, too soon."

A cool, moist cloth dabbed his eyelids.

"Enough." The cloth lifted. A moment later, hot breath blew against Ritter's ear. "Open your eyes."

It was the first voice. Deep, loud, and commanding. The words hammered Ritter's ears, and a flash of anger raced through his chest. His lips pulled back in an automatic snarl, and the gentle voice gasped.

"You still thirst." The voice yet held the authority of command, but the words trembled. He, too, feared. "Open your eyes, and you'll drink."

Ritter's eyelids were so heavy. He longed to leave them closed, to dive back into the comfort of sleep, but his stomach ached for more life-giving drink. He forced his lids apart. A thin line of brightness seared them shut again. "Too bright."

Silence, then footsteps, followed by comforting darkness. The commanding voice: "Open your eyes."

His lids lifted more easily this time. Blurry shapes shifted and sharpened into two eyes, a straight nose, thin lips—a face, topped by short brown hair. Though the room was dark, the details were clear, down to the pale blue color of the eyes. "What is your name?" the face asked in the commanding voice.

"Breitmann. Ritter Breitmann."

The man straightened and jotted something on a clipboard. The pencil made scratching noises against the paper. Though his expression stayed neutral, the man's heart raced in a panicky beat. Ritter could hear it, and when a scrawny, dark-haired man stepped beside him, Ritter heard the rhythm of his heart as well. "What happened to me?"

The commander looked up from his notes. He wore a white lab coat, and Ritter suddenly realized he must be some sort of doctor. "Have I been ill?" Ritter asked.

"How much do you remember?"

Chaotic images swirled through Ritter's mind. Desert, tanks, a hospital. "I remember being wounded and sent to the hospital in Munich."

The pencil scratched. "Anything else?"

"Something about a secret assignment, a dangerous one. And a miracle weapon." He struggled to sit up. "Is that what happened? I remember coming to Dachau. Was I injured working on the new weapon?"

More scratches, then the clipboard lowered. "In a way. Do you recognize me at all?"

"No."

"My name is Übel, Doctor Karl Übel. I worked with you and your comrades for two weeks before starting the experiment."

"Experiment?"

"Your secret assignment." Übel's lips pulled into a cool smile. "You weren't working on the new weapon. You were becoming it."

"I don't understand."

"A country can only do so much with equipment—tanks, planes, and bombs. In the end, a war is won by the soldiers fighting it." Übel set the clipboard on the bed beside Ritter and leaned over him. His voice thrummed with missionary zeal. "I discovered a way to make superior soldiers, soldiers who are stronger, faster, harder to wound, quicker to heal. Soldiers who can march all night without rest, and whose very appearance strikes terror into their enemies."

"And I am one of those soldiers?"

"Yes."

"But I'm so weak, I can't even sit up."

Übel picked up his notes. "An unexpected complication. Wiggle your toes."

By the time Übel had finished his examination, Ritter was sweat-soaked and exhausted. The doctor tucked the clipboard under his arm and turned to the dark-haired man. "Release and feed him."

Übel spun around with parade-ground precision and marched from the bedside. A door closed, and a lock clicked.

Ritter lay limp on the bed. It felt as if someone had parked a tank on his chest. His muscles ached, his throat burned, and his empty stomach howled for more of the wonderful drink. He wrenched his head around so he could see the remaining man's face—pasty pale with hollow cheeks and huge, dark brown eyes—and managed to force one question past his parched lips. "Is it later, yet?"

The eyes stared a moment, then the bloodless lips twitched into a smile. "Yes." He disappeared from Ritter's sight and returned a moment later with a large ceramic stein. He inserted a glass straw and held it to Ritter's lips. "Drink."

Ritter's mind grew clearer with each sip. After he slurped up the last drop, he lay back and grinned at his benefactor. "Thank you."

Instead of smiling back, the man stiffened. He was wearing a striped suit of thin cotton cloth. It was cool in the basement, too cool for such light clothing, but dots of sweat appeared on his forehead and dripped past his eyes and down his cheeks. A tantalizing savor filled the room. Fear, Ritter realized. He could taste the man's fear.

The doctor had exuded fear as well. Suddenly, he remembered the doctor's parting words. "What did Herr Doktor Übel mean when he told you to release me?"

The man's mouth opened and closed without making a sound.

"I'm tied to the bed, aren't I?" Ritter tried again to sit up, and it seemed to him that he could feel a wide swath of cloth pressing his torso into the mattress. "Because the doctor fears me?"

The man's head bobbed up and down. His voice came out as a hoarse whisper. "Yes."

"I'm as weak as a newborn chick. What is there to fear?"

There was no answer. In the growing silence, Ritter's confusion hardened into anger. Something had been done to him, something terrible, and he had to find out what it was. His gaze locked on the terrified man. "You fear me. Why?"

The man started wringing his hands. "Please, I'm just a prisoner. Don't…"

"Stop!" Something—a force—poured from Ritter's lips, and the man's hands stilled. Though fear still darkened his eyes, all expression drained from his face, leaving it as empty as a desert. He stood as if waiting for an order, so Ritter gave him one. "Untie me."

The fear grew stronger, but the man stepped forward and leaned down. Ritter felt a tug, then the band of cloth loosened. He sat up and rubbed his chest. "Again, thank you."

The man straightened. Though his expression hadn't changed, Ritter sensed less fear. "You know what happened to me, don't you?"

"Yes."

"You can tell me. I promise not to hurt you, whatever it was."

The man stood without moving, like a wind-up toy waiting for a key.

Ritter lost all patience. He swung his feet over the side of the bed and stood. The room tipped, but he ignored the vertigo and grabbed the man's shoulders. "Tell me what you saw!"

Eyes as black as hell looked back at Ritter. There was no anger in the gaze, no hope, only resignation. "A hundred soldiers at attention by their beds. The doctor with his blood red syringes. Soldier after soldier falling to ground, bleeding. Blood, blood everywhere. Prisoners carrying out the drained bodies."

"They died? The soldiers? All of them?"

"All but four. Four stopped bleeding, slept, and changed."

Dread rippled through Ritter's chest. "And I'm one of the surviving four. I used to be a soldier. If I changed, what am I now?"

"*Nosferatu.* A vampire."

Chapter Thirteen

Waukegan, Illinois
August 23, 2014, early morning

Ritter swerved to avoid another pothole. Faith's head rolled with the turn, and a teardrop glided down her cheek. "I don't look like a monster, do I?"

"No." The word squeezed past lips stiff with horror. *Gott im Himmel*, the metallic glint in her eyes had to be a trick of the light—a coincidence, nothing more. The past was dead. Faith's safety was the issue; he must concentrate on that. "Tell me your new address."

"I can't. It's a secret."

"I need it to take you home."

Her lips curled into a pout. "I promised Miles not to tell anyone but the police where the lab is." Her expression brightened. "You can ask John."

Lingering shock and growing frustration roughened Ritter's voice. "Your policeman is busy with Cole. Once Cole escapes—and believe me, he will—Cole will come after you. My apartment is the first place he will look for you. Your old apartment is the second. I need a third option."

Faith turned her face to the window. "I promised," she said with the stubborn insistence of the very young or the very drunk.

"*Himmel*." The traffic light ahead turned red, and Ritter eased off the gas. He recognized the intersection, Green Bay Road and Washington Avenue. Inspiration struck. He flicked the turn signal and pulled into the right-hand lane. The answer to his problem was only half a block to the north.

Faith didn't say anything until the car bounced over a speed bump in the parking lot. "Where are we?"

"At a motel." Ritter pulled into a space by the lit office. Thank goodness for the modern penchant for twenty-four-hour service. Turning off the ignition, he turned to Faith. "Stay in the car. I will get your room." He set the parking brake and climbed out of the car.

"Wait a minute. I didn't say I—"

Ritter closed the door on Faith's protest and loped to the office.

The room contained a high plastic counter, painted to look like wood, and a couple of metal chairs. There was no attendant, but muffled snores drifted under a door in the wall behind the counter. A sign on the door read *Private*. Ritter scanned the counter top and found an old-fashioned concierge bell half-hidden behind a display of maps and brochures. He slapped the bell, and the snores ended in a sleepy curse. The private door opened. A bleary-eyed youth stumbled into the room. He insisted that Ritter fill out a registration card, show identification, and pay for the night's lodging, before he handed over a plastic rectangle with a black magnetic strip on the back, the room's electronic key. "Number 113. It's around the back."

"Excellent." Ritter took the key and hurried outside.

Faith had not obeyed his instructions to stay in the car. She teetered in the parking lot, clinging to the car's open door for support. "My legs won't work right."

The plaintive tone in her voice chased away Ritter's irritation. "It's the drug. You will feel better in the morning." He helped her back into her seat and drove around the building to her room. The space in front of the door was empty. He pulled into it and turned off the engine. "I will open the door. Remain here."

Ritter left the car and ran to the room. He slipped the key into a slot in the door and, at the green light, lifted the handle. Hot, stale air wafted across his face as he stepped into a small room dominated by a large bed. Faded wallpaper, worn carpet, cheap but clean-looking bedding. Hardly elegant, but acceptable. He flicked the light switch and returned to the car.

For once, she had followed orders. Her eyes were closed, and her head lolled on the top of her seat, baring her enticing veins. His lips went dry, and when he called her name, it came out a breathless croak.

She didn't stir. He opened the door and gently shook her shoulder. "It is time for bed. If you can't walk, I will carry you."

Her eyes flew open. They were gray again, unfocused. "It's bedtime?"

"Yes."

She grabbed the dash with one hand and swung her legs out the open door. A moment later she stood beside the car, arms at her sides, swaying slightly.

"Can you walk?" Ritter asked.

"Of course." Like a film run on the wrong speed, she slowly lifted a foot and leaned forward. She leaned too far and toppled into Ritter. He wrapped his arms around her to keep her from falling. She was soft and smelled of flowers and exertion. And pulsing life.

His teeth ached for that beautiful throat. Ritter bit the inside of his lip, and the bitter taste of his own blood bolstered his control. He couldn't abandon Faith in the parking lot, not in her condition, but the bloodlust was growing stronger. He had to get her to the safety of the room and leave before it shattered his control. He reached down and slid one arm behind Faith's knees. Supporting her back with the other, he lifted her to his chest.

Her arms twined around his neck, and she rested her head on his shoulder. Her eyes drifted shut. "You're so sweet."

He didn't feel sweet. Hunger throbbed through his body, not just the bloodlust, but the hunger of a man for a woman. Heat flared where her body touched his and raced down his belly and beneath his too-tight jeans. Doing his best to ignore his arousal, Ritter turned and carried Faith across the threshold and into the room. He hadn't thought to pull back the covers, so he kneeled and lowered her to the bed-spread. It was covered in a riot of roses: cream, pink, and red. The colors echoed the pallor of her forehead, the blush of her cheeks He pulled his arms free, but remained crouched by her side.

Eyes closed, she sprawled across the roses, arms and legs askew, her hair a dark halo around her lovely face. Her chest rose and fell in the gentle rhythm of sleep. Ritter smiled. Sleep was what she needed most. A long night of it would wash the drug from her system. Unable to help himself, he leaned forward and pressed his lips against her milky temple. "Sweet dreams, *Liebchen*." Though the night was warm, he stood and walked to the closet to see if there were a spare blanket to throw over her.

"Ritter?" He turned toward the bed. Eyes half open, Faith pushed up on her elbows. "My purse, where's my purse?"

He remembered the little satin bag that had held her car keys. "It must have fallen to the floor of the car. Lie back; I will get it."

Leaving the blanket on its shelf, he hurried from the room, care-ful to close the door behind him. The bag lay in front of the passenger seat. It had opened and scattered its contents across the floor mat—a packet of tissues, a hairbrush, a lipstick, an ID holder, and a three-pack of prophylactics. Heat crept up Ritter's neck, but he scooped up her possessions and shoved them in the bag. After locking the car, he threw in her car keys and ran back to the room. It only took him a moment to take the card from his pocket and open the door.

Faith had kicked off her shoes and now stood at the foot of the bed, nearly steady in her stockinged feet. He hesitated, and her eyes locked on his. "Close the door."

The purse dangled forgotten from his fingers. He stepped for-ward and let the door swing shut behind him.

"I can't reach the zipper," she said, her voice low and rich with promise. She turned and lifted her hair off her neckline. "Would you?"

The years fled, leaving Ritter as awkward as the youth he re-sembled. The room key slipped from his hand. Faith's purse dropped to the carpet. He walked on trembling legs toward her, and his fingers fumbled with the tiny silver tab. The fabric parted. Without his volition, his hand rose. His forefinger traced the zipper's path down the flawless white skin.

She lowered her arms and shrugged her shoulders. The dress flowed off her body and pooled at her feet.

Faith had broad shoulders, a taut waist, and deliciously rounded buttocks. Except for the stockings that rose high on her thighs, she wasn't wearing any underclothes.

"I must go." The words caught in Ritter's desert-dry throat and died before they escaped his lips.

Faith turned. Her breasts were high and conical, with tight, dusky nipples. Her legs were impossibly long, the thatch of hair between them, as dark and curly as the hair on her head. She glanced at a scrap of lace lying on the floor—her panties—and smiled.

Ritter shook his head to jolt some sense into it. "You don't know what you are doing. It's the drug."

Faith giggled, swayed toward him, and touched her finger to his lips. "You talk to much."

"But—"

She silenced him with her mouth. Her lips pressed against his; her tongue darted past his teeth. For all his years, in the art of kissing, she was more experienced than he. She snaked her arms around his waist, flattened her breasts against his shirt. The pressure made his fangs and groin both ache.

His arms wrapped around her, pulled her closer. Her hands slipped past his jeans, beneath the band of his briefs and spread across his bare skin. Ritter gasped. She pulled her mouth away. "You have great buns."

Before Ritter could imagine what bread had to do with anything, she dropped her head to his shirt. Her tongue flicked across the mesh until it found one of his nipples. Her fingers tightened. Her teeth nipped. Ritter's control snapped.

He pushed her back against the bed and fell after her, pinning her body to the mattress. Faith's hands were everywhere, pulling at his shirt, his pants. She kissed his chest, his neck, the line of his jaw.

The hot scent of blood rose from her in dizzying waves. It ebbed and surged in time with her heartbeat. Ritter lowered his head and licked the blue lines that fanned across her breasts. Her heartbeat quickened. He followed the veins over her collarbone, up the column of her throat. The blood called him, and the licks became kisses, deep, suckling kisses that drew the blood to just beneath the barrier of her skin.

She arched her back and thrust against his straining pants. "Ritter, please…"

She bucked beneath him, and the fragile skin tore on his fangs. Blood poured into his mouth. His stomach embraced the offering and howled for more. He swallowed another mouthful, but an edge of bitterness spoiled the savor. It rose from the back of his tongue, a hard, cold taste that reminded him of his own blood.

"*Himmel!*" Ritter pushed himself off Faith and sprang to his feet. A few more swallows, and he would have lost the ability to stop. Thank God, the drug tainting her blood tasted bitter. If the flavor hadn't shocked him back into control, he could have killed her and not known until it was too late.

"Ritter?" Faith sprawled across the flowered spread, arms out, open and inviting.

Desire surged through him, as demanding in its own way as the hunger had been. He longed to tear off his clothes and join her. He didn't dare.

Ritter turned and fled the room.

Chapter Fourteen

"I'd trade my own grandmother for a bite of Christmas stollen."

Ritter lay on his bed, hands behind his head, and gazed at the light fixture above him. The bulb at the top of the stairs blazed like a small sun, but the other lights were off. Except for Dr. Übel's visits, they remained off. Ritter's eyes had grown so sensitive, he could see the dark bulbs behind the wire cages. Bright light blinded him, and his comrades fared no better. To them, darkness was a balm.

Sighing, he sat up and turned toward the speaker, Fritz Heine. Heine hadn't smiled or said a pleasant word since he awoke to find that his friend, the big dairyman, had died during the transformation.

Ritter felt sorry for Heine. Without his friend, he seemed to have no one, nothing. At least Ritter still had Greta and his mother to go home to. "My mother makes wonderful stollen. The war will be over by next Christmas. Spend it with us, and she'll make two, to celebrate."

Heine was sitting three feet from Ritter, cross-legged, on his bed. Four beds huddled together in the corner of the room farthest from the stairs. The white pillows, sheets, and blankets blended with the white walls and floor. The rest of the room was cavernous and empty without the other soldiers; a great, white void. Ritter had been cooped up in the basement for nearly two months, and he longed for a bit of color—blue, green, yellow, red—any color but white.

Heine's lips spread, to reveal eyeteeth longer and sharper than a man's. "She could bake a dozen—it makes no difference. I can't eat your *Mutti's* stollen, and neither can you. We can barely keep down milk."

Heinrich Schmidt, the corporal who had greeted them when they arrived, looked up from the game of solitaire spread across his blanket. "I'm sick of hearing you complain about what you can't eat. There's more to life than food."

"*Ja*, there's women. And as far as we know, we can't enjoy them either. Übel's experiment may have turned us all into eunuchs."

"Shut up."

"Make me."

Schmidt lunged off the bed, scattering his cards. Heine snarled and jumped to the floor. Ritter rolled off his mattress and stepped between the two men. "Heine, sit down." He turned to Schmidt. "You, too."

"Go to sleep. It's nearly noon." The muffled voice came from beneath a pillow on the fourth bed. Dieter Klug had been drafted from his family's bakery to serve the fatherland. Of all the survivors, he seemed the least affected by their transformation. Though not as strong or fast as the others, the stout baker could stomach milk, eggs, apples, and bread. Bright light didn't bother him, and he'd even managed to stand in the sun several minutes before blistering. He was Dr. Übel's prize experimental rat, and there were days when Ritter hated him.

But not as much as Heine did. "Shut up, Dough Boy, before I roll you into a ball and stuff you down your own throat. And you," he said, turning to Schmidt. "You probably wouldn't know what to do with a woman if the *Führer* himself put one in your bed. All you think about is drinking blood and kissing Übel's pretty pink ass."

Schmidt lunged for Heine. "You little—"

"Stop."

A shimmer of power accompanied Ritter's order. He didn't dare let a brawl start. Übel reeked of fear whenever he entered their basement prison. If the doctor caught Schmidt and Heine fighting, heaven knew what he would do. Bind them all to their beds, at the very least. At worst, he might declare Ritter and his comrades casualties of war. A forced march outside at noon would make it so.

Schmidt froze in midstep.

"Sleep."

Heine fell back on his bed and was snoring before he could swing his legs up. Schmidt stumbled back to his cot and toppled into it. Klug started to snore.

Of all the survivors, only Ritter could control others with his voice. At least he hoped he was the only one. So far, the others had shown no sign of the strange hypnotic ability. He had kept his power a secret. Only he and Übel's prisoner-assistant knew, and Ritter had ordered the man to remain silent.

He walked over to Heine and lifted his legs to the mattress. Then he made sure the others were comfortable—he didn't want them waking with awkward questions.

Certain they'd all sleep until sunset, Ritter threw himself on his own bed. He stared at the ceiling, nervous and excited. Tomorrow was Christmas, and he'd promised himself a present. His voice worked on the prisoner and on the other survivors. Tomorrow, he would try it on Übel and the men who guarded their prison. Tomorrow, Ritter was leaving the basement and going outside.

"Fröhliche Weihnachten!"

Ritter groaned. For an instant, he longed to plant the pillow over his head and escape back into sleep. A visit from Herr Doktor Übel usually meant a painful and humiliating examination. Then the doctor's words sank into his sleep-fuddled mind. *"Fröhliche Weinachten."* Merry Christmas. In a burst of excitement, Ritter threw off his pillow and sat up. Tonight he walked free.

"Where's the Jew?" Heine crossed the floor to halfway between his bed and the stairs. "I'm hungry."

Übel stood alone on the stairs, no assistant, no guard. His fear spiced the air, and Ritter's stomach rumbled. The other survivors sat up and turned toward the doctor. Heine slowly licked his lips, and Übel's face grew as pale as the walls. He turned and called up the stairs, "Hurry!"

Übel's assistant appeared in the doorway with four tall steins on a tray. Fear had abandoned him weeks ago. He carried the tray past Übel and held it out to Heine. His striped trousers flapped around his bony ankles as he walked, and Ritter suddenly realized how thin he'd grown.

An uneasy feeling prickled Ritter's scalp. The assistant had grown weaker as the survivors grew stronger. Surely, Übel wasn't feeding them his assistant's blood. The steins they received three times a night were filled with the blood of cows or pigs, not men. They had to be. Not even Übel would bleed one man to feed another.

The assistant left Heine and carried the tray to Ritter. A greeting flickered in his dark eyes, but he said nothing, just held out the tray. Pushing his worries aside, Ritter chose a stein and drained it in three swallows. The blood cooled his lips and warmed his stomach. Strength and confidence filled his body, and with it, renewed purpose. Tonight, he'd test his voice on the guards and escape his whitewashed prison. For a few hours, he'd walk outside and breathe free air. Maybe he'd even find the assistant and learn answers to questions he dared not ask in the presence of his comrades. Questions like, where did Übel get the blood that kept them alive?

A jolt to his shoulder jerked him back to the basement. "Move over and let us drink." It was Schmidt, with Klug hovering at his elbow.

Ritter stepped back and they lunged for the last two steins. The sound of their greedy gulps filled the room. In the following silence, the assistant gathered the steins and carried them back up the stairs. Heine sauntered to his bed and dropped to the mattress. He glared up at Übel. "So it's Christmas. Why are you bothering us tonight? What do you want?"

The doctor shrugged, a casual movement that fooled no one. Fear still hung thick around him. "To throw you a party."

"A party? Without food or beer, music or women?" The words spat from Heine's lips like machine-gun bullets.

"No food or beer, but I do have women."

Heine stared, mouth open and silent. Ritter's groin clenched. Women? He hadn't seen a woman since the nurses in the hospital.

"For us?" It was Klug. Only he would ask such a stupid question.

"Of course for you. A group of French whores to use as you please. And a battery-powered radio for music"

Heine jumped to his feet. "Who needs music? Just bring the girls."

A tendril of power uncurled with his words. Übel stiffened. "Bring the girls." His voice was flat, emotionless. He turned and marched up the stairs.

Heine gazed after him, a puzzled frown on his face. Ritter bit his lip to keep from cursing. It was only a matter of time before Heine realized what he'd done, what he could do. Ritter had been careful while exploring the range and power of his voice. Heine was reckless. He'd do something stupid, and Übel would discover his experimental rats were even more dangerous than he feared.

Ritter shook his head. All the more reason to test his voice tonight. Now, before the women could tempt him to stay. Not that he was interested in Übel's whores. He had Greta, and he'd promised to stay faithful.

"If Übel asks where I've gone, tell him I'm on the can." Ritter tilted his head toward the curtained corner that served as their privy and waited for his comrades to nod. He increased the power in his voice. "Don't see me leave."

Their faces grew still, and Ritter knew he had them. "Enjoy your party, and don't think of me until I return."

Heine blinked and turned to Schmidt. "Ever been with a French whore? I had one in Berlin once. She had the whitest thighs and the biggest..." Ritter didn't wait to find out what. He jumped from his bed and ran toward the stairs. Heine's increasingly obscene description chased him up the short flight. As he'd hoped, Übel hadn't thought to lock the door. Ritter turned the knob and silently opened it.

Two soldiers lounged against the wall, one on each side of the door. Ritter took a deep breath. This was it, the test to see of his voice could compel a man to act against his duty.

He summoned the power, let it fill his mouth, then spoke. "Don't move."

The soldiers stiffened at the first word, but didn't turn. Ritter stepped through the doorway. He listened, but heard nothing but the soldiers' breathing. The corridor leading from the door was empty. Übel must have left to get the whores.

Ritter turned toward the guards. "You saw no one leave this room."

"No one," they said.

"You can't see me now, and you won't see me when I return. If

Übel asks, you saw no one cross this threshold."

"No one," they repeated.

"Good. Return to duty."

The soldiers relaxed into watchful stances, but they ignored Ritter as he walked away from them to the door at the end of the corridor. It, too, was unlocked. Ritter slipped from the house into the night.

The street was empty. Praying his luck would hold, Ritter raced through town. The wind from his passage whipped at his shirt and pants. Though ice crunched beneath his feet, he felt no cold, only a swift flight of air and a prickle inside his nose.

Ritter ran until the houses thinned to fields, then slowed to a walk. Even so far from town, the holiday scents of pine, orange, nutmeg, and clove sweetened the air. He thought of Christmas in Schwarzdorf and smiled.

A distant church bell tolled twelve times. "Merry Christmas," he whispered. As if in answer, voices drifted over the field, a church choir singing his favorite Christmas carol, "Silent Night."

He stood in the middle of the deserted road and sang along. Calm filled him. The night was beautiful—deep, velvet sky, stars so bright, they cast blue shadows on the snow-dusted stubble. If only Greta were with him, the moment would be perfect.

The song ended, and Ritter continued walking. He followed the road around a turn. The scents of the town faded, and the smell of snow and earth took their place. The breeze shifted, and a new sensation brushed his tongue, faint but plain: the flavor of fear.

Ritter stopped. Not just fear, but despair as well, and horror, desperation, and rage, thousands of combinations, all different, blended together like cheap wine. He must be approaching the nearby work camp. He'd heard his comrades talk of it during the long nights in the basement, this camp outside of Dachau. They said it was huge, built to hold dissidents, prisoners of war, and Jews.

The breeze grew stronger, and the prisoners' fear filled his mouth. His teeth began to tingle, and his stomach began to ache. A shiver ran down Ritter's arms. What had he become, that the suffering of others stirred his appetite?

He still had a few hours before dawn, but freedom had lost its savor. Ritter turned and jogged back to town.

He'd hoped the pine and spice of Christmas would scrub away the tantalizing fear, but its flavor still taunted him as he left the fields and ran past Dachau's neat, half-timbered houses. They all looked similar, but only one had six soldiers in front of it—the one he had to enter before dawn.

Ritter ducked into the shadows. Holding his breath, he strained to make out the soldiers' whispered words.

"How much longer?"

"As long as it takes. Übel's pets get them first; you know that."

"But I'm freezing."

"Then go back to the barracks. No one ordered you here."

"I want to see the women."

The others murmured agreement.

Ritter sagged against the brick wall in relief. The soldiers were waiting for the women, not him. Still, he wasn't sure he could bemuse all six of them. He'd better try the back way.

He was edging along the wall toward the nearest alley when he heard a door open. A familiar voice called, "Return to your barracks."

Übel stood in the doorway. His eyes were black holes in a pasteboard face. Terror radiated from him in dizzying waves.

The soldiers didn't seem to notice. They groaned at the announcement. "What about the women?" asked the complainer.

"Forget the women," the doctor shrieked. "Go."

Shooting each other uneasy looks, the soldiers backed away. Übel lingered in the doorway until they turned down a side street, then disappeared inside the house. The door slammed shut.

Ritter slipped from the shadows. Something had frightened Übel to the point of panic. Cold dread filled Ritter's stomach. His life and the lives of his comrades depended on the doctor's good will. He had to find out what had happened, before Übel decided to terminate both the experiment and their lives.

He hurried to the door. Übel had locked it. Ritter grasped the doorknob and twisted. The knob snapped. The door swung open. He smiled grimly. Not all the consequences of their transformation were unfortunate.

He stepped into the house. Muffled moans rose from the basement, but he ignored them. He had to find Übel. He stretched his hearing. In the second room down the corridor, someone was breathing in short, desperate gasps. Ritter ran to the door and threw it open.

The first thing he noticed was the smell: fresh, hot blood. Übel crouched on the floor next to a pair of striped pajama legs.

Ritter couldn't tear his gaze from the man on the floor. It was the doctor's assistant. He lay in a lake of blood. Fresh rivulets ran from wounds in his arms and throat. His eyes were shut, his only motion, panting breaths. Ritter could almost see his life ebbing away. He wanted to feel sorrow, but instead a surge of hunger gripped his throat. It was an act of will not to throw himself on the unfortunate man and lap at the gathering pool.

Ritter swallowed, forcing down his hunger. "What happened?"

Übel lunged to his feet. He clutched a cross in his right hand, a large wooden cross, like the ones found on church alters. "In the name of God, be gone."

Striding into the room, Ritter snatched the cross from the doctor's grasp. "Answer me." He filled his words with power. "Who injured your assistant?"

Übel's horrified expression smoothed, though fear lingered in his eyes. "The vampires."

"What?" Cold sweat trickled down the back of Ritter's neck. "Explain. Everything."

"I sent the Jew into the basement to get the whores and—"

"Not . . . the Jew." Eyes still shut, the assistant spoke in short, breathless bursts. "Ezra …Baruch. Let me…die…with my own name."

"He screamed." The doctor kept talking as if no one had spoken. "The door opened, and he flew into the corridor as if he'd been thrown. I dragged him in here so the others wouldn't see."

Ritter pushed the doctor aside and knelt beside the dying man. "Ezra Baruch, can you hear me? Can you tell me what happened?"

"Blood everywhere. The floor. The walls." The dark eyes slowly opened. "You…weren't there."

"No." Dread settled over Ritter like a shroud. What had happened to his comrades? Had Heine gone insane and attacked the rest?

"I tried…to stop them. Too…late." Ezra arched in a convulsion and sagged into death.

Ritter stared a long time into the lifeless eyes. Finally, he stood and grabbed Übel's arm. "Come."

He dragged the doctor out of the room and down the corridor. The smell of blood and fear grew stronger as they approached the door to the basement. It stood ajar, unguarded.

Ritter pushed the door wide and squinted against the glare of the stairway light. The moaning had stopped, and the room was silent except for a faint creaking. He couldn't see his comrades, only a blinding wash of red. Red streaked floor. Red splattered walls. Red beds, red sheets, red blankets. Even the air tasted red.

Eyes tearing from the light, he pulled Übel down the stairs. There were lumps on the beds. Ritter released Übel and ran to the nearest one. Klug sprawled across his bed. His chest rose and fell in silent breaths. Beside him lay a naked girl. Black wounds gaped from her breasts and throat. Blood stained her thighs. Ritter reached forward and touched her cheek. Her skin was cold. She couldn't have been more than fifteen.

A grunt spun Ritter around. The lump on Heine's bed jerked and lay still. It was Heine. Ritter ran over, grabbed his shoulder, and hauled him off the bed. Two girls remained. One was dead, with eyes wide and staring. The other's eyes were squeezed shut. Shallow gashes marred her arms, her chest, her thighs. A jagged tear at the base of her throat had flooded the valley between her breasts with blood. The thickening flow oozed down her side and soaked into the stained sheets. The girl lay motionless, as if she wished she were dead, but her heart fluttered behind her ribs. She was alive.

"Breitmann?" Heine sprawled on the floor. His voice was slurred, as if he'd drunk too much schnapps. "Where've you been? You missed a helluva party."

Ignoring him, Ritter leaned over the living girl. "Can you stand?" She didn't move.

Ritter quickly scanned the other beds. His was empty. Schmidt slept beside another corpse. He turned back to the girl and poured power into his voice. "Open your eyes." Her eyes flew open. "Get up."

Moving like a mechanical doll, she crawled off the bed and stood in front of him.

She looked like a half-starved waif, not a painted whore. Ritter stripped off his shirt and wrapped it around her shoulders. What was he going to do—with her, with Übel, and most of all with his comrades? He'd left for a few hours, and in his absence, they'd turned into monsters.

He glanced at Übel. The doctor hadn't moved. From what Ritter could see, he hadn't even blinked. "What went wrong?"

"Sexual situation. Subjects too dangerous, too unstable. Must abort experiment."

"Abort?"

"Abandon the experiment, neutralize the specimens."

"Neutralize." A pretty word for kill. Ritter nodded toward the girl. "And her?"

"She goes back to the camp."

Where she wouldn't last a week. Ritter took a deep breath, then wished he hadn't. Despite his horror, the mixed scents of blood and fear made him burn with thirst.

"No," Ritter whispered, but the blood had no mercy. It taunted him, the blood on the walls, the blood on the bed, the blood between the girl's small breasts. And her fear. Ritter's mouth went dry; his teeth throbbed. It was hard to breathe, hard to think. He ached to lick the gore from her skin, to plunge his teeth into her pulsing throat. He moaned and leaned forward.

A loud, nasal snore filled the room. Like the others, Heine had passed out, drunk on the blood of his victims.

Ritter jerked back. He grabbed the girl's arm and thrust her toward the stairs. "Go! Run and don't stop until dawn!"

Her steps were shaky at first, but soon smoothed into long strides that carried her up the stairs and out of sight. Ritter watched her go, then stalked toward Übel. His teeth itched to rip out the doctor's throat, and this time Ritter welcomed the feeling. "You. You did this."

Fear flared in Übel's eyes, but his voice remained emotionless. "I just brought the girls. I didn't know what would happen. Once the carnage began, I didn't know how to stop it."

But Ritter did. If he hadn't left his comrades alone, he could have used the power of his voice. Klug, Schmidt, and Heine weren't evil. They would never have killed those girls if Übel hadn't injected them with his serum. Übel had stolen their souls. Only Übel could give them back. "Can you reverse the transformation?"

"Perhaps, with time and study."

Time. Ritter nodded. He could give Übel time. If he were careful, he could control the others and keep them from killing, until Übel's study bore fruit.

He stepped away from the doctor. "Go. Have a guard bring sponges, water, and clean bedding, then forget everything that happened here tonight. Everything."

"Everything." Übel turned and trudged up the stairs.

"And *Doktor*," Ritter called after him. "Find a way to turn us back into men."

Chapter Fifteen

Waukegan, Illinois
August 23, 2014, late morning

Faith hurt. Every muscle, bone, and tendon ached. Her eyes scraped against their lids like sandy marbles, and her mouth tasted like dirty socks. Worse yet, if she didn't get to the bathroom soon, she was going to explode. She groaned, sat up, and opened her eyes.

All thoughts of the bathroom vanished. Where was she? The room was dim, but enough light seeped around the closed curtains to make out the cheap plastic lamp beside her and a TV on the dresser. She was in a motel room, and she had no idea how she got there.

A rattle and clank from under the window announced a blast of cold air. The room's air conditioner had kicked on. Faith shivered as the chilled air wrapped around her. She looked down for the covers and stifled a yip. Except for the hose that bit into her thighs, she was naked.

"Shit." Faith jumped out of bed and landed on a pair of lace panties. Her pumps lay in two different corners of the room, and her shift was a blue puddle near the end of the bed. She didn't remember getting undressed, or who, if anyone, had been with her when she did. "Oh, shit."

She closed her eyes and tried to remember the night before—who she'd been with, what they might have done—but all she got was an insistent warning from her bladder. Toilet now, or else.

Faith ran to the bathroom without bothering to turn on the light and left it off while washing her hands and face. The cool water washed the grit from Faith's eyes and returned some order to her brain. Miles had lent her a car, she remembered, and she'd packed for a weekend in the city. She had a toothbrush and a change of clothes in her overnight bag. Faith ran to the door, squinted through the peephole, and felt like cheering. The loaner was parked right outside the door.

She scanned the room for her purse and found it on the floor near her feet. An electronic room key lay beside it. Stooping, she picked up both purse and key.

The car keys were in the purse, jumbled with everything else at the bottom of the bag. Faith fished them out and frowned. She always kept keys in the change compartment, so they'd be easier to find.

The keys jingled in her hand, and an image flashed across her mind. A dizzily reeling parking lot. A man saying something about keys.

A shiver rattled Faith's teeth, and the memory vanished. Or dream—she wasn't sure which. Only one thing was certain; she had to get warm. Closing the purse, she grabbed the bedspread and wrapped it around her shoulders.

A combination heating-and-cooling unit was under the window. The thermostat was on the wall near the head of the bed. Faith ran to it, hoping to find an *off* switch for the air conditioner. She found the switch and a thermometer. Though the room was dark, there was enough light to read numbers. It was eighty degrees. The room wasn't cold; Faith was. She had to put on some clothes.Her silk shift was badly wrinkled after a night on the floor, but she picked it up and slipped it on. When she reached for the zipper, another memory drifted through her mind—cool fingers tracing her backbone. Her chill deepened. This one wasn't a dream. She didn't know who, but someone had helped her out of the dress last night.

She just stood there, zipper tab caught between her thumb and forefinger. Faith had been hoping beyond hope that she'd stumbled into the motel room by herself and fallen asleep before she had a chance to finish undressing. An unlikely scenario, but one she preferred to the alternative, that she'd spent the night having sex with an unknown partner.

Faith forced herself to finish zipping the dress. It was too late to worry about last night. First things first. She had to go outside and get her overnight bag. Praying that no one was watching, she grabbed her purse and room key and hurried out the door.

Daylight blazed across the parking lot, bright enough to hurt her eyes. And hot. Heat rose from the asphalt in waves that lapped against Faith's chilled skin. She paused to soak in the warmth and to let her eyes adjust. The parking lot slowly pulled into focus. Except for the car Miles had lent her, the lot was deserted.

Faith skip-hopped over the burning blacktop to the trunk and danced from foot to foot while she opened it. Her overnight bag was where she'd left it. Feeling grateful to the point of tears, she hauled it out of the trunk, relocked the car, and ran back into the room.

She threw her purse, car keys, and room key on the night stand and opened the bag. "Thank goodness!" Not only had she packed a change of clothes, but she'd included a pair of sneakers and a set of sweats, in case the weather turned chilly. Her makeup and emergency medical kit were underneath them.

Faith slipped off her dress and rolled down her hose. She winced as the elastic peeled off her thighs. She preferred thigh-highs to pantyhose, but they weren't made for sleeping in. Shoving her dirty clothes to the bottom of her bag, she grabbed the shampoo and travel scrub from the makeup kit and hurried into the bathroom. Hopefully, a shower would clear away the sludge in her brain, and she'd remember what had happened the night before. She clicked on the light and, blinking against the glare, climbed into the shower stall and turned the faucet all the way to hot.

The first blast was chilly, but the water quickly warmed. After adjusting the temperature to just below scalding, she turned the low-flow shower head to high and let the jets pound her head, neck, and shoulders. When her face began to sting from the heat, she stepped out of the water and washed her hair. The familiar scent of her shampoo soothed her as much as the warmth.

Hair rinsed and skin scrubbed, she climbed out of the enclosure into a bathroom white with steam. The towels were stacked on a shelf over the toilet. They were scratchy and smelled of bleach. She dried herself, then wrapped a towel around her hair and another, sarong-like, around her body.

Now to do something about the scummy coating on her teeth. Her toothbrush was still in the makeup kit. She walked into the bedroom and hit the light switch. Colors leaped at her, red and pink from the bedspread, green from the wallpaper, orange from the lampshade. A mirror over the dresser reflected it all, including Faith. Her skin looked pale, nearly as white as the towels, except for the blue and purple contusion running the length of her neck.

Her hand flew to the injury. What had she done to herself? She walked closer to the mirror and leaned forward for a better look. There was no pain when she probed the site, just a little tenderness near the jaw line. No swelling, no heat. No symptom except the discoloration. She'd never seen a bruise like it.

Faith straightened with an indrawn hiss. Oh yes, she had, seventeen years ago after an all-night necking session with her high school boyfriend. The mark on her neck wasn't a bruise; it was a hickey.

And suddenly she remembered. Not images; but she remembered weight pressing against her open thighs and kisses burning across her breasts and up her throat. She remembered writhing and clinging. And she remembered begging, "Ritter, please..."

"No!" Her denial shattered the memory, leaving only the ache of remembered desire. It had to be a dream. She hadn't seen Ritter in months. He was a student; it was summer. He was probably home in Germany.

But the voice in the parking lot had been Ritter's. And the fingers down her spine had held his cool assurance. She vaguely remembered flipping through the campus newspaper, looking for the University Film Club schedule. Maybe she'd gone to the movies and run into

Ritter there. Faith stepped away from the mirror until the back of her knees hit the bed. She sat and buried her face in her hands. Why couldn't she remember?

Because she'd been drugged. Faith didn't know how she knew, but the information slammed into her, cold, hard, and certain. Someone had spiked her drink. Considering her amnesia, probably with one of the date-rape drugs, GHB or flunitrazepam.

Had Ritter drugged and raped her? Faith didn't believe it. He might be arrogant and conceited, crazy and a drug addict, but she couldn't imagine him stooping to rape. Truthfully, she didn't even believe he was behind the break-in of her apartment. His friend Cole, maybe, but not Ritter. Ritter seemed to have an old-fashioned sense of honor. Besides, he could have taken advantage of her months ago, when she fell asleep in his apartment, and he hadn't.

No, Ritter hadn't spiked her drink, but Faith was pretty sure he'd driven her to the motel. From the evidence at hand, he'd done more than drop her off with a kiss on the cheek. From her fragmented memories, she'd begged him to do more.

A chill snaked past the shower's lingering warmth. Faith grabbed her purse from the night stand and dumped its contents on the bed. She tossed aside her ID, her hairbrush and lipstick, and reached for the pack of condoms that she always carried, "just in case," but had never used. She fumbled the box open. The packets were all there, untouched.

She wasn't sure whether to be relieved or more worried. She hadn't woken with the stickiness she associated with unprotected sex, but that didn't mean anything. Ritter could have brought his own condoms, or he could have...

Erotic possibilities raced through her mind. Her breathing grew faster, until spots appeared around the edge of her vision. She forced the stale air from her lungs and slowly sucked in fresh. It wouldn't do her any good to panic; she had to think. What did she *know*? She knew that she'd woken up in a motel room, suffering from hypothermia and amnesia. She ached all over, but the only visible injury was a painless bruise on her throat. She knew that someone, at some point, had slipped her an illegal drug. And she knew that she'd spent at least part of last night with Ritter.

If she wanted to know more, she was going to have to call Ritter and ask. She didn't know his phone number, but she remembered his address. A quick call to information should do the trick. There was an old-fashioned landline phone on the night stand. She reached for the receiver, but pulled her hand back before touching it. What was she going to say? "Hi, Ritter. This is Faith. Did we have sex last night?" No way; not over the phone. She had to watch his face while he answered. She had ask him in person.

She took her sweats out of the bag and quickly dressed. The collar wasn't high enough to cover the whole bruise, but a dab of foundation hid the worst of it. She slipped on her sneakers, brushed her hair, and repacked. So much for the easy part. Now she had to summon the courage to face Ritter and demand the truth.

☙ ☙

Faith checked out of the motel around twelve-thirty and spent the next hour looking for Ritter's building. Fallen Way was a tiny street and wasn't on the map she'd bought from the motel attendant. She drove through Waukegan three times before stumbling across it. The neighborhood looked older than she remembered, with cracked sidewalks and barred windows. She drove past rust-spotted cars to the loading zone in front of Ritter's building, parked, and turned off the ignition.

Heat shimmered across the hood of the car and beat against her face. She'd left the car's air-conditioning off, and sweat glued the fleece sweatshirt to her breasts. For a moment, she was tempted to run back to her apartment and find something more suitable to wear. Right; as if different clothes would make talking to Ritter any easier. Disgusted at her cowardice, she threw the car door open and climbed out. The air was blazing hot, but she locked the car and strode up the stairs to Ritter's building.

The air was cooler inside. She wiped the sweat out of her eyes and read the names by the mail boxes. She found *Ritter*, pushed the button next to his name, and waited. Nothing. She pushed the button again, a little longer this time. A distant buzzing assured her the doorbell worked. Maybe he wasn't home.

She was trying a third time when she remembered Ritter worked nights and slept days. She yanked back her finger, but it was too late. A speaker next to the mailboxes crackled. "I told you she is not here. Go away." Though distorted, it was Ritter's voice. He sounded angry.

There was another button by the speaker. She pushed it. "Ritter?"

Crackle. "Faith? What are you doing here?"

Embarrassment flooded her. This was harder than she'd expected. "I'm sorry if I woke you up, but we need to talk. Face to face. Can I come in?"

Silence. Then, "Now is not a good time. I'm in the phone book. Call me tomorrow."

Faith's embarrassment exploded into white-hot anger. "Tomorrow? Now that you got yours, you're not interested any more; is that it?"

"Got mine? What are you talking about?"

"You tell me. I don't remember."

He muttered something in German she couldn't quite catch, then, "This is about last night."

"Of course this is about last night. What happened? How did I end up naked in a motel room?" Faith didn't realize she was shouting until one of the first-floor doors opened. A teenager in shorts and a halter top stormed into the foyer and threw open the inside door.

"Fight with your boyfriend some place else. I just got my baby to sleep."

Faith's cheeks burned hotter than the street outside. "I'm sorry, I—"

At the same moment, Ritter's voice crackled from the intercom. "Go home. I will explain tomorrow."

Embarrassment forgotten, Faith slammed the intercom button. "The hell with tomorrow. I'm not going anyplace until you tell me what happened last night."

The young mother gave Faith a curious look. "That the man in the basement?"

Faith nodded.

"Come in." She held the door open, and Faith walked past her into the lobby. Behind them, Ritter's voice called, "You can't stay. It's not safe."

The young woman reached into her pocket and pulled out a ring of old-fashioned brass keys. "I'll let you into the basement. After that, you're on your own. Keep it down, okay?"

"Okay."

She selected a key and opened the door. "Good luck."

"Thanks." Faith crossed the threshold and shut the door behind her.

The basement light was dim after the afternoon sunshine, and the air grew chillier with each step she took down the stairs. Too soon, Faith was standing in front of Ritter's door.

Though her heart fluttered like a captive sparrow, she raised her fist and pounded on the door. "Ritter."

"How did you get in the building?" Though he had to be on the other side of the scarred oak door, his voice sounded as clear as if he were standing beside her.

"Cut the ventriloquist tricks and let me in."

"No."

"I'm not going to leave until you talk to me."

His sigh whispered against her ear. "What do you want to know?"

"I'm not going to do this through a closed door. Let me in."

"I can't."

"Why? Because you've got a girl in there?" Faith hadn't considered that possibility, but once the words were out, she realized they were probably true. Ritter could have spent part of the night with her and then gone home to his full-time sweetie. Something hot and green twisted in her chest, but Faith kept her voice even. "I don't care who's there. I just want to find out about last night. Have your girlfriend stay in the bedroom if you don't want her to hear."

"There is no girl. I'm worried about Cole."

An image flickered before Faith's eyes. Ritter's dark and scary friend dressed like a seventies disco king. "I saw him last night, didn't I? Is he here now?"

Silence settled over the basement, heavy and still. Faith could almost see Ritter weighing lies, but when he spoke, the reluctance in his voice told her he'd settled on the truth. "No. He came last night and will return. That's why you must not stay. If Cole sees you, he will kill you."

Kill you. The tired words carried almost no emotion. Ritter wasn't threatening her, he was stating a fact.

His cold certainty raised goose bumps on her arms. She was almost tempted to leave. Almost. "I'll take my chances."

"You don't know what you ask. We can talk tomorrow. I will answer any questions you have. For now, just go." Ritter's voice wrapped around her like a cashmere shawl. "Please."

Faith wanted to say yes, she really did. And she might have, if she hadn't recognized the warm tingle of attempted hypnosis. "Nice try, but I'm not going anywhere. If you don't let me in, I'll camp on your doorstep until you're tired of hiding from me."

The warmth shut off. "I am not hiding."

"Then let me in." Frustration burned the back of her throat. She swallowed and tried again. "Ritter, please. Last night is a hole in my mind. It's driving me crazy. Please, *please*, let me in, and tell me what happened."

More silence, then footsteps and a double click. "Come."

Sudden reluctance weighted Faith's arm, but she lifted her hand and grabbed the doorknob. It turned easily and the door opened. She barged into the room before she could lose her nerve. The door swung shut behind her.

She'd forgotten how dark Ritter's apartment was. It was like walking into a blindfold.

"Ask your questions, then leave."

Faith squared her shoulders. If Ritter meant to intimidate her, he'd chosen the wrong way to go about it. She turned toward his voice. "Can I turn on the light?"

"No."

"But I can't see."

"Your problem, not mine."

Faith sucked in a breath and let it out slowly. "You're not making this any easier."

Gears ground and the cuckoo cried twice. Ritter sighed. "A moment, please." Quiet footsteps grew even quieter as they moved away from the door. "Walk forward two steps. You'll find a table with a lamp on it. Click it once, no more."

Faith slid her feet forward until her toe bumped into the table leg.

She fumbled for the lamp and turned the switch.

The lamp flared, but the glow barely covered the table, couch, and chair. Faith still couldn't see Ritter.

"Better?" His voice sounded rough, as if he were in pain.

Faith looked around the room. "Are you all right?"

Ritter stood behind her and to the left, just outside the circle of light. It caught his hair and cheekbones, but left the rest of his face in shadow. "Just ask your questions."

Faith stepped toward him. "Last night in the motel room, did you...I mean did we..."

"We did not make love, if that is what you're wondering."

"Oh. Good." The sinking feeling in her stomach had to be relief. She couldn't possibly be disappointed. "What did happen?"

"We were at a rave. Someone tampered with your bottled water— added a drug to strip away inhibitions. Cole was also at the rave. He saw you and started after you. I...distracted him, and we left. I drove you to the motel when it became clear you were in no condition to drive yourself home." His voice lightened, as if he were smiling. "You refused to tell me your new address."

Faith couldn't help but smile back. "I get stubborn when I'm drunk."

"I paid for the room, carried you inside, and helped you undress. Then I left."

His story didn't jibe with what little she remembered. Her smile slipped away. "That's not all you did." She pulled the collar of her sweatshirt below the line of makeup. "What about this?"

The hiss of air told her he hadn't noticed the hickey. "*Liebchen*, I—"

"I mean, we must have done something, unless I got this before the rave."

"No." His voice was even rougher now. "I lost control for a moment, but stopped before I did anything...irreversible."

Faith didn't remember the rave or the drive to the motel, but his words brought back a wave of a desire that made her legs wobble. With it, came more memories. She remembered spreading her hands across his bare, muscular bottom, remembered biting his chest, pulling him down on the bed. And she remembered Ritter running from the room while she begged him to stay. She'd wanted him more than anything. God help her, she still did. She forced herself to meet his shadowed gaze. "I threw myself at you, didn't I?"

"You were drugged and did not know what you were doing."

But she had known. "I'm sorry if I embarrassed you last night. I won't bother you any longer." She turned toward the door.

"*Liebchen*, wait." He stepped into the light.

Ritter's skin was the flat, cave-fish white of a corpse. Shadows bruised his eyes, and dark hollows underlined his cheeks. Only his eyes held life. They shone with feverish light. Faith hadn't seen anyone look that bad since her residency in infectious diseases. "You're sick."

"No."

"I have a medical kit in my overnight bag. There's a thermometer in there, some ibuprofen and antibiotics. It's in the car. I'll get it and be right back." Faith ran toward the door. Her hand reached for the doorknob.

Without seeming to move, Ritter was beside her. He grabbed her wrist. His fingers weren't hot; they were icy. "I don't need your drugs."

No, he needed his. The revelation rocked her. He was ill all right, but not with infection. Ritter was sick with withdrawal. Another thread wove itself into the tapestry of her memory. She pulled from his grasp. "You weren't looking for a girl last night. You were looking for a fix."

"It's not that simple."

"And here I thought you left the motel out of some sense of decency. Ha! You just wanted to get high more than you wanted me. Don't worry, I won't keep you any longer. Sniff or shoot up or do whatever it is you do. Just leave me out of it." She yanked the door open and stormed out.

"That's right, run!" Ritter's voice chased her up the stairs. "Go back to your secret apartment and your secret laboratory. Go back to your secret life, and leave me to mine."

✲✲

Her footsteps clattered up the wooden steps and vanished with the slamming of a door. The flavor of her humiliation lingered. Ritter sank to the floor and covered his face with his hands. He could have told Faith the truth, how much he wanted her, how hard it had been to leave last night. He could have soothed her hurt and saved her dignity. But he hadn't. Heaven help him, he had sensed Faith's vulnerability and used it to drive her away.

He looked up. She had left him no choice. Her blood had called to him even before she bared her throat to his starving eyes. When he held her wrist and felt her pulse against his fingertips, it had taken all his control not to pull her close and lose himself in her warm, life-giving embrace. If she had remained, he would have finished what he started the night before.

He bit his lip, but his body was empty, and no blood flowed. Even his eyes remained dry, despite the stinging glare of the lamp. Ritter pushed himself to his feet, stumbled to the table, and clicked off the light.

Faith was in terrible danger. Until last night, Cole believed she had left the state. Now he knew she was nearby and would stop at nothing to track her down and kill her. Ritter dropped to the couch. He had to protect her, but how? He couldn't think with hunger howling in his mind. He had to drink. Soon. If only he had followed Cole's example and stolen a pint or two from the blood bank. Now he had no choice but to seek a victim the moment dusk deepened to a tolerable level. He knew of a place where desperate women sold themselves for drug money. He would find one and pay her for a sip of life.

In the meantime, he must sleep. he stretched out on the cool leather and closed his eyes. His breath grew shallow; his pulse slowed. Soon, the only thing that separated him from the corpse he resembled was the hunger gnawing at his dreams.

Chapter Sixteen

Faith drove to Banat's complex with her windows down and the radio blasting loud enough to make her ears ring. She couldn't think with music pounding her brain, and right now she didn't want to think. Unfortunately, the volume also made it hard to navigate. She passed the entrance twice before she recognized it. Except for a discreet sign, there was no hint that on the other side of the manicured woods lay the biggest research facility in western Lake County.

She turned onto the narrow, tree-lined drive and followed it up a rise and down into the hollow that cradled the compound. The radio died in a burst of static. She turned it off and pulled up to the locked gate. She grabbed her purse from the passenger seat, intending to show her ID to the guard manning the military-style guard post. One thing she had to give Banat: he took security very seriously. But the gate swung open while she was rummaging in her bag.

"Good afternoon, Dr. Allister."

Startled, Faith looked up. The guard was in his early twenties, a special-forces wannabe with blond, buzz-cut hair and a thick, weight lifter's neck. Faith didn't recognize him, but there were a lot of guards around the compound, and most of them had thick necks. "Hi, ah…" She quickly scanned his blue Banat & Sloan uniform but couldn't see a name tag. "I'm sorry, I forgot your name."

"Sorenson, ma'am. We've never met."

"How did you know to let me in?"

He nodded toward a flat-screened monitor. "You're on my list. It came up when you drove over the sensor. 'Car 11, on loan to Dr. Faith Allister until Monday.'" He grinned. "Did you have a good time in Waukegan?"

"How did you—" Faith answered the question herself before she finished asking it. Miles must have told security that he'd lent her the car and why. He probably assumed she'd be going back to her old apartment and had told them that, too. Miles had a real problem respecting her privacy. Shaking her head, she thanked the guard and drove through the open gate to the lot that separated the apartments from the lab building. Miles' parking space was still empty, and she pulled into it.

Turning off the engine, she grasped the steering wheel and rested her forehead against the warm leather. God, that was weird, how the guard had seemed to know so much about her weekend. She appreciated the security, but there were times when B&S felt more like Gestapo headquarters than a scientific research facility. It gave her the creeps. Thank goodness there was no way for anyone to know where she'd really been, what she'd really done.

For the last forty-five minutes, Faith had used loud music and the mechanics of driving to keep from thinking. Now silence settled over her, and all her thoughts and feelings came rushing back. She was an idiot—a complete, addle-brained idiot. Ritter was too young for her, too pretty, and too sure of himself. Even before she was stupid enough to confront him in his apartment, she'd strongly suspected he was a drug addict. Yet she'd gone anyway, looking for…what? Information? She'd known in her heart of hearts that they hadn't had sex, at least not full-blown vaginal intercourse. No, now that she thought about it, she'd gone to Ritter for reassurance. She'd wanted to believe that pretty sentiments hid behind his pretty face. She'd wanted to hear him say things like "I wanted to stay, but I couldn't take advantage of you" and "It was so hard to leave you. Now that you're here, I'll never let you go."

Right. Faith tipped her head and glared at the mirrored windows lining the first floor of the laboratory building. She knew life didn't work that way. Love and lust were hormonal processes, and it was just her bad luck that Todd Ritter sparked every single one of her hormones. Because that was what last night was about: hormones. She'd had them and he hadn't, at least not enough to keep him beside her after his cravings hit.

Faith had always been too wrapped up in her research to make time for relationships. The few she'd tried had all ended badly. Logically, she knew she was better off without Ritter in her life, but his rejection still hurt—more than any of her other break-ups. Why did she care so much about losing a lover she'd never had?

Faith let go of the steering wheel and sat back against the leather seat. That was the problem: she cared. Despite his arrogant manner, she liked Ritter. It wasn't just his face and body. It wasn't even that he'd run to her rescue the night they met. She liked his intelligence and his old-world manners. Like a schoolgirl with a crush, she wanted him to like her back. Maybe she should bury herself in romance novels until the feeling passed. A half-dozen treacly happily-ever-afters should cure her. Either that, or torture her with longing for something she could never have.

Faith snorted. She didn't have time for romance. She had a virus to craft and a disease to cure. She needed what she'd always needed—her work. A few hours in the lab, and she'd forget all about the sting of Ritter's rejection. She might even forget how much she still wanted him.

She climbed out of the car and, after a moment's thought, took her overnight bag from the trunk. She might run into Miles, and he'd want his car back. Then she locked up and headed for the lab. She'd left Friday in the middle of tabulating chromosome shifts—repetitive, mind-numbing work that she usually hated. Today, mind-numbing sounded good.

The building was locked on Saturdays. She swiped her ID through the slot for after-hours entry. A sultry female voice said, "Dr. Faith Allister. Access granted." The door swung open, and Faith stepped into a blast of refrigerated air.

Glad that she was still wearing sweats, she hurried through the window-lined foyer to the elevator. It was open and waiting. She rode up to the third floor and hurried to her lab.

The door was unlocked. Darn that Miles, he'd promised to lock up for her. Muttering to herself, she shouldered the door open. The light was on, and Miles sat at her desk. He wore a pair of headphones, and his head nodded in time to music she couldn't hear. She couldn't read the computer screen from the doorway, either, but she was willing to bet Miles was going through her files. She shoved the door hard enough to bang against the wall. "What the hell do you think you're doing?"

Miles jumped and turned, yanking a portable CD player off the desk. "Faith, you're back."

"Ya think?"

As usual, sarcasm was lost on Miles. He slipped off the headphones and stuck the CD player in his lab-coat pocket. "I wasn't expecting you until Monday morning."

"And I didn't expect to find you at my desk." She walked over to the computer and saw a grid of empty columns. She spun to face Miles. "I was in the middle of tabulating chromosome shifts. If you've lost that data—"

"I didn't. I backed-up and saved everything." He pushed the chair from the desk and stood. "This is a file for another experiment. Banat asked me to infect adult blood with the viral prototype."

Faith leaned forward and studied the grid more closely. It looked exactly like the one she'd designed to compare fetal chromosomes. "Adult blood? Why?"

Miles shrugged. "To see if the virus poses a danger to medical personnel exposed to it."

"It's awfully early in the process to worry about liability. Besides, we designed the virus to be fragile. It could never survive outside laboratory conditions."

"That's what I told Banat, but he ordered the trial anyway. ASAP. That's why I started without you. Now that you're here, I'll let you do it. The blood samples are there." He nodded to a rack of test tubes by the sink at her lab table. They were labeled with subject number and blood type. "Treat them like the fetal samples. You know the drill."

She did, all too well. In the last year, she'd prepared thousands of petri dishes, infected millions of cells, and recorded the results in hundreds of studies. They'd all been fetal cells, though. It might be interesting to see the virus' effect on mature, differentiated cells. The virus might act as a normal infection and kill the cells, or it might enter into a symbiotic relationship, as it did with fetal tissue. And there were always the immunological ramifications to consider. Faith had gone to the lab hoping for a boring, mind-numbing task to distract her, but this was even better. "What have you done so far?"

Miles' lips curled in a smug grin. "Just started entering the subject numbers in the grid. Everything else is set to go. Let me know when you get results." He turned and left the room. The door whispered shut behind him.

"Good-bye to you, too," Faith said, but she wasn't really upset. The possibilities of the new study filled her with an excitement that didn't leave room for other feelings. She dropped her overnight bag and slipped into the chair. It only took a moment to finish the data grid. A quick wash of her hands, and she was ready to begin the real work.

❧ ❧

Four hours later, she slid the ninety-fifth petri dish into the incubation oven, closed the oven door, and stretched to work out the ache in her lower back. God, she was tired. Her excitement over the new study hadn't cooled, but she was beginning to feel the effects of her late night. At least she was almost done. All she had to do was fix a slide from the blood remaining in the test tube and she'd be finished with sample nineteen. Then one last sample to prepare—five bloody petri dishes to infect, and one slide to make—and she could go home.

She centrifuged the test tube, fixed a slide with red blood cells, and slipped it into the rack that held the other eighteen. The slides rattled, and she realized her hands were trembling. That cinched it. She was definitely cutting out after setting up the last sample. She'd get a good night's sleep and come in early tomorrow to record the original DNA profiles.

Faith picked up a clean pipette. The phone rang just as she was inserting it into the last test tube. She jumped; the tip caught on the edge of the test tube and snapped off.

"Damn it." Faith glared at the tiny glass circle floating in Subject 20's blood. Contaminated by microscopic shards of glass, the sample was useless to her now. It looked as though she'd have to settle for a study with only nineteen subjects.

The phone rang again. It was probably Miles checking up on her. Throwing the broken pipette into the biohazard container, Faith stomped over to her desk and yanked off the receiver. "This had better be important."

"Faith?" The voice was deep, male, and definitely not Miles. "John O'Connor here. Did I catch you at a bad time?"

John O'Connor, the police officer? Another fragment of memory slipped into place, a dizzy twirl ending with her head on his shoulder. She'd danced with him last night, ballroom steps to the latest rave beat. How had she gone from waltzing with a policeman to necking in a motel room with Ritter? Maybe O'Connor could tell her. "Not at all. What can I do for you?"

Static crackled over the phone line. He must be calling from an old-style cell phone. "You asked me to call you."

Her fickle memory remained completely blank. "I did? I mean, of course I did."

"You don't remember, do you?" He sounded relieved, not disappointed. "When does *your* memory lapse start?"

"*My* memory lapse?"

"I don't remember anything after you wrote your home number on a matchbook cover and asked me to call. I don't remember leaving the rave, driving home, nothing. I woke up this afternoon with a devil of a headache and a blank space where last night should be. I can't even find the matchbook. That's why I called you at work." He sounded embarrassed, like a puppy who'd missed the newspaper. The thought made her smile.

"I remember less than you do. I'm not even sure how I got to the rave. I remember dancing with you, though. It was nice."

"Yeah, it was." More static. "Would you like some dinner? I know a good Italian place in Highwood. We can compare notes while we eat."

"Not tonight, I'm bushed. Maybe some other time."

Crackle, snap, pause. "No problem." Now he did sound disappointed.

"Like tomorrow. Give me the address, and I'll meet you at the restaurant; say, eight o'clock?"

"Great." She could hear his grin. "I don't have the address on me, though. I'll call back with it."

"I won't be here. I'm leaving in five and going straight to bed. Leave a message at my home number, and I'll pick it up in the morning." She gave him the number, and they both said good-bye.

This was just what she needed, Faith thought, as she picked up the contaminated test tube: a date with a man her own age. So what if John O'Connor wasn't movie-star pretty? He was a nice man, and if her memory could be trusted, a great dancer. Dinner tomorrow should be fun and just the distraction she needed to keep from brooding about Ritter.

As she turned toward the biohazard container, her gaze brushed the tube's label. Subject 20 had type O, Rh positive blood. So did she.

She whistled. Why hadn't she noticed before? The study didn't have to make do with one less subject; she could substitute her own blood for the ruined sample. Certainly there would be differences between her blood and the original donor's, but in a preliminary study like this, those differences shouldn't matter.

She threw away the contaminated test tube, then rummaged through the lab-table drawers for a blood-sample kit. It only took a minute more to wrap the rubber tourniquet around her upper arm and puff up a vein. One thing she'd inherited from her mother were nice, showy veins. A stick with the needle and the tube quickly filled with blood. There was a trick to replacing the needle with a cotton ball without getting blood over everything, but she'd learned it in medical school. Bending her arm to hold the cotton tight, she snapped the needle off into the biohazard container and labeled the plastic tube. After that, all she needed to do was to put the tube in the refrigerator and slap a bit of adhesive tape over the cotton. She could prepare the sample in the morning, and in the evening, she'd have dinner with John O'Connor. Dinner with John. She tried the words out loud. They had a nice ring to them. As she locked up and headed for her apartment and bed, she tried to pretend the weight in her chest was just fatigue, not longing for the man she couldn't have.

≈≈

Ritter didn't notice the stop light until it was almost too late. He slammed the brake, and his left foot missed the clutch. The engine coughed. Halfway over the crosswalk, Greta shuddered to a stop and died.

Even at eight o'clock at night, the intersection was busy. The cars raced past, inches from Greta's front bumper. Luckily, there was no one behind him. Ritter restarted the engine and backed Greta to safety.

The traffic light glared from its post. Red and malevolent, it pulsed to the beat of his heart, mocking him. The urge to accelerate into the light, to knock it down and shatter it into a thousand pieces, swept over Ritter. He clenched his hands around the steering wheel. The bloodlust mocked him, not the signal. The madness was closer now than it had ever been, but it didn't control him, not yet. A pint or two of blood would mute its voice, a pint or two more would drive it back into oblivion.

The light shifted to green, and Ritter crossed the intersection and drove with exaggerated care to his destination, the Waukegan Greyhound terminal.

The remodeled terminal was clean, bright, and secure, with comfortable benches for passengers, and guards to keep the homeless from them. Ritter stopped at an automatic gate and took a ticket before driving into the fenced parking lot. He parked beneath an eye-searing arc light near a surveillance camera. Whatever happened tonight, at least Greta would be safe. Smiling grimly, he slipped the ticket into his pocket and, instead of entering the terminal, abandoned the light for the desolate shadows of the surrounding neighborhood.

Ritter felt a kinship with the shadows. Dressed in black, from shirt to sneakers, he, too, was dark and dangerous. He needed blood and couldn't wait for a victim to stumble across his path. Since his forced withdrawal had closed the blood bank at the hospital, the only place that promised instant gratification was Paradise Walk.

During business hours, patrons of its newly renovated shops and cafes called it Genesee Avenue. The shops and cafes closed at six. By eight, the street had a new name and a new set of patrons. In the twelve years Ritter had lived in Waukegan, he had never walked the Paradise. He had heard ravers bragging about the drugs and women they bought there, but had dismissed most of their rantings as drunken hyperbole. Occasionally, though, a spark of recognition would glitter in a predator's eyes when the street was mentioned. It made him suspect the stories were true, and Paradise was the place to obtain the unobtainable.

He walked the two blocks from the terminal to Genesee Avenue, past the Babcox Justice Center and the attached police station. When he stopped to think about it, he had to appreciate the irony of building police headquarters a block from the most notorious street in the city. On his more cynical days, he wondered how many bribes had been paid to protect the street's after-hours trade from official interference.

Tonight, though, he didn't think; he just stretched his legs into a yard-eating pace that startled the only person he passed, an elderly woman pushing a cart full of garbage bags. Her mute stare slowed his strides. For a moment, he considered pulling her into the Justice Center's entryway and taking a sip, just a swallow to hold the madness at bay, but the woman was too old. Ritter didn't trust himself to stop at just one swallow, and the loss of more blood might injure her. He clenched his teeth against the hunger and ran on.

Urban renewal had widened and repaved Genesee Avenue, repaired its buildings' brick facades, and planted old-fashioned gaslights at regular intervals to illuminate the sidewalk. During the day, the effect must have been charming: small-town America at its wholesome best. If so, the wholesome air vanished with the sun. Girls in micro skirts and transparent tube tops had taken over the street. Ritter counted more than a dozen leaning against the gaslights' iron poles or strolling beneath their yellow glow.

The selection was impressive: women of every size, shape, and color. Most looked to be in their teens or early twenties, though he saw a thin oriental girl, who couldn't be more than twelve, talking to a well-cushioned black woman, who looked old enough to be her grandmother. At the end of the block, he spotted a couple of tall, well-coifed whores with jutting jaws and five o'clock shadows. The rumors were true. Paradise Walk had something for everyone.

"Hey honey, you just looking, or you want a date?"

The words were bold, but the voice wavered. Ritter turned to face it. The speaker slouched beside the doorway of a chain clothing store. She wore the uniform of a modern streetwalker—short skirt, tight top, high heels, and mesh stockings. A circular bruise on her throat marked her as a drug user. Intravenous aerosols, the new drug injection system that did away with needles and the diseases they spread, often left such bruises. Despite the dim light, she wore sunglasses that hid half her face.

Ritter saw all these things, but what drew him to her were the blue veins running up her arms. Her skin still held the bloom of health, and under the pall of cheap perfume, she smelled of life.

"A date." The words squeezed from his throat in a rough whisper. Ritter stepped into the doorway, reached into his pocket and pulled out a money clip of folded hundred dollar bills. "How much?"

"A hundred bucks to blow you." Bright smears appeared beneath the rouge on her cheeks, and her voice faltered to a whisper. "Two for a standing fuck."

He pulled three bills from the clip. "I have something else in mind."

An ashen pallor replaced the blush, but she snatched the bills from his hand. "Three hundred buys you an hour. The Berkshire rents rooms, but it's extra."

"I don't need a room." Ritter stepped closer and took her hand. The girl flinched, but didn't pull away. Her heart raced. "Relax," he said, kissing her knuckle. "I won't hurt you."

"Hurt?" Her fear brushed his tongue, and his hunger leapt. His lips pulled back. She gasped.

"Stand still and silent." He stared into her eyes and wove what was left of his voice into a spell that froze her before she could run or scream. He turned her wrist and buried his fangs into her vein.

Blood, hot and sweet, spiced with opiate, filled his mouth. He swallowed, waited for his mouth to fill and swallowed again. The flow from the wrist was slower than from the throat. That was why he had chosen it. He didn't want to kill by accident. If the blood kept flowing, he was dry enough to drink her empty. The blood slowed to a trickle after the third mouthful; the wounds were closing, thanks to the healing properties of his saliva. Ritter moved his lips up her arm, bit again, and drank.

She tasted young, fresh, wholesome. The next time the bleeding slowed, Ritter pulled back and studied the girl. Her blood held the bite of heroin, but not the underlying accommodation an addict's blood made to it. She had used heroin recently, but she wasn't yet addicted.

Ritter examined her face, pale now under her makeup. Her eyes were closed behind her sunglasses, and her heavy eyelashes lay on cheeks still round with baby fat. "How old are you?"

"Old enough."

Ritter added a thread of power to the question, just enough to guarantee the truth. "How old?"

"Sixteen next month."

Her heart had slowed to a steady rhythm that made Ritter's teeth throb, but the madness had eased. He licked his lips for the lingering blood, but didn't bite again. "A child."

A voice spoke behind him, deep and tinged with anger. "These days, most hookers start off as runaways."

Ritter dropped her arm and whirled around. "Cole. What are you doing here?"

Cole strode from a concealing shadow, dressed for hunting, in a black denim jacket and jeans. "I followed you." The anger grew stronger. "Figured you owed me one after that trick you played last night."

"You figured wrong." Ritter turned back to the girl. He would deal with Cole later. "Is that what you are, a runaway?"

"No." The answer was soft, barely a whisper. "I fell for a biker. I didn't find out, until it was too late, that members of the gang don't break up with their girl friends—they sell them."

A hand grabbed his shoulder and spun him around. "Where the fuck is the pretty doctor?"

Ritter shrugged off Cole's hand and filled his voice with sincerity and just a hint of power. "I don't know."

Cole shook his head, as if annoyed by a fly. "You're too dry to work voodoo on me. Where is she?"

"I tell you, I don't know."

"I have to go." It was the girl. Her eyes were open and dark with fear. "Dan'll get mad if I don't turn more tricks."

Ritter's voice should have held the girl for much longer. Cole was right; he was weak. Not too weak, though, to compel a frightened child to tell the truth. "Where do you want to go?"

"Home." She paled as she spoke and looked over his shoulder as if afraid someone on the street might hear her. "But I can't."

"Where's home?

"Don't tell me you're going to pull your white-knight crap on a hooker," Cole said.

At the same moment, the girl answered, "Winnipeg, Manitoba. But Dan won't let me go."

"She's a hooker and a junkie. Shit man, just look at her throat. It's too late to save her."

Ritter ignored them both. "The bus terminal is only a few blocks away, and the money I gave you is more than enough for a ticket home. I will walk you to the station and see you on the bus."

"You can't—" began Cole.

"I can't—" began the girl.

"Enough!" Ritter poured his strength into his voice and silenced them both. He tackled Cole first. "The girl is not an addict, not yet, and I will not stand by and watch her life drain into the sewer."

He turned to the girl. "Why can't you go home?"

She pulled off her dark glasses. Her right eye was colored by an ugly fist-sized bruise. "Dan caught me trying to leave. Next time he'll kill me."

Ritter couldn't tell which angered him more, the beating, or the hopelessness it had engendered. "I won't let him hurt you."

Cole snorted. "How you going to stop him? Look at you, you couldn't keep a kitten off a mouse right now."

True, but it didn't matter. Ritter took the girl's hand. "Come."

Leaving Cole in front of the clothing store, they started toward the bus terminal. Though her steps were unsteady, the girl followed Ritter without complaint. They were halfway to the Babcox Justice Center when the rumble of a motorcycle joined the traffic noise from Genesee Ave.

The girl stopped. "Dan."

Ritter's body had absorbed the girl's blood, and his strength was returning. With it came confidence. He let it fill his voice. "You will be on the bus before he realizes you are gone."

More motorcycles joined the traffic a block away. Ritter couldn't tell how many. He hurried his steps, pulling the girl into a jog. A single pimp he could handle, but he was too weak to face a gang.

The roaring engines died, as if cut by a single switch. He glanced over his shoulder, but the street behind them remained empty. Ritter was beginning to breathe easier when he heard a sharp crack followed by Cole's voice beside his ear. "Look out, Ritter, he—" Another crack, and the voice stilled.

"*Himmel.*" Ritter stopped and gazed back up the street. The girl stood beside him, panting. He threw his voice, aiming it for Cole's ears alone. "A gun?"

The answer he got was faint, pain-filled. "Forty-five, semiautomatic. Loaded with fucking dumdums."

A chill wrapped around Ritter. Cole was strong and tough, but not invulnerable. A bullet, particularly a hollow-point bullet, through the head or heart, would kill him as easily as the proverbial wooden stake. Enough wounds elsewhere, and he could bleed to death before he healed.

The girl's fingers dug into the back of his hand. "We've got to go."

Ritter gently pulled from her grasp. He caught her gaze and willed her obedience. "The terminal is down this street. Go to the lobby, buy your ticket, and sit on a bench until your bus comes. Do not leave the terminal for any reason. Wait for your bus, get on it, and go home."

"Home." Her voice was empty, proof she was under his control.

Praying the compulsion would hold until she was on the bus, Ritter nodded. "Go.

He waited until she started walking toward the terminal, then turned and ran back to Genesee.

The prostitutes had disappeared, as had the cars that cruised past them. Half a dozen motorcycles lay in the street, a black and chrome barricade. Six men in leather jackets too warm for the evening clustered around the clothing-store doorway, swinging their steel-toed boots into a crumpled form on the sidewalk. Cole.

Ritter hesitated at the corner. In his half-starved state, he wasn't strong enough to take on six men physically. He sucked in a breath, but his hunger reared at the scent of blood, making it impossible to concentrate. His voice came out thin, shaky. "Stop!" The closest three men froze in mid-kick, but the others merely paused.

One, taller than the rest, with an impressive paunch and a gray-streaked ponytail, looked up and frowned. He flung out his arm in a dismissive gesture. "Get lost, kid."

The man mistook him for a would-be customer. Good. Being thought harmless was the next best thing to being in control. Pulling the shreds of his power together, Ritter started toward them. "Leave."

The three men who had fallen under his spell turned toward the bikes. The others shuddered, but didn't move.

"What the fuck was that?" The older man, the apparent leader, shoved the others aside. In his hand, he held a large, bluish pistol, a forty-five semiautomatic.

The barrel rose.

Ritter lunged to the right.

A crack, and a bullet whined past him. Ritter jumped over Cole and kicked the biker square in the chest on the way down.

The gun went flying.

Three motorcycles roared to life.

The biker collapsed, stunned. Ritter rolled off him and sprang to his feet. The other two gang members stared open-mouthed at their leader. Ritter grabbed the closest by his rattail braid. Jerked him back. Palm on each ear. Sharp twist to the right. A snap. The biker crumpled to the ground.

The other dove for the gun. Ritter kicked at his face. His foot caught the biker's shoulder and flipped him over. The man flailed desperately, grabbed the gun, and shot.

The bullet went wild. Ritter ripped the gun from his fingers and threw it through the store window. The glass shattered. A ringing alarm filled the air.

He didn't have much time.

He seized the biker by his leather jacket. Ignoring the kicks and punches, Ritter pulled him off the ground. The biker's head tipped back. Fangs tingling, Ritter ripped them through his enemy's exposed throat.

Blood flew everywhere. Blood Ritter craved. Blood Cole needed to survive. Cole huddled on the cracked sidewalk, his whole body jerking with the effort to keep breathing.

Ritter hauled the dying man to Cole and threw his bloody carcass next him. Cole didn't move. He was farther gone than Ritter had feared. Lifting Cole's head, Ritter placed his mouth on the wound. "Drink."

For a moment, Cole just kept gasping. Blood filled his mouth, trickled down his chin. Then his lips closed. His throat bobbed. Long arms shot out and pulled the body closer. Cole's lips locked on the wound. With a shuddering sigh, he fed.

"*Gott sei dank*," said Ritter. Thank God. Cole was going to be all right. Ritter straightened and was beginning to turn when a heavy weight slammed into the back of his head.

The unexpected blow knocked him over Cole. Ritter tucked his chin and rolled down the sidewalk and up on his feet again. Snarling, he spun to face the new attack. The leader of the bikers stared at Cole, a look of horror on his face. A length of chain dangled forgotten from his fist.

The hesitation was all Ritter needed. He ran past Cole, yanked away the chain, and buried his fangs in the biker's left carotid artery.

The biker's own heart pumped blood into Ritter's mouth. Hot, rich, and surprisingly clean blood, flavored by only a hint of alcohol. Ritter gulped it down, swallow after swallow, cup after cup. The blood made him dizzy, and still he drank. The biker's legs buckled. Ritter caught him under the arms and kept drinking. He didn't pause until the pulse faltered. Ritter let go, and the man fell to the ground. He convulsed once and lay still.

A shrill siren cut the silence. Ritter had to get Cole out of there. He turned to see his friend sitting beside the empty corpse. Ritter crouched beside him. "The police are coming. Can you walk?"

"Give me a second." Cole took a deep breath, grabbed Ritter's shoulders, and heaved himself to his feet. He frowned at his blood-soaked shirt.

Ritter slipped his arm around Cole's waist. "Lean on me, but come. The police will be here soon."

The first step left Cole hissing with pain. "We've got to get the bullet out first."

"It's still in there?" The few times Ritter had been shot since his transformation, the bullets had slid through him, leaving a wound that was painful, but quickly healed.

"I told you, it was a dumdum." Cole lifted his shirt and Ritter gasped at the hole in his friend's stomach. "They spread when they hit, get all jagged and nasty. You've got to reach in and pull it out before it cuts something a little blood can't fix."

The sirens were getting closer. There was no time to argue. Ritter spread the wound with one hand, and while Cole's fingers dug into his shoulder, dug for the bullet.

Luckily, it hadn't penetrated deeply; his fingers were only past the second knuckle when they brushed metal.

Cole stiffened. "Go on," he said through clenched teeth. "Get it out."

Easier said than done. The mangled bullet was barbed and slick. Wishing he had surgeon's tools with him—forceps or even a pair of tweezers—Ritter pushed further into Cole's belly and impaled his fingertips on the razor-sharp edge.

It hurt, but the rush of fresh blood made the pain bearable. Ritter tightened his grip until metal grated against bone and slowly pulled his fingers back. The bullet came with them.

The rough bit of metal looked smaller than it felt. Ritter threw it aside, and pulled Cole's wound closed. With the bullet out, he should heal quickly.

"Can you walk?" Ritter asked. Cole nodded.

Blood dripped from Ritter's fingers, his and Cole's. Resisting the urge to lick them clean, Ritter once again slid his arm around Cole's waist and helped him stagger around the corner and into the flashing lights of three police cars.

Two sped around the corner, but the third slowed. The siren shut off. A blinding light flared beside the driver and swept over them.

Cole hesitated.

"Keep walking," Ritter said. He turned his voice toward the officer in the car. "You see two drunks. Drive on."

The light vanished; the car accelerated on to Genesee.

Cole's admiring chuckle ended in a gasp of pain. "I forgot how good you are with that voice shit."

Joyous strength surged through Ritter. He tipped back his head and laughed. "The blood gives me power."

"The blood makes you wasted. How long's it been since you drank your fill?"

"Too long." Another laugh burbled out, and Ritter realized Cole was right. He was intoxicated. "We'd better hurry to my car before I become too drunk to drive."

"You're going to let me bleed over your precious Greta?"

"No. I am going to wrap you in a tarp."

They walked as quickly as Cole was able to the parking lot and Greta. Cole's strides strengthened with each step. His breathing grew stronger, his posture straighter; but blood continued to ooze from the wound in his belly. Ritter took the canvas cover from the trunk, shook it out, and spread it over the back seat. "Lie down. You will be less conspicuous."

With a curt nod, Cole squeezed past the front seat and curled on the tarp. Ritter tucked the edges over him, covering him completely.

Cole shoved the cloth from his face. "I still gotta breathe."

"Breathe after we get to my place. I don't want interfering motorists to see you and call the police."

"Right." Grimacing, Cole began to pull cloth back up.

Ritter glanced at the terminal. "Leave it down for now. I want to check on the girl, make sure she made it to the terminal."

Cole pushed the cover away from his face. "You still worried about that little streetwalker? What kind of white knight are you, can't tell the difference between a princess and a whore?"

"I may be a fool, and she, a whore, but what does that make you, who took on six to protect us?"

"Stupid."

Ritter grinned. "Rest. I will return shortly."

His hands were still sticky with blood. He shoved them in his pockets and hurried toward the terminal. Halfway to the entrance, he heard the rumble of an engine. A Greyhound bus pulled through huge arched doors and followed the curving lane toward the street. The sign over the windshield read, "Minneapolis/St. Paul, Duluth, Winnipeg." The windows were tinted, but Ritter could make out the faces of the people next to them. The girl he had saved was the in the third seat from the back. Her cheek pressed against the glass, her expression a mixture of hope and fear.

The bus turned onto the street and accelerated. Ritter watched its taillights shrink to pinpricks, then walked back to Cole.

His eyes were closed, and he lay in the death-like stillness Ritter had come to associate with a sleeping vampire. Good: after blood, sleep was what Cole most needed to heal. When Ritter leaned down to pull the cover over Cole's face, his eyelids flew open. "That was fast. Did she cut and run?"

Ritter straightened. "I saw her bus. She's on her way home."

"You can't just pull a whore off the street and call her saved," Cole said, but a smile lurked behind the words. His eyes drifted closed. "She'll probably bolt at the next stop."

"Perhaps, but it will be her decision, not a pimp's."

"Boy Scout." A long, shuddering breath followed the words, leaving Cole as empty and motionless as a corpse. He had gone back to sleep.

Ritter gazed down at his friend. "Fraud." Cole might be ruthless, violent, and crude, but he chose his prey as carefully as Ritter did. Pimps, bullies, and murderers, he hunted them all with the same tenacity he had turned against Faith. In his own way, Cole was as idealistic as Ritter was. Ritter pulled the cover over Cole's face, leaving room for his barely perceptible breathing.

The blood smears on his fingers looked black in the harsh light. Without touching the door, Ritter leaned over and opened the glove compartment. He took out a pack of cleansing tissues. The moist wipes were designed for busy mothers, but they worked as well on blood as on finger paint and peanut butter. He cleaned his hands and the smudge from the compartment's latch. His clothes were still presentable, any splatters hidden by the black fabric. Another tissue to remove traces of blood from his lips and chin, and he was done. Ritter shoved the soiled wipes into the trash bag beneath the dash and climbed into the driver's seat.

The parking attendant didn't even look up when Ritter stopped at the exit and handed him a twenty. Quarters rattled down the automatic change machine, and the gate swung open.

Ritter scooped up the change and drove onto the street. For once the lights were with him, and he whizzed through the intersections toward the safety of his apartment. He was halfway home when Cole surprised him by speaking.

"Hey, Ritter."

"Yes."

"Thanks. For coming back, I mean. I owe you one."

Ritter's lips spread in a slow smile. "I know."

Chapter Seventeen

It had to be a mistake. Faith cleared the file and carefully reloaded the data. Twenty DNA profiles sprang onto the computer screen, profiles from the blood samples Miles had dumped on her the evening before. Nineteen male and one female. The nineteen original samples and her own blood. Faith's fingers flew across the keyboard, ordering Banat's supercomputer to once again run an anomalous DNA comparison on the samples. One by one, the first nineteen dropped away, no anomalies found. The twentieth profile was different. The computer chimed, and Faith's chromosomes remained on the screen, along with the message, "Anomalous genes found: 14, 23."

Faith rubbed her sore eyes. Since she didn't suffer from a genetic defect, she'd probably triggered a computer glitch, a bug that mixed data from two files. Either that, or the technician at the electron microscope had swapped her sample with a slide from an earlier experiment. In either case, it looked like she was dealing with an infected sample. There was one way to find out. Selecting the twenty-third pair, she ordered the computer to enlarge and highlight its anomalies. One of the Xs lit up in the familiar pattern. The other remained dark.

A chill slithered across Faith's neck. She had never seen an instance where the virus struck one X chromosome in a female sample and left the other untouched. She was looking at a pattern more likely to be found in the carrier of an inherited condition like hemophilia or Tay-Sachs disease.

Her brother had died of Stoker's syndrome, a disease so rare that, until the incidence started rising in the last decade, the medical community assumed it was the result of random mutation. Her research was close to proving the syndrome could be caused by a virus. If there was no computer bug, and the technician hadn't mixed up the samples, she was staring at evidence that the syndrome could also be inherited...and that she was a carrier.

The image of her brother, tiny and pale in the incubator, flashed through her mind. The chill sank to her stomach. She knew she should be elated—evidence that the disease could be inherited supported her theory—but, no matter how good it would be for her research, she didn't want to carry the threat of Stoker's in her genes.

Faith shut off her computer and stood. A mistake was still the most likely explanation. She'd call tech support on Monday to check out her computer. To rule out a sample error, she needed to draw more blood, prepare a new slide, and double-check the results. She glanced at the clock. Past six already· too late for more work tonight. She'd have to wait until Monday. Right now she had a more urgent problem—her date with John O'Connor

She locked her lab and ran across the parking lot to her apartment. She'd been having second thoughts all day—had actually picked up the phone twice to cancel, only to hang up without dialing—but now she was glad for the excuse to get away from the lab. After a quick shower, she slipped on her favorite sundress—the white one, spotted with sunflowers—and a pair of strappy sandals. The outfit was perfect, except for one problem: the dress's neckline plunged well below the hickey on her throat.

She had avoided mirrors all day. The hickey was too sharp a reminder of the night she couldn't remember. Still, people's stares would be even harder to deal with. She ran back into the bathroom to get some concealer, cleared a circle from the fogged mirror, and gaped in surprise. The long bruise that had seemed so vivid yesterday had vanished. The only sign that she hadn't imagined it was a faint purple smudge near her jaw line. Faith shook her head and reached into the drawer for a hair brush. Obviously the drug had lingered longer in her system than she'd realized. It must have warped her perceptions and turned a slight blemish into the beacon she'd thought she'd seen. She ran the brush quickly through her hair and, moments later, was in the borrowed car on the way to Highwood and her date.

The address was easy to find. The little storefront restaurant sat on the main street, sandwiched between a liquor store and a Mexican bakery. John O'Connor paced in front of its curtained windows. He looked good in a dark greenpolo shirt and khaki slacks. Faith honked. He looked up, smiled, and pointed to an empty space just north of the restaurant. She pulled into the spot and opened the car door to John's cheerful, "Glad you could make it."

Faith sneezed. Aromas from the restaurant scented the warm, humid night: oregano, toasting cheese, and, of course, garlic.

"Bless you." John took her hand and helped her from the car. His grip was strong, his skin warm and dry.

She gently pulled her hand away. "Thanks." The garlic in the air slipped into her mouth and tickled the back of her nose. Her eyes began to water; her nose began to drip. Damn, she'd forgotten to take an antihistamine before she left. She sniffed and fought the urge to sneeze again.

"Sorry," she said, fumbling in her purse for a tissue and a pill bottle. "I should have warned you. I'm allergic to garlic."

John's smile broadened until it crinkled the corners of his eyes. "No problem. If you don't like Italian, we can go someplace else."

"No, Italian's fine. This will take care of the sniffles." She showed John the pill before swallowing it dry. "As for the hives, I'll just order something that doesn't have garlic in it."

His eyebrow rose in mock disbelief. "Italian without garlic? This I have to see."

Faith fell in love with the restaurant the moment they stepped through the door into Frank Sinatra's version of "The Lady is a Tramp." There was no receptionist, but a moment after the door closed behind them, a middle-aged waitress hurried from the back of the restaurant. She had an aggressive bust and bottle-blond hair, but the smile she flashed looked completely genuine. "Hi, John! Your booth's ready."

"Thanks, Ada." Taking Faith's arm, John guided her past a noisy family eating pizza to a booth snuggled into the back of the restaurant near the bar. The aromas drifting from the kitchen made Faith's eyes water and her stomach growl.

She slid into her seat. Before she had a chance to unfold her napkin, the waitress arrived with menus and a cloth-covered basket. She set them all in the middle of the table. "Can I get you anything to drink?"

"Just water for me," Faith said. She sneezed again and hoped the antihistamine would kick in soon.

"Bless you." John turned to the waitress. "Same here. I have to work later."

"Be back for your order in a minute." The waitress shot John another brilliant smile and hurried away.

Faith spread the napkin across her lap. "You must be a great tipper."

John looked startled. "What? Oh, Ada. She likes to feed people, and I've got a big appetite. What are you going to have?" He picked up a menu. "I'd suggest the veal vesuvio, but it's full of garlic."

Faith chose steamed mussels in white sauce. The waitress didn't even blink when she asked for it prepared without garlic. John ordered the same with a side of fettucine.

Ada jotted down the order, then lowered the pad. Her voice dropped to conspiratorial tones. "Mario just pulled out a fresh tray of tiramisu. Want me to save you a couple of pieces?"

John grinned and caught Faith's eye. "Dessert?"

"Always."

"Good." He turned to the waitress. "Better hold us three."

Faith and the waitress both laughed.

Dinner was fabulous: good food, quick service, pleasant company. Faith even stopped sneezing. By the time Ada poured the after-dinner coffee, Faith's stomach felt that warm, mellow contentment usually reserved for Thanksgiving.

Ada left to get dessert, and John leaned forward. "Ready to compare notes?"

About last night. The food in Faith's stomach turned into a indigestible lump. "I don't really remember anything, just bits and pieces, until—" She broke off, too embarrassed to go on.

"Until?"

"The next morning."

John looked at her a long moment. "What's the last thing you remember before your blackout?"

Ritter's weight between her legs, his lips on her neck. Heat rushed up her face. "Dancing with you."

If John noticed her embarrassment, he didn't show it. "I remember getting your number and your boyfriend showing up."

"Ritter is not my boyfriend."

His eyes narrowed. Faith's good-natured date had turned back into a police officer. "Then you do remember seeing him."

Faith sipped her coffee, hoping to buy time until she could think of a good answer. She was not about to admit to anyone, much less John O'Connor, what she remembered about Ritter that night. As she struggled to come up with something to say, the fog in her mind cleared from another memory. She set the cup down. "Before we went into the rave. We had a fight in the parking lot."

"Was there a tall black man with him?"

"No."

John picked up his spoon and tapped it against the side of his cup. "What did you fight about?"

"I...I don't remember."

"Was it drugs?"

"No. The only drugs I take are antihistamines for my allergies."

"What about Ritter? Does he do drugs?"

"I—"

"Here you go!"

Faith jumped, and, from the look on his face, John was as startled as she was. The waitress set three plates on the table, each containing a huge cocoa-dusted square. Faith had never before seen tiramisu that wept liquor and sagged under the weight of its sweet cheese topping. Normally, she would dig right in, but John's suspicions made her stomach cramp. She stood. "I have to go."

Ada frowned at John. "Did you turn cop on the poor girl?"

He ignored the waitress. "Please sit down. I'll behave. Promise."

The waitress humphed. "You better."

John glared at her. "Don't you have tables to clear?"

"No, you're the last one." She tucked the tray under her arm and stalked back into the kitchen.

Faith looked around the room. Except for a man at the bar, they were the only customers left. A touch on her hand brought her attention back to the table.

"I'm sorry," John said. "About the questions, I mean. But I've got this hole in my mind. I can't remember much, and what I do remember doesn't make sense." Frustration and fear battled in his eyes. "I keep getting these flashes of memory. Some of them are weird, crazy."

Faith dropped back in her chair and slipped her hand around his. "You're not going crazy. I think we ordered drinks and someone spiked them while we were dancing."

John's expression cleared, and he slowly nodded. "I remember you drinking bottled water."

"Spiked drinks would explain both the blackout and the hallucinations."

"I keep forgetting you're a doctor."

There was something in his thoughtful tone that made the food jump in her stomach. "I did not put anything in your drink."

"What about your friend, Ritter? The last thing I remember clearly is you saying his name."

Faith yanked her hand away. "Why are you obsessed with Ritter? There were over a hundred people at that rave; any one of them could have slipped something into our drinks."

"Yeah, but he was the only one there who might have a reason to."

"Why would Ritter want to drug us?"

Frank Sinatra's voice crooned in the background, accompanied by laughter from the kitchen. "I'm a cop." John finally said. "What better way to put me out of commission?"

"But—"

"As for you—" John glanced around the deserted restaurant and lowered his voice to a murmur. "For some slimeballs, drugging and seducing pretty women has become the new national pastime."

Broken memories flashed through Faith's mind. Her begging. Ritter leaving. The horror in his voice when he saw the evidence of his kisses. A burn ran up her throat and across her face. "Then I know he didn't do it."

"Over the last six months, dozens of women have disappeared from raves and campus parties. The lucky ones wake up in bed, with no memory of how they got there. Others wake up in alleys or cheap hotel rooms. Some don't wake up at all."

"But Ritter—"

"According to witnesses, many of the girls were seen leaving a party or rave with a man, blond, medium height, good-looking. Sound familiar?"

"Sure. Add a minibeard and spiky hair, and you've got half of the boys at the rave last night."

His eyes narrowed. "I thought you didn't remember the rave."

"You are so suspicious." She took in a breath and tried to blow her annoyance out with it. "I don't remember much, but I do remember feeling like I was at a hedgehog convention."

The corners of his mouth twitched, as if he were fighting a smile. Then they straightened into a grim line. "Someone is saturating the North Shore with designer and date-rape drugs. Every time we nab a scumbag that's selling, another takes his place. We need to get higher on the food chain, nab the distributor, close down the lab, something. I've been working on the case since winter, but now that I've gotten a taste of it myself—" He shook his head. "I've got to stop those bastards."

Faith leaned forward and laid her hand over his. "Ritter might be a user, but he didn't drug us. I'm not sure of much about last night, but I'm sure of that."

John turned his hand and laced his fingers through hers. "I hope you're wrong. He's the only lead I've got."

"Is that why you asked me out, to get information on Ritter?" Faith knew she should feel betrayed, but John's grim, almost desperate expression knocked away her anger. "I'm not wrong," she said gently. "But I still might be able to help. You say you're looking for a lab. What kind?"

"Small, probably mobile. Most look like commercial semis, only there's a laboratory in the trailer instead of cargo. Sometimes they park in a deserted area, but more often they work on the move. Unless the driver gets stopped for a traffic violation, the only chance of finding the lab is if we catch it at the drop-off."

"Drop-off?"

"Where the lab delivers the goods. It's usually at a warehouse, but could be anyplace. I've seen drop-offs at truck stops, rest stops, even at weigh stations. Unfortunately, all the tips we've gotten so far have turned up dry."

The overhead lights sprang on. Ada pushed through the kitchen door. "Sorry folks. We're closed." She walked over to their table, set down the bill, then frowned at the untouched desserts. "Shame on you, letting good food go to waste."

John grabbed the bill from under Faith's fingers. "The only waist these babies are going to is mine. Pack them for us, would you, Ada?" Turning on his megawatt smile, he handed her a credit card.

Ada smiled back. "Sure." She scooped up the plates, took John's credit card, and left.

Faith reached for her purse. "How much do I owe you?"

"Dinner's on me. Work expense."

"Thank you." Faith set the purse in her lap. "Except for the third degree, it was a pretty good dinner."

"Pretty good!" Ada had returned. Glaring at Faith, she slammed the slip and card on the table.

"The best, Ada, the best." John signed the slip and reclaimed his card. "Now, about our desert..."

Ada humphed, but hurried away and returned a moment later with three Styrofoam containers. John thanked her and added a wink that brought back her smile. Balancing the containers on one palm, he offered Faith his arm and walked her to her car.

Somehow, all three ended up in her trunk. She closed the lid and turned to John. "I had a good time. Thanks."

He stepped close, put his hands on her shoulders, and leaned his lips into hers. It was a nice kiss, neither sloppy nor rushed. But it didn't burn. Kissing John was like kissing one of her male cousins: friendly and safe. A hungry ache settled low in Faith's stomach. She didn't need friendly, she realized. She didn't need safe. Neither would dispel the chill that lingered from last night. She needed heat: mind-melting, bone-searing heat. She needed Ritter.

Faith pulled away from John and hoped her pasted-on smile hid the horror erupting inside her. She barely heard his good-bye, barely felt the door handle when she opened the car and climbed in. Her fingers shook as she slid the key in the ignition. She managed a wave, then drove out of sight. When she was sure John couldn't see her, she turned the corner and parked behind a busy pizza parlor.

Grasping the top of the steering wheel, Faith rested her forehead on her hands. Instead of helping her forget the night before, John's kiss had made her ache...for Ritter, had made her hunger...for Ritter. There had to be a logical explanation. Maybe the drug from last night?

Faith didn't even bother completing the thought. A drug might loosen her inhibitions, blur her memory, even knock her unconscious, but it wouldn't make her long for one man over another. Besides, the drug had worn off hours ago. She was suffering from something more insidious, like a worm that infects a computer and lurks unseen until a specific date or program triggers it. Something like a posthypnotic suggestion.

She took a deep breath and looked up. What had Ritter done to her?

≈≈

A hundred motorcycles chased Ritter through the burned-out streets of Dresden. Scorched pavement. Skeletal buildings. Thick, swirling smoke. Choking, gasping, running, he darted away from the earthshaking roar and into the last standing structure, a shop.

Unbroken windows. Clean-swept floor. Fragile china figurines on pristine shelves. The scent of vanilla and baking. Behind the counter, a vision in pink and gold smiled and lifted her arms. The sweetest voice in the world. "Ritter."

He, too, lifted his arms and stepped forward. Their fingertips almost touched. Shelves rattled. Figures danced. Windows shattered. The door buckled. A wave of black and chrome swept around Ritter and—

"Greta!"

Ritter shot off the couch into darkness and a discordant buzz. For a moment, he thought he was still in the nightmare, but the darkness solidified into the familiar shapes of his chair, tables, and lamps. He scrubbed his fingers through his hair. The noise made it impossible to think. Why was he sleeping in the living room? Cole, that was it. After they returned to the apartment, exhausted and giddy with blood, he had given his injured friend the bed to rest and heal in. Ritter had retired to the couch, intending to read until the blood-rush faded. He must have fallen asleep before he could turn on the light.

The buzzing continued.

Cole had little tolerance for fools and wouldn't appreciate being woken by one. Ritter stumbled to the intercom and slammed the button. "Go away."

The noise stopped. A crackle and, "Let me in. I have to talk to you."

Ritter's blood stopped cold. "Faith?"

"Yes, Faith. Let me in, or I'll—"

He didn't wait to hear the rest. If Cole woke up, he would rip out her throat and call it a good day's work. Ritter raced to the door and up the stairs to the lobby, praying Faith would keep talking and not push the buzzer again.

She stood on the stoop outside the building, bathed in light from the nearly full moon. Ritter yanked open the door separating them. "Go away. Cole is downstairs."

"Liar."

Ritter nearly choked. "You don't believe me?"

"You tried that line yesterday, remember." She dropped her voice to a parody of his. "That's why you must not stay. If Cole sees you, he will kill you."

"But he is here. Now. In my bed."

For a moment, surprise washed the anger from her face. "Your bed?" Then the anger returned tenfold. "I don't care who you sleep with. I just want you to take away the posthypnotic suggestion."

Her anger beat against him, but her words made no sense. "What?"

His confusion must have shown, because her frown deepened. "Take it away, bring me out of it, whatever. Make it so I can kiss another man without thinking of you."

A swirl of emotion hit Ritter like a punch in the solar plexus. Anger, jealousy, elation. "You kissed another man and thought of me?"

"Don't look so pleased. It's one of your frigging mind tricks. And I don't like it."

Ritter stepped over the threshold and let the door close behind him. "*Liebchen.* Believe me, I have not played any 'mind tricks' on you."

She backed down a step, and her glare deepened. "Yeah, right."

"On the grave of my mother, I have not."

Her expression softened. "Your mother's grave?" She shook her head and her scowl returned. "She's probably alive and well and keeping house in a suburb of Berlin."

Not Berlin, but once in Dresden. Ritter struggled to keep his voice calm. "My mother died when I was twenty. And as far as mind tricks go, you seem to be immune."

"Then you admit you tried."

A sharp pain shot through his jaw, and he realized he had clenched his teeth. He forced them apart. "I admit to trying to keep you safe. Which is why you must leave. Now."

She crossed her arms. "I remember you putting John in a trance at the rave. And—guess what—he doesn't remember anything after you broke in on us. I don't remember much after that either. Kind of suspicious, don't you think?"

"I admit to influencing your policeman, but I did not wipe his memory. Cole must have done that."

"So now you're trying to tell me your homicidal friend is also a hypnotist?"

The door behind Ritter opened. He spun in time to see Cole framed in the doorway. Cole's lips spread into a fanged smile. "No, pretty doctor. He's telling you I'm also a vampire."

Chapter Eighteen

"We're vampires. It's time we started acting like vampires."

Fritz Heine's voice cut the still afternoon, waking Ritter from a doze.

He blinked at the dark fixture above his bed. "Are you two fighting again?" His breath puffed white, but he wasn't cold beneath the thin cotton blanket. The transformation that made him lust for blood also kept him warm.

Bare feet slapped the tile floor. Ritter didn't have to look to know Heine was pacing, from stairs to bed and back again. The footsteps stopped. "What else are we to do? Übel keeps us caged like animals."

"Herr Doktor Übel is our commanding officer." Schmidt sprang off the bed, boots hitting the floor with an angry thud. "If he orders us to stay in the basement, then in the basement we must stay."

"Until we can rejoin our comrades and lead them to glorious victory?"

As usual, Schmidt missed Heine's sarcasm. "Precisely."

"We're not even human anymore. What is a war between mortals to the likes of us?"

"It is our duty to serve the fatherland." Pride seasoned Schmidt's voice. "To think otherwise is shameful; to say otherwise is treason."

"And what will they do if we refuse? Hang us?"

Ritter rolled his legs off the bed and sat on its edge. Heine and Schmidt glared at each other from opposite ends of the room. "Enough, both of you." He turned to Heine. "We are still men. Germany is still our country. Even if we have changed, our duty has not. As for the 'war between mortals,' you know as well as I do that we're not immune to death. Look at what happened to Klug."

Heine shrugged. "Klug was a fool."

"Klug is dead."

"Only because he was stupid enough to stand in the sun."

Ritter sighed. For nearly a month after the disastrous Christmas

party, he had remained in the basement. But the white walls had begun to creep in on him, and early one morning, in the silent hours
before dawn, he slipped out while his comrades slept. While he *thought*
they slept. Klug must have awakened and followed him into the night.
Ritter hadn't heard him, hadn't realized Klug was gone, until he returned an hour later to find him missing. Übel brought in Klug's charred
body later that day, as an object lesson in the dangers of sunlight and
disobedience. Heine was right; Klug had been a fool. "True. But the
point remains that the transformation did not render us immortal.
We are still men, in some ways more vulnerable than most."

Heine and Schmidt both snorted.

"It's true and you know it. All the enemy needs to do is bomb this
house from over our heads. The sun would do the rest."

"But the enemy doesn't know that," said Schmidt. "He would come
after us with guns, and bullets cannot harm us. That is why me must
join the war."

"Nonsense." Heine stalked up to Schmidt. "We don't know we're
immune to bullets. We don't know anything of being vampires—beyond a thirst for blood and a fear of the sun." He reached under his
shirt and pulled out a crucifix. "The old stories are full of lies; but
we'll never learn the truth in this damned basement. We have to leave
and discover for ourselves what it is to be a vampire."

Schmidt sneered at the cross dangling from Heine's fingertips.
"We don't have time to chase Catholic superstitions. Our first duty is
to our *Führer*."

"Our first duty is to ourselves."

The door at the top of the stairs burst open, and Übel hurtled
down the stairs. "They're coming!" His face was as white as the walls,
his hair uncombed, his blue eyes streaked with red. Sweat and enough
fear to make Ritter's teeth itch soured the air around him.

"Calm yourself." Ritter wove power into the words, enough to
soothe Heine and Schmidt, as well as the distraught doctor. "Who is
coming?"

Übel stumbled to a halt at the foot of the stairs. His breathing
smoothed, his heartbeat slowed. "The Americans. They've reached
the west bank of the Rhine."

Heine made a rude noise. "That's nearly three hundred kilometers from here. Why are you panicking now?"

"They know."

A chill Ritter hadn't felt before ran down his neck. "Know what?"

"About the experiment. About you." Übel pulled a folded sheet of
paper from inside his jacket. "Word came today from headquarters
about an English spy ring. Over the last year, the spies stole hundreds
of top-secret papers, among them memos about this project."

The chill grew deeper. "And headquarters thinks the English will
tell the Americans?"

"Headquarters thinks the Americans already know." Though his expression remained calm, fear oozed from Übel's pores. "I must dismantle the experiment, destroy the evidence, and flee."

"Destroy the evidence?" Heine strode up to Übel. "We are the evidence. What are we supposed to do, march out at noon and fry?"

Schmidt's throat worked, as if he were trying to swallow, but he pulled himself to attention. "If duty requires the ultimate sacrifice, an honorable man embraces it."

"A stupid man, you mean."

Face taut with rage, Schmidt lunged at Heine. "You—"

"Silence." Ritter poured power into the word, and the men froze into three breathing, blank-eyed statues. He sank to his bed and buried his face in his palms. What was he to do? Unlike his comrades, he understood how fragile their existence was. All Übel had to do was set the house on fire and make them choose between the flames or the sun. Ritter couldn't let that happen, but he couldn't let his comrades loose on the world, either. He'd wiped the Christmas bloodbath from their minds, but visions of the drained and ravaged girls still haunted him. Left on their own, his comrades would kill again, and soon. No, he had to keep the group together, keep the experiment going until Übel found a way to return their humanity.

He straightened and stood. "Herr Doktor, pack your notes and summon a train."

"A train?" Though flat, the doctor's voice held a hint of question.

"Yes. We must move to a safer location." But where? A place far from the front, but big enough to provide medical equipment and facilities. A small village wouldn't do. They needed a city, but one the enemy wouldn't bomb. A peaceful city, not associated with military industries and the war machine. Ritter smiled. The answer was obvious. "We go to Dresden."

Chapter Nineteen

Waukegan, Illinois
August 24, 2014

Before Ritter could stop him, Cole lunged at Faith. Though he moved with vampire speed, his hands closed around empty air. She had bolted, down the stairs and along the sidewalk toward the white sedan Ritter had driven Friday night.

Cole snarled and dove after her. Hands outstretched, he arced through the air and caught her knees on the way down. Faith crashed to the ground with Cole on top of her. In a heartbeat, Cole flipped her over and went for her throat.

"No!" Ritter poured all his freshly fed power into his voice. "Stop!"

Cole froze, bared fangs inches from Faith's carotid artery.

Faith didn't. Though she had only one arm free, she slammed the heel of that hand into Cole's nose. His head snapped back. Cartilage cracked. Blood spurted. "Get off me," she shouted, but Cole couldn't move, not while Ritter's control held. Kicking and writhing, Faith pulled her hand back to hit him again.

"Faith, wait." Ritter ran toward them. Cole was already fighting his control. Another blow like that would knock him free. "Don't—"

Too late. Fingers outstretched, rigid, she went for his eyes.

Cole screamed and reared back.

One more stride brought Ritter within reach. He grabbed Cole's shoulders and flung him away from Faith. Ritter had forgotten the strength a full stomach gave him. Cole soared off the ground and landed in the street on the other side of the parked cars.

"How did you do that?" Faith was on her feet. Adrenaline flavored the air around her, fear and anger mixed. Her heart pounded, her breath raced. Her forehead was bruised, the tip of her nose scraped and bleeding. She was so beautiful, it made his heart ache.

Ritter took her hand. "Come. Back to my apartment. I can keep you safe there."

She jerked her hand free. "I'm not going anywhere with you."

"But Cole—"

"—is probably a hypnotically induced hallucination. I bet when I get home tonight, there'll be no sign of—" She glanced at her right hand, and her voice died. Raising her arm, she stepped forward and held her hand under the glow of a streetlight. Cole's blood darkened her index and middle finger. She touched the blood with her thumb, and her expression grew troubled. "It feels so real, though. He felt so real." She took a deep breath and lowered her hand. Her cheeks had grown pale, but her voice was brisk. "If he is, call an ambulance. I think I took out an eye."

"Faith—"

"I'm real all right." Cole rose from behind the cars. Blood dripped from his crushed nose and flowed from beneath a closed and sunken left eyelid. His smile revealed all four of his fangs. "I'm going to enjoy killing you."

Ritter stepped in front of Faith. "I won't let you harm her."

"You can't stop me forever."

"I can kill you."

"You're too much of a Boy Scout." Cole stalked through the cars and onto the sidewalk near Ritter's steps. The light from the lobby lit his face, and Faith gasped. Cole's smile broadened. "You pack a mean punch, pretty doctor. Want to see the damage?" He opened his closed lid and a misshapened glob rolled on to his cheek and hung there.

"Dear God." Faith's whisper was half prayer, half sob.

Still smiling, Cole pushed the eye back into its socket and grimaced. "Fucking thing itches."

As if on cue, he began to heal. The blood stopped coursing down Cole's cheeks. Though dried blood still stained his lips and chin, the fresh blood soaked back into his skin, into his nose, into his eye. His nose straightened with a pop, his eyelid filled. He blinked twice, then looked at Ritter through eyes clear, brown, and whole. "All better."

"No. That's...that's..." Faith's breaths were coming in quick shallow gasps.

Keeping one eye on Cole, Ritter turned to her. "I can explain."

"...impossible," she said. And fainted.

❧❧

"Not this time."

The words drifted to Faith from far away. The hushed voice was male and vaguely foreign, a good voice. It kindled a warm glow inside her.

"She's spinning you, man. And you're falling for it."

This voice was deeper, harder, colder. A jolt of fear stripped away the comforting warmth. Faith's eyes flew open, and she found herself staring at a heating duct and a white plaster ceiling. A man leaned over her. Ritter. She was in Ritter's apartment. On his leather couch. Worry lined his forehead. "Are you all right?"

"I don't know." Fragments of memory whirled through Faith's mind, crazy, impossible images. She struggled to sit up. The room spun twice, then settled. The movement made her forehead throb. She touched it and felt a knot as big as a tennis ball. No wonder she had a headache. "What happened? Did I hit my head?"

The lines eased. "In a manner of speaking."

"Cut the amnesia crap."

The hard, cold voice came from behind Ritter and to the right. Wincing at the pain, Faith turned her head. Ritter's crazy friend Cole leaned against the door to the kitchen. "Nothing can save you now."

Ritter spun to face him. "We have an agreement."

"For tonight only. What happens after that depends on the doctor." Cole folded his arms across his chest. "So tell me, pretty doctor. Why shouldn't I kill you?"

"Tell him about your work," Ritter said, turning back to her. "Explain what it is you are trying to do."

The shattered images in Faith's mind suddenly clicked together. Her date with John. The furious drive to Ritter's apartment. Cole's attack, her defense, the miraculous regeneration of his eye. Her fear vanished in a wave of wonder.

Ignoring her pounding head and the unsteady floor, she stood and stumbled toward Cole. His eyebrows lifted in surprise, but Faith rose to tiptoe to palpate the nose that should be broken and examine the eye that should be blind. "How?" She dropped back to her heels and swayed on the tipping floor. "How did you heal so quickly?"

Ritter caught her arm to steady her. "It's a long story."

Cole's gaze swept her face, and the hard lines softened. "You're right, she doesn't know."

"Of course I am right." Ritter slipped an arm around her waist and turned her toward the couch. Faith wanted to argue, to stay and examine Cole further, but her stomach chose that moment to turn inside out. Nausea rolled over her, symptom of a possible concussion. Struggling to keep down her dinner, she let Ritter settle her on the couch.

Gears ground and the cuckoo called five times. Faith had spent most of the night passed out on Ritter's couch. She closed her eyes, leaned back, and concentrated on breathing. One, two, three deep breaths to calm her stomach. When she was sure she wouldn't disgrace herself, she opened her eyes and turned to Ritter. "You said you could explain?"

"Yes." The couch cushion dipped as he sat beside her.

Cole strode into the room and dropped into the easy chair. He leaned back and stretched his legs beneath the coffee table. His lips pulled into a wide, fanged grin. "Yeah, Ritter, explain."

Ritter shot him a look. "You are not helping."

Though his lips only lifted enough make the words, Faith caught a glimpse of too much white. She leaned forward. "Smile."

"What?"

"Smile. I want to see your teeth."

Cole's grin grew broader. "Yeah, smile for the lady."

Ritter leaned forward and put his hand on her arm. "If you would just let me explain—"

"Smile!" Before he could stop her, Faith wrenched her arm free and pushed back his upper lip. Twin fangs glistened where his eye-teeth should have been. Her hand dropped to her lap. "Those aren't fake, are they?"

"No."

"You're both vampires?"

"Yes."

Faith's hands began to tremble. She clasped them together and struggled to stay calm. "That's scientifically impossible."

"How can you say that?" Ritter snapped. "In an era where babes grow in test tubes and the blueprint of humanity is open to revision, how can you say anything is impossible?"

"That's different. In vitro fertilization and genetic research are based on demonstrable fact and testable theory. Vampires are—" She struggled for the right words. "—superstitious nonsense."

"The doctor needs proof." Cole chuckled and ran his tongue over his glistening fangs. "How 'bout I bite her?"

"Shut up." Ritter sounded more tired than angry. "I have better proof to offer." He stood and strode to a bookcase at the end of the room. His fingers trailed across the spines until they rested on a thick black volume. Ritter pulled it out and opened it. "This is Trent's *Diagnosis and Treatment of Rare Diseases*," he said. "I presume you are familiar with it. Care to hear what it says about Stoker's syndrome?"

The room grew uncomfortably hot. Faith shifted on the couch. "I know what it says. I know all about the sun sensitivity, dental malformations, and digestive problems characteristic of the disease. I also know that, in the past, the victims of Stoker's were thought to be the progeny of vampires. Innocent people were burned because their babies suffered from the disease. But that was in the past. We know better now."

"Sometimes the past is right." Ritter returned the book to the shelf and stood a moment, facing it. "Your brother died of Stoker's syndrome, correct?"

"Yes. And that proves my point. My parents weren't vampires."

"No." Ritter slowly turned to face her. His expression hadn't changed, but it suddenly seemed a mask. Ancient and exhausted eyes peered through it. "Your grandfather was."

"My grandfather? That's crazy. Grandfather Allister was a Baptist minister. As for my zeyde—Grandfather Meyer—he was the gentlest man in the world. He always said he was the world's lousiest soldier.

He fainted at the sight of blood."

"Meyer was the soldier who liberated your grandmother?"

Faith nodded.

"No doubt he was a fine man, but he was not your grandfather."

"How can you say that?"

"Because I knew your grandfather."

"Zaide died when I was fifteen. You were what, three years old?" Faith jumped off the couch. "I've heard enough. I'm out of here."

She turned toward the door, but Cole was already there. "You have to get through me first."

"When was your mother born?" Ritter had stepped beside her. His voice was gentle. "How soon after the wedding?"

Faith swallowed. "Only a few months, but it was hard to get a marriage permit, and they were young and—"

"Your mother was born in the fall of '45, wasn't she? Late September or early October?"

"Yes, but—"

"The Americans liberated Dachau and the surrounding area in April. You do the math."

She never had. The comfort of family legend had kept her from adding the dates together. Now she did, and the result made her stomach hurt. "Poor Bubbie. She got pregnant in Dachau, didn't she? No wonder she ranted about monsters. Monsters and...vampires." The strength drained from Faith's legs, and she dropped back to the couch. "How did you know?"

Ritter's sigh carried the weight of decades. "Because I was there."

Faith wanted to dismiss his claim as impossible. Ritter was lying, he had to be, but he sounded so sad, so sincere. It was hard not to believe him. She realized she was slowly shaking her head, back and forth. She lifted her gaze to his. "Are you doing that hypnosis thing on me again?"

He barked a short, bitter laugh. "My dear Faith, if 'that hypnosis thing' worked on you, we wouldn't be having this conversation."

"I didn't believe him either, the first time he told me his age." Cole sauntered back to the chair and sat down. He rested his hands on his knees and leaned forward. The light reflected off his fangs. "It's true, pretty doctor. Ritter was a German soldier in World War II."

Faith couldn't keep the horror from her voice. "A guard at Dachau?"

"No!" Ritter sounded so offended, she had to believe him. "I was a soldier, ordered to Dachau—the town, not the camp—to take part in a secret assignment. I thought to work on a new kind of tank, but what they wanted was a new kind of soldier."

"Are you telling me the Nazis tried to create an army of vampires? That's crazy."

"Not crazy, desperate. We were losing the war and had to do something." He sighed again and sat beside her. "They didn't mean to create vampires. There was a prisoner in Dachau who was incredibly strong, incredibly fast. Who refused to waste away, no matter how they starved him. The *Werhmacht* decided it needed soldiers like that. Elite shock troops to push back the invasion of the fatherland."

Ritter looked up. "I used to wonder why he didn't leave the prison, just walk into the night. Maybe he was too afraid."

Cole snorted. "He probably liked the atmosphere and the all-night buffet dining. Not everyone is as squeamish as you are."

Ritter shot him an annoyed glance but kept talking. "Doctors back then didn't know about viruses or genes or Stoker's syndrome, but they realized the secret lay in the prisoner's blood. One day, guards fell upon him while he slept and drained him. They put the blood in vials and injected the vials into men already proven to be strong and resilient. But the experiment failed. Instead of creating superior soldiers, it killed most of the men and left the rest monsters. One hundred began the experiment; only four survived to its end. I was one. Your grandfather was another."

Faith stared at Ritter. He didn't look crazy. What if his story were true? While there was no record of a Stoker's syndrome victim surviving to adulthood, it was theoretically possible. What if the Nazis had found an adult Stoker's victim? To survive so long, he'd have to be strong and tough. According to her theory, his blood could be used to infect others with the virus. According to her theory, an adult strong and healthy enough to survive the initial acute stage of the disease could adapt to the permanent abnormalities Stoker's caused. According to her theory, the abnormalities could be passed on genetically to the survivor's children and their grandchildren. Ritter's story would explain why her brother was born with Stoker's and why her DNA showed some of the distinctive markers. Her huge orthodontia bills as a child, her sensitivity to the sun, even her garlic allergy: it all fit.

Faith buried her face in her hands. The story even explained why her mother looked so young at fifty, before she developed skin cancer.

She'd told Ritter about her brother, but she'd never mentioned her mother. She'd told nobody the results of her DNA scan. Ritter couldn't have used it to make up his story. Maybe it was true.

No way. Faith lowered her hands. She didn't remember much from the night she'd been drugged. She might have mentioned her mother or her grandmother. A good con man could take Bubbie's story, extrapolate a bit, and come up with something just plausible enough to be convincing. Faith didn't believe in vampires, but she did believe in con men. She turned to Ritter. "What do you want from me?"

Ritter's smile shook her certainty. He looked so relieved. "Tell Cole about your work. Explain about viruses and birth defects. Prove to him that you seek the cure, not the disease."

"Tell Cole about my work, huh?" Banat had insisted she sign a confidentiality agreement, that she keep her work at the lab secret until he patented the viruses she engineered. She'd thought Banat was being paranoid, but maybe she was wrong. "In general, or do you want details?"

The chair creaked as Cole sat back. "As much detail as you can give me. Unlike this fossil here, I've kept up with the times. I'll follow your explanation."

Anger knotted Faith's gut. She just bet he would. It was beginning to look like this was all a trick to steal her work. The question was, how to give them enough information so they'd let her go, but not enough to compromise her research.

A gentle touch on her arm pulled her out of her thoughts. Ritter was looking at her, brow furrowed. "Are you all right?"

God, it was like he could read her mind. Faith forced a shaky smile. "Not really. How would you feel if you just learned your grandfather was a vampire?" The words made her skin go cold. She didn't believe Ritter's crazy story, and yet . . . "He's not still around, is he?"

The lines in Ritter's forehead deepened. Then he sighed, and his expression cleared. "No, he died long ago."

She didn't believe his story, but relief washed over her anyway. "Good."

Cole growled. "Cut the chatter, and tell me about this work of yours."

Faith nodded. Now for a tightrope walk. "If you follow developments in viral genetic research, you've heard of my boss Miles Odell and his work isolating viral strains."

Cole's nostrils flared. "I know all about Odell's work."

"Well—" Faith groped for a way to say as little as possible, as convincingly as possible. "According to my theory, one of those strains is the virus responsible for Stoker's syndrome. Are you familiar with the disease?"

A quick, bitter laugh. "Yeah."

"So far, my research has shown that embryonic cells infected with the virus show genetic changes consistent with the disease. Now I'm trying to develop a countervirus, one that would return the genetic code to its original pattern." Heart pounding, Faith stood. A faint line of light had appeared on the floor below the window. It gave her an idea and hope. "All my notes are in my briefcase. Let me get them, and I can show you my progress so far."

Cole rose to his feet. Even with the coffee table between them, he towered over her. "You're not going anyplace without me."

Faith pointed toward the window. "You can't come, the sun's already up."

"A little sunlight won't hurt me. Come on," Cole grabbed her arm and started pulling her toward the door.

"Stop." Ritter appeared beside them. "You can endure the sun, but I cannot."

Faith fought down a surge of triumph. She was right. They were going to stick to their story that they were vampires. In the excitement of the moment, Cole had forgotten, but Ritter had covered for him. Very clever. And very good for her. Their story was a two-edged lie, one she could use against them. She slid her feet sidewise, intent on edging around the table.

Cole glowered at Ritter, but he let go of Faith's arm. "So stay home. I already promised not to hurt her."

"You promised not to hurt her last night. It's day now, and knowing you, the promise has expired."

"Damn it, Ritter." Cole's sudden anger drove Faith back a step. "She's a fucking scientist. So she didn't know everything Odell was up to—she's still dirty."

"This woman is under my protection, and I will not let you harm her."

Cole stared at Ritter. The anger drained from his gaze. "This isn't about the doctor, is it? This is about Greta."

"Greta?" Faith looked from Cole's now compassionate expression to Ritter's stony one. "Your car?"

Ritter shook his head. "This has nothing to do with Greta."

"You promised to protect her, and you couldn't. Now you're determined to protect the pretty doctor. Damn it, Ritter." This time, his voice was almost gentle. "You picked a hell of a time to go soft on me."

A sharp and edgy feeling—curiosity? jealousy?—pricked Faith's heart. She turned to Ritter. "Who is Greta?"

"A woman I knew. She died long ago."

"She been haunting you ever since. Let it go, man. It wasn't your fault."

It was too weird, hearing Ritter's monstrous friend spout pop psychology. Faith slid another step closer to the door. "My briefcase is in the car. I'll just run out and get it."

Cole was in front of the door before she'd taken another step. He had to be on something. No normal person could move that fast. Of course if he *were* a vampire…Faith shook the notion out of her head. She was a scientist for Christ's sake; she refused to believe in fairy tales.

His mouth spread in a snarl. "You're not going anywhere."

"Yes, she is." A warm draft stirred Faith's arms. It seemed to be coming from Ritter. "Step aside and let her pass."

"She's playing you. There are no notes. She just wants to get out of here." But Cole moved away from the door.

"Perhaps, but she will return." Ritter turned to Faith. "Even if you don't believe my story, can you risk abandoning the possibility that it might be true? Do you want to lose the opportunity to study two adult survivors of Stoker's syndrome, to examine our blood, our bodies' accommodations to the disease? Bring back your notes, prove to Cole that you seek a cure, and we will help you with your research."

Cole shot a glance at Ritter, full of dawning respect. "Yeah, and Odell might want to take a look at us too."

Something passed between the two men. Faith didn't know what, and at the moment she didn't care. All that mattered was that they were letting her go. She darted for the door. It was unlocked. She threw it open and ran out.

No one stopped her on the stairs. No one stopped her in the lobby. Expecting large, impossibly strong hands to seize her at any moment, Faith burst out of the building and sprinted for her car. Grab the keys, open the door, turn the ignition. Slam the accelerator. The wheels squealed as she took the corner too fast, but the farther she got from Ritter's apartment, the safer she felt. Her breathing slowed, and the tension began to drain from her shoulders.

She was safe. All she had to do was return to the research campus and stay there. Thanks to Banat's paranoia, it was hidden, both physically—behind carefully maintained woods—and on paper—behind a maze of false corporations. Ritter and his murderous friend would never find her. As long as she stayed on the grounds, she'd be safe. Stir crazy, maybe, but safe. She'd never have to see Ritter again, never have to look into his young-ancient eyes, or feel his velvet voice flow over her. A pang of regret tainted her relief, but she pushed it away. She never wanted to hear his lies about vampires and her grandmother again. Not ever.

Faith recognized one of Waukegan's main thoroughfares and turned onto it. It was early enough that the roads were still deserted. Less than an hour later, she pulled into a parking space behind her new apartment. Leaden legs carried her around the building and over her threshold. She stumbled through curtain-filtered light to her bed. It only took a moment to strip off her sundress and fall between the sheets.

Her eyes closed. In the darkness, pairs of letters danced: swirling As and Ts, Cs and Gs, the building blocks of DNA. Music started, an odd, beeping tune, and the letters waltzed into a twisting ladder. The ladder spun, and Faith saw a baby clinging to it as it dipped and twirled, a tiny infant with translucent skin and a tuft of black hair. Her brother. His head turned; his mouth opened, revealing long, jagged teeth. "Help me!" he cried. Faith jumped forward, but the ladder jerked him away before she could reach him.

"No!" Faith shot off the bed, heart beating so fast it made her chest hurt. The letters were gone, but the beeping continued. It was her phone. She fumbled for the receiver. "Yes?"

"Faith? This is Miles. I dropped by your lab this morning to go over that trial with you, but you weren't there. Is anything wrong?"

Faith squinted at her alarm clock. It read 8:16 AM. She'd gotten maybe two hours' sleep. She stifled a groan. "No, just had a late night.

Give me time to shower, and I'll be there. Say around nine?"

"Take your time." Miles sounded disgustingly cheerful. "Nine-thirty would be fine." He hung up before Faith could say good-bye.

Faith settled the receiver on the hook. Knowing Miles, he'd want to see the pretrial data. She'd hoped to have more time before showing it to him, time to discover if her anomalous DNA reflected error or reality. Oh well, she'd just admit to breaking the pipette and ask Miles to draw another sample. That way she could forget about the whole thing.

Her sheets clung to her legs, damp and twisted from the nightmare. Faith sighed. Who was she trying to kid? She couldn't just forget her genetic profile. She untangled herself, climbed out of bed, and stumbled into the shower. Damn Ritter and his stupid story; she couldn't forget that, either. If the profile turned out to be correct, she'd have to examine him. She refused to believe he was a vampire, but she'd have to prove his claim a lie. She owed it to herself. She owed it to her brother.

Chapter Twenty

Lake County, Illinois
September 2, 2014

Faith squeezed her eyes shut and prayed the data on the screen would change by the time she opened them. Didn't. She had waited a long, nerve-wracking week and all of Labor Day weekend until it was finally time to check her trial samples. She'd slipped her cell nuclei in with the samples from the virus-infected cells and had sent them to the electron microscope to be processed by a different technician. The data came back picture-perfect and in record time. Faith would have been delighted if it hadn't been for the results. Her DNA showed the same anomalies as before.

She pulled her genetic profile from the trial folder and saved it in a separate file. Clicking off the computer, she sat back and rubbed her aching forehead. She'd almost talked herself into believing the initial results were due to lab error, but she could fool herself only so far. She didn't want to admit it, but the evidence was consistent with Ritter's ridiculous story. So much for avoiding him for the rest of her life. She had to examine him.

Unexpected warmth filled Faith's chest. Though she tried to squash the feeling, it rose into a smile. She wanted to see Ritter again. The exam would undoubtedly expose him as a fraud, but she didn't really believe he was a con man. He seemed too honorable to use her to get to Banat's lab. She expected the exam to confirm her original diagnosis—that Ritter was a drug addict. She'd read that the modern hallucinogens left some users with lingering delusions. Maybe she could show Ritter the article and use the results of her exam to talk him into a drug treatment program.

The absurdity of the notion hit her like a winter gale. She didn't believe in vampires, but was a psycho-druggy with a sense of honor any more realistic? Drug addicts would do anything for another fix. She knew that. The fact that he was delusional made Ritter even more unpredictable.

A sharp rap yanked her away from her thoughts. She swung her chair around in time to see Miles open her door and barge into her office. "I was just in the electron microscope lab. Jane told me you'd picked up the results for the trial I have you running. How do they look?"

Faith's headache cranked up a notch. "The door was closed for a reason."

"I knocked, didn't I?" Miles' puzzled expression pulled into a frown. "What's the matter? Did something go wrong with the experiment?"

Faith sighed. Maybe she should invest in a nice set of padlocks. "No, though about half the samples showed genetic changes consistent with Stoker's syndrome. Good for our research, not so great for Banat's liability concerns."

"His problem, not ours." Miles stepped toward the door, then looked back over his shoulder. "You haven't seemed yourself this last week. Is everything all right?"

Ritter's crazy story must be worrying her more than she realized, if even Miles had noticed. It hadn't occurred to her to run the story past her boss, but maybe she should. After all, he'd been studying Stoker's since she was in diapers. She leaned forward in her chair. "Miles, have you ever heard of an adult contracting full-blown Stoker's and surviving?"

His brow bunched into deep ridges. "Why do you ask?"

There was something in his tone, an undercurrent of anger or fear. Faith shrugged. "I was just wondering. I mean, if my theory is correct, someone at some point must have contracted Stoker's and survived long enough to have a baby."

His brow smoothed. He walked over to her desk and perched on the edge. "There's nothing recorded in the literature, but you're probably right. According to our theory, though it would be rare, the Stoker's virus must occasionally infect adults. My guess is, the effects of the virus are much milder in the adult and have routinely been either ignored or misdiagnosed."

"*Our* theory?" Miles just looked at her, a parody of innocence on his face. Faith hadn't eaten or slept well all week. Her worry, hunger, and fatigue suddenly exploded into temper. She shot out of her chair. "According to *my* theory, Miles, not yours, not ours. Mine."

Miles waved away her protest. "Don't get so excited. I only meant—"

"I know what you meant. You may have isolated the virus, but we're testing *my* theory. And *my* theory predicts that the Stoker's virus must occasionally strike adults. Well, guess what—I found one."

"Where, in a supermarket tabloid? There's been nothing published about Stoker's in any legitimate journal in months."

"I'm not talking about an article, Miles. I'm talking about a living, breathing, Stoker's survivor."

He jumped off the desk and grabbed her shoulders. "Where?"

"Let me go." She twisted from his grip. Her shoulders ached where his fingers had dug into her skin. She rubbed the sore spot and glared at him. "What's wrong with you?"

Miles lowered his arms and took a deep breath. "I'm just excited. An adult with proven Stoker's syndrome would help confirm your theory. I'd like to meet him and examine his medical records."

Faith tipped her head to one side. Miles' words were reasonable enough, but he looked and sounded scared. She couldn't figure out why. It wasn't because she was angry. Miles had seen her mad before, and he usually met her anger with a supercilious smirk. "Nothing's proven, yet. I haven't even examined him. But if you want to be here when I do—"

"Not here; you can't bring him to the lab." Panic simmered under the words. Miles glanced around the room and leaned close enough for his whisper to tickle Faith's ear. "Banat wouldn't like it."

Suddenly, Miles' reaction began to make sense. He was afraid Banat would cut off their funding. And Banat just might, if he thought their research jeopardized his facility's precious security. "We'll get Banat's okay first. If we explain to him what a breakthrough this is, I'm sure he'll understand. I'll conduct the screening exam in Ritter's apartment and only bring him here if the initial results are promising."

As she spoke, Miles grew as white as computer paper. "Impossible," he whispered.

"It can't hurt to ask."

Miles blinked. "What? Oh, yes, Banat. I'll tell him right away." He walked to the door, opened it, then turned back to Faith. "Tell me before you bring anyone here. No matter who, no matter why. Understand?"

"Yes, but—"

"No 'buts.' Just tell me." Miles stepped over the threshold and disappeared down the hall before the door closed behind him.

Faith dropped into her chair. Of all the conversations she'd had with Miles, that had to be the strangest. Shaking her head, she turned to her desk, picked up the phone, and dialed for an outside line. A moment later, the electronic operator was reciting Ritter's phone number. Faith chose the automatic dial option and waited until his voice came on the line. "Leave a message. I will return your call."

She had to smile. Even Ritter's answering machine was bossy. "Hello, Ritter? This is Faith. Are you there?" She waited. Nothing. Of course. With the hours he kept, he'd have to sleep in the middle of the day. "I thought over what you said last week, and you're right, I do need to examine you. It will take me a day to get the equipment together. Can we meet at your apartment tomorrow evening, say around eight? Leave me a message at…" She rattled off her old phone number. Her voice mail was still active, and this way, Banat couldn't accuse her of breaking security rules. "Let me know. Thanks. Bye."

She had a lot to do before tomorrow evening. Clicking on her computer, she pulled up a blank document and started composing a list. She was halfway through it before she remembered that Ritter wasn't the only one she'd be examining. She was going to have to examine his psychotic friend Cole, too.

≈≈

"I told you Faith would return." Ritter hit the replay button and handed the phone to Cole.

As he listened to Faith's message, Cole's frown melted into a broad grin. "You sneaky bastard. Are we going in tonight?"

Ritter took the phone and hung it on the charger. "Tomorrow. I called Faith and left a message that eight is too early. She should arrive here after ten. Her stubborn curiosity will keep her ringing the bell for at least an hour, giving us plenty of time for us to find Odell, learn his plans, and destroy the facility if necessary."

"Got the address?"

"Not yet, but I will." Ritter reached into his pocket and pulled out the matchbook he had carried since the rave. "I already checked the number she left on her message. It connects to her old apartment. This is her new number. We can use it to find the address."

Cole snatched the matchbook from Ritter's hand. "You've been sitting on this over a week. Why?"

"I don't want Faith hurt." Ritter strode to the computer and woke it with a keystroke. He opened the browser and typed in one of his favorite websites. "Find out anything about anyone," it claimed. Ritter had used it before to keep track of comrades and old enemies. He held out his hand. "Give me the number."

Cole closed his fist around the matches. "You want her out of there before we go in, don't you? That's why you set this whole thing up. Not to get Odell, but to protect the lady."

"As long as we stop Odell, what does it matter?" Ritter snapped his fingers. "The number."

The computer hummed. The cuckoo clock ticked. Cole slapped the matchbook into Ritter's palm. "This better work."

"It will." Ritter set the matchbook on the desktop. His fingers flew across the keys. Moments later, the computer chimed and a PO box number appeared on the screen. Ritter frowned.

"Give me that." Cole grabbed the matchbook and picked up the phone. He dialed and a murmured conversation followed. Finally Cole hung up and turned to face Ritter. An arrogant smirk had replaced his scowl. "Your pretty doctor's working out of B&S Developments, just west of Grayslake on Route 120. Here's the address."

The matchbook now contained a scrawled address under Faith's number. Ritter took it from Cole. "I called the phone company for the address before you came, but the young woman refused to help me.

Have you learned to project the power of your voice over the phone?"

Cole chuckled. "No. A lady friend of mine works for Ameritech. You should get a steady girl, Ritter." His grin spread to show all four of his fangs. "Some women like their lovin' dangerous."

Ritter shook his head. Vampires and love didn't mix, he knew that. Cole had been lucky so far, but his luck wouldn't last. Someday he would go too far with one of his women, lose control, and drain her beyond recovery. Ritter turned toward the computer with a sigh. Between the dangerous games Cole played with women and his penchant for hunting high-profile prey, it was amazing he had lasted as long he had.

A quick series of clicks brought up a map site. Ritter typed in the address, and moments later his printer spat out a map and a list of possible ways to get from his apartment to Faith's lab.

Cole leaned over his shoulder. "That where we're going?"

"Yes. Come here tomorrow, just before dusk. We will leave after the sun sets and take one of the less-direct routes." Ritter allowed himself a smile. "We don't want to run into Faith."

"I still think we should go in tonight. If your lady doctor mentions us to Odell, he might bolt."

"Which is why we must wait. If Odell knows of Faith's appointment to see us, tomorrow night is the one night he will feel safe enough to return to the lab. With any luck, we will catch him in the middle of packing his notes."

"And get everything at once. You're a smart son-of-a-bitch, I'll give you that." Cole's expression sobered. "We still have to deal with the pretty doctor. It's not just her work, Ritter. Even if she's not helping Odell grow baby vamps, when she comes back to find the lab smashed and Odell's dead body, she'll know we did it. I say we hang around the lab and take her out when she comes back."

"No."

"If we don't shut her up, she'll sic the cops on us: probably that bulldog you saddled me with last week." Cole swung his arms in a gesture that took in the whole room. "I'm used to disappearing, but you've put down roots. You ready to give all this up, just to protect her? She's the enemy, a scientist, like the bastards that made us. Fuck her all you want, but—"

Ritter jumped to his feet. "You will not speak of Faith that way."

Cole's eyes widened, and he let out a long, low whistle. "You're in love with her."

"Don't be absurd."

"You're fucking in love with her. Damn it, Ritter, I thought you had more sense."

"Love has nothing to do with it. I—" The words caught in Ritter's throat. Cole was right; he did love Faith. Not as he loved Greta. Greta had been a child: a beautiful, docile child. She basked in his adoration and accepted his suggestions with flattering trust. Greta had been a joy and a precious burden. A responsibility he had failed utterly.

Faith was a woman: intelligent, independent, aggravating. She rarely agreed with him and never did what he told her to do. He found her annoying, intriguing, and...irresistible. He loved everything about her, from her curly hair to her sharp tongue, from her deceptively lean body to her brilliant mind. He relished their arguments, the way her eyes flashed, the way her lips tipped up before she made a strong point. Better yet, in those precious moments when she had stolen his control, Faith had made him feel almost human. He still loved Greta, but, heaven help him, he loved Faith more. And he would not fail her. Even if it meant losing her forever.

"I will not let you harm her. She searches for a cure, Cole. If she continues her work, maybe she will find it."

"Right. And then you'll go out at dawn and watch the sunrise together." Cole's sigh sounded a hundred years old. "I'll wait until tomorrow to go after Odell. You better pray your pretty doctor gives us time to find the bastard and smash his lab. I won't go after her, but all bets are off if she gets in my way."

A tightness in Ritter's chest, that he hadn't noticed until that moment, loosened. Cole's word was good, and he had just given it. As long as Faith didn't interfere with Cole's vendetta against Odell, she was safe. "Fair enough."

"In the meantime, I need to eat. Want to come?"

Hunger gnawed at Ritter's gut, but he ignored it. He had eaten more than his fill a little over a week ago. He might long for more, but like a great snake, he didn't need it to survive. "No. You go ahead."

Cole gazed at him a long moment, then shook his head. "Didn't your mamma teach you not to do important work on an empty stomach? I still got those two pints from the blood bank. I'll bring 'em by later."

"That's not necessary."

"Yeah it is, if you plan to be my backup." Cole's mouth spread into a small, but genuine, smile. "You get weak and wimpy when you're hungry."

Ritter's lips twitched. "Wimpy?"

"Whiny, too. See you later." With a wave, Cole strode out of the living room. A moment later, Ritter heard the front door close.

He put the computer to sleep, grabbed his keys from the table, and turned off the living room lights. It was too warm and restless an evening to stay home. Grabbing the directions to Faith's lab, Ritter left his apartment and jogged the three blocks to Greta. Tomorrow was still the best day to hunt Odell, but it wouldn't hurt to do a little reconnaissance tonight. He could verify the map and find the best routes for getting in and out of the laboratory complex. He might even find Faith. It was foolish, but he longed to see her. Cole was right. If they succeeded tomorrow, Ritter would have to disappear. Tonight was his only chance to say good-bye.

⁓ ⁓

Faith stepped from the laboratory building and paused to let the breeze warm the air-conditioned chill from her skin. It was a lovely night, too hazy for stars, but a half moon dangled just above the tree-tops. Its glow silvered the leaves before disappearing in the florescent glare of the parking lot.

Though it was well past midnight, she was tempted to stay up and go for a walk. The laboratory and apartment buildings, parking lots, and supply sheds of Banat's research campus were surrounded by acres of park-like woods, laced with paths and dotted with ponds. In the last, sleepless week, she'd explored the woods near her apartment and discovered a field of prairie flowers. Tonight she could check out the paths on the other side of the lab.

A yawn caught her by surprise. No, as restless as she felt, she was too tired to wander. She needed to go to bed, to at least try to sleep. Tomorrow was going to be a very long day.

A breath of cold air tickled the back of her neck. She glanced over her shoulder, but the door to the lab was still closed. The breeze died, but the tickle continued. Someone was watching her.

She swept her gaze across the empty parking lot and peered into the shadows under the trees beyond. She wasn't frightened, not really. There were too many guards around for her to be in any danger. Still, it was creepy, being watched by invisible eyes. "Who's there?"

"Don't be afraid." The familiar velvet voice came from a shadow near the corner of the building.

"Ritter?" The name stuck in her throat and came out a whisper.

He stepped into the parking lot. "Hello, Faith."

Her heart ricocheted off her sternum. The harsh lights that bleached her face to a two-dimensional mask brightened Ritter's to unearthly radiance. It caressed his lips, glinted off his eyes, and ha-loed his hair. His polo shirt hugged his shoulders. His jeans molded around the muscles in his thighs. How dare he look so good? "What are you, some kind of stalker? How did you find me? What are you doing here?"

"So many questions. Do you want answers to them all?"

"Just tell me what you want."

"You." Ritter strolled to her. "I want to talk to you."

"Couldn't you wait until tomorrow? I'm coming to your apartment. Unless—" Faith swallowed. "You haven't changed your mind about the exam, have you?"

"No. But I need to see you tonight. Tomorrow evening will…" Something—pain, longing, maybe both—darkened his eyes. "…change your perception of me."

He looked so lost, so vulnerable, like one of Peter Pan's boys, who wanted to go home but couldn't. Faith laid her right hand on his arm. His skin was cool, the muscles beneath it rigid. "The exam won't change anything."

Ritter shook his head. "After tomorrow, everything will change. I will become a subject for your investigation." His smooth voice trembled. He grasped her left hand and lifted her knuckles to his lips. "Please, *Liebchen*, let me spend one last night with you as a man."

From anyone else, it would have been a come-on, and a lame one, at that; but Ritter wasn't just anyone. He wasn't trying to talk his way into her bed. He was afraid she'd turn him away.

Faith trailed her fingers down his right arm until she could give his hand a squeeze. "I was going to take a walk before turning in. Want to come?"

Ritter's smile was blinding. Again, too much white. Faith pushed the thought from her mind. Tomorrow was soon enough to worry about that. Ritter was right, she should know him better as a person before she made him part of her research. Holding both his hands, she nodded toward an opening in the trees. "There's a bench down that path. We could talk there."

Ritter let go of her right hand but clasped the left one tighter. He turned toward the woods. "Lead on."

A few feet down the path, darkness closed around them. The lights stopped at the edge of the parking lot, and thick leaves blocked all but the occasional splash of moonlight. After working so many late hours, Faith was used to walking in the dark. The trickle of light through the leaves was enough for her to make out the bumps and turns in the path, but she was surprised that Ritter didn't have more trouble. He strolled beside her, as confident as if it were midafternoon.

The path dipped and wound through a hollow, then broke free of the trees and rose to a moon-kissed vista. A manicured lawn spread from the trees and curled around a small pond. Fireflies danced over the grass to a symphony of crickets.

"Beautiful." The word whispered past her ear, even fainter than the breeze.

"It is, isn't it? Whoever designed the complex did a nice job on the landscaping."

"I wasn't talking about the landscape."

Faith turned. Ritter was staring at her, eyes glittering. "Moonlight becomes you, *Fräulein Doktor*."

He released her hand and bracketed her face between his palms. His fingers felt cool against her cheeks. Ritter leaned forward and brushed his lips over hers. It was a tiny kiss, short and chaste, but it burned the strength from Faith's legs. She stumbled back. "That bench I told you about? It's over there." She pointed toward the pond. A bench just long enough for two sat on its bank.

"Come." Ritter wrapped his hand around hers and led her to the bench. "After you."

Faith sat and Ritter sat beside her. "So, what do you want to talk about?" she asked.

"You."

The answer surprised a laugh out of her. "Me? You know all about me."

"I know much about Faith Allister, the scientist. Tonight, I want to learn about Faith Allister, the woman."

"Only if you'll tell me about Todd Ritter, the man."

Ritter's smile was small and sad. "If you wish. But you first. What is the one thing, in all the world, that you most desire?" Faith opened her mouth to answer, but he raised his hand. "Not as a researcher, but as a woman."

Faith closed her mouth. He was right: her first impulse had been to tell him about her work. She shook her head. When she thought about it, her life was awfully one-sided. "I'm not sure," she said finally.

"There must be something."

Ritter stretched his arm along the back of the bench. His hand cupped her shoulder, pulled her close. Faith found herself leaning against his side, her head pillowed against his sleeve. "Well, when I was little, I wanted a house like Bubbie's."

"Your French Jewish grandmother?"

"Yes. She had the prettiest house. It was tiny, white with blue shingles, and had a yard full of flowers. Inside it always smelled like cookies. When I was a girl, I visited every summer." Faith smiled at the memory. "If I could have anything, I'd choose a house like Bubbie's, a husband like Zaide, and a baby all my own."

A deep croak punctuated the cricket song. "A sweet dream." Ritter's voice was low, barely above a whisper. "I hope you attain it someday."

Faith tipped her head to look at his face. "What's yours, the thing you want more than anything else in the world?"

He smiled. "You."

She elbowed him in the ribs. "I'm serious. I told you my secret longing; I want to hear yours. What is it you want more than anything else in the world?"

His smile died. He sighed and looked out over the water. The sadness Faith had glimpsed in his eyes filled his voice. "When I was a boy, I wanted to be a mechanic and open my own garage. I planned to rise every dawn and work hard all day, until I became rich enough to marry my sweetheart."

"Greta?"

He tilted his head and gazed into her eyes. "Yes."

"What happened?"

"She died." The words were flat, emotionless.

Faith reached up and traced the faint lines framing his mouth.

"Cole said it wasn't your fault."

He jerked from her touch. "Cole wasn't there."

"What happened?"

Ritter was quiet for so long, Faith began to wonder if he would answer. When he did speak, she could barely hear him over the crickets. "I worked in the city; she lived in the country. She came to see me." His lips twisted into a heart-wrenching smile. "A surprise visit."

"Something happened to her in the city?"

"Yes. An...accident. If it hadn't been for me, she wouldn't have been there."

"Oh, Ritter." Faith hugged him, hard. "Cole's right. You shouldn't blame yourself."

"Perhaps not, but old habits die hard." Ritter wrapped her in his arms and held her close, cheek against his chest. She shut her eyes and let herself float on his slow, steady breaths. Finally, he kissed the top of her head and let go. "No more sad stories. I brought a present."

A sharp stab of pleasure shot through her. She sat back. "For me?"

"Of course for you." Ritter reached behind his head. He was wearing something around his neck, she realized, something on a fine-link chain. He unhooked the clasp and took it off. An oval pendant shone in the moonlight: a locket with a pair of entwined rosebuds engraved on the lid.

"Oh, Ritter, it's beautiful, but—"

"I've carried it a long time. Now it is yours."

She shook her head. "I can't accept it. Tomorrow you'll become part of my study. It wouldn't be appropriate."

"Then return my gift tomorrow. Tonight you are just a woman, remember? And I am just a man. For tonight, accept this as a token of my...admiration."

She meant to refuse, but she couldn't resist the longing in his voice, the sorrow in his eyes. Ritter fastened the chain around her neck, then dipped his head and brought his lips to hers. They lingered this time, softened, warmed. He brushed his tongue against her mouth, and she opened it. But instead of deepening the kiss, he moved it. He covered her face in kisses, her cheeks, her temples, the bridge of her nose, the line of her jaw. Her skin burned where his lips touched. One hand moved behind her head, the other cupped her breast. The kisses moved down her throat. Their heat swept through her and pulsed between her legs.

He nuzzled aside her shirt, and something sharp caught on her collar bone. Faith gasped.

Ritter pulled back. His eyes were huge and black. His breath came in open-mouthed pants that showed the ends of needle-pointed fangs. With his moon-enhanced pallor, he looked every bit the vampire. In a distant corner of her mind, Faith waited for fear, but none came. The grip on her head tightened, then fell away. Ritter's hands dropped to his sides. "I should go."

Faith reached up and touched the warm trickle where Ritter had nicked her skin. She looked at her bloodstained finger and then at Ritter. She'd never paid much attention to vampire lore, but she was pretty sure they weren't supposed to look horrified when they bit someone. "Walk me home first?"

Confusion wrinkled his brow. "Are you sure?"

"Positive." He just sat there, so Faith took his hand. "You're an enigma, Todd Ritter, but I know one thing. You're no monster."

He dropped his gaze. "I wish you were right."

"I am for tonight, at least. Remember, I'm just a woman and you're just a man? Be a man, and walk me home."

His head rose. His lips twitched. "How can I refuse such a gracious invitation?" He stood and draped her hand across his arm. "Which way?"

"Back down the path and across the parking lot. I'm in 2B."

Their feet fell into rhythm as they walked to the apartment. They didn't speak, and a comfortable silence settled over them. It didn't break it until they stood by her front door. Ritter took her hand from his arm and held it. "Goodnight, Faith." He kissed her cheek.

"You're not getting off that easy." She pulled him closer, and wrapped her arms around his neck. Careful of his oversized canines, she kissed him: a real, open-lipped, tongue-darting kiss. He stiffened and then sighed into her. His arms enveloped her, his tongue danced with hers. Faith was hot and breathless when their lips finally parted. "Stay with me tonight."

"Oh, *Liebchen*. If only I could." He kissed her forehead, lowered his arms, and stepped back. "Good-bye, Faith."

"The night's not over yet. Why won't you stay?"

His smile was a hundred years old. "Because, dearest Faith, I am not a man. No matter how much we both pretend, I never will be."

Chapter Twenty-One

Dresden, Saxony
February 10, 1945

Frantic footsteps pounded outside Ritter and his comrades' new prison. The door flew open, and Übel burst into the room.

The deserted warehouse the doctor had found for them in Dresden was larger than the basement, with a maze of crates along the back wall and a door with chinks that let in burning bits of light. Luckily, the weather had been cloudy since they arrived in Dresden a week ago: cloudy, windy, and chill.

Übel paused just inside the doorway, panting, his breath white and flavored with fear. He clutched a telegram in his gloved fist. "They know!"

"Know what?" Heine lay on his cot, eyes closed. "What are you pestering us with now?"

"Yes, what is it?" Ritter swung his legs off his cot and stood.

"The enemy knows where we are." Übel scuttled across the room and thrust the telegram at Ritter. "I sent a report from Leipzig. Less than a week later, the British and Americans firebombed the city. Fire to destroy vampires. They know, I tell you. The enemy knows."

"The enemy has been bombing Leipzig for years." Ritter took the telegram and quickly read it. "It says here they bombed Chemintz, as well, and Berlin. The train didn't carry us anywhere near Berlin."

He handed back the telegram. "Stop worrying," he said, with just a touch of power. "The English and Americans are our enemies, but they are not monsters. Dresden is a peaceful city, a refuge for those fleeing the Russians. We are safe here."

Übel's fear drained away. His shoulders straightened, and his voice grew brisk. "As you were, men. The tests resume this evening." His heels clicked as he turned and marched toward the door.

Heine snorted. "We don't need more tests. We need more blood. Übel, bring us blood. Now."

The rush of power raised the hair on Ritter's arm. Übel was half-way across the room when it hit him. His back twitched. He shuddered, paused. "Bring blood. Now." He quickstepped to the door and disappeared into the brightening dawn.

Ritter wanted to curse. Heine's voice was growing stronger, and he was using it more frequently. Behind him, boots hit the floor. Schmidt walked up. "What was that? Did you feel it, like a summer wind, only sharper?"

"It was nothing." The words crackled with power. "Forget it."

Schmidt's expression went blank.

Heine sat on his bed, brows drawn together. "Something happened. I felt it. I spoke and—"

"Forget." Ritter poured strength into the word and prayed that the Berliner had not grown immune to his voice. Heine stiffened. Ritter breathed out a sigh. Heine became harder to control every day. Someday soon, Ritter would be unable to smooth away his memory. Thank heavens, that day had not yet come. "Nothing happened. This morning is like all other mornings. Go to bed, sleep, and forget."

Heine flopped back on his cot. Schmidt stumbled to his own and began snoring before his shoulder hit the mattress. Ritter was the only one awake when Übel returned with three steins on a tray. Still puppet-stiff, he carried the tray to the crate Ritter and his comrades used as a table. Ritter took one of the mugs and drained it in a gulp. Heine was right. They did need more blood. The stein merely whetted Ritter's appetite. He took the other two and drank them as well. Warmth flowed from his stomach and filled his body. He smiled at the unmoving doctor. "Tonight, bring double rations for us all."

"Double rations." Übel spoke in the monotone that meant he was still under control, but Ritter tasted panic building under the artificial calm.

"Fear not." The blood had strengthened his voice, and its power shimmered in the chill air. "We are no danger to you."

"No danger."

Ritter returned the last stein to the tray. "We are your men. You are our commander. You are safe with us. Always."

"Safe. Always."

Übel's fear had lessened, but its tempting undercurrent still seasoned the air. During the long months in the basement, Ritter had discovered the doctor's secret dream. He used it now to chase away the lingering anxiety. "We will make you famous, a hero of the fatherland. The *Führer* himself will thank you."

"The *Führer*." Übel remained still a moment. Then his shoulders squared, and his arm shot into a salute. "*Heil* Hitler."

Ritter returned the salute, and the doctor marched from the room, into the dawnlit front office. Even after the door closed, afterimages of Übel in the blazing doorway chased Ritter to bed and lurked behind his closed eyelids. The blood-fed warmth quickly ebbed. He was running out of time. The doctor's tests hadn't yet revealed a way to return

Ritter and his comrades to humanity. If the next round proved equally futile, their days were numbered. Not because of Übel—Ritter's control over the doctor grew daily—but because his comrades were growing stronger, more dangerous. One day soon, Heine would break free of his control. Schmidt wasn't far behind. When that happened, there would be nothing to protect the people of Dresden from their appetite for blood.

Blood. Though he had just drunk his fill, Ritter's teeth ached for more. The hunger—no, lust—for blood pulsed through him, as inescapable as his heartbeat. It, too, grew stronger with each passing day, stronger and harder to resist. There were days when it took all his self-restraint to keep from ripping out Übel's throat. Those days were becoming more frequent.

Ritter's fists clenched. He refused to let the bloodlust overwhelm him, refused to let monsters loose upon the world. Before he let that happen, he would rip off the roof and give them all to the sun.

❧ ❧

The evening's tests started late and ended early. Disgust filled Ritter as he watched Übel scurry from the room. The doctor was no closer to returning them to the human state than he had been the day they awakened. The answer was in their blood; Ritter was sure of it, but Übel couldn't even draw it. The needle pricks healed before blood could flow. Tonight, Ritter's body had actually ejected the needle, pushed it from Übel's grasp to clatter on the floor. Ritter stood beside his cot and stretched. He would worry about Übel's latest failure tomorrow. Tonight, he had other plans.

Heine rolled from his cot. "Hey, Schmidt, ready to lose another game?"

"Lose? Last night I wiped the board with you." Schmidt leaned over and pulled a dog-eared chessboard and box of wooden chessmen from beneath his bed. "Take white. You need the advantage."

Heine pulled the crate over to Schmidt's bed and started laying out the lighter-colored pieces. "I don't need it, but I'll take it."

Ritter grinned. Schmidt had taught Heine to play chess, and now the two spent most nights hovered over the red-and-black checked board. The games made Ritter's nightly excursions easier. "Make the game a long one." He wove power through the words. "Enjoy yourselves, and forget about me."

A moment of silence, then Heine and Schmidt's banter continued, as they set up the pieces. Certain that they would be busy for hours, Ritter slipped from the warehouse.

Every night since their arrival, Ritter had wandered the streets of Dresden. Avoiding the patrols, he had paced the whole city, from the widest *Strasse* to the smallest byway. He explored both banks of the Elbe and examined the parks, churches, and even the *Stadtschloss*, the old castle on the south bank of the river. Now he turned his feet to the one place he had been avoiding. Tonight, he would visit his mother.

According to her last letter, she still lived with Aunt Hilde and helped in Hilde's china shop near the *Altmarkt*, the old market. Ritter had walked by the shop every night, had gazed at the heavily curtained window of the upstairs apartment, but had been unable to force his feet to Aunt Hilde's door. A nearby church chimed the hour, nine o'clock: too late for a visit. Ritter sighed. It was always too late, but he couldn't wait any longer. The way Übel's experiments were going, this might be his last chance to see his mother.

There were two bells by the shop door, one for the business, one for the apartment. Ritter stepped up to the shop and pulled the second. A faint tinkle sounded overhead. Silence, then raspy hinges and hesitant footsteps on creaking stairs. A thin voice: "Who's there?"

Ritter's heart leapt to his mouth. "Mother?"

"Ritter!" Fumbling clicks and the door flew open.

She had shrunk. The top of her head barely reached his shoulder. Her blue cotton dressing gown had faded to gray and hung from stooped shoulders. She held an oil lamp in one hand, and its yellow glow highlighted her careworn brow and darkened the hollows beneath her cheeks. It glinted off new silver streaks in her long bedtime braid.

"You have grown." Her voice cracked. She blinked and wiped at her cheeks. "Where are my manners? Come in, come in." She grabbed his hand and pulled him over the threshold.

Ritter wrapped his arms around her. Though she felt as fragile as the figurines around them, she still smelled right, like the lavender sachets she kept in her dresser drawers. "Oh, *Mutti*, I missed you so much."

She looked up with a smile that wiped away twenty years. "We already ate, but there is some soup left. It will only take a moment to warm it for you."

"Thank you, but I, too, already ate."

"Then let me wake Hilde. She will be nearly as happy as I am to see you."

"Let her sleep. I can only stay a minute." Ritter gently pulled from his mother's embrace. "Orders."

"Orders." Her smile dimmed, then brightened again. "Will you be in Dresden long enough to share Sunday supper with us? I could invite Greta."

Just hearing her name made his heart beat faster. "Greta? Is she here?"

Her chuckle was fond, knowing. "She is still in Schwarzdorf, but I received a letter from her last week. Come upstairs, and I will show it to you."

A few minutes later, she settled Ritter at a small wooden table.

Setting the lamp on its scarred surface, she hurried to a nearby bureau and returned with an envelope addressed in Greta's rounded handwriting. Ritter pulled out the letter and imagined Greta's voice as he read:

Dear Frau Breitmann:

I hope this letter finds you happy and well. Mother sends her regards, as does Herr Rheiner. Schwarzdorf is the same as always, dull and quiet, but people grow frightened by the news from the front. They say the Russians will soon cross the border and enter Germany. Mother thinks we would be safer in Dresden. Perhaps we will join you there soon.

Today, I received a letter from Ritter. Did you know that he, too, is coming to Dresden? Do you know if he has arrived? Have you seen him? Please give him my love when you do.

Affectionately,
Greta

"I will write and tell her how handsome you have grown." His mother lit the stove and set a kettle to boil for tea. She turned, and worry creased her brow. "Too pale, though. You should eat more meat."

"I eat what I can."

"I understand. One can hardly buy a bit of sausage these days, much less a nice beef shin." She sighed. "Still, even if the people starve, the *Führer* should feed his troops. Let me cut you a slice of bread."

"I eat well enough, don't worry about that." He patted the chair beside him. "Sit. I want to hear about everything that has happened since your last letter."

She stepped toward him, but the kettle whistled, and she turned back to the stove. She spooned tea leaves into the pot and added steaming water. "There's no milk."

"Black's fine, thanks."

She placed the teapot and two china teacups on a plain metal tray and carried them to the table. "So, are you stationed near here?"

"On the other side of the city. You can write me there, if you want." Ritter gave her the address of the abandoned warehouse. Übel kept an office in one of the front rooms, where he received mail. "Don't try to visit. My work is secret, and security is heavy."

"Of course." Ritter's mother poured the tea and watched while he took a sip. The tea dropped to the bottom of his stomach and lay there like stone.

He forced a smile. "Mm, good." And it *was* good—not the tea, but sitting next to his mother in Aunt Hilde's homey kitchen. It tore Ritter's heart to think this might be the last time he saw her, but the pain was eased by the sweetness of her smile. He set down the cup and drew her into a hug.

"Ouch! You're hurting me."

Shame burned his neck. He dropped his arms. "Forgive me."

"Don't be silly!" She laughed and settled into the chair beside him. "I am glad my son has grown so strong. Now, did I tell you about Mrs. Kirchner's cat?"

She told funny stories about the shop and the neighborhood around it, while the tea grew cold. The church bell tolled ten. Ritter regretfully pushed back his chair and stood. "I must go."

"So soon?" She rose from her chair and touched his lips. "You haven't smiled all evening. What worries you so? The war?"

Ritter lifted the corners of his mouth, but kept his lips low to conceal his teeth. "You always could read my mind." He hugged her again, careful this time not to hurt her.

She held him a long moment, then dropped her arms and stepped back. Tears stained her cheeks. "You came to say good-bye, didn't you?"

"I will try to come again, but..." He struggled for a way to warn her without revealing his awful secret. "The way the war is going, who knows?"

"You will come back." His mother spoke in the firm tone she had used when he was young and had misbehaved. "Even if they send you to the front, you will return to me. Until then, do your duty. I will write Greta and tell her how well you look."

She walked him down the stairs and past the figurine-lined shelves to the front door. Ritter opened the door and turned. "*Auf Wiedersehen.*"

She hugged him again and kissed his cheek. "*Auf Wiedersehen*, Ritter. *Ich liebe dich.*" I love you.

After the bright kitchen, the street looked black and forbidding. A chill ran across Ritter's shoulders. Shrugging it off, he strode over the threshold and away from the shop. He didn't look back, though he knew his mother still stood in the open doorway. He turned a corner and, a moment later, heard the door close. The quiet sound echoed in his heart throughout the long run back to his prison.

≈≈

The next evening, Ritter and his comrades woke to the smell of fresh blood. The tray and three steins sat on the crate, near the remains of Schmidt and Heine's chess game. Übel bent over it, but he bolted upright at their stirring, as if caught in an immoral act. Heine was the first out of bed. He snatched his stein, frowned, and shoved it toward Übel. "Mine's half empty. Fill it."

The doctor stumbled back. "I can't."

Schmidt leaned over the remaining steins. "None of them are full. First you keep us prisoner, now you starve us?"

Neither Heine nor Übel seemed to hear him. Heine advanced on the doctor. "Can't? What do you mean, *can't?*"

Übel retreated across the room.

Ritter jumped out of bed and started after them. "Heine, wait."

"Find a pig. Bring us more blood!" Heine's order exploded in an avalanche of power. The doctor stiffened. Ritter shivered in the backwash.

"Pig. More blood." Übel's lips barely moved. Awkward as a wind-up toy, he turned and jerk-stepped from the room.

"You did it!" Schmidt ran up and clapped Heine's arm. "I didn't believe you last night, but you really did it. Übel will dance to our tune, now."

Heine's eyes narrowed to gold slits. "Breitmann's not surprised, are you comrade? How long have you been bewitching us?"

Ritter's mouth went dry. "What do you mean?"

"'Stop,' you say, and we stop. 'Sleep,' you say, and we sleep. How long have we been your puppets? Tell me!"

Heine's voice crashed over Ritter. It froze his limbs, numbed his mind. Only the warmth of his own power kept Ritter from turning to ice. His lips started to move of their own accord, and it took all his will to bend them to his desire. "No."

"It's true, then." Schmidt turned on him, cheeks flushed with anger. "You have been clouding our minds, forcing us to sleep while you drink our share of blood."

"You kept us weak when we should be strong, prisoners when we could be free. Why?" Heine's question slammed into Ritter hard enough to make him sway.

"To protect—" The words slipped out before Ritter could stop them. He clamped his teeth together before any more could escape.

Heine frowned. "To protect? Whom? Übel? Speak!"

The force of Heine's will knocked Ritter to his knees. "All of us. All of them. Until Übel discovers how to turn us back into men."

"Turn us back to men?" Heine's laugh cut like a March wind. "Fool. We are gods. Why would we wish to be men again? Sleep." Heine shoved his shoulder, and Ritter toppled to the floor. "Sleep, and pray I let you live until you wake. Sleep!"

"Yes, sleep!" Schmidt's voice was weaker, a whistling draft compared to Heine's gale, but it was enough to snuff out the last flicker of Ritter's resistance and plunge him into darkness.

～～

He woke on the floor, stiff and cold. The door to the warehouse stood open, but a shadow blocked the lamplight from the outer room. Ritter pushed himself to his feet. "Herr Doktor, is that you?"

Instead of answering, Übel walked into the room. He held a tray between his hands.

Ritter glanced around the warehouse. The beds were empty, the makeshift privy deserted. Heine and Schmidt had escaped. Ritter shuddered. Heaven help the city, he had waited too long.

Übel carried the tray to Ritter. Steam rose from the steins, steam thick with the scent of blood. Hunger flooded Ritter's mouth. It had been hours since he had eaten. Telling himself a moment's delay wouldn't matter in the hunt for his comrades, he grabbed the closest stein and drained it in a gulp.

The blood hit his stomach like liquid lead and began to roll. Ritter doubled over. The stein slipped through his fingers and clattered to the floor. "What is it?" He groaned as another cramp hit him. "Poison?"

"Pig's blood." Übel's voice was still wooden.

"Pig's blood?" The words turned his roiling stomach to ice. "What kind of blood have you been feeding us?"

"Jew's."

Ritter's gut clenched, bucked, and spewed its contents over the floor. He stumbled back and dropped onto the nearest bed. "You bleed men for us?"

The doctor blinked and lowered the tray. "Of course." He sounded angry. Heine's control must be wearing off. "It was easier in Dachau. Thousands of Jews with blood to spare. But here? I brought prisoners along for the journey, but thanks to your greedy appetites, they didn't last long. Tell me, where am I to get blood? From Jews? In Dresden, there are no Jews. From prisoners of war? The commander in charge of the prisoners refuses. I begged a few pints off the blood drive, but the rest is gone, sent to the front."

Übel's words made Ritter feel even sicker. He and his comrades were worse monsters than he had feared. He should have let Übel kill them all after the Christmas massacre, but he had clung to unreasoning hope. Now it was too late. Schmidt and Heine were out of control, free, and hunting in the unsuspecting city. Ritter stood. He had to find them, stop them before they stained the streets with blood.

"Wait here," he ordered Übel. "Stay until I return."

The power flowed around Übel, and the doctor went rigid. "Until you return."

Satisfied, Ritter ran from the stench of vomit and clotted pig's blood, through Übel's office, and into the sharp tang of winter.

A heavy silence closed around him. Though a glow still lingered in the west, the buildings around him were dark and empty. He stretched his hearing, but caught nothing but the distant barking of a dog. It came from farther down the river, near the elegant buildings and church spires of the city's heart: as good a direction as any. As he ran toward it, Ritter prayed that this time he wouldn't be too late.

Warehouses gave way to tenements; tenements, to shops and row houses; row houses, to the stone edifices of church and state. The dog stopped barking, and, except for Ritter's hammering footsteps, silence reigned. He ran for hours, until his search brought him to the *Altmarkt*.

The shops were as dark and silent as the rest of Dresden, but the murmur of voices drifted down the alley behind his aunt's shop. He ran to the front door. It was locked, but the voices were clearer. Though the churches had tolled midnight, his mother was still awake. Ritter glanced up at the window. As if commanded by his gaze, the heavy black-out curtain drew back and his mother's face appeared. The room behind her was dark, but the stars gave enough light to see the worry etched between her eyes. Something was very wrong.

Ritter pulled the bell. It tinkled above him, and his mother disappeared. Hurried footsteps rattled the stairs, the lock clicked, and the door flew open. The woman behind it was not his mother. She was older, with sunken cheeks and red-rimmed eyes. "It's about time you two showed up. I have been worried sick!" She scowled, then leaned to one side, as if she were trying to look behind him. "Don't you hide behind that scamp. Come out and let me see you."

"Greta?" More footsteps, and Ritter's mother stepped up behind her. Ritter suddenly recognized the older woman, and his gut twisted into a knot. Though she had lost weight and her hair had gone white, it was *Frau* Hofmann, Greta's mother.

Frau Hofmann looked up, and the angry color drained from her cheeks. With surprising strength, she grabbed his arm and dragged him into the shop. "Where is she? What have you done with my Greta?"

"I left her in Schwarzdorf three years ago." Ritter looked over her head to his mother. "What happened?"

She answered in a strained whisper. "Greta and her mother arrived this evening. The front draws closer every day. With her father and brothers in the army, they were afraid to remain in Schwarzdorf. They came here—where else had they to go? Your Aunt Hilde and I made them welcome, and I told Greta that I had seen you." Ritter's mother seemed to shrink. "I showed her the address you gave me."

"My baby took it while we were cooking dinner. Took it and left the house without a word. After dark, after curfew. Where could she have gone, but to see you?"

"I was out all evening." Out chasing monsters. The knot in his gut tightened. *Gott im Himmel*, Greta might still be at the warehouse, waiting for him. He had to get back before Schmidt and Heine tired of their freedom and returned to find her. "She is probably still at the ware—barracks," Ritter said, stumbling over the word. He gently pulled from *Frau* Hofmann's grasp. "I will find her and bring her back."

Without waiting for a response, Ritter turned and raced from the shop. His mother called to him, but he didn't stop. He couldn't. Greta was alone in the monsters' den. He had to reach her before the monsters came home.

⌘

Ritter burst through the warehouse door into the scent of blood and the taste of fear. He stumbled over a lump near the door and realized it was Übel. The doctor sprawled chin up, eyes open. A gash split his throat. The flesh spread like a second pair of lips, but gray and lifeless. Dark splatters stained the floor beneath the body, but there was no blood on the wound. It looked as if it had been scrubbed clean.

Ritter forced his gaze from the lifeless husk and scanned the room. Someone had knocked over the crate-table and scattered the chess game. A stein lay near the wall in a puddle of pig's blood. Clearly Heine and Schmidt had returned, but where were they now? Where was Greta?

Stomach churning, Ritter stepped around Übel. "Greta?" Silence. Perhaps she was hiding among the crates or under one of the beds. "It's me, Ritter. Come out and I will take you to safety."

"Too late."

Ritter spun around. Heine stood in the doorway. Sometime during the night, he had picked up a flick-knife. The bare blade glinted in the dim light. Schmidt loomed behind him.

Ritter's mouth filled with ash. "What did you do to her?"

"Your little girlfriend? See for yourself. She's over there." Heine nodded toward the cots.

They were empty. Ritter dragged his feet toward them. The floor behind crawled into view. The toe of a black laced boot. An outstretched hand. A strand of blond hair. Ritter shoved the cots aside. "Greta!"

She was no longer beautiful. Her blue eyes stared at him, glazed and lifeless. Color had abandoned her cheeks, and her gray lips spread in a silent scream. Her modest blouse had been ripped open, and bloodless wounds marred her throat, her breasts. Her skirt bunched around her waist, and more wounds dotted her thighs.

"We had Übel for dinner," Heine's voice whispered in his ear. Ritter jerked around. The two vampires still stood by the door. A grin spread Heine's lips. "Your girlfriend made a sweet dessert."

Ritter launched himself across the room. One stride, two, and his hands closed around Heine's throat.

The smaller man's eyes widened. His face turned red, then blue. Somewhere in the distance, Ritter heard Schmidt yelling, felt him grab his arm. He squeezed harder. Then fire slashed his gut.

Ritter clutched his stomach, dropped to his knees. Blood oozed from between his fingers, dripped from Heine's blade.

"Bastard!" Heine kicked Ritter in the stomach. The pain knocked him over. Heine kicked him again, this time in the head.

The room dissolved into blackglitter. "Your sweetie showed up asking for you, right after we finished Übel." Kick. "She started screaming. I told her to shut up. She did. I told her to lie on the bed and spread her legs. She did. I told her to moan and beg for more. She did. And after Schmidt and I were both too tired to fuck and too full to drink, I told her to die. And—" Kick. "—she—" Kick. "—did."

A final kick rolled Ritter across the room. "Now it's your turn. Die, you bastard. Die."

Heine's voice wrapped around Ritter's heart like a tourniquet of ice. Cold crept down his limbs, fogged his brain. He couldn't think, couldn't breathe. He was falling down a well, tumbling farther from the light with each breath he didn't take. Schmidt leaned over him. "Is he dead yet?"

"Almost. It will take a minute, like it did with the girl." Schmidt disappeared. Cloth rustled, and something silver swung into Ritter's line of sight. Greta's locket. "A pretty trinket to remind me of a pretty whore."

Something hot and pulsing flared in Ritter's torn gut. Rage. It melted his heart, freed his lungs. He gulped a breath.

Shock flashed across Heine's face.

Ritter rolled to his knees, forced himself to stand. A sharp pain raced up his stomach and vanished. He looked under his torn shirt. The skin was whole: not even a scar to show where the blade had entered. He lifted the cloth so Heine could see. "I guess I am not that easy to kill, comrade."

Heine dropped the locket and snatched the knife from his pocket. He flicked it open. "I should have gone for the heart. Hold him, Schmidt."

Schmidt grabbed at Ritter's arms. Ritter dodged and ran toward the overturned crate. He loved movies; he had seen *Nosferatu* twice. The sun wasn't the only way to kill a vampire.

He stomped the crate, seized the sharpest slat, and turned. Schmidt raced toward him. With all his strength, Ritter thrust the jagged end into Schmidt's chest.

The makeshift stake caught on a rib. For a moment, Ritter feared he had made a mistake. He shoved. Something snapped. The stake jerked forward and lodged in Schmidt's heart.

Schmidt's mouth moved, but no sound came out. His knees buckled. He toppled over and lay still.

Bile filled Ritter's throat. He had never killed before, not face to face. Swallowing the bitterness, Ritter snatched up another board and turned to Heine. For a moment, Heine's gray-gold gaze met Ritter's, then he spun around and bolted out the door.

Ritter started after him but slipped in Schmidt's blood. He staggered, went down. It only took a moment to regain his feet and race through Übel's office and into the street beyond. Too late. The street was empty, silent. Heine had escaped.

A distant bell tolled, and Ritter cursed. Dresden was a large city, and dawn was near. He would never find Heine before daybreak. Heart in his boots, Ritter returned to the warehouse.

Übel and Schmidt's bodies were dark mounds on the floor, but Greta's locket glittered in a streak of starlight. He picked it up. The chain was broken, but the locket seemed undamaged. He flicked the catch. Greta had put in two pictures, hers and his. Her smile cut deeper than Heine's blade. Ritter closed the locket, slipped it in his breast pocket, and stumbled to Greta's side.

Her pale face shone in the darkness. He knelt and gently closed the staring eyes. Warmth lingered on her skin, and he suddenly wondered if the old stories about vampires were true. Did their victims rise on the third night, themselves vampires?

Greta looked dead, but sleeping vampires were supposed to look dead. Schmidt and Heine had. Once asleep, their skin had gone cold and their breathing had slowed. They had bitten Greta so many times—had they infected her with their curse? If so, she would eventually awaken, confused, terrified, and hungry, but alive.

Hope hurt almost as much as grief. Ritter smoothed loose strands of hair from her forehead. "Don't worry, *Liebchen*. I will care for you." He glanced around the warehouse. Greta had been abused and terrorized here. She needed to come into her new life gently, in a place untainted by the memory of pain and the scent of death. Ritter pulled off his overcoat, wrapped it around her, and scooped her into his arms. Even in the heavy wool, Greta felt as light as a doll.

He carried her from the warehouse, over the Elbe, and east toward Schwarzdorf. Their hometown was twenty miles from Dresden, too far for a man to bear such a burden, but he was no longer a man. "I will take you home," he murmured, as his quick strides ate up the miles. "You will be safe there."

The night was nearly over. When the horizon began to pale, he hid in a barn and held her stiffening body close through the long daylight hours. Her limbs loosened as night fell, surely proof that his hope was true. He picked her up and ran on. The moon set before he reached Schwarzdorf, but he needed no light to find Greta's house. He broke open the locked door and carried her to her room.

It was as he remembered, small and neat, with pink flowers on the wall. He laid her on the bare mattress and kissed her still lips. A draft stirred her hair. He looked for a blanket, but could find no bedding: not in the room, not in the house. *Frau* Hofmann must have brought all her linens to Dresden. He returned to Greta and buttoned his coat up to her chin. The heavy wool would have to suffice until she could drink blood to warm her.

He shut the door and moved her bureau to block the window. Then he sat on the floor beside the bed and waited. Day came. No change. Night dropped. No change. Another day. Another night. Greta remained motionless on the stripped mattress.

Just after dusk of the third day, Ritter could wait no longer. He reached over and touched her cheek. "*Liebchen*?" Her skin felt cold, waxy. He grabbed her shoulder and shook it, hard. "*Liebchen!*" Her head flopped like a dead fish. Despite the room's chill, a hint of decay tainted the air. Ritter's eyes stung, but no tears came. Like the burning cross, the rising victim was only a myth.

Except for a mouse chittering behind the wall, the house was silent. Ritter lifted Greta and carried her outside The town, too, was silent. No man spoke, no dog barked, no chicken rustled. He looked down the street. All the houses and shops were dark. It looked as if the whole village had fled to Dresden. On legs as heavy as stone, Ritter carried Greta to the old churchyard and the Othmann family crypt. A fitting place to leave her until her family gave her a proper burial.

The crypt's door was closed but unlocked. He shouldered it open and carried Greta inside. An ornate sarcophagus dominated the small stone room. Kneeling, Ritter settled Greta on its lid and kissed her one last time. "Sleep well, *Liebchen*."

He rested his forehead against hers. How he longed to join her. The crypt faced east. In the morning, the sun would stream through the open door. He could lie down beside his love, close his eyes, and wait for the sun to free him. A burst of pain, and he would be with Greta forever.

No. Ritter sighed and straightened. He couldn't rest until Heine was dead. Though he had failed Greta, he could return to Dresden, hunt Heine down, and ensure that he wouldn't hurt other innocents. Besides, he had promised *Frau* Hofmann he would bring Greta back. The old woman had already waited three days. Knowing her, she was sick with worry. He couldn't tell her that Greta had been raped and murdered by vampires, but he could invent a plausible story and use his voice to make *Frau* Hofmann believe it. And he could tell her where to find her daughter's body.

He reached beneath his jacket and pulled out the locket, meaning to leave it with Greta, but he couldn't. The locket and the picture it contained were the only bits of her that remained to him. He shoved the necklace back into his pocket, stood, and walked from the tomb. Once outside, he started to run. He didn't think. He tried not to feel. He just ran.

A ruddy glow appeared on the horizon. Ritter slowed to a walk. Dawn was hours away, and this glow rose from the west.

Ritter sneezed. Smoke scented the air—smoke he had smelled for some time, but only now noticed. His heart tripped over a beat. Could Übel's fears be true? Had the enemy intercepted the doctor's reports and sent bombers to destroy what he had undoubtedly exaggerated into an army of vampires? The British *had* firebombed Leipzig after Übel sent one such report. He had sent others since. Had the enemy traced them to Dresden?

Ritter's legs started pumping before he finished the thought. His mother was in Dresden. If the city was burning, he had to get her out.

He had already lost Greta. He couldn't lose his mother, too. Ritter stretched his stride and ran like the monster he had become. Towns passed in a blur of empty streets and startled night laborers. He ran without pause to the outskirts of the city and the first signs of devastation.

Flames swept shattered buildings. He dodged the worst of the inferno and kept running. Perhaps the planes had missed the *Altmarkt*. But no, the entire area had been flattened and burned. He found the pile of bricks that had once been his aunt's china shop. Though the rubble still smoldered, he started digging. If his mother had made it to the cellar, she might still be alive. The heat blistered his hands, but he tossed aside bricks, charred beams, and ceramic shards, until he found the cellar door.

Ritter ripped it from its hinges. A dim light flickered in the room below. "Mother, Aunt Hilde, are you there?" Silence. He plunged down the undamaged stairway. The flickering was from a dying flashlight. It lay on the floor at his mother's feet. She slumped on a bench next to her sister and *Frau* Hofmann. "*Mutti?*"

Nothing.

Fear as bitter as bile filled Ritter's throat. He ran to his mother and shook her shoulder. Her head rolled back, revealing open, sightless eyes.

A circle of light bobbed across her face. "Any survivors down there, Corporal?"

Ritter spun to face the stairway. A lieutenant stood on the top step, a flashlight in his hand. Lines of fatigue and sorrow etched his blackened face. Ritter forced air into his lungs, words past his lips. "They don't look injured, sir, but they're not breathing."

The officer sighed. "It is the same all over the city. The flames sucked the air out of the underground shelters. Thousands suffocated who thought they had made it to safety. I found my wife and daughter in the subway station near the ruins of our home." He choked back a sob. "Damn British! Why did they bomb here? Dresden was no threat to them."

But Dresden had been a threat. Because of Ritter, Dresden had sheltered Übel's miracle weapons, his super soldiers. What better way to kill vampires than to burn them?

Without a word, Ritter ran up the stairs. He pushed past the lieutenant and raced through the smoke-filled streets. It didn't matter where he went. Everyone he loved was dead, and he had killed them.

The east began to brighten. Ritter longed to stay outside and meet the sun's deadly embrace, but he didn't have the right. Heine and Schmidt had revealed their true natures Christmas night, but he had refused to act. Though they grew daily more monstrous, he had waited. Driven by fear and false hope, he had waited too long. His indecision cost Greta her life, killed his mother, and destroyed a city. A stake in the heart finally stopped Schmidt, but Heine had escaped. Ritter's one-time comrade had probably perished in the fires, but *probably* wasn't good enough. Ritter had to know for sure.

He spotted the ruins of a vegetable shop and dug open the door to the root cellar. It was empty, except for a withered cabbage. Ritter settled on the floor but did not rest. He must find Fritz Heine. Dead or alive, it didn't matter. Ritter had failed to protect Greta, had failed to protect his mother, had failed to protect the people of Dresden. He would not fail again. No matter how long it took, Ritter would find Heine, tear open his chest, and crush the bastard's heart with his own hands. Then, and only then, could he rest.

Chapter Twenty-Two

Lake County, Illinois
September 3, 2014

Ritter's smile was a hundred years old. "Because, dearest Faith, I am not a man. No matter how much we both pretend, I never will be."

"But—" Faith stopped because she didn't know what to say. How could she convince him that tonight nothing mattered? She didn't care about his drug-triggered vampire delusions. At the moment, she didn't even care about her work. She only cared about Ritter. She wanted him. Needed him. Now.

As if he could read her thoughts, he smiled. "Good-bye, Faith." He blew her a kiss, turned, and disappeared down the stairs.

"Wait!" Faith raced after him, through the corridor, down the stairs, into the night. "Ritter!"

Only the crickets answered.

Faith didn't break pace. Banat's compound was stuck in the middle of nowhere. Ritter must have driven, and the only road out of the complex passed her building. If she hurried, she could catch him before he drove away. Listening for the roar of an internal combustion engine, she sprinted toward the parking lot.

She tore around the corner and skidded to a halt. Three cars remained in the lot. All were dark and silent. None was a 1964 Mercedes 280SL. Ritter had vanished.

Body humming with frustration, Faith sagged against the building. She tried to tell herself that Ritter had done her a favor, that it was best he'd left before she made a complete fool of herself. She didn't believe it.

A mosquito whined past her neck. Faith slapped at it and hit the necklace Ritter had given her. She slid her fingers down the chain until they reached the locket.

It was only about as big as her thumbnail, but heavy. Holding it in her hand, Faith stepped into the parking lot and under the nearest light. The metal was silver, the design more intricate than she'd first realized. She flicked the catch, and the locket sprang open.

Two photos stared back at her. One was black and white, the other tinted. The colored portrait was of young girl, sixteen or seventeen, with braided yellow hair coiled around her head. Her cheeks were baby-doll pink, and her blue eyes tilted into a sweet smile. Of her dress, only her little round collar showed. It was white, with embroidered flowers on the edge.

The other photograph was of Ritter. He seemed younger, though Faith couldn't say why. In contrast to the girl's smile, his lips were straight. He must have looked at the camera when the picture was taken, because his gaze seemed to lock onto hers. Ritter looked stern, determined, and proud. Though the photo had obviously been trimmed to fit the locket, Faith recognized the dark cap and collar of a World War II *Wehrmacht* uniform.

She snapped the locket closed. It had to be a fake, like the pictures she'd seen of Civil War reenactors in their blue and gray uniforms. Maybe Germans had WW II reenactments. Ritter could have attended one and had his picture taken there. The girl looked old-fashioned, too, but it was easy enough to buy antique photographs.

A faint roughness on the back of the locket teased her fingertips. Faith turned it over. Cursive shadows marred the smooth back. *Du bist wie eine blume.* You are like a flower. Faith recognized the line. She didn't remember the name of the poem or the poet, but she'd read the words and liked them years ago, when she'd taken German literature in college. Below the line were a name and a date: *Ritter 1941.*

Faith dropped the locket. It fell back against her blouse. Ritter couldn't have been twenty years old in 1941. The locket and its photos must be fake, part of his elaborate delusion—unless his incredible story were actually true. She shook her head and turned toward the building. She must be more tired than she thought.

The locket could have belonged to Ritter's grandfather, or maybe Ritter had it engraved when he was in a delusional state. Letting the possibilities shuffle through her mind, Faith turned toward her apartment building. She'd just stepped into the shadow between the brightly lit parking lot and the walkway when a low rumble joined the cricket song. She froze. Could it be Ritter? Now that she thought about it, he had appeared from around the corner of the laboratory building. Maybe he'd parked in one of the more-distant lots.

But the sound was coming from the wrong direction, from the gate, not deeper in the compound. The rumble grew louder, too loud for Ritter's little roadster. Moments later, a pair of lights stabbed the darkness, and an eighteen-wheeler roared past the parking lot toward the other side of the laboratory building.

The engine's roar shifted to a rumble and a loud beep-beep-beep. The tractor-trailer rig must be backing into the lab building's loading dock. Faith listened a moment, then headed for the lab's entrance.

She was too wired to sleep anyway. While she couldn't imagine why laboratory supplies would be delivered so late at night, checking out the shipment would give her something to think about besides Ritter. She'd cut through the building to the loading area and see what new toys Banat had bought for them now.

She swiped her ID. Ignoring the door's greeting, she pushed into the foyer, walked past the elevator and through an unmarked door to the service corridor at the back of the building. The corridor was empty except for the murmur of voices. The voices grew louder as she approached the loading area.

"Can the operational details." It was a man's voice, sharp and angry. "I have an order for a hundred thousand to fill tonight and another half mil by next week. Work around the clock if you have to, but get me my pills."

Faith stopped. Pills? Why would someone deliver pills to a research facility that had no subjects to take them? She heard footsteps, and two men emerged from the loading area. She shrank against the wall, but they turned without a glance and walked away from her. The taller man, gesturing broadly, made a series of excuses, but it was the shorter man who caught Faith's attention. She was too far down the corridor to be sure, but he looked like Banat's partner, Phillip Sloan. He had the same bleached hair, expensive suit, and salon tan. The men turned a corner and and disappeared from sight.

Faith shivered, and it wasn't just the air-conditioning. John O'Connor was looking for a portable drug lab and its drop-off point. Could this be it?

She crept forward, ears primed for the slightest hint of Sloan's return. When she reached the door to the loading area, she peered around the jamb. Two men in B&S uniforms were carrying boxes from the truck to the freight elevator. Behind the boxes, she caught a glimpse of a well-appointed chemical laboratory. John was right, the drug lab was on wheels, and she had found it.

One of the men set down his load and turned. His eyes widened when they fell on Faith. "Hey!" he called, but she was already running toward the elevator.

She sprinted to the lobby. Instead of hitting the elevator call button, she pulled open the door to the stairs and pelted up the two flights to her lab. The first place the guard would look for her was the parking lot. The second was the elevator. Taking the stairs should buy her the time she needed to call John and tell him about Sloan's sideline.

Her ID unlocked the door to her office. She hit the lights and wasted precious seconds rifling through her briefcase to find John's card. Once she had it, she reached for the office phone. Her hand stalled inches from the receiver. Call her paranoid, but she wouldn't put it past Banat to bug the lab phones. Faith grabbed her cell phone instead. It rang four times before John's voice came on.

Faith twitched with impatience as he said his name, repeated the number, and invited her to leave a message. Finally, the machine beeped.

"Hello, John. This is Faith. It's about—" She glanced at her desk clock. "Three-thirty Tuesday morning. You know that mobile drug lab you're looking for? I think I've found it. It's—" The phone jerked out of her hand before she could finish the sentence.

Faith spun around. Miles stood behind her, in rumpled slacks and a stained lab coat. He looked tired and irritated. He was holding her cell phone.

"Give it back." Faith lunged for the phone, but Miles grabbed her arm. For a skinny guy, he was surprisingly strong.

"Faith, what the hell do you think you're doing?"

She pulled and twisted, but she couldn't make him let go. "I was calling the police."

"I can't let you do that."

Faith stopped fighting and tried to gather the frayed edges of her temper. "Listen to me, Miles. I stumbled across an illegal drug lab this evening, hidden in a tractor-trailer rig. The eighteen-wheeler pulled right up to the loading dock, and Banat's guards started unloading crates of pills. They could be making anything in that lab, GHB, Ecstasy, God knows what. There's been a flood of drugs into the North Shore. Kids have been dying. I can't turn my back on that."

"Keep your nose in your research and out of Banat's business."

"But—"

Miles shook her hard enough to make her shoulder ache. "Where do you think the money's coming from anyway, some old fart's charitable trust? For your own good, for the good of your work, shut up and take the money."

Heavy footsteps thundered down the hall. Miles tightened his grip. "Damn."

A broad face appeared in the doorway. The guard had caught up with Faith.

Miles hauled Faith past the guard into the corridor. "It's okay, Donnelly. She's with me."

"Good. You explain to Banat what she was doing at the loading dock."

The elevator dinged, and Banat appeared at the end of the hall, jacket off, sleeves rolled to his elbows. His shoes squeaked as he marched toward her. His expression, angelic smile topped by dead, cold eyes, made Faith shiver.

"Found her, Mr. Banat." Donnelly called.

Banat's lips stretched, and Faith gasped. His false smile hid a pair of canines every bit as sharp as Ritter's. "Bring her downstairs."

Miles let go of her shoulder and stepped forward. "Dr. Allister is one of the best researchers in the field. We can't afford—"

The smile vanished. "I decide what we can afford. If you don't have the stomach for it, go home."

Banat's words were as sharp as his teeth. Faith took a step back, hoping to make a break for the fire escape, but the guard's hand wrapped around her arm. "Come along, Doctor."

Leaving Miles in the hall, the guard pulled Faith after Banat, down the corridor, and into the open elevator. Banat pulled out a card, swiped it through a slot next to the door, and hit a button. The elevator closed and began to sink. Faith's heart dropped with the descending numbers. She tensed, ready to bolt at the first floor, but the elevator kept moving, past the basement, past at least two more floors, before finally jerking to a halt. The doors opened onto a corridor lit with red bulbs like a photographer's dark room. Banat strode into the hallway. The guard hauled her after him.

Without turning or slowing, Banat began to speak. "Miles is right. You are the best researcher in your field. I studied your work before approving your VSI grant. You're very talented, Faith. What would it take to keep you on my team?"

Faith's mouth was so dry, she had to swallow before she could answer. "I don't work with drug dealers."

Banat shrugged. "A means to an end, nothing more. Your work is important, Faith, far more important than saving squalling brats. I'm using your virus to create the next step in the evolutionary chain, the true *Übermensch*. Your research guided its conception; now you can be part of its birth."

He turned a corner and kept walking. The underground labyrinth was larger than the lab building above. Finally Banat slowed in front of a door with DANGER written on it in bold black letters. He swiped the electronic key through the door's lock. The lock clicked. The door opened. Banat stepped inside. The guard let go of Faith's arm and motioned for her to follow. He remained just outside the doorway.

The room was even darker than the corridor, with a single red bulb in the center of the ceiling. Faith could barely make out two rows of beds.

Banat moved to the wall and twisted a dimmer switch. The bulb brightened enough for Faith to see a sheet-covered mound on each mattress. "Observe your handiwork. Ten men, pioneers in the great cause. Thanks to your gentled virus, of twenty volunteers, fully half survived the first days of transformation. For that alone, you will go down in history as one of the world's greatest scientists."

The implications of Banat's words filtered through Faith's numbed brain. "You infected those men with my Stoker's virus. They're the donors for the samples Miles gave me, aren't they?"

Banat's smile was back in place. "Very good, Faith. For a human, you are quite remarkable."

Ritter's story flashed through her mind: how the Nazis had tried to create an army of vampires. How four had survived: Ritter, her grandfather, and two others. Banat's declaration of the *Übermenschen*, the master race. Good God, could it really be true? "Mr. Banat, how old are you?"

His smile showed his fangs again. "Like you, older than I look."

Faith thought back to the night Ritter had visited her lab. How old had he claimed to be? "Ninety-five? A hundred?"

Banat's eyebrows shot up. "How did you know?" Faith was groping for a good lie when he answered his own question. "Odell, of course. What did he tell you?"

Miles had stood aside and allowed Banat to haul her away. Why not let Banat blame him now? "Not much. He mentioned Dachau and an experiment gone awry."

"And his pathetic experiments during the Vietnam War, did he tell you about those? He took army rejects, criminals mostly, and tried to turn them into supermen. The idiot! He had to burn the lot."

Cole's face flashed through Faith's mind, his anger when she mentioned Miles, his obvious hatred of scientists. Had he been one of Miles' guinea pigs?

"But Odell's incompetence isn't the issue here," Banat continued. "I'm offering you an opportunity, Faith. Join me, support my great work, and I'll make you the most famous scientist of the age."

"Your great work is growing vampires, isn't it?" The words sounded ridiculous, but Faith didn't feel like laughing.

"Yes, if you want to use the old-fashioned term. I prefer to call us *Übermenschen*. We are, after all, the ultimate master race."

"What do you want me to do?"

"Continue your work. Most of the weaknesses ascribed to vampires in the common lore are superstitious nonsense. *Übermenschen* have nothing to fear from crosses or holy water. We are stronger, faster, tougher than ordinary men, but we suffer some inconveniences. We can't face daylight and our diet is…limited." He reached out with lightning speed and took her hand. "You can change that, Faith. Continue to work with the virus, tinker with it. You've made it less deadly; now soften its effects. I have many men to draw from. Make as many trials as you need. When you've perfected the virus, I'll infect us all again, and we will rise to greet the dawn, pure, perfect, and superior."

Banat's eyes glinted with a metallic light. Faith had thought Ritter was crazy, but Banat's plans made his story look positively sane. "You never wanted a cure, did you?"

"A cure? For superiority?" Banat's laugh was the scariest thing Faith had heard all night.

She forced herself to take a deep breath. She had to convince Banat she needed time to consider his proposition. If left alone, she might be able to escape. Or John might get her interrupted message and trace the location of her cell phone. A police rescue sounded really good right now. And then there was Ritter. Maybe Ritter would come looking for her when she didn't turn up at his apartment. Strangely, that was the most comforting thought of all.

"Your offer is...amazing," Faith said. "But it's too much to take in all at once. I'd like some time to think about it."

"Of course. Donnelly will show you to one of the guest chambers. It's spartan, but it will do for now. Get some sleep and think about my offer." Banat squeezed her hand hard enough to hurt. "Think very carefully, Faith. You won't like the consequences if the answer is no."

≈≈

Faith paced the perimeter of her cell. Four paces. Turn. Four paces. Turn. Pace past the door to the tiny washroom, to the bed. Turn. She dropped to the mattress. It felt as if she'd been pacing for hours, but according to her watch, she'd only been awake fifteen minutes. Despite all her anger and fear, she'd fallen fully dressed on the narrow bed and had slept for more than ten hours. In a way, Faith wished she were still asleep. Her dreams had been sweet and peaceful. Her waking thoughts were anything but.

The room was hot and airless, but Faith felt cold. Vampires were real. Bubbie's monsters were real. Her nightmares hadn't been caused by her decaying synapses, but by the vicious assault of creatures like the one that now held Faith prisoner.

Banat was a vampire. She hadn't believed Ritter, not even when he told her straight out, but she believed Banat. One look into his soulless eyes was enough to convince her that evil was real and she was looking at it.

The door clicked and opened. Faith sprang to her feet. A guard walked in—Donnelly again—carrying a covered tray. There was no table in the room, but he set the tray on the end of the bed and took off the cover. Two eggs, sunny-side up, sat in a pool of brown grease next to a stack of limp toast. The smell made Faith queasy.

She shifted her glare from the plate to the guard. "I'm not hungry."

Donnelly stepped back, leaving the tray on the mattress. "Mr. Banat said to bring you breakfast. Around here, what Mr. Banat says, goes. If I was you, I'd eat." He turned and left the room, pulling the door shut behind him.

Faith lunged for the door, but it was already locked. She stalked back to the bed. The eggs looked worse the second time round, but the guard had a point. She didn't want to openly defy Banat, not until she had to. He didn't need to know she didn't want his damn breakfast. The toast didn't look too bad, so Faith nibbled on a triangle while she carried the plate to the toilet and dumped it in. One flip of the handle and the evidence swirled away. She was sitting on the bed be-side the empty plate when the door clicked again. Faith rose into a relaxed but ready stance. If the guard gave her a chance, she was running for it. The door opened, and Banat walked into the room.

Faith blinked. "It's three-thirty in the afternoon. Why aren't you still in your coffin?"

He smiled, that closed-lipped, beatific smile that Faith was begin-ning to hate. "Coffins are for the dead."

"But I thought—" Faith bit back the rest. Now was not the time to accuse Banat of already being dead. "I mean, don't vampires sleep during the day?"

"Most do, but only because we can't abide sunlight. The UV radia-tion is the problem, not the hour." Banat lifted his arm in a sweeping gesture. "Here in my underground facility, I rise when I wish."

"Are there many more...vampires here?"

"At the moment, no. But there soon will be. Thanks to your work."

Banat walked closer and grasped her arm just above the elbow. "Odell wanted to keep you ignorant of my higher purpose. Claiming you refused to share your findings, he borrowed some of my men to search your laboratory. He even arranged for them to ransack your apartment. He wanted your notes, Faith, but not because you were secretive. The fool wanted to claim your work as his own."

So Miles had been behind the theft of her slides and the break-in of her apartment. Miles, who should have supported her research, had been working for Banat the whole time. A sudden thought struck her. "Four men tried to attack me in May, big guys. They came out of nowhere and disappeared just as quickly. Were they yours too?"

Banat's fingers tightened. "No. But there are those of my kind who don't share my vision, who feel threatened by the publicity sur-rounding your research. That was one reason I brought you here: to protect you."

Banat's words sent chills up Faith's arms and thighs. She shiv-ered them off. "What do you want me to do?"

"Continue your work." He spoke slowly, his gaze never leaving hers. "Tame the virus and make more."

"So you can make more vampires?"

"Yes."

"What happens to everyone else?"

Banat's smile hardened. "They become food."

"Mr. Banat, I—"

"Silence."

Icy prickles swept Faith's body. Strangely familiar prickles. Ex-cept for being cold instead of warm, they felt like Ritter's attempted hypnosis. Banat was trying to hypnotize her into helping him. Faith closed her mouth and waited. Now that she was aware of Banat's mind games, she didn't think they'd work. She'd play along with him, though.

If he thought he had her under control, he might get careless and she could make a break for it.

"Come with me." Banat pulled her toward the door.

Faith let the prickles swing her legs into strides that matched Banat's surprisingly quick gait. They followed a maze of corridors to the room with the danger sign. Without letting go of her arm, Banat unlocked the door and hauled her inside. "Your patients, doctor. Examine them."

Faith had grown used to the eerie red lighting of the basement corridors, so the room didn't seem as dark as it had the night before. Once Banat turned the dimmer up, she could see the men's faces clearly. They were all B&S security guards. The one nearest her was Sorenson, the special-forces wannabe who had opened the gate for her after her aborted weekend off. His eyes were closed, and his shallow breaths barely stirred the thin sheet covering his chest. At first glance, he appeared to be asleep, but a closer look revealed sunken cheeks and wasted, almost shriveled flesh.

All the men looked that way, as if they'd suffered a prolonged fever. They reminded her of something she'd seen recently, but Faith didn't have time to remember what. The men appeared to be dying before her eyes. She had to do something. Now.

She hurried to Sorenson's side and checked his carotid pulse. Faint and dangerously slow. Her fingers left indentations in his neck when she let go. She turned on Banat. "These men are severely dehydrated. They need fluids. I want a normal saline drip started on all of them, followed by a complete blood work-up. From the looks of them, their electrolytes are shot to hell." She frowned down at Sorenson's face. Even taking into account the red light, he looked dangerously pale. "You better bring blood, too. They might need transfusions."

Banat just stood beside the light switch, smiling. "An excellent diagnosis. The men have lost a great deal of blood and are in desperate need of fluids."

"Then why aren't they getting them? I want them prepped for an IV. Now."

"Odell tried to administer intravenous fluids." Banat motioned toward a cluster of IV stands at the back of the room. They stood between a heavy metal door and what looked like a supply cabinet. "But in addition to being less deadly, your virus works faster than the old one. The changes started almost immediately."

Faith looked from the abandoned IV stands to Banat's deceptively benign expression. "I don't understand."

"There are bags of saline and needles in the cabinet. Hook up one of the men and see what happens."

Faith hadn't inserted an IV since her residency, but she couldn't let those men die without trying to save them. She hurried to the back of the room, grabbed a bag of saline, and hung it on the stand. She took a needle out of the supply cabinet, unwrapped it, and attached it to the long tube. A dribble to clear the air bubbles, and she was ready.

She wheeled the IV stand to the nearest bed. If anything, the man looked worse than Sorenson. His veins had sunk deep into his dehydrated flesh, but Faith managed to find one in the back of his hand. She inserted the needle, started the drip, and turned to get tape to secure the IV.

She'd seen some rolls in the cabinet next to a couple of prefilled IV aerosols. Faith's hand was closing around the tape when a strange sound, almost a squeak, stopped her. It came from the bed. She spun around in time to see the IV needle pop from the vein.

Banat appeared beside her. "You see the problem."

The tiny wound had sealed shut. There was no blood, no mark, not even a dimple to show where she had inserted the needle. The only sign that she'd tried to hydrate the man was the saline dripping in a spreading circle on the sheet. She thought of Cole, and the ruined eye that had healed while she watched. "The needle won't stay in because they heal too quickly?"

Banat's smile spread to show his teeth. "Very good, Faith. Odell tried a dozen times before he came to the same conclusion."

The man beside Faith shuddered. "These men will die if you don't do something," she said. "Have you tried using a nasogastric tube, or rousing them enough to give them fluids by mouth?"

"They can't been roused, not yet. But don't worry, Faith. My men will rise soon enough, and when they do, I have plenty for them to drink." Banat walked past her and opened the door beside the IV stands. Cold air swirled into the room in a foggy mass, and Faith found herself looking into a walk-in refrigerator. Dark, pint-sized plastic bags lined all the visible shelves "Not your saline, but blood. That part of the old stories is true. We *Übermenschen* must drink the blood of lesser men to survive."

Faith scanned the ten faces, all white and sunken like recent corpses. Like Ritter. Faith gasped. That's who they reminded her of. Ritter had shown the same symptoms—flat white skin and sunken cheeks—the Saturday she'd burst into his apartment demanding to know if they'd made love. At the time, she'd assumed he was going through drug withdrawal, but the hunger in his eyes hadn't been for drugs. Ritter had needed blood. "My God," she whispered.

"Of course, fresh blood is best." Banat continued as if she hadn't spoken. "This is merely insurance. Live donors will ease their thirst when they awaken."

Somehow, Faith didn't think the vampires would stop at one pint per "donor." Not only had Banat infected a room full of men with her virus, but if they survived the infection, he planned to kill innocent people to feed them. She had to get free and find some way to stop Banat before the vampires woke up and people started dying.

"You are afraid, but you don't need to be. While you support the cause, your safety is ensured." A chill wind, sharper than the gust from the refrigerator, bit Faith's arms. "Join me, Faith. Forget your scruples and embrace your destiny. Become the mother of a higher race of man."

Banat was trying to beguile her into helping him. She had to make him think it was working, but how? She'd seen Ritter hypnotize people: Sloan, for instance. At the first warm prickle, the man had stiffened. He'd repeated all Ritter's orders in a flat, emotionless voice. Faith held herself as still as her trembling legs allowed and tried to keep her voice steady. "Forget my scruples. Embrace my destiny."

Banat nodded. "Good. It would be a pity to lose you so soon." He turned back to the shelves and frowned. "Miles has the temperature set too low. The bags are nearly frozen. Wait here while I reset the thermostat.

The thermostat was beside the back shelf. Banat stepped over the raised door seal into the refrigerator. His back was toward Faith, his attention fixed on the numbered dial. This might be her only chance.

She slammed the refrigerator door and jammed one of the IV stands under its handle as a makeshift lock.

"Stop!"

She felt, as well as heard, Banat's order. A freezing wind raised goose bumps on her legs, but she ignored it. Faith tore out of the room, kicking the door shut behind her. With any luck, it would lock. She sprinted down the corridor, faster than she'd ever run before. Banat might be able to force his way out of the refrigerator, might be able to unlock the door. She had to find the bank of elevators and get out of the building before he escaped and ordered his goons after her.

A shriek of tearing metal rose behind her. Faith raced around a corner. There they were, the elevators, right in front of her. Half a dozen steps, and she'd be home free. She stretched her gait until her feet barely touched the floor.

One stride.

Two.

Something hit her back and knocked her to the floor.

"That was ill advised." It was Banat. He hauled her to her feet and spun her to face him. His smile had vanished, and a hard light glittered in his eyes. "Stop breathing."

An icy band wrapped around Faith's chest and tightened until her heart slammed against her ribs. It hurt, and the pain turned Faith's fear to anger.

"Stop it!" she cried, with the little air she had left. Banat's eyes widened. The band around her chest loosened. Fresh air flooded her lungs.

"You defied me." Banat sounded more amazed than angry. "How can you resist my order?"

"Resist your order?" Faith was panting as if she'd run a marathon. Her words came out in spurts. "What did you expect, that I'd hold my breath until I passed out?"

"No, until you died." Too quickly for Faith to see, much less react to, Banat switched his grip to her arm. "You're a brilliant, talented woman, but you're only human. If I can't persuade you to join my cause, you're a danger to it. An expendable danger."

The cool precision of Banat's voice made his words all the more terrible. "Mr. Banat, I—"

"Silence." Banat hustled Faith down the hallway toward the room she'd just escaped.

She tried to pull her arm free, but Banat's fingers tightened like titanium clamps, threatening to break her arm. She stopped struggling. Faith couldn't break free; she was going to have to talk her way out of this. "I didn't refuse to join your cause. I...I just panicked," she began. "Vampires take a lot of getting used to."

Banat didn't respond until they reached the room with the vampires. The door lay on the floor. The shriek she'd heard must have been the hinges tearing. He hauled her through the room to the open refrigerator and stood, facing her. His tongue darted from his lips, reminding Faith of a snake tasting the air. "There's no panic. Only fear mixed with repulsion and anger. And curiosity. I'd hoped to use that curiosity, but I can't trust you if I can't control you." One of the sheet-draped men moaned, and Banat sighed. "If only I had more time."

Time, that's what Faith needed. The longer she stalled Banat, the more likely John would be able to trace her call and come after her. "You're in charge. Make the time."

"And now hope. You are a remarkable woman, Faith. Pity I won't get to know you better." With lightning speed, Banat reached into a drawer and pulled out an aerosol syringe. He thrust it against Faith's throat and pressed the plunger before she had time to flinch.

The injection felt like a hard, quick poke. It left a cold circle that quickly spread, up her throat, down her chest. "What was that?" Faith jerked her arm, and Banat let her go. That scared her more than anything else. A horrible thought formed in Faith's mind and chilled her whole body. "Did you infect me with the virus?"

"No. I had hoped to, eventually. We'll need female *Übermenschen* if the race is ever to breed true. But an uncontrollable vampire is even more dangerous than an uncontrollable human." Banat lifted the empty syringe. "Odell prepared these to keep my men calm and still until their transformation was complete. It's a mixture of tranquilizers and muscle relaxants. Takes effect almost immediately."

Faith couldn't feel her feet. Or her fingers. She tried to run, but her legs tangled, and she fell. She struggled to get up, but her legs refused to work. Desperate, she clawed at the floor, pulling herself away from Banat and his monsters. He didn't move, but stood watching her inch past the beds. Soon, her hands grew clumsy, her arms heavy. Finally they collapsed, useless, beneath her.

Faith's heart hammered her ribs. It was the only part of her moving. Banat's shoes appeared beside her. Then his shoulder as he bent to pick her up. Faith wanted to push him away, but she couldn't even close her eyes. Banat carried her to a bed and laid her beside the man already there. The mattress was so narrow, Faith knew they had to be touching, but she couldn't feel anything except distant warmth. The warmth grew and wrapped around her. She was still afraid, but her fear became a tiny voice, muffled in a soft and comforting cocoon.

Banat leaned over her. "What is this?"

Faith's view shifted as he lifted her head. Her head dropped back. Ritter's locket dangled from Banat's fingers.

"A pretty trinket. Imagine finding it here. Pity you can't tell me where you got it." He slipped the locket into his suit jacket. "Your time is almost over, Faith. My men will soon awaken. The scent of your blood will draw them. They will sink their fangs in your veins and drink."

Banat's hand appeared over her face. The red light disappeared as he drew her eyelids closed. "Sleep well, and dream of your contribution to the new world order."

Chapter Twenty-Three

Waukegan, Illinois
September 3, 2014

The cuckoo welcomed Ritter home, four calls for four in the morning. He had left Faith little more than an hour ago. He kicked off his shoes, grabbed yesterday's newspaper, and sprawled on the couch. The content was the same as always—gossip and local politics—but the black-and-white columns helped block her final plea from his mind. She had asked him to stay. It had taken all his control to turn and walk away. Leaving had been the right thing to do, the only thing to do, but the memory of her kiss burned. Ritter swore and threw the paper down. It hurt to want Faith so much, hurt more to know he would never hold her again.

The front door clicked. It flew open, and Cole sauntered in. He grinned and flashed a set of lockpicks. "Just practicing."

Ritter didn't bother getting up. "Go away."

Still grinning, Cole reached into his deep coat pockets and pulled out two frost-covered plastic bags. "Blood-bank take out. Still frozen, but a couple minutes in the microwave will take care of that." He lowered the bags. "You do have a microwave, don't you?"

"I am not hungry."

"I'll put them on ice. You can eat later." Cole disappeared into the kitchen. The refrigerator door opened, closed. Cole walked back into the living room. "How's the pretty doctor?"

"Get out."

"That's where you went, isn't it? I came by an hour ago. You weren't here."

"I told you to leave."

Cole flopped on the easy chair and stretched his legs under the coffee table. "What the lady do, slam the door in your face?"

Ritter sighed. Cole must have eaten well. A full stomach always left him expansive and gregarious. Unfortunately, when he was in such a mood, nothing short of compulsion would drive him away. Ritter swung his legs off the couch and sat up. "Faith asked me to stay."

"So why you here bitching at me?"

"I couldn't stay." Ritter rested his head on the back of the couch. "She...shakes my control."

"You and your fucking control fetish. Chill out, man, you'll live longer."

"My survival is not the issue."

Cole's voice grew harsh. "It ought to be. A little sip and snuggle tonight could keep you alive tomorrow. We're going after Odell, remember? No telling what surprises he'll have for us."

"Odell is a fool."

"Who nearly took us out." Cole sat forward. "Don't be a fucking asshole. Go hunting, get laid, whatever, but can the martyr routine. It'll get us both killed."

He glared so fiercely, Ritter had to smile. After a moment, Cole smiled back. "Knowing you, you scouted out the place before looking up your lady. Fill me in on what you learned."

Ritter pushed off the couch and walked over to the desk. He took out a piece of paper and started sketching a rough map. "The address your friend gave you turned out to be an abandoned farm. Luckily, I caught Faith's scent and followed it to the laboratory complex. The facility is very secure. A single road in, guarded by a well-manned checkpoint."

Footsteps, and Cole appeared beside him. He pointed to blank space between the county road and the research facility. "What's this?"

"Open space. Woods, grassland, a few ponds."

"So we park on the highway and hike in?"

"The abandoned farm is no more than a mile from the complex. We can park Greta in the barn."

Cole nodded. "That way your license doesn't show up on the state troopers' watch list. Good thinking."

Ritter pointed to the laboratory building. "Faith's lab is here. I suspect Odell's is, as well. If we—" The door buzzer cut him off.

Cole scowled. "Who the fuck is that?"

Who but Faith would demand entrance at such an hour? Ritter ran past Cole and hit the intercom. "Yes?"

"Police," said an angry male voice. "Open the door."

Ritter's finger froze over the intercom. *Police?*

"Fuck."

Ritter spun to face Cole. "Is this your doing?"

Cole's eyes opened in a white-rimmed parody of innocence. "Who, me?"

"Cole." He put enough power in his voice to compel the truth.

The scowl came back. "I went hunting, but no one saw. No one followed me here."

The intercom buzzed again.

Ritter hit the button. "Do you have a warrant?"

Silence. "Yes."

Ritter sighed and turned to Cole. "I better let them in. I'll find out what they want, then adjust their memories if necessary."

"Need help?

"No. Go to the kitchen and wait."

After Cole left the room, Ritter pushed the button to unlock the outside the door and listened for how many feet trampled overhead. To his surprise, he heard only two. A moment later, the door to the basement rattled.

"Wait." Ritter projected his voice so the man in the lobby would hear him. He left his apartment, ran up the stairs and unlocked the door, then retreated to the shadows. "Come."

The door opened and Faith's pet police officer, John O'Connor, dressed in street clothes, charged across the threshold and down the stairs. Hostility and anger radiated from him. Beneath the anger, Ritter tasted a deep undercurrent of fear.

When he reached the door, Ritter stepped beside him. "Where is your warrant?"

O'Connor spun around. The anger increased. The fear did not. He wasn't afraid for himself, Ritter realized, but for someone else. "Fuck the warrant. Where's Faith?"

"The last time I saw her, she was standing in front of her new apartment."

"When? Where? I want specifics. Now."

Somewhere overhead, a baby began to cry. "I thought she gave you her new address."

The police officer's anger spiraled upward. "The address was bogus, nothing there but an old barn."

So Faith had given the police the same address the phone company had. Interesting. "Come in," he ordered, wrapping his voice around O'Connor. "Come in and sit on the couch."

O'Connor's expression smoothed into an obedient mask. "Come in. Sit." Ritter opened the door, and O'Connor walked into the apartment and perched motionless on the edge of the couch.

Ritter closed the door and leaned against the jamb. Though he kept his body relaxed, a dozen questions crowded his mind. He asked the first and loudest. "Why are you looking for Faith?"

Despite Ritter's control, a wave of worry swept O'Connor's face. "She called me at three-thirty this morning. I was asleep and didn't catch the phone in time."

Ritter frowned. Three-thirty, half an hour after he left her. Faith should have been safe in bed. His concern deepened. "Go on."

"She left a message. About finding the drug lab. The message cut off midsentence. I put a trace on the call, but the damned signal must have been scrambled. The tracking system put it in the middle of Lake Michigan." O'Connor struggled to rise. "She's in trouble. I've got to find her."

Cole walked into the room. "Stubborn SOB, isn't he? Kept fighting me, too."

Ritter gestured for silence. He couldn't afford any distractions until he had forced the whole story from the police officer. "The drug lab. Tell me about it. Everything."

O'Connor did. He told Ritter about the drugs flooding Lake County, about rape victims and overdoses, about a mobile lab every law enforcement agency in the county sought and none had been able to find. His anger grew with each word. "Faith called. Said she'd found the lab." O'Connor pushed off the couch. "If you or your druggie friends have hurt her, I'll—"

Fear for Faith shot through Ritter. It added strength to his voice. "Silence." O'Connor's mouth snapped shut.

Cole sauntered past Ritter to O'Connor's side. "Sit, bulldog."

O'Connor sat.

"Sounds like Odell's into drugs as well as vamps." Cole shook his head. "The bastard always struck me as too uptight to get high."

"He is selling, not using. The important thing is Faith is in danger."

"You can't do anything about that now. Look at the time. The sun's nearly up."

"I can't leave Faith to Odell's mercy."

"You have no choice." Cole's words hit Ritter like a blow to the gut. "Even I couldn't make it out to western Lake County, rescue the girl, and get back before burning. You'd be ash before you got to your car."

Unable to stand still, Ritter paced across the room. "It doesn't matter. I must go to her. Heaven knows what Odell will do to her once he discovers she tried to call the police."

"According to the bulldog's story, Odell already knows." Cole's voice was uncharacteristically gentle. "It's too late, Ritter. The bastard's already done his worst."

"No! Odell is a coward. He may have Faith, but he hasn't summoned the courage to hurt her. Not yet. It may be too late for me to intervene, but perhaps the police can get there in time." Ritter spun to face O'Connor. "Faith is in danger. Go to—"

"Wait!" Cool power shimmered around Ritter and startled him into silence. "If the police barge in there, Odell will get away."

"I'll order O'Connor to arrest him."

Cole's voice dropped to a deadly quiet. "I don't want the bastard in jail. I want him dead."

"I won't trade Faith for vengeance."

"This is not a fucking business deal." Cole's anger beat against Ritter in frigid waves. "Thanks to your girlfriend's help, Odell may be hatching a batch of new vamps right now. You know what will happen if the police stumble across them. You want that bloodbath on your conscience?"

"I..." Ritter's voice died. Cole was right. The police would be powerless against newly hatched vampires. O'Connor's blundering into the situation would place him, his comrades, and Faith, all in deadly peril. Ritter couldn't send O'Connor to Faith's rescue. He would have to wait until sunset and pray it wasn't too late. Ritter slammed his fist into the wall. *"Himmel!"*

The plaster cracked. His knuckles split and bled. Agony, sharp and nauseating, raced through his hand and up his arm. He welcomed the pain. Broken bones felt better than the guilt flooding his heart. Too soon—before the plaster flakes finished falling—the hurt faded, and his broken hand healed. Ritter stared at the exposed lath and wondered if God heard the prayers of monsters.

"I'll take that as a 'no.'" Cole stepped beside him, put a hand on his shoulder. "You're right. Odell is a cowardly little shit. He'll take at least a day to decide what to do with the pretty doctor. Don't worry. We'll find her and get her out of there. In one piece."

Cole's dark eyes held a warmth Ritter had seldom seen in them. "We?"

Cole shrugged. "I wouldn't leave a dog in Odell's hands. Besides, I'm beginning to like the lady. She has guts."

"She is going to need them." Ritter turned to O'Connor. The police officer still sat on the couch, but his expression twitched with anger. "What about him?"

"Wipe his mind. Send him on his way."

"It won't keep. See how he fights my control?" Ritter sighed. "If I let him go, he may return with backup, perhaps more men than I can handle. He has to stay here."

O'Connor struggled to his feet. "Faith—"

"Is safe." Lying hurt worse than breaking his hand. He strengthened his voice. "Sleep."

"Sleep." O'Connor's knees buckled, and he dropped to the couch.

"Sleep until I awaken you."

Cole appeared beside him. "Sleep." The shimmer of his voice entwined with Ritter's. O'Connor sighed. He lay down and stretched out. His face grew slack, his breaths deep.

Ritter turned to Cole. "Thank you."

Cole's gaze swept Ritter's face. "You look like shit. Go to bed. Get some sleep."

"But O'Connor—"

"I'll keep an eye on the bulldog. Go on," he said when Ritter hesitated. "You won't be any good to the pretty doctor if you're a wreck tonight."

Again, Cole was right. Nodding, Ritter walked to the bedroom. Anxiety and fatigue weighted his steps. He turned at the door. "Wake me in a few hours. You, too, need sleep."

"Deal."

Ritter entered the comforting darkness of his bedroom. He closed the door, stripped off his clothes, and slipped between the cool sheets. He lay on his back and stared at the ceiling. Despite the darkness, he could see the pattern of tiny cracks in the old plaster. Pushing his worries about Faith from his mind, he started counting them, hoping to lull himself to sleep. When Cole knocked on the door, hours later, he was still counting.

∂↝

A storm began late that afternoon. The clouds thickened. The sky darkened. The air grew still and heavy. The first crack of thunder rattled the windows of Ritter's building. The second shook the foundation.

The door to the bedroom opened. Ritter put down his newspaper. Cole stood in the doorway, eyes still half closed. "What you doing out here, playing with dynamite?"

"A storm blew in about an hour ago."

"Hell of a storm." Cole walked over to the window and peeked under the curtain. "What time is it?"

"Quarter to five." Two hours to sunset and counting.

"Take a look." Cole lifted the curtain. The window glass reflected back Ritter's living room.

Ritter's heartbeat kicked up a notch. He stood and walked to the window. Pulling the curtain all the way open, he peered out. The alley outside his window was shrouded in gloom. The streetlight at the corner was on, but the glow huddled around the bulb and didn't reach the ground. He looked up. The sky was a deep, gray green. His face tingled, but the clouds filtered out most of the afternoon sun.

"Dark as sin out there," Cole said.

Ritter nodded. "Dark enough, as long as the clouds don't break. Come, Greta is in a garage three blocks from here."

A flash of light split the sky. A single hailstone bounced off the pavement. Then a dozen. Then thousands. Their clatter drowned out the answering boom.

"We can't go out in that." Cole's voice was sharp with frustration. "It's a fucking avalanche out there."

"Stay, then, if you fear a little ice." Ritter strode to the door and snatched up his keys.

"It's not me. I heal. But those stones'll pound Greta to scrap iron."

Ritter hesitated, but only for a second. "Metal can be replaced."

Cole whistled. "You that worried about the pretty doctor? Man, you do have it bad." Ritter glared, and he raised his hands in mock surrender. "I'm coming. Just let me grab my stuff and an umbrella."

"Here." Ritter pulled an umbrella from the stand and threw it at

Cole. When Cole caught it, the point was less than an inch from his chest.

He frowned. "You almost staked me."

Ritter snorted in disgust. "It is an umbrella, not a stake."

"Still sharp." Cole nodded toward the sleeping O'Connor. "What about him?"

Ritter walked to the couch. "Continue to sleep," he said, weaving his voice into a blanket of power that covered the policeman from hair to heel. "Ignore the storm, the door, the phone. Sleep until the cuckoo strikes four. Open your eyes and remember Faith's message. You arrived to find an open door and an empty apartment. There is a map on the table. It will lead you to the place you seek."

O'Connor groaned in his sleep and rolled over. Ritter set the map he'd drawn Cole on the coffee table, where the police officer would see it when he awoke. After a moment's thought, he took out a pen and wrote B&S Developments across the top of the sheet.

"He's going to wonder what happened to Wednesday."

Ritter straightened. "Not immediately. He'll think it is still this morning and follow us. It will give Faith another chance if we fail."

The clatter outside softened to the pounding of rain. Ritter walked to the window and lifted the curtain. The rising wind caught the heavy drops and flung them against the window in loud splatters. Cole sighed. "Might as well leave this here. It's blowing too hard to use it." He hurled the umbrella—point first—at Ritter. "Nice catch."

With a grimace, Ritter propped the umbrella beneath the window. "Come."

Cole put on his broad-brimmed hat and duster. Ritter threw on a hooded slicker. They ran up the stairs and out the door into the downpour. The rain slipped under Ritter's hood and drenched his face; he sucked in drops when he breathed. His shoes filled with water as he ran at full speed the three blocks to his rented garage.

Cole rushed inside after him. Taking off his hat, he shook the water from it. Despite the wide brim, water streaked his face. "The only good thing about weather like this is that no one else is stupid enough to be outside to see us run. You got a towel in here?"

Ritter opened Greta's trunk, shoved the tarp to one side, and took out the hand towels he kept to wipe bird droppings off Greta's hood. He tossed one to Cole. "Don't worry, it's clean," he said, at Cole's suspicious look. He used another to dry his own face.

Though he begrudged every second, Ritter picked up Greta's roof and settled it in place. If the storm blew over before sunset, he and Cole would need protection from the sun. He fastened one catch, two, but couldn't line up the third. His hands were trembling too much.

"Fuck it. Let me." Cole pushed him aside—none too gently—and clicked the other catches into place. After a quick shake to make sure the roof was secure, Ritter opened the garage door, stripped off his slicker, and jumped behind the wheel. Cole threw all the rain gear into the trunk and dove into the passenger seat, as Ritter turned on the windshield wipers and accelerated onto the rapidly flooding street.

The drive was a nightmare. Ritter's frustration grew as the seconds ticked by. The forty-two minute drive of the night before stretched into an hour, and then two, with whiteout conditions, ten-mile detours, and flooded viaducts. The sun had set by the time Ritter pulled onto the boggy lane and drove into the deserted barn.

Cole threw open his door and uncoiled from the seat. He stretched his legs and grimaced. "Damn sardine can."

Fear for Faith wound around Ritter like a black shroud. "This way." He started running toward B&S Developments.

Cole's footsteps chased him through a field of thistles and beneath dripping oak branches to a tall fence topped with razor wire. A metal sign every ten feet warned that the fence was electrically charged. Ritter jumped and easily cleared the top of the fence.

Cole landed beside him. "Razor wire *and* high voltage. Impressive."

"Come." Ritter ran, and Cole loped beside him. A few minutes later, they emerged beside a large gray building. Ritter pointed across the parking lot where he had seen Faith the night before. "Faith's apartment is over there."

"What about Odell?"

"How should I know?" The words came out harsh. Ritter took a deep breath and projected a confidence he didn't feel. "The apartment building is a good place to start looking for them. The only road from the complex leads past it. Even if Odell is not there, if he tries to leave, we will hear him drive by. We can be out the door and at his car before he reaches the gate."

Cole's eyes narrowed, but he finally nodded. "Lead on."

The apartment hallways were deserted, silent, and filled with the smell of curing paint and new carpet. No rustle of movement, no clatter of dishes, no smell of cooking. If Odell lived in one of the apartments, he wasn't there now.

They reached Faith's door, and Cole made short work of her lock. Hot, stale air puffed out. Ritter ran inside and searched the two small rooms and bath. The apartment was tidy, impersonal, and empty. The only hint of Faith was the faint scent of her bath powder. She hadn't been home in at least a day.

"Ritter, your lady's not here." Cole stood by the bedroom window. He pointed to the lighted building across the parking lot. "I say we look for your lady and Odell over there."

Ritter glanced around the room one last time. Faith's apartment held the only hints of human occupation in the whole building, and she wasn't home. He nodded.

They raced from the apartment to the laboratory building. As they approached it, Cole slowed. His brow furrowed. He stopped and motioned for Ritter to stop, as well. "That's not an office building, it's a fucking fortress. Reinforced glass, electronic lock, laser alarm, digital vid for face recognition, everything except fingerprint and retinal scanners. What do they keep in there, diamonds?"

"Or vampires. Can you get us in?"

"There isn't a lock made I can't pick." After examining the camera, the door, and the electronic mechanism beside it, Cole reached into his wallet and pulled out a plastic rectangle about the size of a credit card. It was white on one side and red on the other. Each side had a black magnetic strip. "A multiplatform, electronic lockpick. Reads and replicates the last key used."

He passed the card, white side up, through a slot in the electronic lock. Then he reversed the card and drew it through again. The mechanism whirred, the lock clicked, and a feminine voice said, "Dr. Miles Odell. Access granted."

"Odell was the last one through the door," Cole said with a triumphant grin. He kissed the card before putting it back in his pocket. "This baby cost a fortune, but I knew it'd come in handy."

They hurried inside. The entrance was deserted, the guard station empty. Odd, considering the tight security. Ritter shrugged off the thought. The important thing was to find Faith. He hurried to the directory by the elevator. She was the first listing; her office was on the second floor, room 212. Odell was further down the board, his office directly below hers, room 112.

Cole stepped up beside him. "The bastard's here on the first floor. Let's get him."

Ritter turned to Cole. "What about Faith?"

"We'll ask about the pretty doctor before I rip his throat. Odell's a weasel. He'll tell us anything, if he thinks it'll save his skin."

Anything, including a lie; but Ritter would use his voice to compel the truth. Odell was their best hope for finding Faith quickly. Ritter nodded. "Go."

The corridor leading from the bank of elevators to Odell's office was as deserted as the entryway. The door was locked. Cole opened it, and they stepped in. The only light came from an Escher-style screen saver. While Cole searched the office, including the coat closet and toilet, Ritter extended his other senses. Hearing, smell, even taste. The room smelled of aftershave, ink, and cleaning solvent. The computer hummed, air whispered through a nearby vent, and overhead, something creaked softly. Cole slammed back into the office. "Where the fuck is he?"

"Quiet." To capture Cole's attention, Ritter wove a thread of power through his voice. "Listen."

There it was again, a repetitive creaking from the room overhead: Faith's office. Cole studied the ceiling. "Someone's up there. Odell?"

"Or someone who knows where he is."

Cole shot out of the room and was halfway down the hall before Ritter caught up with him. "Don't kill him until he leads us to Faith."

Cole just kept running.

Disdaining the elevator as too slow, Ritter ran with Cole up the stairs to the second floor and down the hall to Faith's office. Cole didn't pause at the closed door. He barreled into it, shoulder first, and knocked it from its frame. The hinges popped. The metal door slammed to the floor, and Cole leapt across it into the room. Ritter raced in after him.

Odell was sitting in a swivel chair in front of a computer. At the sound of the crash, he spun around. The doctor had grown thinner in the last thirty years. Lines bracketed his mouth and eyes, and his hair had gone white. A bit of plastic nestled in one ear. It looked as if Odell now used a hearing aid. Instead of a military uniform, he wore pressed slacks, an open-collared shirt, and a white lab coat. A wire ran from the hearing aid to the lab coat pocket. The flavor of fear clung to Odell like smoke.

"Good evening, doctor." Ritter strolled past Cole to Odell's side.

"What's happening, man? Long time, no see." Cole flanked his other side.

The color fled Odell's face as his gaze shifted from Ritter to Cole. The fear grew sharper. "Morgan? I knew about Breitmann, but I thought you—"

"Burned with the rest?" Cole's grin spread, but his voice grew hard. "No such luck."

Ritter pulled Odell to his feet. "Where is Faith?" He added enough power to the question to ensure the truth.

Odell shuddered as if suddenly cold and shoved his hands into his pockets. "With Banat." A high buzz, like the whine of mosquitoes' wings, accompanied his answer.

Ritter scowled at the irritating noise—probably from Odell's hearing aid—and concentrated on controlling him. Cole had little patience. Ritter had to find Faith, and quickly. "Where?"

"He took her to the underground facility beneath this building, level two, probably. Banat's dangerous. Go now before it's too late."

Cole grabbed a handful of Odell's lab coat and pulled him to tiptoe. "What underground facility? The directory doesn't show any floors below the basement." He dropped the doctor and turned to Ritter. "The bastard's bullshitting us. I say kill him now."

"No!" Odell's protest was more squeak than word. "It's not listed on the directory. You need a special key to get there." He pulled out a white plastic card from one of his jacket pockets. "See?"

Ritter snatched the card from Odell's fingers. "Show us."

Cole glared at Ritter, but stepped aside and waved Odell toward the door.

Odell stumbled in his haste to get from Faith's office to the open elevator. Ritter and Cole kept pace beside him. "See," he repeated after they stepped inside. He pointed to a slot above the buttons. "To get to the lower levels, run the card through the slot and hit the button. One for the first level, two for the second. Banat works mostly on the second level. I think he took her there."

The mosquito was louder in the cramped confines of the elevator, loud enough to make Ritter's ears itch. "You don't know?" he snapped.

"I haven't seen Faith since last night." A momentary tinge of something—sorrow, remorse?—leavened Odell's fear.

Ritter swiped the card and punched the second button. He filled his voice with power. "Find her."

Odell's expression stiffened. "Find her."

Something was wrong. Too much fear hung in the air, fear and...anticipation. The buzzing grew louder. The elevator doors began to close. Odell tensed. The anticipation grew.

Ritter reached for him. "Stop!"

Too late. Odell hit the alarm button. A high pitched siren ripped through Ritter's head, a hundred times more painful than the blast of a rave's amplifiers. Odell dove through the closing doors, but Ritter couldn't follow. He was frozen by the clamor in his brain.

"Fucking bastard!" Cole shoved the elevator doors apart and ran after Odell.

Forcing himself to move, Ritter yanked the alarm button. The noise died. He waited for the ringing in his ears to still, then stepped from the elevator. He expected to find Cole standing over Odell's body, but the corridor was empty and silent except for the distant hammer of running feet. Either the blast of sound had slowed Cole, or Odell had gone to ground and Cole now searched the building for him.

A glint from the floor caught his attention. A silver disk and length of wire lay near the elevator door. Ritter stooped and picked them up. The disk was a miniature CD player, the volume set to high. The wire connected it to an earbud speaker. Ritter swore. Here was Odell's "hearing aid." The doctor had used amplified music to block Ritter's voice.

Disgusted, Ritter dropped the player and returned to the elevator. Odell was Cole's concern now. Ritter had to find Faith. Once again, he ran the key through the slot and pushed the second button. The elevator dropped, picking up speed as it passed the basement. Still, the descent seemed too slow. Ritter's muscles ached with frustration by the time it lurched to a stop and the doors opened.

"*Himmel!*" Any doubts he had about Odell's plans vanished. Ruddy light filled the hallway. The lighting would be dim to human eyes, but soothing to a young vampire's changed vision. He stepped into the corridor. A hint of emotion, fear laced with anger and determination, seasoned the air. Beneath it, he caught a whiff of flowers: Faith's perfume. Once again, his loved one had wandered into the monsters' lair.

Fear for Faith squeezed his heart.

Please, God, let me be in time.

But first he had to find her. Her scent faded as he hesitated, the victim of a modern air-filtration and cooling system. The faint draft brushed his face and whispered in his ears. Though he twitched with impatience, Ritter remained still and stretched his hearing. Faint and far away, he caught the murmur of voices. Abandoning all pretense of being human, he raced toward them, swift and silent. The corridor branched and branched again. He ran past dozens of closed doors but saw no one. The voices grew louder. Finally, he stopped in front of yet another closed door. His heart sank. He had hoped to find Faith, but both voices belonged to men. They were arguing.

One speaker was loud, defensive, and young. The other sounded older, his voice filled with quiet anger. Dread crawled across Ritter's shoulders. Something about the second voice hinted at a distant and unpleasant memory he couldn't quite reach.

Ritter tried the knob, but the door was locked. A quick twist and shove should have opened the door, but it was sturdier than the one to Faith's lab. Ritter gained a sore shoulder and lost the benefit of surprise. The voices stopped. Ritter heard footsteps. The knob turned. The door opened.

At first glance, the man behind it looked old, in his sixties at least. He was short, with thin hair combed over a large bald spot. His posture, though, straight and strong, belonged to a much younger man, as did the smooth, unlined skin. Strangely youthful eyes glittered. Recognition squeezed Ritter's heart even before the lips spread into a pointed smile.

"Ritter Breitmann. Greetings, comrade, I thought you were dead."

Chapter Twenty-Four

Karl Heine's appearance had changed, but not his voice. He spoke in German, in the same wheezy tenor Ritter remembered from their first meeting. "Until this afternoon, when I realized you might still live."

Ritter responded in the same language. Despite his shock, his words came out smoothly. "I thought you burned with Dresden."

"I fled before the bombs fell." Heine's brow wrinkled a moment, then smoothed. "Enough of the old days. The past is dead; let me show you the future."

He opened the door wide and switched to English. "Allow me to introduce my partner, Phillip Sloan." With barely veiled contempt, Heine gestured into the room. It was set up for a meeting, with a large oblong table in the center. Sloan stood beside one of the surrounding chairs, a metal and plastic exercise in discomfort.

Sloan blanched. "You—you're the one in my dreams."

Ritter lifted his lips in a humorless smile. His shock was beginning to thaw into rage, and Sloan was an easy target. "Raped any children lately?"

"You know each other?" Heine asked.

Ritter switched to German. "You kept better company when your comrades were vampires."

Heine shrugged. "At times I find it necessary to work with inferiors."

"Speak English so I can understand." Sloan was obviously trying to assert his authority, but a quaver in his voice ruined the effect.

Heine motioned Ritter into the room. "This is my comrade, Ritter Breitmann," he said in English. "We served in the second world war together."

"Heine—" Ritter's warning was meant for his ears alone.

"I have no secrets from my partner, do I Phillip?" Heine cast a smile at his partner that made the man shudder, then turned to Ritter. "I call myself Banat now, C.W. Banat. I researched our progenitor, the one whose blood transformed us, and discovered he came from the Banat region of Romania. I changed my name to honor him."

A mixture of old anger and new fear swirled through Ritter. Anger at the smug monster who had killed Greta, fear that he now held Faith. Ritter bit his lip to keep from snarling. He had to play along with Heine—or Banat as he now called himself—until he discovered where Faith was and what Banat had done to her. "What is this future you spoke of?"

Banat's eyes grew bright. "Remember our *Führer*'s dream of a master race?"

"Your *Führer*, not mine."

Banat shrugged. "It doesn't matter. The Nazis were fools. I've learned one thing in the last seventy years. White, black, Aryan, Jew, all men taste the same." He leaned forward until his breath washed across Ritter's face. "You and I are different. Stronger, faster, longer-lived. We and those like us are the true master race."

Ritter shook his head. "We—"

"Hear me out!"

The thread of power in Banat's voice gave Ritter pause. He could feel the strength of it, the depth of Banat's control. Banat had learned much since they last met.

"Übel's experiment was a farce," Banat continued. "He started with a hundred men and created ninety-six corpses. He was a fool; his science, flawed. I am not a fool, and science has progressed. A few weeks ago, I started with twenty volunteers. Half survived and will soon awaken to their new lives. Would you like to see them?"

"No," Sloan broke in. "It's too dangerous."

Banat curled his lip like an angry wolf. "Silence while your betters speak."

Sloan stumbled back. "Sorry, Mr. Banat, I didn't mean—"

A high-pitched siren cut him off. Though quieter than the punishing clamor in the elevator, the noise pummeled Ritter's ears and frayed his already fragile control. Unless he was mistaken, the siren meant Odell was alive, well, and calling for help. Cole had failed.

Sloan glanced toward the ceiling. "Someone tripped the intruder alarm."

Banat grimaced and nodded toward the door. "Shut it off and investigate."

With a nod, Sloan darted from the room. A moment later, the alarm stopped.

"A spineless worm, but he has his uses." Banat's smile was brief and wry. He took Ritter's arm. "Back to more important matters; come see my progeny."

Revulsion crawled up Ritter's arm. Snarling, he tore free.

Banat frowned.

Himmel! Cursing his ragged control, Ritter took a deep breath. He couldn't afford to antagonize Banat, not until his onetime comrade told him where to find Faith. He forced his voice to blandness. "I'll look at your vampires later. First I need to find Fai—Dr. Allister. We had an appointment for this evening.".

"An appointment. I can imagine what kind of appointment you had with the lovely doctor." Banat took something out of his jacket pocket and tossed it to Ritter.

It was the locket, the one he had given Greta and then Faith. Ritter's guts twisted into knots. "Where did you get this?"

"I took it from her throat."

"Her throat?" Ritter's voice rose. "What have you done to her?"

"I? Nothing. I left her to my children. Once they awaken, she'll be their first taste of immortality."

"No!" Ritter grabbed Banat's shirt and shoved him against the nearest wall. "She's a brilliant scientist and a beautiful woman. You can't use her as fodder."

Banat remained infuriatingly calm. "She became too inquisitive and hard to control. She left me no choice. I must eliminate her."

Ritter molded his voice into a cudgel, each word into a blow. "Take me to her."

Banat shuddered, but didn't break. "Why do you care? She's a mortal, like any other."

"She is under my protection."

"I admit she's a tempting morsel, but a dangerous one. Find another playmate."

"She's not any kind of morsel. Good heavens, man, you can't leave her to die. She's your own granddaughter."

Surprise flared across Banat's face. "Impossible."

"I made you forget; now remember." Releasing Banat, Ritter slipped the necklace into his pocket and concentrated on his voice. He honed it to a scalpel, sharp enough to slice away years of forgetfulness. "Übel's party that first Christmas, the blood, the girls. Remember!"

Banat waved off Ritter's command as if it were an annoying insect. "I remembered years ago. The whores died, and Übel burned their bodies. No woman has survived a night with me since my rebirth."

"One did. A half-starved waif with Faith's curly hair. You ravaged her that Christmas but left her breathing. You passed out; she escaped. Karl, she bore your child, Faith's mother. You can't let one of your own blood be torn apart by mindless hunger."

A parade of emotions flickered across Banat's face: shock, wonder, disdain. "Why not? She is still a mortal, born to bleed and die. And she threatens the future."

"I want her. Now." Ritter poured all his power, all his control into his voice and prayed it would be enough.

Banat's smile grew hard, contemptuous. "If you want a woman, find another. There are millions of mortals with warm thighs and full veins. Easy, stupid creatures like that little whore in Dresden."

Ritter lunged at Banat.

"*Halt!*" Banat ordered, and the air grew as thick as cold porridge. Ritter forced his arms up, reaching for Banat's throat, but Banat batted his hands aside. "Think you can defeat me? Fool! I spent years learning the extent of my strength and powers. What have you done, besides hide among lesser beings and try to ape their inferiority? Don't look so surprised; Odell told me about working with you in the seventies. About your pathetic attempts to become human again. That's what you are: pathetic and unfit to join the new master race." With negligent ease, he backhanded Ritter.

A man's neck would have broken. Ritter's head snapped to one side, and an agonizing jolt shot from his cheek to the soles of his feet. Knocked off balance, he staggered sideways but pulled himself erect before falling. At least he could move again. He molded his voice in bullet-like bursts. "Where. Is. Faith?"

"Idiot." Banat slammed his fist into Ritter's solar plexus. The blow traveled all the way to Ritter's spine. Bent double, he stumbled back, unable to breathe.

"Her fate is already sealed. As is yours." An uppercut caught Ritter's jaw, flinging him across the table and into one of the chairs. The hard plastic and metal collapsed beneath him. The jagged edges ripped his shirt and flesh.

There was no air. Ritter struggled to pull in a breath as the room dissolved into dots. Footsteps stalked toward him. Ritter gasped, and Banat appeared, an arm's length away. He pulled a wooden stake from beneath his jacket. "Insurance, in case one of my children proved intractable. I have twenty and can easily spend one on you." He raised the stake and swung it toward Ritter's heart.

Arms still weak and jerky, Ritter grabbed the first thing he could reach—one of the chair legs—and thrust it before him.

The leg was sharp where it had broken from the seat. The metal point took Banat in the shoulder. He screamed and reared back. The stake dropped to the floor

Ritter scrambled after it.

"*Scheisskopf!*" Banat swore and wrenched the chair leg free.

Ritter's fingers closed around the stake. He sprang to his feet, shoved Banat against the wall, and plunged the stake under his ribs and into his heart.

Banat gaped like a fish. Ritter jabbed the stake in deeper and yanked it straight back. Banat's breastbone cracked. Ritter pulled harder. In a wash of blood, he ripped Banat's heart from his chest. Banat's husk crumpled to the floor.

Fierce joy surged through Ritter. He had finally kept his promise. Greta's murderer was dead. He wrapped his fingers around the slick, hot flesh and squeezed. "You crushed my heart," he cried in German. "Now I crush yours."

As the blood seeped through his fingers, his joy drained away. Horror took its place. He had forgotten Faith. She was imprisoned with a group of awakening vampires, and he had just killed the only one who knew where her prison lay. The heart tumbled from Ritter's fingers. Heaven help him, he may have destroyed his only hope of saving her.

≈ ≈

Ritter searched all night. The underground facility was a warren of nearly identical hallways and rooms. Since the air remained stubbornly free of Faith's scent, he wasted precious time breaking down the locked doors before he thought to go back and search Banat's pockets for keys. The rooms he searched contained the accouterments of modern business: tables, chairs, and computer terminals. No people. No Faith. He turned down a short corridor and discovered half a dozen small rooms with beds in them. Faith's perfume lingered in the third room. His heart soared, only to crash moments later. The room was empty. Faith was gone.

According to his watch, it was nearly dawn when Ritter heard the grinding of the elevator motor and the chime of its doors. He abandoned his search and ran toward the sound. Perhaps Sloan had returned. Whoever it was, anyone entering the underground facility at this hour would know of the vampires and their location. At least Ritter hoped so. He had little time before the sun rose and barred his escape.

He sprinted to the elevators. The hallway was empty, but nearby footsteps called him. Ritter raced after them. He turned the corridor in time to see Sloan open a door and disappear inside.

"Mr. Banat?" Ritter heard Sloan's fear even before he tasted it. He slowed his pace and approached silently.

Sloan hovered just inside the doorway. The room was large and filled with beds. A blanket-covered form lay on each. In addition to Sloan's galloping pulse, eleven hearts beat in a slow, steady rhythm. Ritter caught a whiff of perfume. "Faith!"

The forms remained motionless, but Sloan spun around. His face was pasteboard white except for the shadows bruising his eyes. He smelled of fear, sweat, and frustration. He cringed deeper into the room. "Christ, you're covered in blood. Did Banat—"

Ritter pushed past Sloan. The forms on the beds were men, large men, with the sunken, hollow look of sleeping vampires. One of them moaned. Ritter had to find Faith and get her out of the room before they awakened. He turned on Sloan and grabbed his shoulder. "Banat is dead. Where is Faith?"

"Faith?"

Another moan, softer and higher pitched, came from the back of the room. Ritter dragged Sloan toward it. The last bed held two, he realized as he drew nearer. Faith lay hidden behind the vampire. Her eyes were closed. Ritter shook her. She moaned but didn't open her eyes. He tightened his grip on Sloan. "What did you do to her?"

"Me? I didn't do anything. I don't even know what she's doing here."

Ritter could taste the truth in his words. Letting go of Sloan's shoulder, he turned to Faith. Except for a small bruise on her throat, she appeared unharmed. Ritter looked closer. It wasn't a bruise, but the mark of an injection. Banat had drugged her.

As if directed by a single will, ten hearts picked up their pace. The shape on the bed began to stir. The moans turned to sharp cries, the hungry cries of a newborn. Ritter had to get Faith to the elevator and safety before the smell of human blood roused the infant vampires to violence. Hoping the inhuman blood that stained his shirt and hands would hide her scent, he scooped Faith in his arms and turned toward the door.

Sloan blocked the way. "What's happening?"

"The young vampires are beginning to awaken. Leave, now, while they are weak and disoriented."

The vampire closest to the door lurched from his bed. He slowly turned as if searching the room. His expression was blank, his eyes empty except for the hunger. His gaze lighted on Sloan. He tipped his head and howled.

The noise sliced Ritter's ears. "Stop!" The order contained all his power, but it was lost in a chorus of cries. Two more vampires rose from their beds and turned toward Sloan.

The man panicked. Wrapped in a cloud of terror, he bolted for the door. The first vampire leapt after him. Before Ritter could stop him, he grabbed Sloan and buried his fangs in his throat.

Though quicker than Ritter thought possible, the young vampire was still clumsy. He tore too large a hole. Blood spurted around the corners of his mouth while he swallowed in loud greedy gulps. Sloan writhed in his grip and screamed.

Fresh blood perfumed the air. The other vampires ran to Sloan. One took an arm. Another grabbed a leg. Fabric tore, flesh ripped. The screams rose.

Praying Faith stayed unconscious, Ritter stilled his breathing and slowed his heart. With a knot of vampires blocking the door, her only hope was for them to remain unnoticed. The blood of one man would only whet their hunger, but if Ritter stood very still, the vampires might leave in search of other prey.

On the other side of the door, a blur of movement froze into a man's silhouette. "Fuck, a baby vamp food fest. Ritter, you in there?"

He would have thanked heaven, but he didn't have time. He focused his words for Cole's ears alone. "Yes. So is Faith, and she is unconscious. Can you clear the way?"

Cole answered the same way. "No problem." Dark fingers appeared around the first vampire's arm. Cole ripped him from Sloan and flung him aside. Grabbing Sloan's shoulders, he tore the dying man from the other vampires' teeth and threw him after the first. The baby vampires scrambled after them. Finding Sloan's outstretched limbs, they latched on again. The screams gurgled to a stop.

A heavy hand gripped Ritter's shoulder. Sharp teeth slashed his neck. Ritter had forgotten the vampire behind him.

"*Himmel*." Clutching Faith to his chest, he twisted from the vampire's grasp.

"There's another one on your right." Cole ran into the room. The cries of the young vampires grew louder. "Drop her and get out of here!"

"They'll attack Faith if I put her down."

Cole threw another vampire into the wall. "They'll attack her anyway. These babies have jumped straight to the mean and hungry stage. We turn our backs on them, they'll have us down and out in seconds."

"Unless one of us distracts them." Ritter kicked free of the second vampire and leapt toward Cole. "Take her. Carry her to safety. I'll hold the door and give you time."

Cole backhanded one vampire and gut-punched another. "You can't. It's almost dawn."

"I am not leaving Faith."

"You don't have time to be a fucking hero."

"I will not leave her."

"Shit!" Cole heaved the two vampires aside, clearing the path to the door. But others were rising, climbing from their beds. He nodded toward the hall. "Go. Now."

"But—"

"I can take a little sun. You can't. Go on, get your lady out of here before I change my mind."

Ritter bit back his argument. Cole was right. He threw Faith over his shoulder and raced for the door.

"Look out for Odell. The bastard maced me with garlic juice. Nearly took me out."

Ritter was down the corridor and to the elevator before Cole stopped speaking.

Thumps, crashes, and assorted profanities drifted down the corridor before the doors finally opened. Ritter carried Faith inside and hit the button for the ground floor. The doors closed and his breathing eased as the elevator rose. Dawn permitting, he would carry Faith to the safety of her apartment and return to help Cole.

The trip up seemed even longer than the trip down, but after an eternity, Ritter stepped from the elevator into the blare of a radio and the reek of garlic. Miles Odell stood in the corridor, a spray bottle in one hand. Ritter was willing to bet it was Cole's "mace." The other hand held a pistol.

Cole had been right about the dawn. Already, the brightening sky dulled the mirrored windows. Ritter only had a few minutes. After that, if Odell didn't kill him, the sun would.

"You found Faith." Odell didn't sound pleased. "I'd hoped Banat had taken care of her."

"Banat is dead. Move if you don't care to join him."

Odell didn't budge. He raised the spray bottle and a cloud of garlic mist shot toward Ritter.

The first sneeze nearly shook Faith from his arms. He set her on the floor before convulsing with the second. His throat clogged and his eyes swelled shut. Through his tears, Ritter saw Odell drop the bottle and take the pistol in both hands. "Thirty-five years ago, I loaded this against vampires." Ritter heard a loud crack, and a blow slammed into his left shoulder. A second hit his gut and doubled him over. Through the numbing shock, he barely heard the bullets hit the wall behind him, barely felt his body hit the floor.

Odell walked up, his shoes stopping inches from Faith's head. "I tried to make you understand, but you wouldn't listen." He knelt down and pressed the gun to Faith's temple.

"No!" Forcing himself to move, Ritter rolled into Odell and knocked the pistol from his hand.

Odell scrambled to his feet. "The bullets are silver. Why aren't you dead?"

The numbness had already begun to ebb, replaced by the throb of healing. The pain fueled Ritter's rage. He stood, lifted Odell, and shook him, as a dog shakes a rag. "Because, you fool, I am a vampire, not a werewolf."

He threw Odell at the window, head first. Odell's neck snapped. The body fell to the ground, leaving a spider web of cracks across the glass.

The fight had taken too long. The mirrors were windows once more. Even filtered through tinted glass, the light stung Ritter's face.

He turned to Faith. She slept on, unharmed by Odell's betrayal. Ritter picked her up and stifled a gasp of pain as her weight hit his shoulder. Weakened as he was by the gunshot wounds, the sun could kill him in minutes. He gazed longingly at Odell's body. A quick drink would speed his healing, but nothing could protect him from the full glare of the sun. He had to go now, while the sun still clung to the horizon. His only hope, and Faith's, lay in speed. Saying a prayer to the God who had abandoned him seventy years ago, Ritter ran into the day.

≈≈

Faith opened her eyes to the familiar sight of acoustic ceiling tiles. Sunshine sifted through curtained windows, giving them a golden sheen. She stretched, and her hand hit the back of the couch. Had she fallen asleep in the living room again?

No. Memory slammed into her. The mobile drug lab. Banat's vampires. There were worse things than drugs in Lake County, and the threat of an even more terrible epidemic. She had to call John and warn him. Faith shot off the couch and lunged for the phone.

She never reached it. The minute her head left the couch, the room began to spin, and a wave of nausea swept over her. It pulsed to the tempo of her suddenly pounding head. Choking back bile, Faith stumbled toward the bathroom.

Ignoring the light switch, she dove for the toilet. Her stomach emptied itself in a series of heaves that left her weak and trembling. When they finally stopped, she grabbed the edge of the sink and hauled herself to her feet. Water cooled her face, soothed her raw throat. She took another sip to wash the bitterness off her tongue.

Banat's drugs had left her nauseous, but that was quickly fading. Except for a lingering tenderness near her collarbone, she felt fine. From what she remembered, she ought to be dead. Banat had left her to the vampires. How had she gotten back to the apartment? She couldn't imagine Banat changing his mind, but maybe Miles had found her and carried her home. Or John—maybe he'd been able to trace her partial message to Banat's complex. Or Ritter. He might have come looking for her when she didn't show up for their appointment. Someone must have helped her, but who? And where was he now?

Her reflection in the mirrored medicine cabinet was little more than a dark silhouette against the dim glow from the hallway. She reached back and hit the lights. A pile of clothes—jeans and a man's white polo shirt, caked with a heavy, dark substance—sat on the floor near the tub. Water had splashed them, and the resulting puddle was red-tinged. *Blood?* Faith's stomach lurched. Swallowing the urge to throw up again, she bent down for a closer look.

A groan rose from the bathtub. Faith jumped back against the sink. "Who's there?"

No answer.

With a trembling hand, she pulled back the shower curtain. At first, her eyes couldn't make sense of what they saw. Pinkish water lapped the sides of her tub and rose halfway up a bumpy red mound. It didn't look human. It didn't even look alive. The center rose, fell, and rose again. It was breathing, she realized: shallow, labored breaths. At the foot of the tub, a pair of long bony feet stuck out of the water.

Recognition hit her like a blow to the stomach. She knew those feet. She'd seen them hanging off the end of a couch last spring. The strength drained from her legs, and she dropped to her knees. "Ritter?"

He moaned and turned what was left of his face toward her. His features were lost in a blistered, swollen mass. Blisters upon blisters, broken, black, and bleeding. Slits for eyes. No nose. Cracked lips parted. "Faith?"

The voice sounded dry and raspy, but it was definitely Ritter's.

"Yes." Faith braced her hand on the tub—the porcelain felt warm in the cool room—and reached out to check his pulse. She jerked back before she touched him. Not only would the physical contact cause him too much pain, but she couldn't risk exposing him to the germs on her hands. He'd suffered third-degree burns on his face and arms, second-degree burns on his shoulders and chest. The murky water hid the rest of his body, but even if it were uninjured, Ritter needed a sterile environment, IV fluids, and a lot of luck, or he was going to die.

She shot to her feet. "I'm calling 911."

"Wait." A black and blistered hand rose from the water. Though Ritter's face had swollen to a shapeless blob, his hand was withered. "Stay with me."

Faith's legs throbbed with the need to hurry. "You'll die if you don't get to a hospital."

"No hospital can help me. Seventy years ago, it was already too late." He coughed, and bloody spittle flew from his lips. "Don't let me die alone. Sit, *Liebchen*, and let me gaze at you. It won't be long."

"No! I have a medical degree. If you won't go to the hospital, tell *me* what to do." It was against all her training to do nothing while a man suffered and died. But Ritter wasn't a man. The thought doused her like ice water. Ritter was a vampire. She knelt beside the tub. "What happened to you?"

"The sun." His lips twisted into a painful smile. "Do you realize how beautiful the morning sun is? Almost worth the cost."

"If you knew sunlight would hurt you, why—" A sudden thought choked off the question. "It was because of me, wasn't it? You found me, rescued me from Banat and his monsters, and carried me home. You exposed yourself to the sun in order to save my life. Oh, Ritter."

"I couldn't let them kill you." He reached up and touched her cheek. Though they had just come from the water, the withered fingers felt hot and dry. "Seeing you alive and safe is worth everything."

"Ritter, I—"

A wood-splintering, wall-shaking crash cut her off, and a deep, "Ritter?" boomed down the hallway.

Faith jumped up. An apparition in black—boots, duster, and broad-brimmed hat—streaked past the open bathroom door. "Ritter!"

Before Faith could take a step, he reappeared. It was Cole, moving faster than any man could. His gloved hand shot out and grabbed her arm. Eyes blazing, teeth flashing, he yanked her toward him. "Where the fuck is he?"

Chapter Twenty-Five

"Let her go."

Ritter's voice was quiet, but Cole jerked as if it burned. He released Faith and crouched next to the tub. "Shit, man. What the fuck you do to yourself?"

"It was the sun." Faith knelt beside him. "Ritter carried me here from the lab building. Banat drugged me unconscious. I guess the sun was already up, and—"

"He went out in it anyway. Fucking Boy Scout." The scowl Cole turned on Ritter would have terrified Godzilla, but his voice sounded surprisingly tender. "I knew you were in trouble when you weren't in the barn with Greta, but I didn't think you'd do anything this stupid. Didn't your mamma teach you not to go outside without your hat?"

Ritter's chuckle was raw with pain. "I must have missed that lesson."

"I wanted to call 911, but he says it won't do any good." Faith touched Cole's arm with hesitant fingers. "There must be something I can do."

The scowl dissolved into a grin that was just as scary. "You want to help, huh?"

Ritter struggled to sit up. "No!"

A feverish prickle swept Faith.

"Don't bother, man." Cole caught Ritter's arm and pulled him into a sitting position. "You're too fucking weak."

"I forbid it. It's too dangerous."

"Forbid what? You risked your life to save mine. What's a little danger compared to that?"

"He needs blood," Cole said. "You willing to donate?"

"She doesn't understand." With obvious difficulty, Ritter grasped Cole's arm and levered himself to his feet. Except for blue boxers clinging to his skin, he was naked. Though his chest was red, swollen, and covered with blisters, his legs looked almost normal. Apparently jeans protected better than white polo shirts.

"What's not to understand? You bite her, she bleeds, you drink. You heal. She doesn't. Two problems solved." Before Faith could bolt,

Cole grabbed her again. "I'll hold her."

"Let me go!" Faith tugged, but she couldn't free her arm.

"I didn't save her life to take it now. Let her go, Cole."

The gloved fingers loosened, and Faith jerked away. She glared at Cole, furious, but curiously unafraid.

"You don't have any choice," he said to Ritter, voice sharp with frustration. "Clearing out the baby vamps took too long. The sun's too high. I can't hunt fresh blood for you."

"Can I?"

Both vampires turned toward Faith. "You'd lure someone here for him to drain?" Cole's words dripped skepticism.

"No, of course not. But I can go outside." She turned to Ritter. "And I am a doctor. I'll go to the hospital and requisition blood."

Cole shook his head. "It'd take too long. He's got an hour left; two, max. The paperwork alone would take longer than that."

"The pints from the blood bank." Ritter's voice had dropped to a weak whisper.

"Still in your fridge?" Cole asked.

Ritter nodded.

"Greta is a fast little car." It sounded as if Cole were talking to himself. "If the pretty doctor ignores the speed limit, she could get to your place and back again in less than an hour."

Cole reached into one of the duster's pockets, pulled out a set of keys, and shoved them at Faith. "I left Greta in the fire lane out front. Drive her to Ritter's, get the blood, and hurry back. If you don't, I'll hunt you down and eat your liver." Despite the warmth of the room, an icy draft wrapped around Faith, and she recognized the tingle of vampire hypnosis.

"It would probably give you heartburn." She snatched the keys. "How dare you waste time threatening me? Look at him." Ritter leaned against bath enclosure. Fine shivers ran up and down his skin. "He's hypothermic from sitting in that cold water. He needs to be in bed. My sheets aren't sterile, but at least they're clean. Take him to the bedroom, tuck the covers around him and make him some tea, if he can stomach it."

Ritter shook his head. "Your living room—too much sun."

Faith thought a moment. "There's a down comforter at the foot of the bed. Wrap him in it, if you have to. The curtains are thick, so the bedroom itself should be dark enough. I'll be back in forty minutes."

It took her thirty-eight. Greta hunkered down to the road at 150 kph; at 180, she still handled beautifully. Faith raced down the deserted country roads and thanked God that for once there was no traffic. She had to slow when she reached Waukegan, but even with lights and the occasional slow truck, she was back at her apartment with the two pints of blood in less than half the time it normally would have taken her.

She burst into her bedroom. She'd been right about the curtains. With the light off, the room was as dark as death. Light from the living room spilled across the floor and onto the bed. Ritter lay under the comforter with only his face showing. He looked worse, much worse. The swelling was gone, and the skin had shriveled. Black and leathery, it clung like a mummy's to his skull. His sunken eyes were closed, and only the faintest movement hinted that he still breathed.

"Got the blood?"

Startled, Faith jumped and spun around. Cole lounged against her dresser. He'd removed his coat and hat, but the clothes beneath were equally black. She could barely see him, a shadow in the darkness. He pushed off her dresser and stalked toward her. "Well?"

Faith lifted the pints for him to see.

His teeth shone in a sudden smile. Tearing the bags from her grasp, he ran to the bed and lifted Ritter's head. He held the first bag up to his mouth. "Here, man."

Ritter didn't move, not even an eyelid flutter. Cursing, Cole ripped the pint open with his teeth. Blood splashed his hand and ran down the plastic. He shoved the bleeding bag under Ritter's nose. "Drink!"

Ritter's nostrils flared. His eyes opened. He raised the desiccated claw that had once been his right hand and pressed the torn bag to his lips.

The first bag drained quickly. So did the second. Ritter licked the edge of the plastic and dropped back to the mattress.

The improvement was immediate and amazing. His sunken eyes filled out. His lips plumped. Flesh seemed to grow beneath his charred skin. It stretched, cracked, and peeled, revealing healthy pink beneath.

Faith ran past Cole to the bed. She sat on its edge and, ignoring the skin that sloughed off on her fingers, took Ritter's hand. "You scared me half to death."

"Myself, as well." His voice sounded stronger, though it was still raspy. "Thank you."

"You strong enough to walk? The tarp's in the trunk—it should protect you from the sun." The mattress sank as Cole sat on the bed beside her. "I fixed a little surprise for Odell and his pals. We should be out of here before it blows."

"Odell is dead," Ritter said.

"Surprise?" Faith said at the same moment. Then Ritter's words hit her. "Dead?"

Cole grinned. "Tell me about it later. Right now, we have to get the fuck out of here. I found some incendiary grenades in the late doctor's office—probably his insurance against the baby vamps. I rigged a timer to set them off at noon." He glanced at Faith's alarm clock. "We have ten minutes."

Miles was dead, and in ten minutes, the building next door was going to burn. The information sat like an indigestible lump in Faith's brain. Then its implications sank in. She jumped off the bed. "My briefcase—it's still in the lab." Along with the memory stick from her computer and all her notes. If the building burned, they'd burn too. All her work, her hope for a cure, gone in a burst of flame. "I've got to get it."

"Faith." Ritter's voice was weaker again. He struggled to sit up, but couldn't. His flesh shrank, and his skin tightened until it once again hugged his naked bones.

Faith looked at Cole. "What's happening?"

"He's dying." Cole sounded bleak, almost forlorn. "Two pints weren't enough."

"He needs more blood?"

"Lots of it and now. Fuck!" He punched a fist-sized hole in her bedroom wall.

"Don't mourn. I have already lived too long." Ritter's voice was fading again. He stared at Faith a long moment, as if trying to memorize her face. Then his gaze drifted past her. "Cole?"

"Yeah, man?"

"Take her and go."

A hand grasped her arm. "I'm not going anywhere!" Faith yanked free and spun on Cole. "There must be something we can do. Maybe if we both donate blood—"

"My blood's no good. Think I'd stand here and watch him shrivel if a pint or two of mine would help? He needs human blood, probably three or four pints." Cole's face turned to a sneer. "Enough to kill a little thing like you. You willing to die for him, pretty doctor?"

"No!" Ritter's protest was the ghost of a whisper.

"It might not take that much." Faith took Ritter's hand. It was a claw again and burning hot. "We could at least try."

Ritter's fingers closed around her hand in a grip weaker than a baby's. "No. Too dangerous."

It was dangerous. Faith had seen Ritter swallow two pints in seconds. He could drain her and not even realize it. And there was her work to consider. If she died, who would find the cure for Stoker's? The answer was in her notes—she knew it—but it would take other scientists years to replicate her work. Without her notes, they might never succeed.

She glanced at the clock. According to Cole, in eight minutes her notes would burn to ash. Faith had eight minutes to run across the parking lot, up the stairs, into her lab and out again. She once ran the mile in four minutes, eighteen seconds. She could save her notes…if she left now.

Surely Ritter could wait eight minutes, eight tiny minutes to save hundreds of babies. Eight minutes to make her life mean something.

Ritter's fingers fell from her hand. "Good-bye, *Liebchen*." His voice was so faint, she had to lean forward to hear him. His eyes closed. "*Ich liebe dich*." I love you.

Tears stung Faith's eyes. Ritter didn't have eight minutes. He didn't have two. She looked up at Cole. "My blood—how do I give it to him?"

≈≈

In. Out. In. Out. Sweet air filled Faith's lungs. Dry and cool, it tickled her nose. Her hand itched, and her arm throbbed to a distant ache. Something was wrong. Dead people weren't supposed to hurt.

I must be alive.

The thought surprised her awake. She lay on a hospital bed, surrounded by the beeps and hum of modern medicine. The overhead lights were off, but indirect lighting around the ceiling allowed her to see the room. An IV irritated her right hand; white bandages swathed her left arm from wrist to elbow. Her mouth was sandpaper dry, and her arm hurt, but the thing that bothered her most was the damn IV. A funny thing to worry about when she'd expected to wake up dead.

Voices drifted from the corridor outside. They grew louder, until Faith could almost make out words. The door swung open.

"She's under sedation and shouldn't be disturbed." The words crackled with indignation.

John O'Connor strode into view, followed by a young man in a blue lab coat, most likely the resident physician on duty. His reddened cheeks clashed with his carroty hair and freckles. Even with the stethoscope around his neck and the clipboard in his hand, he looked about twelve.

"Hey." Ignoring the continuing sputter, John pulled a chair up to Faith's bed and sat down beside her. His smile didn't chase the worry from his eyes. "How's it going?"

"Not bad." Faith patted the bed until she found the controls and raised the mattress to a sitting position. The room dissolved into spots, then swam back into focus. Yes, she was definitely doing better than she had any right to hope. She glanced at her wrist, but someone had removed her watch. "What time is it?"

"About eight. You slept the day away." His smile faded. "Feel up to talking about what happened?"

"Sure." Faith glanced at the resident who still hovered near the door. "Alone."

The young doctor made a show of studying the clipboard. "The chart says no visitors."

"Let me see."

He began to shake his head. "It's not—"

"I got my MD while you were still passing notes in high school bio. Hand it over."

He did, with obvious reluctance. She took the pen, jotted *Visitors OK* across the top of the sheet, and scrawled her name beneath it. "Now you're covered. Go play doctor somewhere else."

The resident flushed a brighter red. He snatched the clipboard and stalked out. John chuckled. "I hear doctors make lousy patients."

"The worst."

"The ER doctor put you down as an attempted suicide, but you didn't slit your own wrist, did you?"

"No." At least she could tell that much truth. When Faith couldn't bring herself to slice her own skin, Cole had taken the scalpel and opened her vein. She'd placed the bleeding wound by Ritter's lips herself, though, and had cradled his head while he drank. In a way, the admitting physician was right. Though she hadn't wanted to die, the worst damage was self-inflicted.

"I knew it!" John jumped up and started pacing. "I told that idiot in the ER the cut was too smooth, too deep. Most suicides make a few false starts. What happened?"

Faith described the drug lab and what she knew about Banat's involvement. She didn't exactly lie, but she told John that Banat had tried to kill her and let him draw his own conclusions.

When she was done, John turned to face her. "It all fits. The bed where I found you was too clean, just a few drops of blood on the covers. Banat must have cut you first, then moved you."

"*You* found me?"

"Yeah, and almost too late. After I got your message, I wasted a lot of time trying to figure out where you'd called from. Finally found a map at your boyfriend's apartment. I was working on a search warrant when the call came in about the fire."

"At Banat's complex?" In her wonder at waking up, Faith had forgotten about Cole's grenades.

John nodded. "Looks like the Embryo-Rightists who vandalized your apartment and the LifeSource office set fire to the lab building."

If the lab had burned, her notes were gone. Faith's throat closed around a sudden lump. "How bad is it?"

"Place burned to the ground. If Banat hadn't tried to make your death look like a suicide, you'd have burned too."

Her throat ached, and she had to blink back tears. All that work, all those years, and nothing left but ash and smoke. "How'd you find me?"

"Plain dumb luck. Saw the apartment building when I drove into the complex and decided to check it out. Good thing I did. Got there just in time." His pacing brought him back to her side. He settled a gentle hand on her shoulder, and worry creased his brow. "You okay?"

The room door flew open before she could answer. A nurse with steel gray hair marched into the room, shadowed by the resident. She had the clipboard in one hand and a scowl on her face. "Dr. Allister, you may be a physician, but—" Spotting John, she turned her frown on him. "Detective O'Connor, I'm the charge nurse on this floor, and I must ask you to leave. Despite her opinion to the contrary, Dr. Allister is still very ill and needs to rest."

John took his hand from Faith's shoulder. "Looks like we're out-ranked. Take it easy. You can fill in the details later."

The resident followed him out of the room, but the nurse remained behind. "No more notes on the chart," she said. Faith nodded, too tired to argue. With a final, searching look, the nurse pulled the privacy curtain around the bed and left.

Faith sagged against the mattress. The nurse was right, she needed rest; but her mind was swirling. The fire, her notes burned, her work destroyed. The concern in John's voice when he said he'd found her just in time. With the fire in the lab, Faith was amazed he'd even thought to look for her in her apartment. He was right, she'd been very lucky. Faith bolted up. Lucky? She'd bet a month's salary, luck didn't have anything to do with it. John found her because someone told him where to look. The tears Faith had been fighting spilled past her lashes. Her blood had worked. Ritter was alive.

He had to be. The only other person who'd known she was in the apartment was Cole, and he would have left her there. But not Ritter. Pigheaded, infuriating, sweetly anachronistic Ritter. Even if he were too weak to go for help, he'd find a way to save her.

His final words joined the swirl. "*Ich liebe dich.*" I love you.

Ritter loved her.

A fluttery feeling filled her stomach. Faith once thought she needed only her work to be happy, but now she wasn't so sure. The thought of never seeing Ritter again filled her with emptiness. If that wasn't love, what was?

Faith's hand reached for the locket around her neck, but of course it wasn't there. Banat had stolen it. Ritter's token lay in a melted puddle under the rubble of the lab. The thought started another wash of tears.

The door whispered open and shut. Hard-soled boots thumped across the linoleum, and a dark hand shoved the curtain back. Cole loomed in the opening. Faith sat up, grabbed the edge of the sheet, and quickly wiped her face. "What are you doing here?" A sudden thought made her go cold. "Ritter—is he...?"

"He's fine. Still weak, but nothing a good meal won't fix. Here." He stepped toward her and swung something up onto the table beside her bed. Her briefcase.

She stared at the soot-streaked leather. "The lab...I thought...How did you get it?"

"After you helped Ritter, I remembered what you'd said about your briefcase. The grenades had just blown, and I figured I could still get it if I ran." He grinned. "You may be a fucking scientist, but you're all right, pretty doctor."

Hands trembling with excitement, Faith grabbed the handle and hauled her case into her lap. A charred smell clung to the leather. Faith didn't care, as long as the memory stick and notes were still inside. Her heart tap-danced against her throat as she thumbed the combination and opened the lock.

There they were, the memory stick and her hard-copy notes, right where she'd left them. Sitting on the top page were a small white envelope and two dark red vials, one labeled with an *R*, the other with a *C*.

Faith looked from the vials to Cole's sharp-edged smile. "This is blood, isn't it? Yours and Ritter's. How did you manage to draw it? The way you guys heal, the needle must have popped out of your veins after a few drops."

The grin twisted into a grimace. "Don't ask."

A horrible suspicion began to grow in Faith's mind. She picked up the envelope. "And why give me the blood now? Why not wait until I'm better?"

"Ritter's idea. Check his note."

Faith tore the flap open. The locket lay inside, nestled against a sheet of white stationery. She took out the paper and unfolded it to reveal neat, old-fashioned script. "I could have killed you. Good-bye." It was signed *Ritter*.

Faith went numb. "Good-bye?" She crumpled the note in her fist and looked up at Cole. "Ritter's leaving, isn't he?"

Cole's lips twitched up at the corners. "Good-bye, pretty doctor." Almost too quick to see, he strode past the curtain and was gone.

"Wait!" Faith swung her legs over the side of the bed, but the room spun so hard she nearly fell off the mattress. She flopped back onto her pillow, and her tears turned bitter. *I haven't told him I love him.*

∽ ∾

It took Faith three days to convince the hospital to release her. She put the time to good use. Her old lab was still vacant. She rented it through the end of the month. She also persuaded one of the techs in virology to make slides of the vampires' blood, to run them through the electron microscope, and to download the data onto her memory chip.

Ritter had left to protect her. Faith knew that as well as she knew her own name. He thought himself a monster and blamed that monster for the death of his first love. Faith had offered her life to save his, but all Ritter saw was another attack, one that had nearly killed her. Ritter had abandoned his home, the life he'd created, and even Faith herself, to ensure the monster never touched her again.

Ritter was no monster. Faith knew that too, but it would take more than love to prove it to him. Well, that was just fine. She had more than love to offer.

She would have told him so, if only he'd come to say good-bye. She kept hoping he would. Her heart jumped every time her door opened, but it was never Ritter. On Sunday evening, she finally gave up waiting and checked herself out of the hospital.

She didn't go home. She didn't have time. She had to check that data, and the university's supercomputer would be available for only a few more hours. Too impatient to wait for the elevator, Faith trotted down three flights of stairs to the basement. Slightly dizzy from the exertion, she fumbled with the key before she could unlock the door to her lab and step inside.

Nothing had changed. Same table, same chairs, same computer. Feeling as though she'd stepped into an episode of *The Twilight Zone*, Faith turned on the desktop and took out her memory stick while the computer booted up.

Faith was holding the key to Stoker's. She felt it in her gut. She'd already processed the data from Banat's "volunteers" and from her own blood. Two points of reference. The vampires' blood would make a third. Three points of reference from survivors of Stoker's. That had been her mistake all along: she'd focused on the genetic markers that appeared in children who died from the disease. No, if she wanted a cure, she needed to compare the profiles of those who survived. Three points of reference should be enough to define and isolate the common characteristics—if only she recognized the vital ones when she saw them.

The desktop chimed. Praying the hospital hadn't gotten around to updating the supercomputer user list, she typed in the network command and her password.

It couldn't have taken more than sixty seconds, but Faith's heart was pounding by the time the computer chimed again and Essie's icon appeared. Too nervous even to swallow, she slipped in her memory stick, opened the file containing Ritter's data, and started the anomaly search.

Another eternity before twenty-three pairs of chromosomes replaced Essie's icon. Ritter's chromosomes. Another keystroke to magnify and highlight the anomalies. The twenty-third pair of chromosomes lit up in the same pattern she'd seen in all the cells she'd infected, but it was the fourteenth pair that caught her attention. Twin anomalies blinked like beacons from the top of each.

Twin anomalies from the fourteenth pair. Faith's heart shifted into overdrive. Her fingers flew across the keys. She called up her own profile and the profiles from Banat's volunteers and ran a comparison of their *fourteenth* chromosome pairs.

And there they were. Twin anomalies on the top of each chromosome.

"I'm an idiot," Faith whispered. "Stoker's is bidependent, like cancer." Fingers trembling, she saved her work and logged out of the computer. Stoker's was bidependent. It took two separate sets of anomalies on two separate chromosome pairs to create Stoker's. The cure would require fixing both simultaneously, as Fisher's modified rhinovirus did in cancer cells.

She could even use the same microbe. It would take a while, perhaps years, to work through the testing process, but with the information on her memory stick, any competent genetic engineer could manipulate the anticancer virus to undo Stoker's. Faith had her key. Someday, soon, she'd have her cure.

And she'd give it to Ritter. He'd run away, but once the treatment was safe and proven, she'd find him. She'd track him down, destroy the monster inside him, and spend the rest of her life proving to him how much she loved the man.

The door opened behind her. Faith spun around. Ritter stood in the doorway. He looked as he had the night she met him: flawless skin, no scars, no scabs, no hint of the horrible burns she remembered. Her smile made her cheeks ache. "You came back."

He didn't smile. He ran in, grabbed her arm, and pulled her from her chair. "If you would live to see dawn, come with me now."

The End

About the Author

Carrie S. Masek has been telling stories since she was three and discovered she got into less trouble when she provided creative explanations for the chaos that swirled around her. It took her almost forty years to start writing her stories down. Carrie now lives in a comfortably messy house on Chicago's North Shore. Contributing to the chaos are her husband, four children, a ditzy dog and an opinionated house rabbit.

Carrie has written two award-winning novels, *Under a Bear Moon*, winner of both the 2000 EPPIE for Young Adult fiction and the 2000 Dream Realm Award, children's category, and *Room For Love*, winner of the 2002 Lories Award for Best Overall short contemporary romance. Her short stories have appeared in romance genre publications and web sites. "Cybergeist" was her first venture into horror and appears in *Beyond the Mundane: Unravelings*, a 2005 EPPIE finalist from Mundania Press. She wrote the story to exorcise a nightmare.

You can usually find Carrie working at her desk, but if her chair's empty, check the vegetable garden—she likes to dig in the dirt. Carrie also enjoys long bike rides, oatmeal stout cake, and belly dancing.

Printed in the United Kingdom
by Lightning Source UK Ltd.
108527UKS00001B/33